39 BAYSHORE

Bayshore Series – Book One

Donna J. Grisanti

ISBN: 0970886055
ISBN 13: 9780970886057
Library of Congress Control Number: 2016909544
Phoenix Publishing Corporation, Marina del Rey, CA

Dedicated to my sons, Christopher and Stephen

PROLOGUE

On March 17, Lucas Crandall felt excited as he sat back in his over-stuffed dining room chair. Not even his solidly booked day at the law firm, getting him home at 8 PM, could detract from his enthusiastic decision to offer this term's 'cold case' opportunity to the Billie Reynolds' investigation. Lucas knew his solitary pursuit for each year's case for the class he taught at his alma mater, seemed a bit too heavy into criminology and too theatrical to the other lawyers and staffers at the law firm bearing his name, but he'd always enjoyed being known as flamboyant to both his admirers and haters. There was no such thing as bad publicity as long as it was publicity.

His housekeeper had left at 8:15 PM, leaving him a light celebratory dinner just as he had ordered - a chicken Caesar salad and an excellent bottle of Merlot from his wine cellar. After pouring a second glass of wine, all his notes and the hefty volumes of garnered police and private investigator reports on the Reynolds' case filled the table top. The second year law students would clamor to uncover any new leads or find any suspects in this perplexing case!

His eyebrow crooked at a sound from the kitchen. Lucas cursed as he wondered if this was a signal from the feral one-eyed tomcat his housekeeper had adopted. He would have to speak to her in the morning about it. *Was this another indication she had forgotten to feed the pesky animal again?*

The next afternoon, Detectives Andersen and Drake sat at the long interrogation table looking over their notes and crime scene pictures. "Mayor Jenkins and Alderman George are clamoring for new press conference leads on this homicide case," Drake grumbled.

"You know better than anyone else, I'd like to oblige them…and help our careers but this looks like a robbery gone wrong. Nothing flashy," Andersen said as he tried to rub the fatigue knots out of his neck. "Missing $30,000 Rolex watch and rifled wallet from the usual place in the butler's pantry that the housekeeper identified where Crandall habitually left his personal belongings when he got home."

"A few missing electronics, no fingerprints and a dead body of the illustrious lawyer." Drake had been awakened at 5 AM. "The housekeeper said she arrived early at Crandall's residence because she was given permission to have the next day off."

"Her alibi and the next day off story checks out," Andersen replied. "Let's go over the photos again." He raised each one and gave them to his partner.

"Wish I had such a great housekeeper," Drake remarked sarcastically, thinking of the three days of dishes piled in his sink and a week's worth of laundry stuffed in a bag needing to be done. "The polished shine on that mahogany dining table is really something. Table set for one. The only thing marring the "model home" perfection is Crandall's dead body and the spray from the bullet wounds on the wall."

The detectives didn't know it but all the notes and the files were gone.

CHAPTER ONE

Sitting on this red-eye flight, which Carolyn Reynolds's three aunts booked from LA to Baltimore, seemed like the latest faulty move in a long chain of bad decisions. In retrospect, Carolyn clearly remembered those three ladies continually telling her "what fun" they'd *all* have on the flight to Baltimore *and* driving to their destination to see the fantastic "home" they'd bought her. Unbeknownst to Carolyn, they'd pooled some of their $5 million in stock and settlement money from the forced sale of Carolyn's company and now wanted to enthusiastically present Carolyn with —a historic Maryland mansion "fixer-upper" on the East Coast strategically located on the salt flats near open water - which among other things needed a new dock.

None of her aunts ever had to work again, if they were careful and this escapade was not "careful" in the least! Even though Carolyn had twenty times that amount in stock and money now, she wasn't going to waste money or much time for that matter on this wild goose chase. *A fixer-upper on the water with no dock?*

Carolyn now knew time was an increasingly valuable commodity – and she'd wasted her fair share trying to build her company and chase down the hit-and-run driver that had killed her mother, Billie, five years ago, in 2005. Carolyn had to face hard facts in her personal life. Granted she'd been successfully raised by her single-mother Billie, and her three aunts, but she wanted to have a more traditional family *for herself.* Time and biology were against her if she had any chance on gaining this personal dream now. Just like the character, Mona Lisa Vito, in her mother's favorite comedy, "My Cousin Vinny", at 35, if Carolyn was going to enrich her personal life with a husband and children, she needed to make that goal a priority in her life. But she was stuck on this plane, and with this house, for the time being. *Again – time!*

In the kindest of terms, the Internet pictures her aunts showed her with such exuberant delight looked more like an atrocious ruin—seemingly beyond repair. Carolyn would bet her last dollar nothing had been done to the hulking purple disaster of a place in decades. Yes, purple. Carolyn slid her hand down her face. *I'll need a hard hat as well!*

While Carolyn chewed an antacid to ease her pounding head and queasy stomach, she looked at the seatbacks of the three women in question. The aforementioned "mansion buyer-perpetrators" ignored her, sitting two rows forward, chatting amiably while turning home-renovation magazine pages in print and on their electronic devices. The "buyers" were having fun...while Carolyn was working on a migraine.

Their last communication, voiced by her always blunt-spoken Aunt Cass before the plane took off, had jarred Carolyn. "You don't need to tell us you haven't decided what to do with our gift. You might not even have a plan. But you need to get one...and we're here to help." Carolyn should have *refused* to leave LA. *Can I get a parachute?*

Facing the cold, hard facts of these last five years, Carolyn and the police had failed to find her mother's killer. Also, Carolyn's beloved health food company, which she'd birthed from her kitchen, had been sold out from under her. Finally, the efforts for the university law school "cold case" review concerning her mother's case were gone with the death of Mr. Crandall. The newspaper reports indicated it was a robbery, probably due to Crandall's unrepentant expensive and flashy lifestyle. *With all this long-term negativity, I do need a plan.*

In the two-seat row now holding her captive, Carolyn's kind-looking and grandmotherly seatmate, who spoke no English, now opened a redolent wax paper package of dry sausage and crackers. Smelling the sausage caused Carolyn more unbidden pressure on her temples and in the back of her neck.

Carolyn fumbled and lost her grip on the pain reliever bottle in the depths of her purse…just as she had lost her beloved company. The snarky woman reporter from *Business News* intimated as much in today's four-page article titled "Health Gone for Health Bar Maven?" Carolyn didn't know the entire definition of "maven," but she'd probably find out in the crossword puzzle dictionary she'd been given as a gag gift at one of her several farewell parties. *Doesn't everyone know they wrenched me from my passion? Am I not too young to be a maven?*

Carolyn sat in her seemingly too-small airplane seat and took stock. She been to doctors so many times in the last fourteen months, she could state her height, weight and health history by rote. At 5'8 and 160 lbs. her doctors didn't complain. Her mother and aunts always admired her blue eyes and dark, sandy hair but her pale skin made them worry when she was tired or stressed – a common occurrence these last five years as an executive and with her mother's death. Perhaps, the tragedy dove-tailed with what they called her "insatiable curiosity" - always being ready to learn and improve herself or situations. They also said she was a kind and caring person…but they had to, didn't they? She'd have to regain more of a personal life to know and see for herself.

At 35, she was well-respected, well-liked by her employees but alone, again a byproduct of her being a workaholic and chasing leads on her mother's death. OK. No future life plan and debilitating episodes of galloping heart rhythms.

Carolyn knew she'd made an unholy mess of things, throwing all her energies in hounding the police and her private investigators with new leads or clues or in building her company. All Carolyn had to show for it was a cold case, a sold company…and an ailing heart!

In hindsight, besides paying more attention to her personal life, Carolyn wished she'd publicly forced her board and the bankers to eject her from her position by prying her death-gripped hands off the knob of her office door. Instead of continuing that thought, which her LA health therapist said would only lead to more anxiety and galloping heart rate episodes, Carolyn pressed her fingers to her right temple and took a long breath, hoping to calm herself. "Relax instead of feel, relax instead of feel," her therapist would chant. Carolyn's mind skittered back to her aunts.

Cass Williams, who'd chided Carolyn to get a life plan together, stood as tall as Carolyn at five feet, eight inches. Cass's lime-green eyes matched her sharp wit, equally sharp tongue and voluminous mane of center-parted luxuriant brown-black hair. As the best seamstress of the group and an avid gardener, Cass lived in her garden grubby outfits or lounged through life in her handmade exotic, jewel-toned outfits flying about her.

Her second aunt, Muriel Porter, identified her height as five feet, one inch tall. But Carolyn knew Muriel's height estimate would require that Muriel stood on a large metropolitan phone book! No one argued with the diminutive librarian whose shiny, black-haired Buster Brown cut and straight front bangs wreathed her serious brown-eyed face and squarish head. With her bent toward logical approaches to life, Muriel was their historian, researcher and resident fact-finder who also liked studying history and calligraphy.

The third and final conspirator, Bee Elders, acted as the group's head chef, chief cook-and-bottle washer, resident culinary encyclopedia and amateur psychologist, who now loved to blog about her culinary adventures and looking for new and unusual ingredients. The plump, blue-eyed, rosy-cheeked blonde, had a respectable Internet following and remained the group's eternal optimist - always steering everyone in the group to consider brokered compromises.

Bee was always the one to ask questions – even the hard ones. She bustled in her signature caftans or jean outfits to enhance their meals…and their lives.

Carolyn loved her aunts, but she wanted to concentrate on *her needs* as she continued to rummage in her tote for the lost pain remedy. But the steward grabbed Carolyn's water glass in his disposable-gloved hand. "Sorry, we're getting ready to land in two minutes." He wrinkled his nose. "Your mother might want to put away her snack away as well." Carolyn could only reflexively try to regain her glass as her hand fluttered in the steward's wake. No point in trying to set the matter straight. This kind, elderly woman was a stranger, and her own dear mother, Billie, was dead.

Carolyn wondered, if she should risk choking by swallowing the tablets dry; if so, she'd be wheezing until the plane turned off the runway and onto the taxi path to the terminal. She didn't want to spend any time turning blue. If she were to die, this wouldn't be the way or time she envisioned it might happen.

Carolyn tried to concentrate on some other subject. But her mind skittered back to her fury when she'd gotten the surprise news about this cross-country 'sticks-and-bricks' gift from her aunts - the decrepit purple mansion. When they landed, she'd start her speech. Could she, as their niece, divorce the only three re-maining "family" members she'd ever known? *A mansion indeed!*

The three ladies in question, still rock-solid in their mutu-ally crafted plan regarding the dilapidated estate, waited for the plane to land. They'd purposefully picked seats away from Carolyn because they'd already argued with her during the trip to the airport, and they didn't want to risk upsetting Carolyn's somewhat fragile health. They'd just barely managed to get her on the plane.

They'd bought this white elephant, more precisely purple el-ephant of a mansion, using a big chunk of their retirement plans as a "gift" for Carolyn, because several things were crystal clear: Carolyn was still devastated by the double losses of her mother and her company, and Carolyn had nothing going for the foreseeable future. "Remember, this money came from the sale of Carolyn's company and we wouldn't have any of it if it wasn't for her," Bee whispered.

"Someone had to take action…and there's no one else but us," Muriel reasoned. They were trying to provide a safe haven and a therapeutic project for their niece; for growth and rest rather than despair—no matter what came of the purple, decrepit house at 39 Bayshore. To save some of their investment from disaster, they'd turned its property into *three lots* instead of keeping it one expan-sive estate. If this effort turned into a tragic failure, at least they'd be able to get most of their money back. "I know the two lots have sold right away…but I don't know if anyone will want that pile of near-rubble!"

"We've had our marriages and men," Cass offered strongly, thinking of her and Bee's late husbands, as well as Muriel's long relationship with the dear departed Cal Willis. "Carolyn's had only two short relationships in four years, and neither one was worth the powder to blow to Hades!"

"Keep your voice down," Muriel ordered in a low hiss that historically scared patrons at the three libraries she'd headed in her career. "She's said she wants a family...but we can't force her into dating websites or dating brokers!"

"Perhaps, we could have fashioned one or the other because our gift has its own drawbacks," Cass said in a characteristically sour tone, putting her hand to her forehead. "What were we thinking?"

"We were *clearly* thinking buying this rundown mansion would give Carolyn some time away from the bad publicity in LA, give her a chance to regroup, and perhaps give us more time to figure out how to better help her, if she can't help herself," Bee hissed in a softer tone. "It's a project we can all have a hand in and then some..."

"I just can't believe the local LA business press was so unkind. They knew Carolyn had lost her mother and build such a fine company as a young CEO at 35," Muriel huffed, turning the subject a bit.

Cass straightened herself in the seat. "We had to get her out of LA. Everyone's acting like sharks smelling blood in the water because they promote sensation over good sense to help their ratings or websites, and they don't have the manners that God gave a frog. Carolyn's their current target."

"We've got to have backs of steel as Billie would say!" Muriel stated, needing to say it for the hundredth time to bolster her own courage.

"Backs of steel!" Cass said, patting Muriel's hand in agreement.

"Backs of steel!" Bee repeated, adding her hand to her friends'.

All four got off the plane in tired silence, resting in the waiting area before getting their luggage. None of them, it seemed, had gotten any sleep, and Muriel didn't relish Carolyn driving with all her simmering anger and fatigue. "You've got to start living again!" she announced.

Carolyn looked at Muriel incredulously, her dark-circled eyes now radiating shock and surprise. Cass was usually the one who preferred frontal attacks.

Muriel waved her hand at their communal surprise. "We *saw* you in the emergency room, and part of me feared I wouldn't see you again." Muriel remembered the ER episode during one of Carolyn's near two-hundred-beats-per-minute heart rate incidents. "I'd have been sorry to my grave for not telling you sooner to get connected with *living* again…and that means more than just having a business, us, and a heaping bank account."

Carolyn just frowned and refused to rise to the bait. *Besides a family, what does a contemporary woman like myself whose path in life has been smashed to smithereens want now?*

"It's just an example, sweetheart, of how you've devoted all your energies to your work and your hunt for peace about Billie. You'll get started again." Bee, Muriel and Cass avoided mentioning death or anything regarding Carolyn's muddled business life. Bee's last statement was as much of a prayer as a hope for her niece.

"I know I've been preoccupied with things, but before I start discussing modifications in my life, I want to talk *about you* – my would-be mentors in this remodeling project!" Carolyn sputtered heatedly. *Before* her mother died, Carolyn planned to establish her career and graft a more conventional family onto her fairly unique family tree of a single mother and three loving aunts. She'd envisioned marrying a husband who love and respected her and their children to follow, all *within* the company of her mother and aunts in one big, loving package! Those plans all shattered with Billie's hit-and-run death.

"If you're so all-fired ready for me to get a fresh start," Carolyn began. She wanted to let them have a taste of their own medicine. "I think I need to start looking at things *from the beginning.*" *See how they like being the lab rat recipients of all the questions and answers.*

"You mean take the suggestion of that crackpot counselor back in LA, who said everything has its beginnings in your childhood?" Cass's deep frown lines in her brow indicated she thought this wasn't the correct place to start.

"We're got time in the rental car," Bee offered, trying to mollify Cass's anger with Carolyn's suggested approach. "Perhaps we *should* start where your mother and we all met."

"That's right!" Carolyn shot back, not waiting for the time in the rental car. "Let's talk about you!"

Muriel pursed her lips before starting to speak. If that was where Carolyn wanted to start, she would agree to her niece's choice. At least Carolyn would be talking! "It was a unique situation," Muriel began with her dry wit pointing toward the incongruity yet to come – knowing all the facts but not Carolyn's current feelings.

"You mean the unwed mother's home?" Cass accused in her whisky-low voice. "That's where you want to start?"

The unwed mother's home! *Who would have considered those four women would have met in a place like that, let along form the nexus of a family?*

Carolyn cleared her throat. "My mother, Alvira Reynolds, nicknamed Billie, always truthfully repeated all the long-ago facts, whenever I asked." Her three aunts always did the same. "It's where it all started for me – at my conception." But this was painful emotional ground. "None of us should be afraid of the truth!"

"We wanted to talk about the fact that you've buried yourself in your corporate work…and searching for the hit-and-run driver who killed your mother, not the dust-dry facts from our past thirty-five years ago," Cass remarked stubbornly, trying in a final effort to stay on the original topic. Carolyn's problems of the last five years had *nothing to do* with the unwed mothers' home in her estimation.

"It's what I want to talk about *now*," Carolyn retorted, "or do you want me to just do what you want and not to talk at all!"

Everyone recognized Carolyn's infrequently used mutinous tone, so the three looked at each other in silent agreement to let her lead the conversation. If they didn't, just as Carolyn said, there wouldn't be any talk – or possibility for progress.

Carolyn's mother, Billie, had found herself pregnant and mourning the death of her fiancé on the eve of their elopement – alcohol poisoning. It all boiled down to Carolyn's father being a college student who died in a tragic bachelor party accident.

"When I think about my parents, I've fantasized about a college romance, wedding, and happily ever after, which had been undone by some binging by him and the rest of my father's friends," Carolyn began. Billie and her unknown pregnancy survived, but her beau, the young Kenneth Wilton, had not.

Billie had always known from the get-go, she wanted to keep her baby even though Carolyn's father was dead. "Mom often said her sister, Robin Lee, was making big money in California." Billie had no other financial resources beyond working as long as she could before the baby's birth. Billie was forced to call her sister Robin and asked for help. As a bona-fided movie star with several blockbuster films, with a big rental house in the Hollywood Hills and thousands of adoring fans in her fan club, Robin told Billie she'd make darn sure her sister completed her education in LA after the delivery, and they'd live with her in California after the baby was born. "Reporters might come sniffing around, so we need to keep these things hushed up for the time being," Robin told Billie in a phone conversation that indicated Robin was taking care of everything. "My agent will get a fake marriage license and divorce decree so everything will look on the up-and-up."

Things had changed a lot in Hollywood, but thirty six years ago, out-of-wedlock births still gave movie executives shivers. "My agent, Carl Springs, tells me we'll send you to some place nice, so you can have your baby and work up a plausible story from there." So Billie's older celebrity sister had taken her from college with the cover story of her needing her sister as a personal assistant when, in reality, Billie was secreted away to an unwed mothers home.

Surprisingly, the place had been a broken-down dump with the only good things being Cass, Muriel, and Bee. Bonding with these young women, and the thought of living with Robin after the baby was born, kept Billie from complaining to her sister or bolting.

Cass, Muriel, and Bee were already there with worse hard-luck stories. A fellow employee ambushed Cass and raped her one night in the woman's bathroom at work. Getting off when local authorities dragged their heels when the guy's wife and three kids surfaced. The judge gave him probation...and left her alone and pregnant.

Bee had fallen in blind love with an out-of-town guy with a sob story as long as a chorus line. He'd drugged her on the fourth date, left town, and she discovered she was pregnant.

Muriel knew she shouldn't have succumbed to her lover's advances, but her mother, as well as the rest of the family, told her she was "plain as a stick." What Muriel thought was her chance at love ended in pregnancy without marriage. Her family abandoned her, and she suffered a spontaneous abortion several weeks into her stay at the home. Billie and Cass had found Muriel passed out in the bathroom, so they cleaned her up and hid Muriel's miscarriage as long as they could.

So they stayed together, doing the chores they were assigned and fantasized on ways in which they could get revenge on the remaining three men who gotten them pregnant.

"I recovered and resumed my job as a library assistant on the way to my college degree," Muriel said. "Bee lost her baby too when it came so premature." Bee looked down at the floor and shook her head.

"In those days, they didn't have the newfangled treatments they have today. We were living in one of the last of those backwater charity places, and the equipment looked like it had been there since the Civil War. We notified the matron who sent Bee to bed to rest to try to stop the labor, but the child came anyway." Muriel patted Bee's hands, which were now knotted in several tissues. "We couldn't tell the matron or she would have kicked Bee out of the place…and we didn't think they'd be able to hide things about both Bee and me! So we lied again." Muriel shrugged, and her eyes clouded. "We had to do several things. Wrapped the baby girl in a few clean rags and placed her in a cloth-lined shoebox under the bed until it was nighttime and we could sneak out and bury her."

Bee looked up into Carolyn's eyes. "I didn't have anywhere to go. My mother was divorced, and she kicked me out of the house when she found out I was pregnant. Didn't even bother to tell me she moved when I tried to find her to tell her my baby died."

Cass jumped in. "Came up with a plan to hide the fact she'd lost the baby so she could stay there as long as possible to recover." She took a breath as if it were her turn to talk. "Bee only had the clothes on her back and a few changes of underclothes when she came to the home. She borrowed some of our outfits when she went out for jobs. Sneaked back to the home with Muriel and slept there until dawn when it was time for her to do the break-fast shift at the diner where she found work." Cass smiled a bit at the memory.

"Had a nice service in the woods outside of town where we buried my little girl," Bee whispered. "We took the matron's hand trowel she used for some pots of geraniums on the front porch of the place. Tried to remember some Bible verses, but didn't sing because we were afraid we'd rouse the police or something, even though it was dark. Fishy enough four girls, two of them pregnant, all of them crying and standing around the woods in the night…"

Muriel's face was sober. "We were just dumb, fool kids. Perhaps not kids, but fools nonetheless."

Carolyn eyes widened at this. Those negative words seemed like cursing coming from Muriel. She always had all the facts and a positive attitude!

Muriel continued. "The matron had people scouring the bus, train stations, and college campus, always on the lookout for desperate unwed mothers down on their luck. Times were changing. There were other programs, safe programs caring for what happened to the mothers during their pregnancies, giving them help and choices about keeping the babies or giving them up for adoption. This wasn't one of them, but we found that out too late."

"What Muriel's trying to tell you, yet again, is that we learned pretty quickly the place was a baby farm." Cass's arms flew to her face. She still didn't understand why they had to go over the unwed mothers' home story! "Billie started looking around more closely and found blank birth certificates in the drawer of the office. Noticed all the mothers got ether or chloroform and heavy sedation before and after the birth. The babies were out the door in minutes or hours, and so were the girls within a few days of having the babies. Some came back teary-eyed, asking questions and got shooed away by the matron or her assistants haranguing the poor women about all the rent, food, and medical bills they'd incurred during their stay at the home. 'We got you through your problem. You did the right thing. Just start over,' they'd say and show everyone the door.

"That's when we started looking for a way out. They just threw Bee and me out without asking the whys and wherefores about what happened to our babies," Muriel reported. "We could have killed the babies or something—done something fishy. They didn't even ask."

"By this time, Muriel and Bee had a one room flat over the diner where Bee worked, as incentive to help the owner when some of his other help didn't make their shifts." Cass shrugged, and some of her luxuriant hair fell over her shoulder. "Bee's tips were OK to start our savings. Muriel was making enough for the rest of the rent and food money, so we'd have some place to go when we could escape. Then it changed into a place for Billie to escape when her water broke and we knew you were coming."

Muriel took over the story. "Cass was to fake early labor pains and tell the staff she'd found a note from Billie saying she was headed for the bus station. Billie made it over to the diner so we wouldn't raise suspicion. Thankfully, it was a quick labor, and you both were OK. I don't know what we would have done if you hadn't come by nightfall or waited until the next morning to show your pretty, Cupid's bow mouth."

"As we've told you before, we were your midwives," Muriel chuckled, "and at least that part of the plan worked."

"You were such a good baby," Muriel offered as she looked at Carolyn. "The diner owner didn't even know there was a baby up there. At least, he didn't let on."

"By the end, we were all trying to get on with things," Cass said, exasperated, then sad. "As you know, my baby died."

Muriel's hand flew to cover her friend's in a gesture of comfort. "The cord."

All the color left Cass's face. "The cord was around his neck and there were some genetic problems too, as they would say today. Poor baby needed special care and before I could intervene...decide what to do, my baby was dead."

Carolyn had heard bits of the stories over the years. She felt hot and cold at the same time.

"I would have taken him and done my best," Cass whispered. "While the matron wasn't looking, we took his little body and buried him next to Bee's child."

"We all stayed together and then decided to get to a city farther north to make something of ourselves," Bee added, "and that's the way it's been all this time."

"As you know, I did the research about telling the authorities and exhuming their bodies…and our children were put in memorable crypts," Muriel said.

Even though Bee thought they were making progress, the baggage claim area was almost deserted and they needed to leave. In a voice sounding thin and tired, she said, "We'd best get our bags off the carousel or they're going to put them in the unclaimed baggage section…and I don't think we need any more problems *right now.*"

Bee sighed, and Cass recovered from telling her part of the story. Her tone oozed authority. "Let's get on the road!"

Carolyn frowned at Cass's order, still feeling like a lab animal, but she didn't want to say anything to inflame the situation. She took a deep breath. *She was the only one who could decide what to do with the rest of her life.*

Carolyn had taken one action, she reminded herself. She'd agreed with her doctors and therapist that keeping her LA home only reminded Carolyn of her mother…and she needed to move on. Everything had been packed up in LA; a major uptick of action against a heavy stream of loneliness and loss. But whichever columnist wrote that money—from the multi-million dollar settlement Carolyn had gotten from selling her company and home—equaled happiness was wrong.

"Let's get our rental car," Muriel suggested, trying to put some optimism into her voice. It would be grand to see the old Carolyn emerge again. But if dredging up the past helped in some way, Muriel was all for the effort. They'd just have to pray and see.

CHAPTER TWO

After purchasing snacks and stowing their luggage in the rented SUV, Carolyn looked in the rearview mirror she'd just adjusted and waited for the patient, mechanical instructions of the GPS voice to guide her. As if Carolyn were their female chauffeur, Cass, Muriel, and Bee all sat quietly in the backseat, away from Carolyn's pensiveness and wrath.

Carolyn pretended not to notice as she flipped the turn indicator, proceeded into traffic, and unclenched her teeth. The only sound was the tires on cold pavement. To appease these women who loved her, Carolyn drove towards their destination, when all she really wanted to do now was run...in the opposite direction, back to LA.

Fortunately, her aunts didn't know Carolyn had purchased her return flight plane ticket, which allowed for several more days to consider options...and an escape. At this point, Carolyn felt sure her future, or the place for planning, wasn't anywhere near the derelict mansion they were driving towards. *Best start the hard conversation now.*

Carolyn assessed the lighter traffic flow and kept her eyes on the road. "I know you think this cooked-up idea of seeing some house you've bought is *your* best plan for me at this time. That I love learning and challenges…but I remain unconvinced." Carolyn looked in the rearview mirror again.

Cass certainly wasn't going to confirm Carolyn's suspicions, even though what Carolyn said was basically the truth. Instead, she parried the subject with a major salvo. "Carolyn Lee Reynolds. You most certainly said you were coming of your own free will…to see the home we bought for you."

"Don't you remember? Your mother was fond of telling us about the mansion when she accompanied your Aunt Robin when Robin was starring in that film with…with…what's his name?" Bee said, waving her hand in well-bred emphasis.

"Another thing. Using her royalty checks kept you and your mother afloat…and helped pay for some of your college expenses…among other things," Muriel retorted, always good at using logic to its best strategic advantage.

"Being grateful to Aunt Robin's estate and being gifted with a home so far from LA seem to be only thinly related subjects," Carolyn replied, perhaps more sarcastically than was polite. All the old television interviews and news reports indicated her aunt Robin Lee had been no-nonsense and plainspoken. Carolyn wasn't her aunt's niece for nothing. *Score one point for me as the abused niece!*

Muriel added, "Well, we didn't want you to mope *or* get caught in a mistaken grind of having to find something else to do *immediately* after you sold your Four Almonds Company. Giving you a certain period of time for rest and reflection *away from LA*, and all the recent bad press, seemed like a good idea. What else do you have to do right now?"

Bee saw the mutinous look in their niece's eyes in the rear view mirror. "Carolyn, the doctor *said* you needed to rest, dear, and a change of scene."

Even though Carolyn wanted to shout a retort concerning age and wisdom, she kept her mouth shut. *Couldn't a week or two in an island paradise have produced the same result?*

The ebb and flow of their dispute went on as Bee's best negotiating tactics failed to win over either side, as she doggedly continued to restate the positive points of their initiative in the discussion.

Carolyn looked at the gas gauge. "We'd better stop for some gas and something to drink," she said as she pulled into the gas station.

They bought some drinks and used the rest rooms. The older of the two station attendants walked up to them. "Can I ask your permission to look under the hood of the car? Arnie says there might be something leaking from the engine."

Carolyn's look immediately turned to dismay. *Now what?*

The attendant pointed to a few drops of liquid on the pavement under the car. "By the color, I think it's anti-freeze but I can't be sure until I look under the hood."

Carolyn had heard of gas stations trying to rip off unsuspecting motorists in the past, especially unsuspecting women. "This is a rental car and we'd have to contact them if any service is needed."

"This car looks to be brand new, which is puzzling. But I won't know till we open the hood," the man replied.

"Might as well," Cass offered. "We'll look at things with you. We don't want to break down farther down the road."

Carolyn nodded and walked to the front end of the SUV.

"Let's see what we have here," the man replied after he released the lid lock and raised the hood. He looked at engine and frowned. "Looks like several hoses are damaged."

"Several hoses?" Bee repeated.

"And this one belt looks in bad condition, too," the man continued. "You can see the belt threads sticking through, which should be encased in a smooth rubber, if it were in good working order."

He looked at ladies with a frown. "I wouldn't drive this car with things in this condition."

"What do you suggest?" Muriel asked quickly.

"You can call their nearest rental car place. I have the number in the office," the man replied. "They can send you another vehicle and tow this one back."

"How long will that take?" Carolyn asked as her stomach soured. *More delays!*

"About one hour, depending on what vehicles they have, I'd guess," the attendant replied. "Let's go call them and find out. Arnie will pull the car in the shade, so you can sit there and wait. But I must say, I've never seen anything like it. They shouldn't have let you leave the lot with things looking that bad. Be sure to tell them that."

Bee turned to look at her niece. "I guess that will give us more time to talk."

"Do you feel like you want to talk more, Carolyn? These aren't the greatest conditions," Muriel noted.

"We'll keep the doors open for ventilation. Carolyn and I can sit in the front seat with you and Cass in the back," Bee said, offering her plan.

"Best to keep space between the combatants," Cass snapped. She wasn't so sure any of this "talking" was working and she wanted her fellow travelers to know it.

"Now, Cass," Muriel replied. "We're going to have to be here for an hour, if the man's guessimate is correct, so we might as well continue things while we still can remember what's already been said."

"That computer mind of yours, Aunt Muriel, will make sure we *all know* what was said and when," Carolyn interjected. "But I think you're right about continuing our discussions." She went over to the car and sat down behind the steering well. "And nobody's yelling at anyone."

"Yet," Cass added in a flash.

Muriel decided to ignore Cass's sarcasm. She'd talk to Cass later about the virtues of patience and tact. Instead she said, "Billie didn't want the people at the unwed home coming to take you away from her."

Carolyn closed her eyes to remember. Cass had become an underwriter, Muriel was a librarian, and Bee worked as a sous chef. Cass and Muriel were now 61, Bee was 59 and her mother, Billie, would have been 56...if she had lived. Most of the time, Carolyn welcomed the fact she was the 35 year old "daughter" of sorts to them all – except, like now, when they meddled.

"The home burned down about two years after we left," Muriel offered. "The other girls had gotten out, but the matron had slipped on the stairs and broken her shoulder trying to get away from the fire."

"The town tore it down as a hazard; the rest of the girls went to social services–approved homes, and the scandal of the girls and their babies came out after the fire." Muriel took another breath, as if talking about the story was still a raw, painful thing. "The last of the baby mills, the microfiche newspaper files said."

"So that was the way it was—the five of us staying together." Muriel looked directly at Carolyn's profile. "Now we need to consider the times when things got off track for you in Cass, Bee and my estimations."

Carolyn lips puckered, as the conversation slammed into the present circumstances. "Not everything," Carolyn said sharply. A lone tear made its unbidden trail down her left cheek. She whisked it away, hoping her aunts won't notice. They would make a fuss if they did.

So Carolyn started talking again to make sure they thought she was fine. She talked about the mementos from those times, still in boxes in LA: including a smudgy photocopy of her father's obituary and a few small pictures photocopied from the microfiche college yearbook pages when she'd gone on a pilgrimage to find out what she could about her father. She'd hired a private investigator after her high school graduation. "If you think there's something more to learn, go after it," Billie had said. "I didn't have the money to investigate at the time but...I did have you." Carolyn remembered how Billie had smiled widely as she hugged her daughter...and hadn't interfered with Carolyn's wishes for more information.

"The private investigator bill took three years to pay off," Carolyn remembered—her only indulgence in her college career with only a few facts to show for her investment. The investigator reported Kenneth Wilton's family had never known about her, her mother or Kenneth's marriage plans. Kenneth's parents on both sides of the Wilton genealogy were long dead of natural causes. It seemed Kenneth Wilton was the baby, the youngest child of an Indiana family with older parents and Kenneth's much older sister sibling. The private investigator discovered her father's one remaining grandniece and two grandnephews were many years older than Carolyn! Only one elderly brother and a near-centenarian great-aunt on his mother's side were left. Both were fragile, suffering from serious, age-related illnesses, which included some dementia. The uncle lived in nursing home and the great-aunt was cared for by her grandson-in-law in his home.

After college, Carolyn sometimes thought of calling, writing a letter, or showing up some day at the home of her very elderly aunt and uncle if they were still living; telling them about her long-lost story. Perhaps her great-cousins might care. Could they give Carolyn any more than these bare-bones facts? Could they tell her anything about her father as her mother remembered: was his favorite flavor of ice cream really chocolate, was his favorite color green, or perhaps tell her about his dreams for his future? Did his eyes twinkle when he smiled just like her mother said? Did he ever say he'd like to read storybooks if he had children? What parts of him could they see in her? *No,* Carolyn thought, shrugging.

Was there any point in grafting her slim branch into their family tree? *Hi, I'm your long-lost grandniece or great-grand cousin from an unknown relationship right before your Kenneth died.* It was improbable that it might be a positive situation for either her or the Wilton family. At least she'd preserved some memories and facts. Those might be shattered by the pain of rejection or confusion if she chose to intrude.

Then there were Billie's parents. Carolyn tried not to get too angry when she thought of Billie's divorced parents, estranged from her because of her unwed pregnancy—another set of grandparents she'd never get to know. They died within a few years after Carolyn was born.

"After spending the time, tears, hope, and money to investigate what I could, I did a gut check." As she looked at the paid private investigator's bill in one packing box, when moving into her townhouse, Carolyn found no further desire, not even tepid embers, to revisit that part of her past. She just accepted the facts and aimed her expectations toward her own adult life—cementing the fatherless hole in her heart with the satisfaction of her investigation efforts. So Carolyn wouldn't have a father - only her mother's memories. Nothing much beyond his biology.

"I had Billie...and you...and that was enough." Carolyn concluded. "My parents were one mother and three adventurous aunts, an unlikely but excellent survival family, sticking like glue from the time Billie was three months pregnant with me—and you've never let me go."

"But sometimes, too tightly, you think?" Bee remarked, trying to get Carolyn to talk about Billie's death, losing her company and her health.

Carolyn wouldn't be dissuaded from her train of thought. "Aunt Robin Lee was dead, too, dying in a car crash on a torturous Hollywood Hills road shortly after I was born. Alcohol and drugs found in and around the wreck, right?" she asked, knowing the answers. Her aunts only nodded. "After kindergarten, I remember helping the four of you move Aunt Robin's things to a new storage locker in California. You took me to Disneyland and Knott's Berry Farm. I was too young to understand death." Carolyn's face became pale. "Now I understand it only too well." She tried to shake off the sadness and keep going with the conversation. *Might as well get it all out now.*

"It was the second time, Carolyn. The first trip was when we came to your Aunt Robin's memorial service. We scraped up the money to take the bus on our first trip to LA. But you were only a few months old," Bee said.

"Most everything in the will went to Billie's agent and mentor, Carl Springs," Cass remembered. "He fostered her career and helped Robin make the right choices. He loved and protected her...and Robin said she loved him, too. We never spoke to him. He went all to pieces when she died. His secretary, Miss Raymond, took care of everything, and hustled him out of the memorial service as soon as it was over. He looked so grief-stricken and didn't say a word to anyone—just sat there and cried."

"Springs was greatly affected by her death and stayed almost in seclusion," Bee remarked.

"Didn't you say he got ill soon after Robin died?" Muriel asked.

"It's a bit of a muddle for us because we had to leave and get back to our jobs, but Darby Fisher, the president of the Robin Lee Fan Club, said if it wasn't for the care of Mr. Springs's assistant, Eleanor Raymond, his health and business might have suffered much worse than the loss of Billie's sister," Cass said. She shook her head.

"Went into a sanitarium for treatment or something for a number of weeks, Miss Raymond said as I recall, so that's why the service was delayed and we were able to get to out to LA to be there," Muriel said. "Darby said Springs remained so grief-stricken when he did venture out, he didn't look like himself at all—much heavier and pasty. Darby hardly recognized him."

"Couldn't even talk on the phone and stayed in seclusion for weeks after…" Bee added.

"Couldn't get him to participate in the transfer of your Aunt Robin's stuff when Darby put everything into the first storage locker," Cass recalled. "Billie kept up the payments faithfully. Miss Raymond apologized several times when we called…she said she couldn't get him to talk about it!"

"Something about intermittent shock treatments or the like to get over his depression," Bee remembered.

"He became a hermit and gave up his business after that, I think you said," Carolyn said. "Darby says he lives in the San Fernando Valley, right? But besides having a phone number and keeping Miss Raymond on as a personal assistant, he won't agree to go to any of the nostalgia events to this day."

"I think Springs and Miss Raymond got married, didn't they?" Cass asked.

"Yes, about three or four years after Robin Lee died," Muriel replied.

Carolyn wished she'd known her beautiful, charismatic aunt Robin Lee. She'd had a short, shooting-star career-an original in energy and style, it seemed. Her large cobalt blue eyes smoldered behind black, charcoal pencil-etched eyelids and lush lashes in the same hushed tones her agent, Mr. Springs, likened to Marilyn Monroe or Audrey Hepburn in her *Funny Face* movie posters. With her vintage or copied 1930's-to-1950s' wardrobe, Robin batted her eyes and vamped her way to celebrity from under the wispy net of her hats she sometimes wore as props—sashaying herself into history. The time she added her smoky alto voice to the title song she written on a whim for one of her film's soundtracks, kept the song on the best-selling charts for forty-eight weeks. She lived a too-short, sun-hot career, journalists lamented in their obituaries.

"Strong cult interest immortalized her fiery life, escapades, and mostly B-level films," Cass said. "Fans, young and old, still talk about her, always begging Carolyn and Billie, and now, Carolyn, to visit their nostalgic gatherings."

"Your Aunt Robin's estate *has* helped with bread-and-butter issues when money was tight," Billie had said. "Everyone remembers or loves your Aunt Robin."

"Billie inherited the memorabilia and a small percentage of the income from licensing fees," Carolyn noted.

Those payments, minus the storage fees, buoyed Billie and Carolyn's existence beyond their household expenses before Four Almonds had taken off. Small checks, and now, small direct deposits, dotted Carolyn's savings account. Not steaks and caviar, but a grateful posthumous stipend stabilizing their life in the former meager situations.

"Now you allow Darby to work on the Robin Lee things, the fan club, and he's become like another relative of sorts." Cass looked at her friends in the car. "Like us."

Billie and Darby took care of most of it when she was alive, but when she could, Carolyn helped with guest appearances and paperwork now. The Robin Lee legacy fell to Carolyn, Darby and her aunts.

"Sometimes, mom's salary from her work in print advertising ran pretty thin," Carolyn remarked. Carolyn always pitched in, working from about age ten or so with babysitting. As Carolyn grew older, there were other part-time and full-time jobs to save for college. "After an uneventful college career, at 24, I had a business degree and a minor in food and hospitality and I went to work for a hotel chain that moved me to LA."

"We all moved to LA, eventually," Cass reminded her.

After several apartments, Carolyn bought her first place, a fixer-upper townhouse near the hotel, which took most of her salary in mortgage and remodeling costs. For a while Carolyn lived on little money, but a mortgage meant she was building a future. With lots of friendly neighbors, Carolyn joined right in with the tradition of Sunday evening potlucks around the pool or in the community room, if the weather was too cold or rainy.

Carolyn noticed one of the men, who had been down on his luck and in poor health, was no longer joining in the fun because of his radiation and chemotherapy treatments. "He can't keep any food down. Even the smell bothers him," one of the neighbors confided. "He's losing weight like crazy. We're all worried." Carolyn had known of other such cases. No matter what the doctors tried to do to help their appetites and suppress the nausea, these patients just seemed to melt away to skin and bones.

"After dinner, I'll make a batch of granola bars from a recipe I concocted in college," Carolyn offered. "I hope they help."

The man not only ate them, regaining some weight and stamina, he offered bites of them to visitors who asked where he had bought them, and where they could get some for themselves. Her innocent offer of the granola bars changed the course of her career and helped start a company beyond her wildest dreams.

"The burgeoning granola bar sales turned into an after-work obsession with bowls and pans engulfing my small townhouse and consuming all my free time before I moved the operation into a cooperative kitchen space about five miles away," Carolyn said.

Carolyn recalled the worn yellow Formica countertop peninsula separating her tiny kitchen from the dining area in her house; barely fitting her squeaky secondhand table, barely big enough for five chairs when they were all there for meals. In their makeshift production line, Cass grabbed for the filled bowl that Muriel pushed over the counter containing the grain with the dried fruit and nut mixture and wet ingredients, so Cass could spread it onto a commercial-size baking pan, one at a time. Billie started moving too, dabbing her cotton-shirted forearm to her perspiring brow as she exchanged the long-necked metal spoon for the large wooden handle of the rubber spatula she'd be using to mold and flatten the granola-like dough. This was the seventh batch. For a moment, the aunts had shooed Carolyn, who measured all the wet and dry ingredients, to the couch to enjoy a glass of Georgia-style lemonade with lots of ice, sugar, and cut lemons both in the pitcher and her frosty glass.

With Carolyn in the living room, Bee now had enough room to stand in front of the small double sink, fighting to clean the big trays and keep the water off the floor and cabinets. She always said, she had asbestos hands from her years of touching hot trays, pots, and pans, so she volunteered to be the dishwasher; seemingly oblivious to the heat and steam of the awkward space.

That day it had been Billie's idea to spread the mixture on the pan and push the almonds end to end in the sheet and then cut it with a moistened knife. This saved time, and the individual bars were easier to measure before being in their own foil wrappers. She cut sheets of foil hot dog wrappers in half, while they all twisted and tucked the foil ends neatly underneath and stuck the home computer-generated labels on each bar. Small orders of bars were put in plain top-folded brown lunch bags, and larger orders went in brown paper shopping bags.

On one visit, Cass shoved a long white envelope in Carolyn's hand. "We've scrapped up a couple thousand to help you expand."

"I vow to pay you three and Mom back even if I have to sell these things on street corners," Carolyn said with grateful tears in her eyes.

As the business grew, Billie moved in with Carolyn and gave Carolyn her rent money to invest in the business. The money infusion allowed Carolyn to move the cooking from her home to a co-op kitchen.

Carolyn called the granola sticks Four Almond bars because of the line of four almonds her mother first suggested. Soon, with her management's blessings and cooperation, she and Billie started marketing her bars at the hotel where she'd worked. It became a favorite snack of the hotel spa, and gained a national and international customer base.

"Those dark circles under your eyes tell me you can't do both your job at the hotel and grow this business," Billy noted. Before quitting her job, Carolyn wanted to make sure she could pay for her mortgage, car expenses, health insurance, and everything involved in being a budding small business owner.

"I registered the Four Almonds bar name," Carolyn started with a laugh but then, she became more sober. "Growing the company was tough, but I loved it," as the enthusiasm left her eyes. At thirty-five years old, she'd done a lot in a short time, Carolyn thought, as they continued to sit in the car. "Now comes the hard part." She spoke in shorthand or she knew she wouldn't get the words out. "The day my mother, Billie, died started badly."

"I woke up tired with a daylong, plaguing headache." She'd pressed her temples and gritted her teeth, through all the last-minute phone calls on the final touches for the changes in the expansion plan, her assistant needed "yesterday." Carolyn's "little good deed" was now a thriving company. Everyone offered their own remedies during the day, from aspirin to cold tea bags on her eyes, yet the pounding wouldn't stop. She wished for the day to be over, so she could go home and rest. Billie heard the distress in her daughter's voice when she called to make sure Carolyn would be home for their Thursday night dinner, volunteering to go to their favorite restaurant to get some their usual soup and sandwiches. "I'm glad it's Thursday soup night."

Carolyn barely made the car ride home, falling into a chair in the family room, determined to tell Billie, even though her briefcase bulged with paperwork, they were taking the evening off. Carolyn hoped she had the energy to make it through their dinner, and promptly fell asleep until the doorbell rang. Carolyn wondered if Billie had left her door key in the kitchen.

Carolyn got up with difficulty, not wanting to leave the confines of the warm leather. "Please don't tell me you've left your keys," when her brain registered it was dark and two men in plain suits stood at her door. She would have retreated and slammed the door, cursing herself for not looking out the peephole first, but Billie sometimes left her keys at home and had trouble with the garage code box.

The shorter of the two men, with a shaved scalp and mouth wreathed with a thin mustache and goatee, whipped out his badge with the speed of a cowboy gunslinger.

Carolyn didn't hear his name. An invisible empty, cold place, like a block of ice, landed in Carolyn's chest, and her ears started buzzing, "Has something happened?"

She ushered the men into the living room.

"You need to sit down," the bald man said, worried by Carolyn's chalky pallor.

The other, Detective Brandon, indicated Billie parked on the sidewalk in front of Snyder's deli. Every Thursday evening for as long as Carolyn could remember, she and her mother argued at the international news television commentators while eating Snyder's chicken noodle soup with two matzo balls.

"I'm sorry, but we think your mother's life ended with a hasty step off the curb from a hit-and-run driver in a light-colored van," stated the man she now knew as Sergeant Rowen. That was what the detectives, coroner, and official police report would confirm in a few weeks.

Carolyn's world crumbled. Somehow, she functioned enough to call her aunts.

Everything after that smudged into a blur of grief and trying to find out who had callously driven away from her mother's broken body.

There were no eyewitnesses to contradict the detectives' initial information—just a cowardly hit-and-run driver. Carolyn hired private detectives.

Carolyn offered a very hefty reward for information, and used her marketing department to stoke continued publicity for the case...but turned up nothing more. Even with Carolyn's contacts and the six private investigators Carolyn hired, they were tripping over themselves sifting through the same scant information she'd gotten from the police. The case was relegated to the back pages of the front section in the newspaper and then made its way to the cold case category.

Carolyn and her aunts continued working on Billie's case: on the computer, handing out fliers, hanging posters, and talking with the media. Only weeks after the funeral, the police dashed her hopes by telling her in official bluntness, they had nothing more to go on. They repeated the theory they had from the start of their investigation: her mother had been trying to balance their dinner and open the car door when a vehicle vaguely described as a small white panel truck, stuck her at high speed, rushing toward the green light in the intersection. Unfortunately, these types of accidents, especially on two-way streets in the metropolitan area, were all too frequent. Without the truck license plate numbers or more accurate details from the eyewitnesses on that dusk evening, the authorities didn't have much of anything to go on. The pile of competing manila folders on their desks seemed to say the case would stay open, but sharing time with many other crimes...and many other broken people touched by misfortune.

With her mother's death, her own life deteriorated into something she could only describe as a fun house mirror room. Nothing looked or felt the same. No one's advice on how to proceed rang true. Now Carolyn's emotions were like helium balloons floating all over the place, sometimes plunging to despair as if all buoyancy in her life was gone and her world was flat.

Crazy childhood impulses popped up, like wanting her old Pooh bear, lost during a move in her third-grade summer. She again yearned for the crazy, muddy-yellow, long-lost bear whose eyes and patches of fur were gone. Carolyn recalled her sadness as she and her mother traced the path from the old apartment: checking the garbage bin, shaking all the packing papers, and combing every inch of the car, the parking lots and the streets they had driven. A bear-size hole in her heart lasted a long time as she mourned the loss of her bear all those years ago. Now a mother-size one was beside it, begging to be filled and for the physical ache to pass. Her heart began to rebel. "When my mother died, my heart problems started."

Carolyn remembered one event. "It's been a while since your mother's death?" her doctor noted as he looked at his notes, concentration furrows marring his kind, middle-age face.

Carolyn could only nod, not mentioning her Uncle Edgar's recent death as well.

"Just be careful. Your erratic high pulse rate, even though these bursts only occur occasionally, is no joke," her doctor warned in a few heated words. "Running your company and finding answers to your mother's death are important, I know, but not at the cost of these heart episodes." Instead he suggested avoiding the scene of the accident, and getting lots of rest, strongly intimating Carolyn wouldn't get the insurance she needed to grow her company if she continued to stress herself with business and searching for clues in her mother's death. Health facts were facts and couldn't be hidden.

How many times had had her aunts told her to slow down and get on with her life? "Trust your aunts and anyone else who speaks sense," Billie would say. "Cass, Bee, and Muriel show you in a dozen ways that they love you with a daughter type of love. You know that." *Did my mother have an unspoken premonition?* Carolyn thought these pronouncements were morbid at the worst and quirky at best. "Face the facts," Billie would say. "Nobody gets out of this life alive."

Cass started talking. "When we all sat vigil in the ICU waiting room when you were ill, we thought we'd failed you." Prickling, nervous thoughts propelled Cass to want some coffee, breaking her resolution for at least the hundredth time to keep her caffeine consumption down to three cups a day. "People mourn in different ways."

Muriel said, "Then there were the deaths of Edgar, Cal, and Duke."

Bee stayed silent and looked at Cass with troubled eyes. *What more was there to say?* Their coltish niece with the sparkling blue eyes, quick smile, and effervescent spirit had gone underground with her emotional pain, but they were all *reeling* from the deaths of four people in such a short time; each trying to deal with the tsunami of grief.

"Months past, Carolyn, as you dodged question after question regarding you grief and mourning or bushed us off. Sometimes it was agonizing dealing with our own pain while trying to be loving aunts to you," Bee remarked, entering in the conversation.

"Carolyn, you're as stubborn and task-oriented as we all were, but Bee, Muriel, and I shared and cried with each other…and you just went off and carried on your business and investigation crusades." Cass looked at her cup and sighed. "I cried, talked, and could lose myself with fabrics and patterns and digging in the dirt. Muriel and Bee busied themselves with their classic historical and film hobbies and crafts and cooking, respectively. We wrestled with the grief and came out comforted and peaceful on the other side. You just worked and worked and worked."

Carolyn didn't say anything and her aunts' words made her feel equally sad and angry. Angry at them for saying these things, angry that her mother had died and angry that she'd had to chase after a coward of a person, yet unknown, who had done it all and angry her decisions and ill-health had caused her to loss her company.

"Will the three of you please get out of the car for a few minutes, I need to do something," Carolyn asked quietly. "If the replacement car comes, just tell them to wait."

Muriel and Cass looked at Carolyn warily, as if they weren't going to leave, but Bee gave them one of her sternest looks and flicked her head to the car exterior to indicate she wanted them to follow her. Reluctantly, the other two women got out of the car and closed their doors. Carolyn started the engine and drove over to the place farthest away on the lot and away from everyone.

After about thirty seconds, muffled cries could be heard coming from the car interior. "Do you think she needs help?" Muriel took a step toward the car.

Bee restrained her friend and ordered quietly. "I think she needs to be alone for a few minutes."

"What if she...?" Muriel persisted.

"She can't get far in that car the way it is and I've got the license plate and the police on speed dial," Bee replied.

"I'll give her fifteen minutes," Cass said stubbornly.

"We haven't been able to get through to her in several years, Cass. So, we'll give her as long as she needs over there...and pick up the pieces, if need be," Bee ordered.

It took eighteen minutes and an assurance to the gas station attendants that their niece was just having a bad day and needed some time alone. "Sometimes, you get a doo-doo sundae...and the car almost breaking down and this delay was just the cherry on top for her," Bee said to the attendants. "Don't you ever need to de-stress?"

"She's sure got a good set of lungs," Arnie observed as he headed back to the small convenience store counter in the gas station.

All three women looked heavenward and were relieved when the screaming and sobbing stopped, hoping this indicated Carolyn was recovering and putting herself back together.

"Do you think she'll be OK to drive?" Muriel asked.

"All-in-all probably better than when she got to the gas station," Bee replied.

Soon, the rental car engine started and Carolyn drove back to the place where Arnie had originally parked the car. Carolyn looked red-eyed and calm as Bee, Cass and Muriel took their seats, almost as if the conversation had never been interrupted.

"By the time I could afford to put top-level management in place to lead my company and give me a respite, I was too ill to teach anyone," Carolyn blurted hastily, with a sigh and a sniffle. "Episodes of my heart rate speeding up to over two hundred per minute, felt like a trapped, tiny bird in my throat as I panted for breath. If I hastily picked a replacement CEO and made another bad choice, the company might lose market share and momentum…and falter.

"I made inquiries through Mr. Lyon after my last major attack." Carolyn looked at Muriel. "I was lying in my ICU bed, as my cardiologist looked over my EKG tracings and other test reports. 'Your heart can't take much more before you'll be forced to take strong medication and surgery, perhaps a few surgeries.'

"His grim, no-nonsense assessment indicated I really needed to save my health with a long rest from my whirlwind career as owner and spokesperson of Four Almonds." Carolyn bit her lip. "Great success on the outside, but my health…and life…were a disaster on the inside."

Carolyn's lips thinned. "It all could have crumbled if news of my leave of absence spread. The cost of doing business would rise. Debt could be a company killer too.

"So I *very* grudgingly changed course, to say the least, and gave up Four Almonds. Then, in your muddled plan in buying the mansion, I've felt *forced* to jump on *your* bandwagon about this old house. Again, something out of my hands. Loyalty to you and feeling guilty that you'd wrecked your financial retirement stability… got me here." Carolyn waved her arms indicating the gas station. "I loathed the idea of selling my company and that you presented me with this silly 'project' idea of yours. You used the flimsy excuse that 39 Bayshore had appeared as a major exterior shot in one of my aunt Robin Lee's film."

"You never did like being pushed into anything," Bee said.

"The second, third, and fourth opinions from other doctors, and several psychologists, were *not* in my favor either. I couldn't understand why there couldn't be some miracle pill to cure things or why the circumstances stacked everything against me. I was a bit short-sighted on recognizing *my* culpability." Twin shafts of pain caused tears to cloud Carolyn's eyes.

"Regretfully, I sold Four Almonds to Allied Food Brands." Carolyn voice sounded raw. She was now rich and could live quite lavishly - not have to work for the rest of her life. But, pure and simple, it was a hollow victory.

"Getting you here was difficult," Muriel remarked.

"Getting you to do anything you didn't want to do was difficult," Cass noted.

"But you sold the LA house...and were looking for another one. We didn't want you to do anything rash or risk your health further," Bee said. They made their plans as several assistants packed Carolyn's possessions, except last-minute clothes and personal items for the Bayshore trip.

"OK. There wasn't much besides threatening your retirement accounts that could have gotten my attention. I place the blame squarely on my own shoulders. I buried my grief, and my life, under a blistering pace to achieve success with my company and my relentless piggybacked search for Billie's killer." Carolyn sighed. "I chose the wrong road, and in my stubborn numbness, I kept going the wrong *way*. But I wish you had come to me sooner with your plans to come here." Carolyn disliked making snap decisions. "But you three were right in the end. Buying the house was just like something my mother would do. 'Desperate times need desperate measures,' she would always say.

"Immediately buying another house in LA would have been a mistake," Carolyn admitted. "But couldn't it have been something simpler than this yet unseen purple hulk?"

"Well, if it hadn't been such a scatterbrain idea and nothing to do with your Aunt Robin, then you wouldn't have come," Muriel said simply.

"Touché," Carolyn said as she looked over her shoulder. "I think the new rental car is here."

"I don't understand this," the young rental car representative said to his supervisor over the cellphone. "The pictures I've sent you from my phone are really bad!"

"Kid, I don't understand it either," the older man sitting at his corporate desk at the rental car headquarters replied, with an edge in his voice. "Never seen anything like it but we're going to have to investigate everything at the airport garage as well as notify the hose, belt and car manufacturer. That's too much damage for a new fleet car." He looked at the information on the computer screen. "You said the invoice shows four women headed for the shore?"

"Looks like one younger woman is the driver with three older ladies. Her aunts she said. The time indicates they weren't doing anything unusual in their trip since they've had the car." The young man looked from the damaged vehicle being loaded on the flatbed tow truck to the women who were ready to drive away in the replacement vehicle. "I've got, and verified their temporary address."

"Good thing. We'll be looking at everything here. The paperwork from the airport garage says everything was checked...and I know the man who checked it. A long time employee with a flawless employment record," his superior said with an exasperated voice. He wiped his hand over his face. "Just give them the new

SVU with three free days rental with our apologies…and we'll start the internal sabotage investigation as soon as you get the car to the shop. Make sure no one touches it until our team gets down there to check it over."

CHAPTER THREE

As Hesse Silver flexed tension out his neck, he knew this opportunity to talk to his construction business partner, Shealds Jackson, wasn't going to be easy. In their prison days, Hesse, as a black man, *never* had communication problems with Shealds, who was white, or David Molina, their much-younger third business partner, who was Hispanic. *This conversation might be different!*

They'd mutually transitioned from prison life to business life within a few months of each other. From the beginning, the task had been difficult, but they'd gotten permission to work together right and tight from the authorities. Shealds's connections had taken care of all those sticky issues and their paroles were over. The three kept their noses clean and their heads high to prove they'd be rehabilitation success stories. They were clean citizens now.

Granted, they were ex-cons. To outsiders, seeing Hesse as a black man working with a white ex-con and a Hispanic ex-con, ran the gambit of emotions in meeting new people—from fear to bland curiosity. He and Molina owed Shealds a lot for this stable restart of their lives. But now there were two, perhaps three, concerns coming to the surface that might change things…for the worse.

The problem was, most people in prison said they were innocent and they weren't, *not even close.* He and Molina were guilty as sin. Hesse considered he was a decent kid with decent grades. His parents were gone. His father had died of cancer and high blood pressure when he was in middle school and mother had died of diabetes complications before his senior year in college. He'd worked odd jobs for money and high school summers working with his Uncle Jim doing remodeling and small construction jobs – but he wanted more status and more money. He'd used embezzlement and extortion to pay for his out-of-control lifestyle, trying to be a high roller to people who either weren't worth it or those asking for "loans" from his old neighborhood. As the first college graduate on either side of his family, success deluded Hesse into thinking he could *and should* lavish his family and friends with his checkbook and credit cards. They lived the "good life" before Hesse couldn't qualify for any more credit to keep the party going. Instead of coming clean and declaring bankruptcy, his ego got the best of him and he started embezzling from his employer, hoping to pay back his debt and scale back his gifts and lifestyle. The desperate and stupid decision got him fifteen years in prison…and no one visited him, except his Uncle Jim, who hadn't taken a cent from Hesse. Lesson learned loud-and-clear. He'd thrown his life away on fair-weather friends.

Molina didn't talk much. As a prodigy in the gang world, and quiet veteran of urban gang warfare, Molina's parents were dead from drugs and alcohol, two brothers died in gang violence and he was the only one left. At least Molina was literate and gifted in drawing and graphic design. His gang buddies didn't have much use for his constant barrage of doddles and drawings but his abilities were formidable in making schematics to help the gang in their robberies and gun assembly and disassembly for their turf wars. He also cleaned and fixed stolen merchandise and arma-ments for a black market enterprise under the tutelage of his gang brothers. In a police sweep, Molina got caught and given a three years' prison sentence.

Hesse and Molina struck up a friendship while doing laundry detail and Molina acted as his lookout, no questions asked, when Hesse staged a fight to protect Shealds. After that, the three of them bonded as friends behind bars and Hesse and Shealds guid-ed Molina through his GED and some college classes before the state budget cut the funding.

Shealds's story was different. He worked hard: 6'2", like Hesse, and about the same weight – 220. At 41, he had a full head of silver hair laced with black. Shealds was never afraid to get dirty and acted cool-headed and not too edgy when things went wrong on the job. In all his specifics or general talk about his life, Shealds indicated he had a normal middle-class life and education with a gift for business and had amassed his personal fortune in financial ser-vices. Nothing amiss until his half-brother's scheme was uncovered by the authorities.

Shealds continually insisted he was framed - by the government, no less. From the day Shealds was out of prison, he'd straight-up informed him and Molina, that under the tenuous safety of this construction company front, he wanted to prove it.

Hesse and Molina believed Shealds, and Hesse committed himself, as did Molina, to help their friend. But Shealds said the time was getting close now…and the reality of it was sinking into Hesse's bones.

As of now, Shealds's rap sheet included lying to federal au-thorities concerning his knowledge of interstate transportation of narcotics and hazardous materials – all his half-brother's doing. This gave Shealds an eighteen-month stint in prison, the moniker of ex-convict…and the loss of his business and all his securities licenses. He'd been the young, silver-haired poster boy for everything wrong about the banking and investment industry for several years, and the springboard for several political careers out of the federal prosecutor's and district attorney's offices in New York. The problem was that Shealds *pleaded guilty*!

Innocent but pleading guilty? Shealds's situation had been a tangled mess. Hesse still shook his head when he thought of the facts Shealds had shared.

Shealds was also *unlike* any ex-con Hesse had ever met: always honest and truthful, and he tried his level best not to let them down—ever. Rock solid. Shealds was the one to come up with the idea of a construction business once they got out of prison. Shealds said he was interested in architecture and had worked some manual labor in high school and college. Hesse had construction experience with his Uncle Jim and Molina proved in his repair jobs under the tutelage of the prison staff, that he could be an asset as well with his drawing skills and his work ethic.

Besides getting the clearance to allow them to work together after their prison terms, Shealds bankrolled their business and hadn't asked squat in return for either his or Molina's one-third shares, except to work hard and stay clean. They started slow and worked night-and-day, gradually building their business using their own labor, and then, incorporating reliable subcontractors as needed. Shealds worked as long and as hard as they or any of the other people they hired, and didn't seem to miss being a big man back on Wall Street.

Hesse didn't show it but he felt grave concern about sliding down another rabbit hole of failure to go back behind bars...after things had been going so well. If Shealds's personal plan to clear his name didn't work out, Hesse might face prison again as an accessory, having knowledge of and participating in Shealds's crime, which was going to bend, if not break, a number of laws. It would be a second strike on *all three* men's criminal records. So Hesse rehearsed the words he was going to say and prayed things would work out.

Hesse needed more input about what was happening *now.*

Reassuring words and promises were also cheap in their former worlds of his big spending days and Molina's violence-tinged life. A few years of stability against chaotic pasts indicated how fast things changed. *Would they flip back now?*

As Hesse walked into the office, he focused all his energy into convincing Shealds to be careful and share more information. Yesterday's knife-flattened tires on the potential job site at 39 Bayshore seemed worrisome. Shealds had shrugged it off as possible vandals or kids with more time than brains on the path to juvenile detention. Hesse's hard-knock life and convict-honed gut remained skeptical. Hesse's concerns were about Zaugus and the government on the one hand and whispers about Shealds' sister-in-law, Ellen, and the mob on the other. *Better get this conversation over.* He'd try a broader approach. "You're still thinking on how to handle the Bayshore place?"

Shealds Jackson frowned as shadows from his side-parted silver hair hung down to obscure his brown eyes. He didn't lift his head, just nodded curtly, still concentrating on one last item on the architectural drawings of 39 Bayshore.

"Is your situation going to mix with that?" Hesse's tone remained even and quiet.

Shealds stretched his work-broadened shoulders after long hours of being bent over the plans. *There is no need to beat around the bush.* "We wanted to buy 39 Bayshore for ourselves. But I didn't want to cause trouble by throwing money around in such a big investment." Shealds wanted Hesse to understand. "I'm really sorry."

Hesse shrugged to let Shealds know it wasn't a big deal. "It would have been a great place for all three of us—plus plenty of room for the equipment yard...to be hidden from the road and the rest of the property. But there will be other places." He pressed on. "Lucky we bought one of the two freed-up lots from the sale when the new owners subdivided the place...but that's not the only thing I'm concerned about."

"What else?" Shealds asked with an edge to his voice, knowing what was next.

"You're still working to overturn your conviction on the down-low." Hesse knew his grandmother would have kicked him for using so much slang, but Hesse couldn't mince words or tidy up the situation.

Shealds obliged him, because his actions put Hesse, and Molina, at risk. "Don't want our ex-con stink to resurface any more than you want to go back to prison, but I'm *going to* clear my name."

"You've been secretive since you started this," Hesse stated. "So Molina and I are still relegated to a need-to-know basis?"

"You want Attorney General Zaugus and police dogging you if I can't pull this off?" Shealds maintained eye contact until he got up and looked out the office window. "I know I'm putting you both at risk. I don't want *anyone* or our construction business going down in flames...but I've got to prove my innocence, and now's the time to do it."

"I care about *you* and that you're OK...but I'm still praying none of us has to go back...to anything like prison if things go wrong." Hesse followed Shealds over to the window but gave his friend plenty of space.

"I've got my sister-in-law, Ellen, to think of," Shealds hedged as he raked his right hand through his unruly silver hair and headed for the kitchen of their four-bedroom home, which doubled as their construction business address. "Need some coffee?" He passed Hesse on the way to the kitchen coffeemaker. "I couldn't turn away from this job, Hesse. I want to see 39 Bayshore done properly, and it would have raised too many red flags if we seemed disinterested now."

Hesse frowned, but he understood that appearances were everything sometimes. "So you'll tell us when you're ready to start your plan?"

"Yes." Shealds headed back to his desk as he took a sip of the Hesse-strong brew, —all the smaller puzzle pieces still needed to fit if he had a chance to make this all work. Trying not to think about what might go wrong wasn't an easy task. Perhaps taking a ride on his paddleboard might help reduce the stress and this recent spate of bad memories. Shealds headed for the garage and the open water.

Hesse hadn't even gotten to mention his concerns about the mob. He'd wait.

As Shealds paddled his way to deeper water, he remembered the issues, then and now, which lead him to prison and his current construction company work. The first thing he thought of was Ellen's fresh, eager face, all those years ago, looking like a picture out of a cosmetics ad - her easy beauty and intelligence. Shealds mentioned her to his younger stepbrother, Warren. Warren relished the business-related social life—the latest new gossip column girl, the newest runway sensation or the newest, single actress gaining fame on or off-Broadway. Three weeks later, Warren waltzed into the office with Ellen on his arm. Shealds was too busy running the company and fine-tuning the Barkley merger to really think about Warren's intentions.

Only with the long months in a cell, helped Shealds piece everything together. The diamond-hard truth was Warren wanted everything Shealds had, from things he mentioned casually right up to, and including, Shealds's company. If Shealds looked at a watch, Warren had the best model of that brand within days. The same with restaurant reservations, tickets to any venue, vacations…and women. He, as an older stepbrother, was bound to love and protect Warren Preece. Shealds shuddered at his blindness.

His off-handed reference about Ellen had put her in the bull's-eye of Warren's dysfunctional orbit!

Warren and Ellen eloped after knowing each other for five months.

Shealds thought he could help be the eight-years-older big brother Warren needed in order to mature. Shealds's mother had died of a silent, deadly aneurysm two weeks after Shealds had turned eighteen. Until then, Shealds had what he thought was a normal childhood of excelling in a public school environment with plenty of after-school sports and a few trophies. His teachers and classmates called him a "born leader" and he was looking for more of the same with his business undergraduate degree.

His widowed father was not only devastated…but quite incapable of handling the household. Waving away Shealds' assurances that his mother, Marjorie, had taught Shealds rudimentary cooking, washing, and cleaning techniques as part of his youthful training, Carlton Jackson, his father, hired a divorcee, Gloria Preece, as their housekeeper two weeks after the funeral. She frequently brought along her eleven-year-old son, Warren.

His father and Gloria were married ten months later in the gazebo of the family home. Shealds now knew he should have asked his father to wait, to be surer of his decision before remarrying, but he didn't, because he was going off to college and knew his father needed someone to take care of him. *Otherwise, why would he have married again so soon?*

Shealds concentrated on his education and finally started his own investment business. As people began to notice Shealds' acumen, he expanded his businesses and also funded Warren's Ivy League education expenses. After graduation and some serious conversations about life goals and purpose, Warren still flitted from job to job in the company, always telling Shealds at each new desk and assignment, "This will be the right place. I promise."

Shealds was glad when Warren announced he'd given a four-carat engagement ring to Ellen Wolder. Warren would gain stability, Shealds thought, be a grown man with a wife. Then came the quick elopement. Perhaps to stave off his own longing for a home of his own, Shealds paid for a large apartment in Central Park West as a wedding present. "You're on your own now, Warren. Understand?" Shealds prayed he did.

Warren had nodded his ascent and graciously thanked his big brother for all the love and help when Shealds had come by to toast the happy couple in their three-bedroom "wedding gift". After the champagne dinner, he'd only seen his brother a few times outside of work, at family occasions and holiday dinners. Shealds shrugged it off, because he knew Warren and Ellen were newlyweds…and then, new parents.

But Warren's relationships and tactics were a charade; tools of continued deep insecurity and deception. Warren lived beyond his means, and beyond his credit, resorting to money from loan sharks and other illegal sources. Rather than confessing his problems to Shealds or anyone else, Warren had been reeled in like a naive fish, agreeing to use the company's jet to mule drugs, money, and other contraband around the country. Warren's only contact in this illegal behavior, a small time bookie named Ernie, was also dead—a cold-case homicide—and the hunt for any bigger players in the illegal scheme stalled and died as well.

Warren's death-by-sports-car-crash had been a self-centered attempt to free himself from what was going to be a long prison term or death by his mob connections.

The district attorney, Neal Anthony Zaugus, had been like a dog with a juicy bone during the case. Zaugus painted himself as a bold, crusading law-and-order type, when in reality he was a rogue prosecutor with a team of two other lawyers with no compunction of taking advantage of the situation and denying any mercy. Zaugus and his team had been tipped off for several months about

Warren's situation. With Warren dead, there was no one else to go after with any name recognition other than Shealds Clayton Jackson himself. Even though Shealds tried to explain Ellen's fragility and ask for a continuance, Zaugus was undeterred and unrelenting as was Zaugus's handpicked judge. "All you have to do is prove your innocence," Zaugus retorted to Shealds's every request.

Warren was dead, and Ellen was left a young, grief-broken, and pregnant widow with a young child. From the time of the funeral, she'd refused to speak to Shealds directly – blaming Shealds for her husband's death. With the ensuing company scandal, Ellen turned to her mother and shut Shealds off completely from her and her toddler son.

The trusted private investigator firm Shealds had hired years ago for company matters now tracked Ellen and pieced together her family's past. The reports indicted mostly bad news. Shealds understood Ellen's anger, but there was also another dangerous specter in her path. Ellen's mother and her mother's boyfriend affected the family's future as well. "No easy way to put it, Shealds. The mother's boyfriend is tied to the mob. No, let's say he *is* the mob," reported Bob Samples, head of the private investigator and security firm.

Ellen's academic father, Edward, from upstate New York, had older insurance broker and schoolteacher parents, and Edward's college-secretary-to-homemaker wife, Udra, came from an early widowed plumber's home in a tenement and Mafia-ridden neighborhood in Hoboken, New Jersey.

"Joseph, Udra's ex-boyfriend, the mobster, came back into the picture when Edward died from complications of heart disease," Samples said evenly. Joseph was Joey (the Melon) Cantaloupo, who had kept track of Udra's life and stepped in after Ellen's father died.

"Udra's making the payments on her arts-and-crafts family home, thanks to Joey. When Edward died, he left almost nothing: a small pension, an equally small insurance policy, and his books and papers as an eighteenth and nineteenth century American history scholar." Samples turned the file page. "Being a modestly paid professor left a poor widow.

"Udra Wolder told everyone in the neighborhood when Ellen married your stepbrother. With Warren as your younger brother, you the owner and founder of Greene Investment Companies, Udra thought they would all ride the gravy train into the sunset."

Shealds's shoulders tensed. Instead his stepbrother had involved himself in a two-bit smuggling scheme that had ruined them all.

"As you know, your half-brother, Warren Preece, also left a lot of debt behind," Samples offered. The money and credit ran out after Warren's death. Udra looked at the facts. It was no picnic being a plumber's daughter. In their youth, Joey's affection waned and he left to chase more skirts. Then, Udra'd found and lost her academic husband, who left her with nothing. Warren and that gravy train were gone. Now Joey was back...but for how long? And how long were the checks from Shealds going to keep coming?

"Udra's kept above-water with your payments, which she still continues to accept on the sly," Samples continued. "But fearing your generosity can end at any time, Cantaloupo's pressed his advantage. Udra needs security..."

Shealds closed his eyes. Half out of love and half out-of-naiveté, no background checks on *every aspect* of his extended family history were done before Warren's marriage.

Udra contacted a columnist she knew who did society news, and asked if they were in the market for children's pictures during the storm of Shealds's situation and how much were they worth. The sum the smarmy guy quoted was peanuts, but Udra grabbed at the chance. After seeing the pictures of Udra carrying toddler Devin to visit baby Will in the NICU, the press hung out at the hospital.

Shealds knew about pictures. He'd been led off in a well-photographed arrest complete with handcuffs; his brown eyes and square, silver-haired head as well as his other tight, rawboned features, blazed across the then-fledgling business television and specialty print news before, during, and after the proceedings. The twenty-four-hour news monster had to be fed. Digital images lived forever. The press tacked on the new fodder of Shealds sister-in-law and children to the zombie parade of his perp walk as the networks reveled in chewing on him and rerunning the images of his arrest over and over when new business scandals arose.

Overwrought with the unwanted publicity and fear for her baby's safety, Ellen stayed by Will's incubator day and night. Soon Ellen couldn't sleep, and she started talking crazy about her brother-in-law. Ellen wouldn't listen to anyone or slow down, trying to pump breast milk for her premature son, caring for her other child as best she could, and practically living at the hospital. "We kept telling Ellen and Udra the insurance would remain solid. We worked with the hospital and sent in extra twenty-four-hour security anonymously, telling Ellen "we" were hired by the hospital."

Ellen started calling Shealds or his lawyers every hour of the day and night to tell them off about mistreating Warren, mishandling and misrepresenting Warren in the impending court case, and betraying her trust by putting the children in jeopardy. Ellen became as thin as a stick.

At least Ellen wasn't yelling at her about Joey's being in the mob anymore, Udra thought. Warren's brother was now public enemy number one.

Udra thought Ellen would soon calm down and they'd all go back to the Central Park West apartment to consider what to do next. There was always the jewelry and the two mint-condition cars in the parking garage that they could sell...but that didn't happen.

After Ellen fainted in hospital parking lot, no one, including Udra, could get Ellen to stop crying and shaking when she regained consciousness in the emergency room. The doctors diagnosed

Ellen with extreme postpartum depression. At least Ellen didn't fight when they wheeled her gurney to the psychiatric ward.

"Udra stayed skeptical... and didn't know who was going to pay the bills when Ellen and Will were both in the hospital and Devin was still in diapers," Samples said. "She made contacts to try to sell the apartment, but she had no legal standing."

"That's when Cantaloupo tightened his grip?" Shealds said sourly.

"Don't blame yourself; he was always there. Remember, he helped make the mortgage payments on Udra's house," Samples replied.

Cantaloupo was always informed about photographers, paparazzi, and "adult" filmmakers. His capability to provide embarrassing photos of people in high places was a profitable sideline, both in money and needed influence when the police or the legal system challenged his mob connections. With these tools as well as street smarts and talent with guns, he'd risen to the top of his unusual business in the usual bloody fashion. Now he wanted some social credibility, and who better than Udra Wolder from the old high school days across the river, where he worked on the estates of the moneyed families by placing sports and racing bets for the fathers, grandfathers, and their precious children on the side?

Joey knew every smarmy detail about Warren Preece, Shealds Jackson's stepbrother, including his gambling debts and how often he procured expensive uptown prostitutes for himself and Greene Company clients before his death. Maybe Shealds Jackson knew about his brother-in-law's peccadillos, maybe he didn't. Whether Jackson knew about it or not, it was time for Joey to turn over a new leaf, put a layer of respectability between him and the less savory aspects of his business and to smooth things over with Udra as steps in Joey's personal reclamation project. *Why not throw a few "anonymous" facts about Warren Preece, to Zaugus, the district attorney?*

Bad luck for Jackson…but good luck for Joey. Jackson needed to stay out of the picture…and in prison, to give Joey time to solidify his efforts.

Joey wanted Udra squarely in his camp. *Jackson's pile of dirt needs to be bigger than mine!*

So Ellen unwittingly danced with two devils. On one side was a known crime boss…and, on the other, Shealds was, by all appearances, the ex-felon brother-in-law. Ellen blamed Shealds for killing her husband, the premature birth of her son, and the shambles of their lives.

Samples gave Shealds more bad news. "Unfortunately, from all reports, Ellen's continuing personal hatred against you is her prime motivating factor in her recovery." Ellen's medical records indicated her post-clinical challenges: postpartum depression; young widowhood; difficult, closely spaced pregnancies; exhaustion; and grief.

"So it's Ellen and her hatred for me without even considering Cantaloupo's mob connection." Shealds quietly closed the file, thinking of this Damocles' choice as another reason for him to clear his name. Samples shrugged. *Is Joey the one coming after me and causing these accidents?* He'd have to ask Samples to check on these suspicions.

Shealds's considered his company and employees when he decided to go to prison. If he decided to stand trial, tell what Warren had done, and plead his innocence, the court process would take about three to five years, his lawyers said. Until then, his business would be under siege. When the business media needed fodder in slow news times, his beloved Greene Investment Companies headed the list of "talking points" about Wall Street illegalities. They'd snipe, *"How can Jackson be trusted with billions of dollars of pensions, retirement funds and people's hard-earned money, if he didn't even know about his own brother's actions?"* People fully understood black sheep relations and problems, but coupling those indiscretions with investing their money was another matter. Shealds wasn't squeaky clean anymore.

Everyone in the company became associated with the scandal because Shealds was *the sole owner.* For many years to come, competitors would trumpet Shealds's "incompetence" and "dirty dealings" while he sat at his lawyers' offices with depositions and paperwork. If Shealds couldn't keep things afloat, he could still lose the company and have all his employees thrown out of work. How many times had he seen the sad, shell-shocked faces of people who had served their companies well, carrying boxes out of offices and having to face an uncertain life without jobs?

Even though Shealds was innocent, Warren had slung torrents of "dirt" that tainted everything. There would be the dead-to-rights evidence of the Greene plane carrying money, drugs, and contraband in its cargo hold, as well as all the lurid details of his brother's illicit past, including several digital examples of Warren, with clients of the Greene Investment Companies, carousing with women who *were not* their wives, when they was supposed to be out of town and concentrating on business and their work.

Shealds never knew about any of the parties and would have stopped them—if he'd known. *Was blackmail in Warren's future plans, if he had lived?*

Shealds scoured every source. Zaugus didn't have those tapes...yet. Shealds thought he had every copy of the illicit parties...but with digital media, could he ever be sure?

So the facts, taken in total, were bleak. Shealds could probably: one, lose his dangerously premature nephew; two, further fray the sanity of his sister-in-law; three, "blow up" a truckload of other marriages and companies, if any information of these party facts leaked to Zaugus and/or the press; and four, still lose the company for people's loss/lack of faith in him because of the scandal, which would cost more jobs and throw more lives into turmoil!

Shealds looked at it from every angle. Zaugus and his team of-fered a package: selling the company and a plea agreement of five years in a federal prison with an expiration date—of two days. So Shealds told Samples and his lawyers to look at everything again and start the negotiated legal process of trimming the five years Zaugus wanted, to eighteen months in federal prison. Zaugus countered with eighteen months, no early parole, the maximum fine, a sell-off or breakup of his company plus an agreement to give up all his security licenses and to never deal in securities ever again.

He'd gone to his suite of rooms, with room service and sev-eral bottles of good Scotch, and thought about all his alternatives. The incriminating electronic images of Warren and the partying were burned along with all the equipment—except for one copy Samples held in deepest security. Shealds decided he'd go to jail, give Ellen and his nephews' time to recover, save what he could of the company from disaster, and wait until everything blew over *before* he started the fight to declare his innocence.

Shealds pleaded no contest, trying to protect what was left of his family, and accepted the plea deal. But he vowed if he lived through prison, he'd stealthily investigate *everything* in the situa-tion and prove his innocence.

Zaugus made it to the state attorney general's office on the coattails of Shealds's conviction in the next year's election. His two team members were now the district attorney and an assistant state's attorney, just waiting their turns for higher office.

So Shealds sat in prison, conferred stealthily with Samples, and concentrated on his strategic game of cat and mouse to clear his name. When he got out, Shealds exploited his long-known interest in architecture and started the construction business as a good cover far away from New York, to get through his parole and hide his true intentions. These rogue prosecutors were no dummies, so he had to be careful. If all went well, Shealds would make sure they would see what life was like in the felony trenches!

While savoring the possibility of payback, there was Ellen and the boys who needed protection. Things for them before during and after his incarceration were rough. Shealds tried to control what he could.

Shealds remembered adjusting to prison with a few mishaps: a brow wound, the jaw scar, and several cracked ribs. Shealds's poker face, learned in the business world, didn't let inmates know the depth of his pain or self-defense proficiency. Shealds needed to indicate he could protect himself before someone decided to make him a punching bag – or worse. The thought of this balancing act furrowed Shealds's brow, creasing at the line of eleven forehead stitches he'd received during his first incarceration.

Hesse said he had a plan.

The result was a smooth, flat jaw scar, like something from a swashbuckling pirate movie, slashed directly along his left jawbone with only a slight curl under the left ear. To be fair, Hesse had set Molina as a lookout and quietly asked Shealds not to flinch in the prearranged prison yard attack Hesse orchestrated. But seeing the crudely made jailhouse knife coming through the air at his neck unnerved Shealds, making the blade veer off slightly, causing the little curl. But just as Hesse had predicted, after Shealds had gotten stitched up and refused to identify anyone from the prison yard as his attacker, he gained the other inmates' respect. After that encounter, everyone kept off his back for the most part, and cemented his, Hesse and Molina's friendship.

After his time in prison, Shealds wouldn't hide his gray hair or his chin line scar, allowing the amnesia of time and the advent of other more outrageous scandals help to help dim people's memories. Flickers of recognition and suspicion still greeted him, but they were getting less frequent. Women no longer clutched their purses or pulled children closer to their bodies when they saw him.

At first he felt he was climbing Everest, but now getting work had become easier; better prices and quality workmanship with heavy bond coverage and insurance helped to win people over and to allow the former ex-cons on their properties.

Their paroles were finished too. Attorney General Zaugus had monitored his parole and his activities closely, according to his contacts in the state police department. Even though Attorney General Zaugus had no legal authority to do so, Samples warned Shealds, he remained under surveillance as a favor from one state's government to another. *So Zaugus could be causing the recent trouble as well.*

Samples continued to give Shealds frequent updates on Ellen and the boys. Currents reports these last months were slightly encouraging. "Udra and Joey have made some mistakes. I don't know if these infractions might be big enough to shake Ellen from their influence. We'll see. But I think you need to talk to her.

"Joey hired nannies to take care of the boys and was looking at putting the boys in an upstate New York boarding school if Ellen didn't get better," Samples said as he continued to look at his notes. "Ellen fired the nannies, has gone back to work part-time …and won't consider boarding school under any circumstances…but they're living in the family home in New Jersey with Udra.

"There have also been some heated discussions about Udra's relationship with Joey as well. Ellen's made it clear she wants Udra to *give up* her relationship with Cantaloupo." Samples frowned and changed the topic a bit.

"On the brighter side, from all reports we continue to get, your nephew Devin is a whip-smart almost six year old and Will is going on five and loves plastic building blocks," Samples reported.

"Keep on it," Shealds replied. "I'll get the building plans over to the bed-and-breakfast where Ms. Reynolds and her family are staying…and try to get some work there to keep things going till we start the plan against Zaugus."

Shealds delivered the drawings and specifications concerning the 39 Bayshore lots to the Two Cups of Tea bed-and-breakfast. When Molina answered the company office phone, a Ms. Tembrell, who represented the LA lawyer of the new owners, seemed quite specific in her requests. "Please deliver the papers and *leave*. Ms. Reynolds hasn't made any decisions and will contact your company when *she's* ready." In corporate speak, Shealds thought Carolyn Reynolds was looking for other contractors. Shealds would locate any competition for 39 Bayshore and give them better jobs at higher rates to make sure they were made busy—elsewhere.

"The ladies aren't here yet," Nan Stornel, who owned the bed-and-breakfast with her husband, Ed, replied. "Expect them day after tomorrow, though."

Shealds didn't want to appear too anxious for information. "I'm working clear on the other side of the county now. If I need to be available to answer questions, a call would help. Will you let me know?"

"Sure," Nan replied with a smile as she lifted her eyes from the bread dough she was kneading. "Ed or I will give you a call."

Shealds gave a nod and tilt of his head, trying to remain casual. For years he'd been torn apart by intense anger, grief, humiliation, and helplessness, not to mention needlessly losing years of his life to legal wrangling, prison, and rebuilding a life much different than he'd imagined. Now, like a shell game, Shealds needed to keep people looking at his business and upstanding social rehabilitation, while the prized pea of exoneration remained well hidden under the third, and last, shell.

Just a few more puzzle pieces...

He and his partners lost 39 Bayshore, but as a consolation prize, they had managed to buy one of the two adjacent lots for a spec home. Pastor Allred bought the other lot and Shealds hoped to lure Ellen and her boys to safety with the other.

CHAPTER FOUR

As they moved into the interstate traffic, Muriel spoke up as she looked at her watch. "We might as well get a look-see at the property. We can't go to the bed-and-breakfast until three p.m. for check-in."

"We've got a contractor lined up—several really. Given glowing references," Bee reported.

Carolyn's voice coarsened as she changed lanes to drive faster. "But they're *ex-cons* according to my investigators." This was another touchy subject on the tail of so many others since they'd got off the plane.

"Trying to learn from their mistakes and helping others— nothing violent," Bee said as she went inside her purse for tissues. "They're all above board about their pasts. You know your lawyer, Mr. Lyon, had private investigators check their construction company out. Found nothing untoward. Do excellent work."

"Mr. Jackson, Mr. Silver, and Mr. Molina are model citizens now," Muriel added. "Mr. Silver is 43, Mr. Jackson is 41 and Mr. Molina is younger at 26, I think our information from Mr. Lyon said."

Carolyn's jaw clenched again not caring about the ages of these men – but the fact that they'd been *in prison*, as she recalled how her aunts had used her company's law firm throughout this debacle. If only she had been able to dissuade the lawyers from exploring this "secret present for Carolyn" real estate purchase as her aunts had characterized the transaction.

She'd been focusing on larger issues—like the safety of her employees in her company's sale and her health. The frowning face of her cardiologist came to her mind's eye. *Wouldn't dealing with ex-con contractors be stressful?*

"I don't want to deal with anyone with an unsavory past. Period." Carolyn raised her voice at the end. "It's enough to have to be here in the best of circumstances, without having to think about dealing with people having been in prison."

"Your lawyer, Mr. Lyon says that there're some papers and plans waiting for us at the bed and breakfast." Muriel ignored Carolyn's barb, keeping a conversational tone.

"You can look at them and do what you want after that," Cass suggested. "If you think they can do the job, that's great. If not, get rid of them."

They drove in silence as Carolyn reconsidered her position. Carolyn now accepted her aunts' decisions and explanations as well-meaning, but still, the problems of the ugly, little-known-to-her mansion and the prospect of dealing with unsavory people remained unwelcome looming obstacles. *But I'm going to make all the decisions from now on.* "We'll table more discussion for now. In the meantime, we'll head for the property and go in…as soon as I can locate the place."

Muriel grasped on to this positive note, while asking Carolyn to put on her jacket over her sweater. "The Bayshore mansion and land was known as one of the "Jewels of the Chesapeake Heritage" in the 1870's when it was finished. The mansion wouldn't have been there *at all* except the original salts mashes were filled in by an extraordinary engineering effort and the foresight of a Mr.

Elias Payne," Muriel began. "The rock and clean fill came from Mr. Payne's family mines about five miles from the coast which raised the land to provide prominent bay views that are mentioned in many of the references.

"Let me see," Muriel said, grasping for her notes in the folder she'd put with some other papers. "I think they said it took four or five years of earth work before they were able to start the construction on the house which Mr. Payne sited to take full advantage of the inlet views and the vistas of the Atlantic Ocean to the east - on the inlet bay waters but far enough away to blunt damaging ocean storms. Guess he picked the place well since it's still standing after almost a century and a half..."

"Just barely, if the pictures are any indication," Carolyn sniped. "I now have a derelict "Garnet on the Chesapeake" if I recall that purple jewels are called garnets."

Muriel cleared her throat and continued, not wanting to get in another fight with her niece. "Originally, constructed as with great foresight as a three story stone and shingle home with a two and a half story barn and large servants quarters building, the home is still one of the largest in the area," Muriel reported. "Mr. Payne, his wife and children lived in the home as he enjoyed woodworking and separate iron-working and jewelry businesses as well as looking over his family's mining interests while Mrs. Payne dealt with charitable causes, especially those concerning Civil War veterans."

"How did it get to the sad shape it is now?" Bee asked.

"Lose of several heirs who went north, the close of the mines and you'll remember the last occupant was named 'Dorne', so I surmise the house didn't have or lost a male heir at some point," Muriel surmised. "Those points in the record are vague. I need to do more research but there's also an indication the Dornes might have changed the interior somewhat. Later newspaper articles still talk about 'parties, lectures and dances' up until the 1940's. I haven't had the time to do more in-depth research.

"The current buildings as you can see from the pictures show the mansion, the barn and an art studio...but nothing about the servants' quarters." Muriel put down her notes. "I think I remember something being said about beautiful decorative ironwork."

"Can you just imagine? Turning off the road in your carriage or early model car ...and being teased by a thick corpse of trees to get a glimpse of the two and three story buildings - a large compound of beauty and activity!" Bee said romantically.

"Darby said he was going to try to get pictures from the Robin Lee film...which might indicate what the property was like when they filmed the exteriors," Cass added.

"We might look it up on the Internet when we get to the hotel." Muriel looked at her cohorts. Now wasn't the time. If Carolyn saw those pictures and compared them to the current dishevelment, she might bolt for sure. And they'd made a bit of progress, Muriel thought.

Carolyn listened intently about the Bayshore property but she couldn't afford to weaken now, so she's made her one grousing comment about the property "still standing" after all these years and concentrated on punching the address into the GPS. "Thirty-nine Bayshore."

As they neared the property, they saw an impassable bank of dirt and road debris in the path to the access road. Carolyn looked at the hill of trash with disgust. "My, what a welcoming entrance!"

"This continued sarcasm is beneath you in such a situation," Cass chided. "You know it's a mess. We can either go to the bed and breakfast or walk the road to the house—your choice."

"Is your heart up to it?" Bee asked with concern.

Carolyn ignored both the rebuke and the question. "Is this mess from the contractor we've been arguing about, who's splitting up the property on this side of the bridge into two lots?"

"It shouldn't be," Cass replied. "Mr. Jackson and Mr. Allred, who now own the lots, indicated they wouldn't do any of their clearing or staking work until *we* had a chance to see the property and fully outline our plans." The picture of the fortyish, uncharacteristically silver-haired man on trial for securities fraud from the Internet information came to mind when Cass spoke of Mr. Jackson, but Carolyn didn't know much about Mr. Allred. If Carolyn got her way, clearing the lots was all Mr. Jackson was going to get to do. She wanted nothing to do with three ex-cons. Perhaps she'd buy back the lot that this Mr. Jackson or his company seemed to own now.

Carolyn turned to look at Cass. "Mr. Jackson and…a Mr. Allred have purchased the adjacent lots?"

"Mr. Jackson, one of the owners in the proposed construction company, purchased the one that is to be cleared on our immediate right, and *Pastor* Allred has purchased the one on the left," Muriel replied in her crispest librarian-like tone.

Carolyn looked at the acreage beyond. "I can walk in," she said quickly. "Let's get going while we still have some good light." *Would an ex-con and a pastor cancel each other out and make for a good neighborhood?*

As her aunts followed wordlessly in her wake, Carolyn slogged in the thick mulch from what seemed like decades of fallen leaves falling unheeded on the ground. It reached above the level of her pumps. She should have known to wait and put on her hiking boots. "Perhaps we should buy waders!" she called back, referring to the waist-level rubber boots used by fly fishermen. Her aunts were too busy finding their own places to walk to make any comment.

Carolyn felt dumb struck as the hazy outline of the house peeked through the overgrowth. It lay beyond a cheap, bent, and rusted fence, which appeared more like a mangled step above chicken wire than the entrance to a once-grand mansion property. *Where is the "beautiful decorative iron work"?*

Hiding her frank dismay, Carolyn could see some of the disheveled state of the property and the exterior —an abandoned stone-and-shingle mansion painted purple! *Why would anyone paint a house purple?* Thank goodness, at current prices, the price of two lots would cover a good portion of the cost of her aunts' real estate debacle. She'd have to find out if the demolition of the house and the sale of the cleared land on the third lot would repay her aunts' investment.

Her aunts followed Carolyn on the years-deserted road with deep ruts over a small, two-lane brown brick bridge hidden in a mixture of overgrown trees, poorly tended vines and dead weeds. Carolyn hoped the bridge would take the weight of demolition vehicles. She doubted she would rebuild this house, let alone a bridge if it was unsafe! She was glad they were on foot. With her luck so far this morning, she feared their SUV might fall the fifteen feet into the now-dry meandering creek bed that headed out to the inlet beyond. *Did she see a leaf motif on the bridge's weathered rounded stone balustrade as she stopped to empty her shoes for the third time?* Now worse for the mulchy dampness and filth, her suede shoes were probably ruined. Worse was the realization that she was the owner of a humongous rectangular grape, an old barn, and an equally hideous art studio in the style of a completely different era in between!

Carolyn didn't know what else to call this huge hulk of a house bathed in peeling bluish-purple exterior shingle walls and decrepit plywood-covered windows. The grandeur in Muriel's descriptions was no more. A few lonely, surviving windowpanes exposed several broken nine-per-frame style mullions of the three-floor facade of windows and dormers covered with leaf droppings and dead branches from the untended trees. Some of the protective plywood coverings had been ripped away from either the wind or vandals.

"Must have been a sale on that awful paint shade," Carolyn offered, looking at the horrid color of the place, squinting to confirm 39 Bayshore as a shingle-and-natural-stone-style home described in the sale documents. *Who could really tell?*

Most all of the shutters, and many patches of the now-purple wooden shingles, were gone, making the house look like a sad, discarded quilt. There was a large pile of rusted wrought-iron fencing, gates, and other unidentifiable metal decorations in a discarded heap. Most of the rest of what she could see sat obscured by generations of untended conifers; some spindly, malnourished bushes; out-of-control weeds; and if she looked closely, what might be some sort of driveway. "If we cut these bushes, do you think the house might fall down?" Carolyn asked.

"Let's keep thinking 'On the water views! Water views!'" Cass said, ignoring her niece's questions. Dismal thoughts started to invade Cass's thinking. *Perhaps Carolyn should tear it down!* "Let's just keep going!" she sputtered.

After they'd inspected a pile of discarded ironwork, Muriel risked putting her hand on Carolyn's shoulder. The rusted design was the only pretty thing they seen since they left the road. "We've had enough here today."

"We'll look at the views and the other side of the property tomorrow," Bee said, trying to be optimistic that seeing them might let them all feel better about 39 Bayshore.

"Yes," Cass said in a voice stronger than she felt. "We'll see them and use the padlock key tomorrow morning." She motioned with a quick head tilt for Muriel and Bee to head for the road. "We need supplies."

Carolyn knew what she'd seen wouldn't get any better with a second look. "I'll need new shoes. These are ruined."

With a slow afternoon with lots of dry wind and cool temperatures, both Nan and Ed Stornel, the Two Cups of Tea proprietors, greeted their new guests together.

Carolyn stepped through the ten-foot front door crowned with a rectangular stained-glass window sitting like a multicolored hat above the doorframe, as she kicked off her ruined shoes at the entrance.

"The reserved rooms for four customers in the Reynolds party, please?" Carolyn walked on stocking feet to shake both owners' hands. "We haven't eaten much, except gas station snacks, after driving from the airport."

"Looking for a property we've bought in the area," Cass informed. "The access path's blocked."

"I'm Ed, and my wife, Nan, will be with you in a moment." Ed ended the handshake he offered and frowned to himself. Everyone knew these were the people taking on 39 Bayshore. *A Skip Clem scheme if he ever saw one!* Many thought Clem was overreaching in his work as the property executor there. Ed hoped Clem was finished with his meddling.

Clem's escapades concerning 39 Bayshore were well known: "accidentally" painting the house purple; wanting to throw lots of the antique brick posts, ironwork, and those lovely iron gates in the county dump, saying they were rusty and beyond repair; and riling up the neighborhood by taking core samples on the property because he said the mining fill used by Mr. Payne in the nineteenth century in building up the grade might be poisoned by mining arsenic! The tests came back negative!

Fortunately, a few civil-minded people, including Shealds's, Hesse's and Molina's construction firm, could see beyond the rust and disrepair and, at least, had saved the century-old Bayshore front gates from destruction. He'd heard Shealds had stored some of them in his rented construction yard. Some mangled fence pieces still sat in a heap by the mansion door, and they'd managed to keep Clem away from what was the former fenced cemetery on the property.

The remains of the Payne family deceased were gone from the family cemetery and placed in the city cemetery several miles away, but the headstones and antique fence enclosure that remained at

Bayshore told of another time when the Paynes and their loved ones were buried on the property. Efforts to get the home in the Historic Registry had failed so far, and now these four women would take on the place.

Clem, a lifetime resident of their town and its interim mayor, was out for a few vacation days with good riddance, Ed thought uncharitably. Clem told everyone who would listen that reviving the Bayshore property would be a great boon to the community, but at the same time, he'd made the property *less* attractive and *less* saleable by all his actions.

Ed had seen the heavy yellow state construction equipment and crews out on the road a few days ago. Now the mayor was gone, and the road to the Bayshore property was blocked. *Clem's doing he'd bet!*

Ed tried not to appear disgusted, still chafing at Clem's heavy-handed shoving of Evan Smith from the mayor's chair because of Smith's health problems. Being free of Clem's swagger and his equally self-impressed wife for a few days seemed like a vacation to Ed and his family. Ed still hoped for a special election after Skip's stealing of the mayoral seat he'd hammered through as head of the town council. Otherwise, elections were two years away. His guest, Ms. Reynolds, didn't say anything more, so he kept his questions to himself. *Should he push and ask for more information?*

"Why don't you sit down and have a cup of oolong tea?" Nan offered, seeing her husband's frown. Ed retreated behind the dark, hand-carved, comma-shaped oak reception desk tucked under the winding staircase and banister extending to the second and third floor of the single-turreted Victorian. Nan could tell by the set of her husband's jaw, he didn't want her to say anything about Skip Clem or real estate. "I'll set out some shortbread—that shouldn't interfere with your dinner."

Jessie, their sixteen-year-old daughter, came in from the kitchen garden. Seeing the guests, the girl, as if by rote, started getting colorful floral china cups and saucers from Nan's china collection out of the glass doors of the antique dry sink. Nan called. "Get six cups, Jessie…and one for yourself, if you want some tea." Nan had finished her room inspection they'd assigned the group from the dozen in their establishment. "Ed and Jessie will get your bags while you have your tea."

"Could you bring peanut butter cookies or dried cherry sconces?" Ed asked as he took the rental car keys from Carolyn and headed toward the silver SUV sitting in front of the house. "Anybody got food allergies?"

"No. No allergies," Bee said in shorthand, heading for a seat in the dining room while shifting her shoulder bag. "There're several suitcases for each of us, sir, all marked with our names. We'll sort them out for you when you get them in. Your lovely wife is quite right about choosing the tea…and you adding the offer of some sconces. Thank you."

As Carolyn and her aunts enjoyed their impromptu tea before unpacking, a lanky man with wire-rimmed glasses, jeans, and a fisherman's sweater came to the back door.

"Pete," Ed called, momentarily interrupted in his routine. "We were wondering if you were going to come this afternoon." Ed headed for the black-and-white marble-topped buffet to pour a cup a coffee for their visitor. The thirtysomething-looking man smiled at them all, showing feathery lines on either side of his eyes and dimples at each edge of his mouth. "Glad you're back from your psychology seminar. We thought you might need to catch up on your church work and wouldn't come today."

Pete had come to confide in his two friends. As head of the Church Council and a wise trusted friend, Pete wanted to tell Ed about how he'd been dealing with his problems.

After he came through the door, Pete concentrated instead in Nan's cheerful, pleasant greeting introducing Carolyn, Muriel, Cass and Bee.

Pete wanted to meet the new owners of the Bayshore property and welcome them to the community – just at another time. Pete extended his hand. "I'm Pete Allred—pastor of the church about two blocks from here."

"Also our community psychologist," Nan said without pre-amble as she passed the plate of scones. "Pete came this time every Wednesday to see Ed's bedridden mother, Clara, in her last months. He'd talk with her, and then he'd come down for coffee. We've just kept up the tradition." The information was offered in a kind fashion, bespeaking a bittersweet time turned into something comforting and friendly. "Helping people as a pastor and a psychologist, like you did for us and our mother, Clara."

"Pete just got back this afternoon from an out-of-town seminar," Ed added. "Bet you'll be busy the next few days with catching up."

"I'm busy, but I love it," Pete offered, pushing his nighttime insomnia, the splintered episodes of sadness, and this recent trip for help to the back of his mind. *Looking for all the sides of it.* His mother used to call it his love of God and the human mind when he was a boy. Pete pulled out an empty chair at the farther end of the table with an amiable look to Ed and Nan. "And the food's great here too."

Pete raised his mug and the hot, biting liquid slid down his tired throat. He'd been a pastor at the local church for about five years, and he loved his counseling practice. People didn't seem to mind that he supplemented his pastor's salary, and, thankfully, his counseling practice added to his savings account, his retirement fund and afforded the money to buy the Bayshore lot. He'd also helped the community with indigent and emergency referrals, while authorities sought more permanent and better long-term therapy placements, like former prison inmates in their efforts to return to civilian life.

He thought of Shealds Jackson, Hesse Silver, and David Molina. While finishing their post-incarceration counseling requirements, they'd become regular citizens, immersing themselves into the community nicely, and doing well in their construction business. After their series of appointments, he gladly vouched for them and their fledgling company as they continued to show they could work together and not pull themselves back into their former lawless behaviors.

Pete's ground rules had been strict with the three. "Everything you say here will be held in confidence, just as long as you don't have, or share, any unlawful plans or ideas. If so, you'll be jeopardizing my practice and my thoughts about helping people like yourself in the future." His concerns, praise God, had been groundless. They'd all gotten Pete's seal of approval, which helped their efforts to meld into the community and get further referrals.

Pete's focus and gaze came back to Carolyn Reynolds. "I don't mean to pry, but I heard you are the new owner of 39 Bayshore?"

"Why, yes," Carolyn said as she added bluntly, "and *you're* the owner of one of the two other lots on the property."

"Yes, the last of the Payne family line lived there—the Dornes. I'm giving the lot I bought to my aunt as a *retirement present*." The pastor's reply gave some information as to his intentions. "She's got about two years to go before then…and has always been a great help and inspiration to me."

"Mrs. Dorne died about the same time as Clara, didn't she?" Nan offered without enthusiasm, looking at her husband and the pastor for validation. "The state thought Mrs. Dorne should be in a nursing home for some months before that."

"Mr. Clem, the state-appointed conservator, helped her stay in her home until she died, boarded up the windows, and padlocked the doors after the estate sale," Pete said. He didn't want to add anything about its sorry present state or that it had been broken into several times and then see the alarm in Ms. Reynolds' and the other ladies' eyes.

"Yeah, he grabbed that position." Nan, noted for her plain speaking, added, "Saying he was our community's amateur historian after Bess Ruppurt got sick and needed to spend less time in her position down at our local historic society." *Same tactic as becoming the mayor!*

"Mrs. Dorne did her best to keep the place up, but it was too much for her, especially in her elder years. Are you intending to live there?" Pete wanted to reassure the group.

"The property is...an investment," Carolyn said, putting on her business facade. "I don't know what I'm going to do with it." She looked into the concerned eyes of each of her aunts and then into the pastor's calm green ones. *The color of new wheat,* Carolyn thought. "So Mr. Clem, the conservator, knows the property?"

Thought lines ridged Pete's brow, thinking of his client Jackson again. "I'd say Shealds Jackson and his construction company associates, Mr. Silver and Mr. Molina know the place best." He looked to Nan and Ed.

"Think every other interested party, besides yourself, got bogged down with the town council. No one was able to buy it but you," Ed said more sourly than he'd intended. He cleared his throat, trying to disguise his dislike of Skip Clem from both his pastor and his patrons.

"Would you have the time to show us around?" Muriel asked Pete, wanting to keep the subject of the core drilling, with the thankfully negative hazard results, from becoming another sour topic to rile Carolyn. Despite Carolyn's occasional protestations, they wouldn't have bought the property if there had been problems other than the neglect.

"I've got an opening tomorrow morning, before my first appointment," Pete replied, chewing his scone quickly.

"Can we borrow some flashlights tomorrow, Nan, if we can't get to the store?" Bee asked. "We'll probably need them, even in the daylight."

"I'll need to get a few things done this afternoon if I'm going to take you to the property...and will have to say my goodbyes till tomorrow morning. Is 8 AM a good time?" Pete asked. *Talking to Ed and Nan will have to wait.*

"We'll be ready," Carolyn replied.

"Good," Pete replied with a smile. "I'm looking forward to it."

Before Pete could get to the door, Ed pulled him aside. "Thanks for not talking about the vagrants you talked about last week at Bayshore, since you said you thought they were gone. I think the Reynolds' party needs a good night's sleep...and nothing can be done till tomorrow."

Pete looked back at the four women talking amiably with Nan and Jesse. "To tell you the truth, with so much going on, I didn't even remember anything, until you just mentioned it." Pete scowled. "I've been more than preoccupied and I need to talk to you about my progress. But I agree that no one else needs to suffer from insomnia tonight, the kids are probably gone and I'll give everything a good look tomorrow."

"Thanks, Pete," Ed ended as he smiled and opened the door. "Thanks, as always, for being so understanding."

Time passed companionably through the afternoon into the evening. Carolyn felt too tired to talk. Nan ordered some roast chicken dinners with mashed potatoes and green beans from Righter's Restaurant, a local place with a long counter, eight dining tables, and room for six more on the sidewalk during the summer tourist season. "If you will excuse us, ladies, we're headed to the chamber of commerce meeting. Do you need anything?"

"I think we're fine," Carolyn replied, still savoring the taste of the amber-colored homemade chicken gravy.

"I, for one, am going to go to bed early," Muriel said with a tired, thready voice. "Flying half the night and then driving all over God's half acre didn't do me any good." She wouldn't mention all the intense talking they'd done on their ride here.

"You are looking a little pale," Cass said. "Travel's always hard on you. Best get going to bed myself." She and Muriel were rooming together. Bee was in a room by herself, as was Carolyn. The aunts insisted Carolyn take the corner turret room, which scaled the entire street-side corner of the bed-and-breakfast Victorian.

"I think you'll like the window seat in that room," Ed informed her as he handed out the keys. The room's white-curtained windows and lovely upholstered pink quilt seat and back cushions Nan had sewn and quilted, seemed like a place to read a book on a rainy day or to watch traffic on the intersecting streets outside. Filmy gauze material sheers, like gossamer, covered the windows to let in the maximum amount of light. But guests who wanted darkness and privacy need only pull down the hidden scalloped blackout shades provided underneath and on the smaller square window on the opposite wall.

Soon after Muriel and Cass left, Bee and Carolyn followed. In the haze of travel fatigue and hunger, Carolyn had forgotten her mother had usually bunked with Bee during their years-ago traveling.

Carolyn remembered Cass's last words before heading to bed, which Carolyn knew were meant to comfort but now made her feel uneasy. "Plenty of time to talk about everything."

With stabbing clarity, Carolyn felt the loneliness again. First she lost her mother, then her company and her health. *Will things ever seem happy again?*

This house couldn't get her the relationship and new personal goals back on track. *I want a husband and children!* She needed to get back to LA...and start working on those efforts as soon as she got back.

Perhaps, when Carolyn informed her aunts tomorrow, after today's disastrous inspection, that she wanted to demolish

39 Bayshore, she'd feel better. She'd be kind...but firm. Perhaps spending the night in a pink cocoon would help. *Pink makes everyone look and feel better,* Carolyn remembered her mother saying, which gave her a bit of solace as she fell asleep.

CHAPTER FIVE

Pete regretted he didn't get a chance to talk to Ed, his wise and trusted confidant, more before leaving the bed and breakfast. Ed knew all of Pete's dirty laundry, including Pete's family and his past. Now, Pete had two more worries: that his crazy, renegade father, Caleb Faille, would be angry about the development of the Bayshore property...and that he himself was suffering from some profound psychological problems. *A familial genetic defect?* In his own defense, Pete was now trying to take care of his personal problems but he'd feel better once he'd unburdened himself to Ed. The seminar trip...and the conversations there, proved that. Pete knew that once Ed, and Nan, knew what was going on, they could help him.

As for the recent trip, David Molina had tagged along and shared expenses because David had had meetings with several university architectural professors regarding the shingle style homes of the era of 39 Bayshore. It seemed David liked architectural and historical research, as well as construction, and Pete was more than willing to help David any way he could on his road back from incarceration. But Pete felt even better since he'd found some help and strategies...for himself. The truth was, that *before* the trip, Pete didn't want to tell the Stornels, or anyone, that the *real* reason he'd gone to the seminar was that he, as their pastor, and a psychologist, *needed counseling*!

The first night in the hotel room before the "Meeting Today's Pastoral Challenges" seminar had been bad, Pete mused - even by his insomniac standards. All he'd done was toss and turn and pray—getting no sleep whatsoever. No need to interrupt his roommate's sleep just because he was so restless! Pete threw on some clothes as soon as the hotel clock showed the coffee shop was opening. He needed some caffeine—very hot and black. After gulping the first cup with his usual morning prayer, he started thinking about his life experiences...and current problems.

Pete didn't see the man approaching his table. "Mind if I sit down? I think we have something in common, besides your request to speak to me *personally* about needing counseling."

Pete startled. As the half-asleep hostess fumbled from filling the glass coffeepots to seat him, Pete looked up to see a tall, brown-haired man standing at his table with a gold-rimmed pair of reading glasses in his one hand and a Bible and another book filled with papers in another.

"I'm Bill Pearson," the man with kind eyes said. "You're my counseling patient...and fellow insomniac, Peter Allred?"

"Yes. Yes, I'm...I'm also attending your seminar today," Pete stammered.

"Why don't you start by calling me Bill or Pastor Bill? I answer to both," Pastor Pearson replied. "You looked in deep contemplation, and I didn't know if I might be disturbing you," the other pastor said as he sat down. "But I had a feeling."

Pete gave a small, silent laugh that lifted the edge of his stiff-feeling face. "A 'God feeling'?"

"Yes," Pastor Bill replied, knowing he didn't have to explain this phenomenon to other pastors. They both knew many people felt they were prompted by God with feelings or impressions to do things or act in certain ways. "And, no, I don't hear an audible voice."

"I don't either," Pete said wearily. "For me, they're just helpful impressions or feelings on the positive side, and negative feelings or impressions on the other side for me." *Ever since I got out of the hospital years ago.*

"Helping to navigate things for you?" Pastor Bill asked.

"Yeah," Pete replied. "It also helps when I pray about things after these events, even though I forget to do that...at times." *Will I be able to* explain this?

"We all forget at times," Pastor Bill confirmed. "But you're stuck right now?"

Pastor Bill looked as kind as his brochure pictures, the brochure on his other expert topic—helping troubled pastors. "Insomnia, I thought was gone, is back, as well as these strong feelings I get at night...which are now coming in the daytime, too."

"You've already seen your doctor to make sure your health is good?" Pastor Bill asked. It was always good to check to see if there might be physical aspects or exhaustion as root causes before going further.

"I don't want this," Pete replied. "I've tried to go to God first of all."

"Let's do that now," Pastor Bill countered, looking at the pain in the other man's eyes. Pearson prayed aloud, asking for guidance and clarity after closing his eyes. "Amen." He looked up. "Have you been praying for that, too?"

"Yes," Pete replied. "But the thoughts haven't stopped." Pete considered for a moment how things had been going. "I feel such fear and sorrow, as if from another source – not myself. I've had labored breathing, sweating, and heart pounding in recent experiences." Pete's eyes were solemn. "I don't like being out of control...and I've told the Lord that, too. Many times."

Pastor Bill saw the change in the younger man's eyes and the slight stiffening of his shoulders. *What has Pete gone through?*

Pastor Bill might excuse himself and run when he heard what Pete had to say, Pete thought. "I've had difficult life experiences...and I have to know if these feelings are an indication I'm losing my mind."

Pete's hand left the cup, and he wagged it from the wrist in the direction of the other pastor, as if shooing him away. *Wonder what Pastor Pearson will say when he hears it all? Can I articulate it?*

When Pastor Bill didn't flinch or move, Pete blurted. "I...I need to tell you something more." Pete took a gulp of the strong coffee that had come while he was thinking. Getting up enough courage to reveal all the truth. "My father was...is...Caleb Faille."

Pastor Bill's eyes widened as the information sunk in.

The story was common knowledge, a years-ago international news circus when their commune compound had been wrongfully raided by authorities. A false tip from a desperate informer who was involved in petty drug sales said there were illegal drugs and gun trafficking at the commune. Pete had been badly injured, and Pete's mother, Elaine, had been killed trying to shield him from stray bullets. "We'd been sitting at the breakfast table. All early risers...and Dad was out in the barn." Pete twisted the mug in a slow turn in his hands. "The authorities first started shooting at the house, and they got return gunfire from the barn from Dad. Dad wounded the first two agents, who kept the group pinned down...and they didn't find us for what seemed like a long time."

Pete had lain next to his mother's silent body, not having the strength to do much but whisper his love and fear to her chenille-robed back. Then they were taken to the hospital. Pete slowly and painfully recovered from his near-death injuries, his mother was buried, and his father was sentenced to 180 years in prison on fire-arms, conspiracy, and manslaughter charges. But the reason for the raid was wrong-headed and his father never recovered.

"Your father escaped prison, right?" Pastor Bill added.

Pete gave a big sigh to that. His father had not only made what the authorities said was a "cunning" escape, he'd left a detailed outline of the sins people perpetrated in the raid and on the environment: the reason Pete and his family had jointed the commune in the first place.

"My parents, Caleb and Elaine, left their jobs in New York to 'show the world a better way.' I've talked to the Lord many times about that."

Pete looked down at the wood-grained tabletop. "I've looked *ad nauseum* at the traumatic event of seeing my mother die before my eyes, and of me almost bleeding to death, while my father fought the authorities." Pete gulped. "After everything was over, I took her maiden name."

Several times since his escape, his father had shown up where Pete lived. One of the sounds Pete remembered clearly included his father cocking a Magnum 357 close to Pete's ear. Another was the memory of the cold, unforgiving metal on his temple. "You still selling out, Pete?" his father would say as he alternately ranted about the environment and his dislike of Pete's dual professions of pastor and psychologist. Not a hint of love or pride in anything Pete had accomplished.

"I've found my calling in serving the Lord and people, Dad," Pete would always reply, trying to remain calm. "I found peace in God and helping everyone I can – all sinners and mistake-makers under heaven."

His father was unimpressed by his son or his message as he rifled through Pete's belongings, refrigerator, and wallet. "Don't look at me. If the Feds come around, you might do me the service of not helping *them*."

"Can't you just stop, Dad?" Pete asked. The unjust commune invasion had been publicized, but now the authorities had undeniable proof his father had been involved in ecoterrorism attacks since he'd fled the penitentiary. His father remained a wanted man.

"You've never been cooped up in a cage, son."

Pete heard the rage and dread in his father's voice, and Pete had once attempted to comfort his father. He'd been rewarded with a gun butt to the head, followed by a large goose-egg wound and several days of headaches. "Can't trust anyone," his father raged. "Certainly not you, since you've got no sympathy for me or the cause with your religious mumbo-jumbo." Now, Pete knew the personal heartsickness of his father's violent rejection was worse than the physical pain. There was a lot to pray about.

Pastor Bill needed to know the *second situation*. "There's also the fact that one of the largest seaside parcels in my community is being developed, an abandoned mansion and two, as yet, undeveloped lots." Pete stopped for a moment. "I'm the owner of one of the lots now." *Was he even more his father's enemy now with the purchase of the lot?* "It's a retirement gift for my aunt...and she's so excited to come and live by me. She's was wonderful in taking me in after my mother died - turning her world upside-down really. I *don't want* to sell the lot which might be considered an easy fix to all this. When I consider selling, I also get a strong impression, that selling the lot *won't* get rid of the feelings or help my insomnia. It's very confusing."

Pastor Bill didn't interrupt Pete's story. "So you want to determine if your feelings are based in a family history of psychological problems, a warning of your father's possible retaliation toward your property purchase or *something else?*"

"These feelings started *before* I bought the property!" Again, Pete kept a keen eye on the other man. "I can't discount the buying of the lot is involved...but I can't *attribute* the start of the feelings with the purchase."

"Are there any times that the feelings and thoughts are stronger?" Pastor Bill asked.

First and foremost, Pete was concerned because he saw nothing Godly or spiritual in them, just an unknown nuisance. At first, since he was a psychologist as well as a pastor, Pete thought he could take care of it himself. But trying to deal with the shame of having this happen to him *at all* and the insomniac mess he'd become at night, had gone on for too long. What was left was pure ego and foolish pride, Pete now knew, and he had to abandon that strategy of suffering – or face worse side-effects from his problems and sleeplessness and still not get to the bottom of things.

"Does it help to know that I don't think you're crazy?" Pastor Bill replied. "You're asking for help. I'm just asking about corollary things or triggers that might be involved."

"Looking in other areas that might help me, even if they are going over 'cold ground' I already thought I'd dealt with?" Pete asked.

Pete knew he'd be giving a client the same advice if he were the professional dealing with his case. "You think there's some past context I haven't considered?" Pete asked sheepishly. "I've got to be honest. I've thought selling the Bayshore lot might help but my instincts say 'no'…and it seems cowardly to just sell and run."

Pastor Bill looked in Pete's eyes. "You're not a coward…but what I'm going to suggest might seem rather mundane, given the information you've just shared. I look at every aspect of it like it's a puzzle I need to solve."

"And then put that with a fear tolerance scale of one reaction to another?" Pete asked. "Is there any therapeutic importance to know that I haven't thought about being fearful?"

Pastor Bill shrugged. "There might be some therapeutic importance because I'm trying to get at the management part of things, like any problem. If we could gauge or anticipate things somehow, you might be able to lessen your reaction. Truthfully,

I'm looking for *any* clues…besides a knee-jerk reaction of telling you to sell something or act in some way without any clinical effort or enough information. Things like this are never a 'magic eight ball' proposition."

"That's why I've come to you for help," Pete still felt half ashamed he hadn't been able to take care of this himself.

"It's going to take time," Pastor Bill reached into his breast pocket for cards and his pen, which was clipped to his papers and his morning devotional. "I'm willing if you're willing. I'll give you my card with all my personal numbers." He gave the card to Pete. "Just one more thing," he added. "Analyze things as soon after the episodes as possible. Then start moving to consider things in your daily life that might trigger your somnolent reactions, and write them down immediately, day or night."

"Taking a pad and paper with me to bed?" Pete asked. "Try to get a handle on things?"

"Yes, I think the first and fastest impressions are best," Pastor Bill reasoned. Pete was having problems that were affecting his life, and Bill wanted to help. He had to ask another question. "OK, but I have to ask again. Even though you've pretty sure this doesn't come out of past events, after our discussion, are you *really sure* this isn't from your past life experiences?"

Pete deflected the comment. "I know God used dreams and feelings in the Bible to give information. We mentioned those when we introduced ourselves just now."

"Is there any basis in dreams for your reaction in this case? Any reaction from your past?" Pastor Bill persisted, not reacting to Pete's question dodge.

"Not from the past. I've thought about revelatory, instructive, or informational aspects." Pete shook his head. "I don't *feel* like I should take one whit of action, and I don't feel a covering of any of God's great love, care, and compassion in this…at all. That's what's got me concerned…and thinking about mental instability." He looked pointedly into Pastor Bill's eyes. "I know what that's like in prayer and contemplation." Pete shook his head again. "Absolutely no feeling of the Almighty in any of this…yet."

"But there's one more thing," Pastor Bill replied. "We can always pray that the Lord will help to reveal things to us."

"He already has helped, Bill," Pete said. "He sent you to encourage me in my trouble." He smiled a bit. "It's good He sent a messenger to let me know *I'm not going crazy.*"

Pastor Bill smiled back. He was glad Pete used his first name. "That's a lot to be concerned about." He squeezed Pete's shoulder and left him to sit with his now cold coffee. "Let's see if unburdening yourself has helped…and keep up the journal."

Pete extended his hand for a goodbye shake.

Pastor Bill felt obligated to say one more thing even though he knew both he and Pastor Allred were men of peace. "I think you might want to pray about notifying the *authorities.* Your father is much different from the man you knew as a child. He's threatened you several times and, by your own admission, involved in violent acts."

Pete shook his head. "I know and I've been thinking about that, too. But I was truthful when I said I didn't feel any fear." He looked at Pastor Bill. "I'll pray about it and get back to you but I haven't seen my father in months. Getting the authorities involved now might be a waste of manpower and unduly frighten the neighborhood and the Reynolds family, who now own the property where I bought the lot."

"I thought I had to warn you." Pastor Bill got up and headed for the meeting room. "I'll call you in a few days, see how you're doing and see if things are clearer or you've changed your mind." He needed pray for Pete's protection and his finding answers to his problems. Plus, Caleb Faille was a very *dangerous* man.

Pete kept working on his journal and following Pastor Bills' suggestions. As promised he went to the Stornels' bed and breakfast at 8 AM. The Reynolds' followed him out of town to the Bayshore property without incident. They walked in relative silence as he held back the fencing for the women to enter the property.

Pete started the conversation. "I don't really know what to tell you, except Skip Clem, the conservator, invited me into the house to see if the church might use it in some way…and it seemed dated, with repairable damage needed in places, but not decrepit." He thought of anything else he could say to provide information. "Skip asked if we needed more space, so I went to look at the entire place, which was *beyond* my visits when Mrs. Dorne was alive." Pete hoped the second look at the property would leave Ms. Reynolds with a more hopeful impression. "The last occupant, Mrs. Dorne, was a hermit for many, many years before she died."

Carolyn thought the woman probably wasn't a hermit at all, but had been trapped by the dense overgrowth of unkempt trees and bushes choking the house from the outside. "I see," she said, being polite. *Did someone say the woman tried to keep the place up?*

Carolyn hid her white-knuckled apprehension in mundane task-oriented talk. "We're not doing this tedious, mulchy walk after today. I'll get a contractor to clear a path from the road."

Pete looked at the shadowed outline of the Bayshore house. "I'll call my friend David Molina and have his company do it, if you like. They'll be doing work with my aunt when she builds on her lot."

So, Pastor Allred was using the ex-cons' company, Carolyn thought. *Am I being too close-minded about this construction company?*

Pete started talking again. "David told me when the property was first built, the townspeople called it the "River of Stones" because Mr. Payne needed several years and countless wagonloads of rocks and fill to raise the salt marshland to its current grade."

Nothing Pastor Allred said perked Carolyn's interest. Muriel's information told the same story. *Will the glass inside the house from the broken windows be as deep as the rotting leaves?*

"As you can see, there's the garage farther down on the left-hand side of the main structure and a separate artist's studio next to that," Pete remarked. "Someone said Mrs. Dorne enjoyed scenic painting and handiwork." Avoiding any further comments, Pete lead them on a different path from the previous day; this time walking on the side, and around, a fallen long-dead tree.

Carolyn hesitated a bit, not knowing if she wanted to use the padlock key she'd gotten from her lawyer back in LA. *What have my aunts done?*

"Mrs. Dorne had siding put on the house after a big nor'easter wind storm blew some of the original shingle-style facade into the water over several days I'm told." Pete frowned as he tried not to look at the now purple-painted shingles. "Mr. Clem, as the conservator, had the siding removed." He didn't want to insult the man even though the painted shingles and worn sheathing were now one of the worst colors Pete had ever seen.

It had been the windy season in LA when Billie had died, Carolyn suddenly remembered. All at once, memories of her mother and this decrepit house seemed too much.

Pete noticed Ms. Reynolds's grave face get paler with his last remark, the few lone doe-colored freckles sprinkling her nose becoming even more pronounced. His attempts at conversation were only making things worse. "Do you have the key?"

As her apprehension grew, Carolyn's blue eyes looked as bleak as the sky after weeks of cold, steady rain. She woodenly held up the shiny silver key on its black nylon lanyard.

Pete took a deep breath, hoping Ms. Reynolds would do the same; fearing she would become ill if she didn't. "Just look at the water views before you decide what to do. Those remain beautiful even if the mansion isn't in the greatest shape."

Carolyn's face remained blank.

Pete stared back for an instant. *Did she hear me?*

Her aunts remained silent as well as they all walked into house. Best to let the pastor talk and protect Carolyn, they all thought. The ladies closed ranks, Bee and Muriel on one side and Cass on the other, walking as close as Carolyn would let them, all three silently praying the inside of the house would be better than the woeful landscape.

Carolyn's hand shook a bit as she lifted the cold, weather-pitted chain and padlock. It looked the best kept of anything she'd seen so far. Although Carolyn prayed it wouldn't fit and she could get out of there on the first available plane, the key slid in. Pete stepped in front of them and muscled the hinged and bolted triple-thickness plywood sheet covering the doorway—standing like a warped sentinel away from the weather-beaten entrance. "Why did they bother to lock it?" Carolyn asked.

The four women went thought the door with the trepidation of dead women walking. They all, even Cass, continued in silence, steeling themselves against the debris of time, nature, and neglect.

In their most optimistic thoughts before they bought the property, the aunts thought Carolyn could possibly welcome the challenge, and embrace this tie to her famous aunt. The only bright spot now was that they knew Carolyn could tear the place down if she wanted to be rid of it. They just kept their faces as neutral as possible.

Finding her voice after so many minutes of silence, Cass commented, "It smells stale in here, not moldy. I think that's a good sign." Muriel and Bee only nodded, and Carolyn seemed not to hear Cass' comment.

The one thing Carolyn liked about the place so far was the hint of a leaf motif on the creek bridge, but with all the foliage debris between here and the road, she wasn't sure she liked it that much anymore. The second thing, but not enough to entice her to stay, was the delicate scrollwork on the decaying pile of iron fencing about fifty yards from the house—probably mangled beyond saving, like the rest of 39 Bayshore. The warped plywood hid ornate double doors with weather-ruined stained glass sidelights on either side. Stepping forward, the inside entry was only a bit larger than a walk-in closet—much too cramped for such a large home. As Carolyn looked around, her late mother's voice came unbidden into her thoughts. *Always organize the first dozen tasks.*

"Yes. Better to smell stale than wet," Carolyn repeated, meaning she had heard Cass' comment. She ignored the remembered comments from her mother.

Then Carolyn's business sense took over as she looked at the neglected interior. A near expert on commercial real estate, she'd leased space for Four Almonds many times and in many different cities. Carolyn knew a bit about architecture but usually relied on her own personal taste when she made decisions—what she liked and what she didn't. She'd lived a life, of owning a townhouse, followed by a condo and a decent sized house and lot, which she had sold out from under herself in the grief of losing Four Almonds and the advice of her doctors. Carolyn looked at the foyer again. *A dozen tasks, my foot! Try a thousand!*

The bones of her LA home had been contemporary with the large glass windows, open halls, and see-through stairways. She'd just helped the place along by emphasizing the architecture and highlighting its classic features with a few splashes of color and some great art pieces. But the best way to describe *this* old relic's first impression was that of an out-of-character rabbit warren of misshapen rooms, like a Rubik's rectangle instead of a cube—seemingly full of small spaces, dimness, and low, artificial ceilings. "This isn't how it was originally built. I can see by the cheap mid-century materials," Carolyn remarked as she walked forward and turned Nan's borrowed flashlight on. "Just little spice-box rooms in such a huge expanse of house?" She turned to her aunts. "We'd have to tear down a lot of walls. If these are structural, I'm out of here."

Now it was time for her aunts to blink, clearly startled. None of the other three women could quite believe it. In milliseconds, Carolyn's face and manner indicated some interest.

Muriel was the first to find her tongue. "The local library could house some historic books to help us, and there're other people who know about the houses of the area. Didn't you mention some people, Pastor Allred?" Before Pete could answer, Muriel kept talking. "Pastor Allred's also mentioned someone from the construction company. Mr. Molina, wasn't it, who might be interested in continuing his architectural research here." Muriel wanted her voice to sound strong and positive.

"Yes, David Molina, and there's the local historical society down on Fulton Street," Pete mentioned, glad to hear some conversation liven the musty, sad silence and see some color returning to Ms. Reynolds's cheeks. "There's pictures of this place back to the original owners from the Payne family."

"We'll need to come back here this afternoon and tomorrow with more supplies," Carolyn remarked. "Buy some standing lanterns like they use in camping and some space heaters when the weather is chilly so we can evaluate each room. And some fire extinguishers so we don't burn down this ruin before *I* decide whether to raze it or not." She looked over to her aunts and back to the pastor. "Research is definitely necessary. Muriel, do you have your note pad?" Carolyn rummaged in her purse. "How good is the cellular phone service here?"

Muriel reached into her purse for the small spiral notebook she always kept handy. "I've misplaced my pen." Everyone searched until Cass came up with a pen, which sported an advertisement from a restaurant on the other side of the country.

"We'll need more than a note pad," Carolyn said distractedly. "Make a list including packs of yellow pads, a box of pens and phone numbers to set inspections by the gas company and the electric company. Engineers are next, to see if this place is even close to salvageable. I'm warning you…any big negatives from *any* of them, and we'll schedule the wrecking ball in a New York minute. It's not going to be an unnecessary money pit, firetrap, or a 'home' for trysts or transients anymore."

"A business resources book from the chamber of commerce?" Bee suggested.

"Our church publishes one as well," Pete remarked as Carolyn smiled at his input.

Carolyn began ticking off the list in her head and then flicked them off on her fingers. "We'll get a temporary security fence with razor wire, people to board these windows and glazers if the contractor—I pick—thinks we can salvage any window frames. They'll need to have proper insulation value for manageable heating and air conditioning bills to make this place livable." Carolyn squinted and walked closer to areas of murky light. "The place probably needs triple-paned replacements for heating—more than cooling—and they will cost a fortune. I don't like these diamond-paned windows in the back. A first priority would be something keeping with the period…but not so fussy." She turned toward the group. "We'll stay relatively close to the front door and see the rest after the engineers have made a full inspection. They say it's safe, or I'm making airline reservations for LA after we see everything is torn down."

Carolyn looked at the others and smiled again. "I want to thank you, Pastor Allred, for helping us get here. We'll have you for dinner soon. We are all passable cooks, and Bee is our head chef." The happiness faded again. "Your dinner might be something from the local restaurant if we head to LA." Carolyn turned her back to the home's interior.

"We'll also need the water department for a working bathroom or a chemical toilet," Bee suggested. "Checking or replacing a septic tank?"

"Just a shovel and some toilet paper if we get in a pinch," Cass stated dryly. "Plenty of overgrown bushes around here." She stopped for a second. "Think the trees have never seen fertilizer in this or the last century."

Cass, as the resident green thumb of the group, looked more concerned than Carolyn when she saw all the misshapen and neglected landscape. Carolyn turned to their guest again. "Pastor Allred, I'll talk to you tomorrow at the latest. Just let me know about your dinner availability for the next few days when you've checked your schedule."

Pete only "cooked" frozen dinners and macaroni and cheese from the box. "Wednesday and Thursday are the only nights I can't make it, unless I'm out on church or member business." No, he was not a gifted cook. Pete grimaced slightly as he pushed the warped wood back to its original position for padlocking, remembering he'd had macaroni and cheese from a box four times for dinner before going to the conference. "You've got to keep the vagrants out." He decided not to mention the encounter he'd had with the vagrants. The young people seemed to be gone…and he didn't want to see Ms. Reynolds's face pale again, so he kept his mouth shut.

"The razor wire and twenty-four-hour security should keep unwanted people away," Carolyn replied as she closed the lock.

A signal came from Pete's jeans-pocketed device. He held it up to show Carolyn to assure her of remote service. After a quick reply, he responded with a smile, "I'll talk to you again soon, Ms. Reynolds." He hastily scribbled his phone number on a note page Muriel offered, while he quickly scanned the outbuildings before leaving. "Seems deserted here now, but keep the police and sheriff's numbers on speed dial just in case. There have been va-grants here."

Great, Carolyn thought, *more police.* She'd met so many in deal-ing with her mother's case.

CHAPTER SIX

The next morning, getting up felt different, Carolyn mused. She traced the changes to seeing hints of quality and artistry on the Bayshore property, which were hidden in and around the decrepit purple hulk and all the debris. When Carolyn touched the delicate fretwork on the rusted, mangled ironwork pile near the front door of the house, the counterpoint of its delicate yet strong beauty now sparked her interest. With this change of events, Carolyn was glad Pastor Allred's arrival yesterday had stopped her from telling her aunts *immediately* about demolishing Bayshore. *A slight hint of feeling some connection with Bayshore in the neglected iron? Bayshore's neglected iron? My neglected personal life?*

When, Pastor Allred helped her open the door of what seemed like a scene from a B horror movie, instead of dread, her mind, astonishingly and definitely *against her former resolve,* buoyed creatively toward how tearing down walls would open up the front entry. She guessed seeing the inside of the house allowed her to see this relic more like a possible friend, albeit a very needy friend, than an adversary…and wanting to flee.

There was also the *very unexpected* relief, instead of dread, that flowed through her when she smelled the house was not wet and moldy from a leaking roof. If mildew had wafted her way, she would have headed for the hills or, more correctly, the airport. Artistry or no artistry! On her way to her flight, she would have called a demolition company to raze the place and put a for-sale sign on the highway for the last of three scenic view lots!

Pastor Allred was right about the beautiful water views. Carolyn thought there might be thousands of variations to be enjoyed with the right home on this land *in the right time and the right situation.* Shadows and bright sun off the inlet water and the ocean beyond. She'd have to figure out how long a dock they'd need. *Build a dock? Where had that come from?*

Pastor Allred had also mentioned vandals. Vandals. Broken windows had let the elements damage the walls and floors. Carolyn had walked over a charred place on the floor where someone had lit a fire. Yet, to be honest, she'd only seen a fraction of it. *Was the roof made of slate?*

The mansion was a like a down-trodden dowager – a title with no money and no resources. But that was about to change. This long-neglected property needed to be correctly evaluated, or Carolyn's new feeling of purpose would fall in the mud as deep as the ruts from the road to the front entrance. *Her.*

With that in mind, Carolyn and her aunts spent the entire day making so many lists, the papers resembled yellow to-do confetti. Exhausted, they decided to take the evening off and not look at anything related to 39 Bayshore.

The alarm rang early, and Carolyn headed to the window seat with the objective of organizing the lists. Ten clipboards worth, Carolyn estimated. Even that feat of organization only brought more questions. Carolyn had to admit she *didn't want* to rush back to LA as much as she had yesterday. She wasn't going to question why yet or overanalyze her feelings to death right now. She'd just put her "new" personal agenda on the back burner for a few weeks and welcome this respite from the glum place where she'd been stuck for so long – lifted now with seeing this down-on-her-luck mansion rehab project. *Where will we all live in the interim?* "Live here" was a nominal term—like setting herself on a plateau after a difficult climb.

In its present state of disrepair, the Bayshore house was only a hazardous wooden tent with broken windows, no working bathrooms and, at its most recent "update", a more-than-a-half-century-old kitchen. Carolyn doubted she'd be comfortable living in the house while it was redone with the dust and upheaval. She bet her doctors would think quite negatively of that idea as well; whirling clouds of centuries-old horsehair plaster and sawdust would only raise their blood pressure and ire.

Getting another place, whether buying or renting, would mean lots of trips back and forth from the property each day…and for how long? Instead she scanned her screen, looking at modular housing companies in an Internet search. She liked the idea of renting or buying several two-bedroom homes that looked like seaside cottages she'd seen, providing comfortable housing with workable plumbing to septic systems and every modern convenience inside with electrical hookups for the heating and air-conditioning units. They'd fit into the picturesque setting once the landscaping was under control, and they would allow Carolyn and her aunts to stay close to the reconstruction efforts—but away from most of the dust and debris.

Carolyn looked out the turret windows of her bed and breakfast room to admire the coastal scene, the sun streaking through a leaden cloud touching the horizon. Carolyn remembered how things had cascaded into a real torrent of sadness after Billie had died, and things kept getting worse. Five months after Billie had died, Cass's husband of three years, her dear lampshade-wearing jokester, Edgar, died from a stroke. Then, about a year later, a small appliance caught fire on the third floor of Muriel's apartment complex, and everything burned to the ground. They'd picked her and her boyfriend, Cal, up within an hour of the inferno as Muriel and Cal stood on the street curb with two bags of clothes, a few framed pictures, and a beyond-saving, scorched houseplant even Cass couldn't salvage. Cal never recovered, and within weeks he'd died of a pulmonary embolism.

Four months after that, Bee's husband, Duke, sat down after his morning walk, saying he wanted to read the newspaper, and died of a massive heart attack while scanning the sports page. With all those losses and all of her continuing efforts with the police and investigators, Carolyn thought they'd all survived intact until her heart problems started…which ultimately ended her tenure in her beloved health bar company. None of those were happy times. Perhaps now was an opportunity for *all* of them to *really* start over.

Carolyn knew they all said they had worked through their grief. Of course, her aunts' plan were woven around deciding what to do with this historic hulk of a house. The aunts would be happy, and she could show them she was *really* working on getting back on track again *if she stayed*, Carolyn admitted grudgingly.

Carolyn had worked very hard, too hard, and was well off before, but now her newfound money from the sale of her business increased her financial standing exponentially – near mid-nine fig-ure financial independence. She could ease into decisions and cor-rect mistakes, if her judgment proved faulty. Rebuild 39 Bayshore or tear it down. Rebuild or tear down many Bayshore-like projects. Neither would affect her bank balances much. She could easily af-ford this project. *But the time – I'm pleasing my aunts but losing time.*

Suddenly, the bedroom wall seemed to forcibly disintegrate around Carolyn as the curtains and shattered turret windows flew at her like a wave in an exploding torrent of wood and glass shards. Carolyn instinctively turned her shoulder, headed away from the debris coming toward her face, and got up from the window seat. "Oh my God! Oh my God! Oh my God!" she cried repetitively. Her aunts and the Stornels ran as fast as they could from their places in their rooms, the dining area, and the kitchen when they heard the booming crash.

"Everyone, just stay where you are!" Ed ordered after taking three steps at a time on the staircase and hearing his guests' screaming words. He found Carolyn quaking and covered in glass. "Just stand still if you can, keep your eyes closed, and we'll clean you off. Don't move, or you'll cut yourself."

Carolyn didn't know what had happened, but when Ed Stornel said something about being cut, she turned toward his voice. Just as reflexively, she stopped as she thought she might do herself more harm, and she listened to his commands.

"Get some old blankets now, Nan, and the broom. Jessie, get some towels. Some dry, some wet," Ed ordered, his eyes scanning the situation. "Do you have shoes on?"

Carolyn nodded, and a few shards of glass like razor-sharp snowflakes fell down her face.

"I'm sorry for asking. Please don't move anymore," Ed said. "We'll sit you down after we get a chance to clean you off. Nan get another chair from the hall!"

After he laid down the three blankets his wife had brought, Ed excused himself to start making repair calls. Nan and Carolyn's aunts went about getting the glass off her face and hair. Making sure Carolyn kept her eyes closed as they worked around her and carefully extracted her from her now-ruined bathrobe - as if she were a cake on a lazy Susan.

"Should we wash her hair first?" Bee asked.

Carolyn felt better; if she were bleeding badly, they'd have had the paramedics here by now.

"How's your heart rate?" Muriel asked.

Carolyn hadn't even thought of her heart. She was unnerved and frightened, but so far her treacherous galloping heart rate seemed absent.

"OK," Carolyn mumbled from behind the towel Bee held to protect her face as they examined her scalp.

"Oh, Carolyn," Muriel started. "We're so glad you weren't too hurt in this big mess!"

"I seem to be attracting messes," Carolyn replied from under the towel. "Some in LA, one here in this room, and one *big purple one* called the Bayshore property!"

"At least you haven't lost your sense of humor," Cass noted as Carolyn walked gingerly over the old blankets to wash away the debris in the bathroom.

After taking about an hour of examining and making sure Carolyn was free of glass and hidden injury, the foursome sat down to have breakfast.

"Only four Band-Aids on your neck and shoulder," Cass reported unnecessarily, since everyone saw the number that had been needed. No one had left Carolyn's side.

"I've got an appointment for you with Dr. Stephens," Bee said. "Nan gave me the number, and he'll see you as soon as you're finished with breakfast."

"I can't tell you how sorry we are about this." Nan shook her head. "We'll take care of all your bills and refund today's room fee for all of you for your trouble."

"You'll do no such thing, Nan," Carolyn said, wrinkling her nose and shaking her head. "You couldn't help it that a bird flew into the window mullion and shattered the glass panes." Carolyn put down her coffee mug and raised her hands. "I'm OK. See?" She looked at Nan. "Besides, Ed's quick thinking kept me from injuring myself further."

"I know all of you think it's a bird but I'm unconvinced...and I'd like to call the sheriff," Ed said gravely.

Astonished Nan replied. "The sheriff, Ed?!!"

"I just can't get over the damage done here, Nan." Ed tried to appear calm and thoughtful. He was worried. "Just to be sure. Don't want some fool kid or hunter thinking they can shoot their guns here in town, is all."

"Do what you think is right, Ed. Carolyn'll just take another room until that one's fixed," Muriel said, trying to keep everyone calm. "You're going to have enough trouble getting the window taken care of, talking with the insurance people, and getting the room cleared out. We won't hear another thing about not paying."

"Besides, where else can we stay that has such good scones?" Carolyn asked, trying to lighten the faces of her companions. A wry smile came to her face. "But one of you ladies will have to take the next broken window." She looked at her watch. "We've got some people to meet at the Bayshore place...after the doctor's appointment, of course." Carolyn got up and grabbed her purse as Nan headed back into the kitchen.

"Are you sure you're OK?" Muriel walked closer to her. "We could cancel today."

Carolyn waved away her aunt's concern. "I'm sure it was just a bird. Let's forget about this, or we won't get anything done." She looked at the most pressing needs. "Well, I think we need to get recommendations on several things." Carolyn looked more closely at the list. "First off, last night, I looked at the plans the contractor left, but I don't fully understand the preliminary engineering tests done on the house. If this three owner company you keep talking about is competent, we'll talk things over, and I'll ask for them to do more work." Carolyn got a better grip on the car keys. "I've got to ask Nan if we can stay here for at least a few more weeks. My main objective is to stay closer to the site; I don't think any portion of the house is habitable. I'm making calls to modular housing people today and thinking of temporary housing on the Bayshore land."

Carolyn walked down the hall to the reception desk. "I'll talk to the exterminator to check the place, and I'll line up other inspectors and tradesmen based on the engineering reports." Carolyn bit her lip in concentration. "I know we found animal droppings by the half basement built into the subterranean rock that juts out onto the north side of the property, and I'm not about to chance visiting the attic if there are nests and critters up there." She looked at another clipboard. "I don't want to be crushed or injured if the attic's drop-down staircase identified in the property description collapses or releases some swarm or something or other. They'd have three flights of stairs to hunt us down in their anger and possibly infest more rooms.

"The engineering reports are the first thing we need so we can know the structure's safe." Carolyn looked for the number Nan had given her for the second call.

"Then we'll be checking for asbestos?" Bee looked at her list with her half glasses perched near the end of her nose. "The company didn't know if they'd be able to set an appointment for several days. But they've got your phone number."

"Can't tear anything down without their OK." Carolyn made a notation. "We'll need to get ourselves some books and small hobby projects to keep us busy between appointments." Bee needed art supplies and cookbooks, Cass needed a sewing machine and gardening tools, and Muriel would need a printer for her regional and historic research. Carolyn put all the other lists in the SUV's trunk. Thankfully, Ed had kindly traded their SUV rental for a larger one. Everyone could have a seat and still have cargo space for hauling things around.

Carolyn looked up to see the glazing company employees getting the scaffolding in place to cover the broken window. The plywood coverings would make the front of the Stornel's Victorian look like an eye-patched pirate for at least a few days, Carolyn thought.

With the conversation, no one noticed the man coming up the walkway next to the SUV.

"What's happened here?" a short, thin balding man with a thin, pleasant smile asked.

"Broken window," Carolyn replied absently as she searched for her keys.

"Are any of you Ms. Carolyn Reynolds?" the man asked. "I'm Skip Clem, the mayor of this fair city…and your realtor. I have some papers for you." He opened up his black leather briefcase and extracted a magazine-thick stack of papers in a business-standard goldenrod envelope. "Want you to know I'll take the place off your hands if you want to sell, but real estate prices are down."

Carolyn liked people to get to the point, this man's preening tone about being the mayor and trying to suggest a low-ball deal all in the same breath seemed a bit much. "I'm Carolyn Reynolds," Carolyn said with a slight frown, "and I'm on my way to another appointment." She wasn't going to say anything about the doctor or her intentions concerning 39 Bayshore. She handed her clipboard to Muriel and offered her right hand to accept the papers.

"I'm so sorry. My wife and I left for a few days to visit her aunt in Baltimore." The realtor passed a thick legal size envelope to Carolyn. "I hope this information doesn't come as any inconvenience. It's from the zoning commission and coastal authorities, and it might impact your plans." At Carolyn's knitted brows and darkening eyes, he hastened to add. "Perhaps we can sit down and I can explain everything to you." He headed for the front entrance of the bed-and-breakfast. "Didn't your attorney, Mr. Lyon, inform you of this?"

Carolyn's lips compressed. There had been several messages from Lyon's secretary asking her to call. The two messages didn't seem urgent. Besides, Carolyn still smarted concerning Lyon's part in this whole real estate fiasco, even if she'd buried her ill will with her aunts. She felt sure she'd been snake-bit again, looking at the envelope.

"With subdividing the property across the stone bridge, the taxes will be reassessed." He pointed to the packet. "There's also county say-so on the Payne cemetery plot on the other side of the property." Skip wanted to slide that fact in, because lots of people were scared of dead bodies and having had some by the Bayshore house before they were moved in the 1950s, just might send Ms. Reynolds packing. "About ten graves there as I remember."

He was going to use all his personal and public powers to make Ms. Reynolds life miserable in dealing with anything that had to do with 39 Bayshore. *If he and his wife couldn't have the Bayshore house, then neither should anyone else.* Bayshore had been his good luck charm all those years ago with finding that old gold coin. It should be *his* home!

Clem's luck had been slim lately with sales being down in his family's septic business *and* increasing competition for real estate listings, and he couldn't pad his bills to the Bayshore estate any higher without raising red flags. Besides, people were grumping about his mayoral bid after booting out Evan Smith from the mayor's office. Grabbing for the mansion might garner more enemies, and Skip didn't need any more complications if he had any chance of holding office. He thought painting the place purple and taking down most of the fences would scare away any prospective buyers. He thought he could lie low for some months and grab the place at a considerable discount…but his decision had cost him 39 Bayshore—at least for now.

"The lots you subdivided sold almost immediately, and the escrow money is in an account at the bank." He might as well keep pummeling her with facts. "I'll get you the names and addresses if you like. I left them at the office in my haste to get over here." Clem's voice trailed off as if no more air could come from his lungs. He knew full well that Pastor Allred had bought one lot, and Shealds Jackson and his partners owned the other.

Since scraping that pile of road trash into the entrance of the property with county equipment hadn't scared them away, perhaps dribbling out negative information, like the cemetery being on the property and dealing with permitting and legal challenges he'd be surreptitiously throwing their way every few days, might heighten this lady's distaste. Time was on his side. Perhaps he could get some home and road improvements done on her money and come back with an offer to buy if she got tired of the negativity and trying to fix the place up. There were more things certain than death and taxes. Property, houses, and buildings would always be for sale— especially purple ones.

"Do you know my new neighbors?" Carolyn asked in a soft voice, not wanting him to tell him how much she knew already.

"Why, yes," Mr. Clem replied, thinking that keeping such information from Ms. Reynolds would make him appear less than helpful. But he could disguise things and frame his answer to plant more seeds of doubt. He'd hedge a bit, see if he could wheedle her into submission by making Bayshore appear less tony...and less appealing to her rich-woman instincts. "Previous buyers wanted to invest in expansive real estate investment properties and didn't consider *parceling* of the main house with other subdivided lots. But for you, this seems like a perfect solution in welcoming *closer* neighbors into your immediate area and offsetting the costs of the *extensive* repairs necessary for the main house."

Carolyn closed her eyes and recalled the land beyond the house. She couldn't remember much, since the house had consumed most of her thoughts when she'd visited the property.

"Ready to go?" Bee whispered, not liking Mr. Clem's comments. Carolyn nodded.

Carolyn looked into Mr. Clem's eyes. "If nothing needs to be done at this moment, I want some time to look these papers over. I'll get back to you. May I have your card?" she said, turning toward the vehicle door. "We have several appointments, if you'll excuse us." Carolyn started getting in the driver's seat and called, "Nan, could you get Mr. Clem some coffee, since we have to leave?"

When Nan heard Skip's voice, she walked closer to the group and started listening to the conversation, hoping Skip wasn't causing any trouble. Skip was a world-class talker and usually as smooth as a snake. Nan gave her husband the look that indicated Ed should get Skip the coffee. They could talk about the broken window while Nan talked to Carolyn.

"I'll be happy to, Carolyn," Nan said loudly, wiping her hand on a towel as she walked to the driver's side of the car. Nan heard Carolyn's clear instructions to Skip. Wanting to make sure Carolyn and her aunts weren't thrown off by his negativity, Nan looking reassuringly into Carolyn's eyes. "There are no bodies in the cemetery anymore—only markers," Nan whispered.

Thank goodness there are no bodies to have to deal with, Carolyn thought. She closed the door and handed her purse to Cass. "I'm glad," Carolyn replied, not wanting to think of dead bodies. "We'll still have time to buy some folding tables and some chairs before I see the doctor, if we hurry."

Cass piped up from the backseat, "Better add a few brooms, dustpans, rags, and cleaning solution. Plus some buckets. And rubber gloves to protect our hands."

For now, Carolyn didn't mind if the land on the other side of the bridge sprouted houses. Bee didn't mind the cemetery being on the land, and neither did Muriel or Cass. It was just a symbol of heritage and resting in peace...none of them or Carolyn believed in ghosts.

"I think the list needs lots of garbage bags and disposable gloves too, for picking up trash," Cass added. The women consulted their lists as Carolyn drove to the store.

After Ed called the sheriff, he and Skip talked about the window mishap. Nan put a steaming mug on the table. Skip took it without a thank-you and began rummaging through papers in his brief-case. Took all kinds in this world, Nan knew. *Treating me like a servant when there is no one was around to impress!*

Carolyn and her aunts were dear people, just as they seemed like on first impression: down-to-earth and smiling. They liked helping in the kitchen, even though they were paying guests; making them seem more like extended family. Nan almost cried when Carolyn had been so gracious about the broken window. Being in the hospitality industry brought all types to their bed-and-breakfast. It was a hard road sometimes, keeping business and personal feelings apart and dealing with ornery townsfolk like Skip. "You want a cinnamon roll with the coffee, Skip?" Nan didn't add that she thought he had the grace of an ox and the personality of an eel.

Thank goodness, she didn't have to waste her time in conversation with Clem.

After Carolyn and her aunts drove away, a man dressed in a blue jumpsuit started picking up wood scraps and filled several refuse bags which he put in his pick-up truck bed before Nan called out the back door. "Please, don't throw anything away and leave everything in the side yard." The man nodded, but left the garbage bags in the back of the truck while going back to pile the rest of the debris. He worked quickly and pulled away without saying anything to the Stornels.

Ed looked up from his conversation with Clem and another guest to see a three man cleanup crew in khaki uniform pants and shirts arriving to board up the windows. "I'm Roger and we're from the clean-up service sent by your insurance company."

"Leave it all, please. I want to show the damage to the sheriff," Ed instructed.

After ten minutes, the cleanup crew chief waved good-bye to Ed. "Thanks for tidying everything up for us, Mr. Stornel. There's usually a lot more work."

Ed was puzzled. He hadn't done any cleaning and he certainly wouldn't have let Jesse or Nan touch any of the broken wood or glass but just as he was going to say something, Ed was distracted by the fast-paced arrival of the sheriff's car with lights blazing and a smoking-tire stop. "Wish you would have left everything as-is before you started the cleanup, Ed."

"Sorry, sheriff. Calling you just came to mind after calling everyone else...because the amount of damage is what had me concerned - just seemed like too much to come from a bird hit." Ed pointed to the pile of splintered wood and broken glass. "Had the cleanup crew leave the debris though."

The sheriff looked around for several minutes. "No bullet holes, gunpowder or anything to indicate this wasn't an accident, Ed," the sheriff replied. "With this mess, I can't tell you one way or the other. Looks at least like more than one bird or perhaps, something else. I can't tell."

"Well, we'll just stick to the 'bird' theory, because I must say I'm feeling sorry to have botched things up...or to have called you at all," Ed replied.

"Thanks for saving me a pile of trouble, Ed," the sheriff said with relief. "Take a lot of manpower and a big part of my budget, if it were something else." He winked. "We'll just call it a bird hit... and a simple accident. But I will keep an eye out to see if there's anybody messing around for the next few days - just in case."

Pete's Jeep drove up to the bed-and-breakfast only seconds after he saw the sheriff pull away from the curb in the opposite direction.

He nodded to Skip Clem sitting at the table with his coffee and cinnamon roll before heading to see Nan. "What happened?"

Nan explained about the bird-shattering incident and Ed calling the sheriff but kept Ms. Reynolds and the aftermath out of the conversation because Clem was still there – and was such a gossip. When they were out of earshot in the kitchen, Pete asked, "Is the Reynolds' family headed for the Bayshore house?"

"Left about an hour ago, at least." Nan concentrated on kneading the bread dough in front of her, taking her concerns for Skip, Carolyn, and her aunts out on the lump.

Pete saw the empty, greased crockery bowl waiting for its usual path to the deep sink. He'd hoped to talk to Carolyn…about the vagrants. He'd ministered to a young couple there a few weeks ago, knowing they'd used 39 Bayshore's abandoned art studio as their shelter. Ms. Reynolds had looked so shaky yesterday when he had escorted them to the property, so he hadn't mentioned the incident right away. He'd only got to speaking about the problem of vandals in general. Bayshore belonged to Carolyn Reynolds and her family now…and he hoped the two trespassers were many days and truly gone.

Before the Reynolds family had arrived, Pete recalled heading home before he had left for the pastors' conference and meeting Pastor Bill. He'd noticed lazy smoke coming from the direction of the Bayshore studio. Noting the Bayshore house stood empty since the elderly Mrs. Dorne died, he stopped his Jeep and fumbled for his mobile phone, inadvertently sending it into the passenger side backseat wheel well. The house sat six miles from the fire station. A blaze could engulf the studio, house, and barn if the flames caught on the wind and drought-dry timber.

After scrambling to retrieve his cell phone, Pete's new vantage point located a small flame coming from the meadow next to the studio building. On that day, the road to the mansion was clear, not blocked yet by the county road crew. He bent back the rusted fence wire and drove down the path toward the smoke and prayed. Pete had tapped in two of the three emergency number digits, when he saw a girl race from the outbuilding and jump in the high leaf stack, then jump up again as she began to throw the leaves at a taller, bulkier, definitely male companion, who was with her. They looked like they didn't have a care in the world.

As he ran from his Jeep, Pete used his best projecting baritone voice as if trying to rouse someone from sleep in the back row of the sanctuary during a sermon. "Hey! Hey!" he called as he ran, startling the girl and her companion after scaling an old stump. "Didn't you see the 'no fire' warnings on the posts by the road?" Pete ran to the small fire, grabbed handfuls of dirt and stomped the embers. "You could set the place on fire if the sparks fly any-where. Got any water?"

At first, the young people had been silent, looking repentant, as Pete explained about the possibility of the fire spreading. "You've got no hose, water source, or shovel." Pete saw they were like the myriad drifters coming up and down the coast. There'd been an ever-increasing number of break-ins into summer homes, taking up residence for the night or until they were caught - some more lawful than others.

Pete worked on making sure the fire was out as both young people stayed mute and still. *At least they didn't run away.* "You have a name?"

The girl was the first to speak. "We weren't trying to hurt any-thing," she said.

"Do you have food and water for yourselves?" Pete asked, put-ting the welfare of the two before he asked any other questions. He got a card out of his pocket. "If you do need anything, call the church...and I'll see what we can do to help."

The young man gave an angry-faced nod.

"OK," Pete replied, equally succinct. "The property owner is due here in a few days. I'd like you to be gone quickly...and don't set any more fires." He looked into the sullen faces again. "I'll be back tomorrow to check."

But he hadn't been back, with pressing church business, his counseling practice, and his trip. He had a feeling these two young transients didn't mean any trouble. Pete hoped they'd taken his advice and were long gone from the area. There had been no sign of them when he'd come with Carolyn and her aunts to start their property evaluation. *So many lost souls traveling through this area.*

CHAPTER SEVEN

Carolyn had finished with the doctor, getting a clean bill of health, and she now walked on the Bayshore property with the arborist she'd contacted. The sixtyish, tall, thin Mr. Hobbs, talked knowledgeably while giving his straightforward assessment. "I'll check those other trees, Ms. Reynolds, and see if we can save some nearer the house, but don't want to get your hopes up. From what I can see, most are diseased and others are too old or far-gone from lack of attention, water and ice storm damage."

"My Aunt Cass is our resident expert. She says, she'll do any-thing you order," Carolyn replied.

"We may save some of the fruit trees, but proper pruning will take several months of work and cost a bunch. Even with that in-vestment, we'll have to see. The commission overseeing coastal for-estry and wetlands will want some trees planted when they see my report." Hobbs jotted down a few notes.

Even to her untrained eyes, Carolyn knew Hobbs was right. She shaded her gaze from the sun as she looked back at the house. "My aunt Muriel says there's a picture at the library showing other trees on this side of the property." Carolyn watched Bee as she headed out the door with another bag of trash. Carolyn thought they'd need several of the biggest trash Dumpsters available with weekly service, before the first level of cleaning and demolition was done.

The contractor could take care of the Dumpsters. She hoped they weren't jumping the gun on cleaning before getting the engineering report, but her aunts said they needed to keep busy. This place still might meet the wrecking ball. A sigh escaped as Carolyn turned her steps toward the studio building, needing to consult Hobbs about their hopes for salvaging the trees near their lot line. Squinting in the sun, movement and vague shapes flitted before her eyes. Carolyn thought she saw the shapes of two people. A man and a woman, it seemed. Definitely a man, she thought, but she wasn't sure about the other image. Carolyn looked back toward Mr. Hobbs. "Did you bring some other people to help you?"

"Wanted to, but we had other appointments," Mr. Hobbs said. "We'll have crews coming when it's time to do the work. I'll evaluate and tag everything besides giving you a written report. Don't you worry."

Carolyn's brow quirked, and she turned back to the studio. Now no one was there.

The man's brow wrinkled. "Better put out the fire in the fireplace there," he admonished, pointing in the direction in the studio. "They're tricky with this underbrush. Outlawed in fact, until you get the chimney checked." Carolyn was about to reply she hadn't started any fire, and then she took a step toward the long, low building with its patchwork array of remaining shutters lolling with disrepair and wind damage. She hadn't inspected the studio and had only done a cursory inspection on the deteriorated barn with its abandoned horse stalls and decrepit attached living quarters. *How long had they been in disrepair?*

The so-called studio sat at the same elevation as the main house's half basement and was anchored in the same footing line.

It looked out of place in its shape and wood exterior. The architectural drawings showed a lower level, a large rectangular room, undoubtedly designed to her eye as the art studio which had double doors for hiding canvas and supply storage on the far end. Once the weathered plywood coverings were removed, they'd evaluate the floor-to-ceiling windows—or what was left of them.

"Carolyn, the plumber and septic man are here," Cass called in her clear strong voice. "I'll walk with Mr. Hobbs. I'd love his input on replanting."

"I'll...I'll be there in a minute." Carolyn took a few more steps toward the studio and turned, trying to keep her mind on her list of things to do. "We didn't start a fire." She rubbed her brow. The tension caused the beginnings of a headache. "I need you to know I don't own any of the property on the other side of the bridge and creek bed. There might be some changes from the original description of the work needed there since the land has been subdivided and purchased by others." She looked back to the studio. Smoke now curled from underneath the boarded windows. *Who did that?*

Carolyn's feet started running toward the building. "Call the fire department!" she yelled to the startled arborist.

Truth be told, Shealds still smarted from the fact that the Bayshore property sold to some unknown buyer, but he wasn't going to share the depth of his anger with either Hesse or Molina. He'd just swallow his disappointment and finished getting the ironwork casting molds from the foundry for the new owner, hoping they would be redone in their original splendor as a token to get the property contract.

Bayshore sat like a nineteenth-century queen on a huge lot, gazing with an unwavering eye out onto the inlet with the water at her feet. Protected on two sides by wide-spit land and sitting in an untended mature tree area, it seemed like everything there had graced the land forever, even though the historic county and state records showed this was rock and fill land over original marsh-lands. This now shabbily treated regal lady, painted in the ugliest purple color imaginable by their twit of a mayor, sat elevated on the innermost part of the cupped inlet looking out about two miles from the open sea, protected by a broad estuary.

Bayshore towered over the rooftops of other estates a distance away on either side of the inlet. Other people of that era, who were also shaking off the enmities of the Civil War, were building mansions, but nothing was like 39 Bayshore. Elias Barkley Payne, the first owner, spent years building up the site with specially designed mule-wagon loads of rock and clean fill sifted from his mining property five miles inland. Some of his workers had spent more than a few years of their salaried lives making sure the dirt was "clean" or driving to and from this waterfront acreage to fulfill their boss's dream of having the highest property and greatest waterfront views in the state.

In the current day, Shealds and his partners had worked twenty-hour days trying to get enough credibility and momentum for the construction business. Bayshore was going to be their reward—*their* dream property. Others thought Bayshore was a wreck, Shealds knew that in the right hands, Bayshore could, again, be a treasure, and another way to show prospective clients their company's superior work.

He'd already made innumerable topographical drawings restoring the circular brick-paved driveway at the front door of the mansion. The current mansion would house their business offices, public rooms, and Shealds's residence. They'd planned to demolish the studio and restore the true-to-the-era barn for the workshop and the heavy equipment their company owned. Hesse and Molina could each have had a spacious set of rooms on each of the two floors of a newly constructed addition—a reproduction of the two-story servant's wing they'd discovered in old sepia photographs down at city hall. Rot and insects had probably devoured those footings, so that wing had disappeared, and now all the rest of the Dornes, the descendants of the Paynes, were gone as well.

They got the crushing news when he, Hesse, and Molina found out a lawyer representing clients from LA had snatched the property out from under them. Shealds frowned as he skimmed his gray hair with his left hand and straightened his spare metal-framed sunglasses with the other, keeping control of the steering wheel of his large black pickup. *Concentrate on what's going right.* They hadn't touched his money except for an initial loan to get the business started. With the loan repaid to his bank account, every asset of the company was free and clear, including their current house and vehicles. They'd have to see if any other of the old mansions came on the market. There were a few in equally bad or architecturally butchered shape Shealds had his eye on—but they weren't the prize of the Bayshore house.

Shealds had to make it appear he was concentrating on nothing more than his business and make sure he showed everyone he was adjusting to life as an ex-offender. So Shealds would do the work on the house, hopefully talking the owner into going along with his restoration ideas and keep himself busy with the consolation prize of building a companion house near the Bayshore structure intended for his sister-in-law, Ellen, and her boys. If Ellen wouldn't see the truth of the situation after he was exonerated, he, Hesse, and Molina would sell it for a tidy profit.

Shealds's hand rubbed the base of his neck. The soft alto voice of the new owner of the Bayshore property had left two business-like messages, asking questions about his company. Shealds was near Bayshore, wanting to walk the lot the company had purchased once more before considering the recommendations of his architect. Sure enough, multiple tire tracks could be seen on the ground. He'd scraped and breached the county-created mound to allow the new owner unrestricted access. Shealds could see some people and vehicles on the property now. There was also some smoke rising from the area of the decrepit, boarded-up studio!

Stones and mulch scattered under his truck wheels as Shealds accelerated toward the house. His alarm grew as he slid to a halt, jumped from his truck, and watched thick black smoke belching from the broken windows and warped plywood. He recognized Hobbs, a tree and landscaping specialist he'd worked with on several job sites. "You calling the firehouse?" he yelled as he bypassed three ladies tending to two people sitting on the ground.

"Carolyn's still in there!" one of them screamed as he darted past.

Shealds vaulted over the shaky, wooden porch rail as smoke stung his eyes. He bolted into the room and immediately bumped into the back of someone. Shealds knew it was human by the feel of the spine and shoulder blade on his forearm as he unknowingly threw the unknown form closer to the smoke. There was a clanging noise and a choked, coughing sound. The smoke seemed to clear a bit, letting the ambient light from the broken window frames penetrate the gloom. The coughing continued, with an occasional choking sound, now closer to the door. Shealds didn't know what else to do except pull the distressed body with him. As he grasped the body around the trunk, he knew this was definitely a female, as his arm skimmed a woman's breasts and settled to her waist. If he'd had better visibility, he'd have swung her legs into his other arm, instead thinking it better to get fresh air and risk a few bruises.

As he emerged from the smoke, there was a collective gasp of concern and relief. The human bundle he carried struggled to get a foothold back on the ground, while continuing to gasp and sputter as his arm tightened to keep the squirming in check, so he wouldn't lose his balance while heading for the other people. "Stop moving," Shealds growled with a cough. "You'll hurt us both."

"The fire extinguisher," Carolyn said, gasping. She tried to get the words out to explain how as soon as she saw the smoke, she rooted through the bags from the hardware store and found the fire extinguisher. Her arm was still wet from the foamy spray. Her unknown assailant bumped the nozzle and the rest of the setup out of her hand. "The place will burn down." She turned her head to see the smoke ebbing as the big arm loosened, sending her unceremoniously to the grass.

Gaining a sitting position, Carolyn looked up to see a silver-haired man, she suspected, more than six feet tall if her gaze from about eight inches from the ground was accurate. She'd felt the stretched tendon cords against her side as he'd carry-dragged, and then, dumped her. He was Shealds Jackson, Carolyn knew from the digital and newspaper information she'd reviewed. *Wiry and angry. Where did he get such glorious gray hair?*

Carolyn tried to continue talking but coughed instead. She diverted her eyes, anxiously counting heads as she wondered where her aunts were and if they were safe. All three were tending to two strangers. She saw the soot-smudged, scared face of a petite teenage girl, and the sulky frown of a beefy young man, both of whom were sitting on the grass. Carolyn scrambled to her feet, having enough air to make her shaky limbs stay locked and upright.

"We didn't know the fireplace wouldn't work," the unidentified girl explained feebly as she wiped her tearstained eyes and nose.

A thousand questions whirled in Carolyn's mind. She tried to catch the most important ones while keeping her eyes on the angry, brown-haired young man.

"Everyone OK?" Carolyn blinked a bit, also seeing the man she remembered as the local pastor coming behind Mr. Jackson, who was now dusting off his coat sleeves. She couldn't remember the pastor's name.

It didn't matter, because Mr. Jackson started talking. "You know what's going on here, Pastor?" His scowl turned to a sneer on his face as well as in his voice. "Fool kids."

The pastor ignored both of them, heading for the girl and her companion. "I can take care of this, Shealds." Pete's tone sounded as tired as his eyes as they settled on the young couple. He seemed to know them. "I thought I warned you about fire."

The girl, who looked like she was going cry but gritted her teeth instead, stayed silent. She tried to promote a stiff-backed, more aggressive posture in her scarred, thrift-store men's leather jacket. As the girl tried to cross her arms defiantly, Carolyn noticed a tiny pink baby fist escape its confines within the oversize black coat. Noticing Carolyn's eyes, the girl shoved the tiny hand back beneath the voluminous leather folds. "Just give us a second, and we'll be out of here."

Carolyn moved toward the couple and began speaking with a voice seemingly coming from another part of her brain. "Now, young lady, do you think you can come here to meet us without warning? I told you to meet us at the bed-and-breakfast, but, as always, you had to have your own way, and you came out here, I bet. Who's the guy you brought with you?" Sharp-eyed observers would have seen the rigid poses, slack jaws, and saucer-size eyes of the older women surrounding Carolyn, quite belying the story their niece was trying to project. "Bee, you take them into the main house. I'll deal with this new boyfriend later." Carolyn stopped for a moment, having to raise her voice over the emergency vehicles coming down the rutted road. "Welcoming us with a cozy fire was one bad idea!"

By this time, the fire truck had red-lighted its own path to the studio area.

"No one's in there or hurt!" Pete yelled as he headed to let everyone know no one was in the structure. The men nodded and signaled to the rest of the crew as Pete turned toward the chief.

"Always need to make sure the fire's out," the chief called.

"Harry, it's just a teenage relative of the new owner, thinking a fire in the fireplace would be a welcoming idea," Pete called, not really knowing if what he was saying was true. Aligning these transients with Ms. Reynolds and her aunts seemed too farfetched.

"Humph," the lantern-jawed, thickly built fire chief grumbled succinctly. He ran his hand over his face. "Shealds, you got to help me with the report here."

Shealds thought better of a further confrontation with the Reynolds family, and reluctantly headed back to the studio.

By this time, Muriel set herself between the youngsters and the rest of the crowd and pointed toward the old Bayshore house door and its warped plywood padlocked entry, both gaping open from their hasty run toward the studio fire.

"We've got ten folding chairs and four long folding tables," Cass projected in a booming voice, not knowing what else to say. "Relative?" she mouthed silently as a questioning afterthought to Bee and Muriel.

Carolyn joined her aunt, helping the girl get up, as the young man curled his forearm under the girl on the other side. The baby must be sheltered between them, Carolyn thought, giving a sore-throated grunt of her own.

"What are you doing?" Bee whispered, pretending to help Carolyn toward the house.

"I don't know," Carolyn said honestly, astounded by her previous words. Somewhere among the fire, the girl's bravado and seeing the tiny hand escaping the protective bonds of the girl's jacket, Carolyn's anger fell like a crashing boulder, an overpowering feeling of tender protectiveness hijacked her mind...and this ruse began.

Carolyn closed her eyes for a moment, trying to speak again, still feeling Bee at her side. Perhaps, they *could* foist this soot-faced girl as a shirttail relative. Carolyn wasn't sure of anything, except knowing she wanted to see the baby was safe, she didn't want to see these kids in jail, and it seemed difficult to breathe against the pain in her rock-dry throat. *A fraudulent cousin? Another niece for her aunts? A baby?*

The boy pulled a chair a distance from the others, scraping the metal legs on the unkempt slate entry floor. The girl sat with the still-hidden baby in a shadow-filled corner as her burly male friend stood in front of them. Only one frame of what appeared to be a bank of mullioned windows over the two-story entranceway was uncovered, allowing very little light in its interior murky spaces. Cass and Bee began alternately turning on the battery-powered camp lanterns placed around the room.

Carolyn wanted to make sure the baby was all right, or she'd yell for the firefighters to have a look before they called for the police. She turned toward the door to hasten the pastor's exit in order to do so. "Pastor Allred, thanks so much for your help with all this," she said in her best CEO voice as her cheeks flared at the patent web of deception she resolutely wove. "Our family needs some time together after this escapade." She lifted her wrist and fanned her fingers out in a gesture of good-bye. "You'll forgive us, won't you?"

A flat statement and not a question gauged her dismissal. *This is a calculated risk. And when was the last time I used the word "escapade"?* The pastor could throw her lies in her face if he knew the two young people cowering in the dark corner. *Perhaps not.* She'd find out later. She walked toward him. "You'll excuse us, won't you?" she said in a second dismissal statement, lifting her arm to touch the warped plywood exit. "Thank you for everything."

The pastor's eyes flitted between the shadowy corner and the door. "Get yourself...or anyone over to urgent care, if anything happens," he said, relinquishing his spot in the entryway and heading toward the door. "I must apologize, because I knew these kids were here. That's the reason I came over. I told them to leave and not build any more fires…but I didn't know you were related." His eyes remained troubled as he turned to say a few last words, sensing something else was wrong but saying nothing. His gaze returned to Carolyn as he went down the steps. "Take care."

Beyond the wide semicircle portico, the firemen hustled resolutely doing their work to make sure the fire was truly out. Carolyn whirled from the door. Her eyes flashed and her voice sounded husky. "No speaking to anyone. Not any of you, until I figure out what's going on." She punctuated her words with a sharp swath of her index finger. Carolyn looked at Cass and gave out staccato orders like a drill sergeant. "Cass, call for pizza—enough to serve us and the firemen out there…along with enough soft drinks, bottled water, and a gallon of milk. Muriel, call Lyon and tell him not to leave the office." Carolyn stopped. "If they ask where to deliver the pizza, tell them to look for the fire trucks. Tell them we're feeding the crew at the studio here for the active fire scene with four pizzas, on us." She turned back to the teenagers. "Now, let's see the baby."

The aunts gave Carolyn even more astonished looks.

Carolyn ignored them. She needed to get a look at the baby and to think. The overwhelming message from her feelings pinging from her brain was that she would regret turning in these trespassers and this baby for the rest of her life, if she didn't get some facts *first*. They were vagrants and trespassers, who had almost burned down the studio on the property - with a baby in tow!

Carolyn's mind raced and she hoped her heart stayed calm. But the sight of the baby's hand brought back all the things she'd learned over the years about the unwed mother's home, her three aunts losing their babies, her wasted time on ignoring her personal life…and her mother never getting to see her daughter have a child of her own or be a grandparent. Should she take the reins on this or hand this over to the authorities? *A time for more information …and another decision?*

Carolyn's aunts looked at each other, having a million questions themselves but keeping their mouths shut. These kids were strangers but Carolyn wanted everyone to think they were family. *Did Carolyn say - a baby?* Carolyn had *clearly indicated,* she wanted to be in charge in her best CEO tone – dismissing everyone except them and the two teenagers. None of them knew what Carolyn had in mind: protecting the infant, getting the story about the vandalism or both? An unexpected fire, vandals…and a baby? *What am I thinking? What am I doing?*

CHAPTER EIGHT

S omehow, Muriel coaxed the infant girl from the pair of trespassers. Carolyn tried to tamp down her anger at what could
have been an inferno – destroying Bayshore. If anyone was going
to demolish the place it was going to be after a thorough evaluation and *on her order*! As far as this new complication, the baby girl,
who only needed a bath and a bit of diaper rash cream, seemed to
be in perfect smiling and cooing health. *A baby.*

Again reverting to her CEO style, Carolyn swallowed against a
painful, itchy throat, wanting more answers. "Bee, will you be sure
to watch the door?" She turned toward the teens. "OK, you two.
Let's hear it."

"That's the last diaper we have," the doe-eyed girl, tinged from
head-to-foot with soot, offered in with a shaky voice as Muriel
changed the baby.

Thank the Lord for small favors, Carolyn thought. If they hadn't
had one, Carolyn was figuring out if they could assemble a makeshift diaper from the paper towels and masking tape from the
cleaning and organizational supplies they'd purchased.

"I think we killed a chipmunk in the chimney." A single crystal tear etched a clean path down the teenage girl's sooty cheek. "My name is Beth," the girl announced. Then she gestured to the baby using the half-eaten slice of pepperoni pizza in her hand. "And that's Grace Ann."

"She ain't ours," the burly, six-foot, square-headed boy with the box haircut grunted through a full mouth, to the dismayed gasp of Beth as her arm almost tipped over her soda can as she tried to swipe at the boy.

"You said you'd never tell!" Beth cried in outrage, with tears of betrayal.

The boy swatted off her arm with a shrug. "She's slowing us down."

"I've raised her, Joe," Beth stated emphatically, her eyes shining with anger. "Becky couldn't keep her. Didn't even want her, for that matter."

Carolyn waited for more information as she pushed her un-eaten piece of pizza back and forth on the pizzeria's printed napkin, hoping she'd get some straight answers to the million and one questions she had.

"So I guess I better tell the story," Beth said as she swiped at her teary checks. "I'm Beth Seavers, and I got kicked out of my last foster home. There were *only* going to be *two* more full-pay checks coming, they kicked me out and said I ran away." Beth shrugged. "Didn't mean much to me, except it was two months too soon according to the state child services department, but they wouldn't be back for another few months and, like I said, the checks were going to run out anyway. Luckily, it was April, I was almost eighteen, and I could crash at friends' houses until I finished high school in May." Beth shrugged unemotionally, as if she were rattling off a grocery list.

"After that, I got an ID card and decided to see if I could stay with an aunt. My mom told me about her before she died. Lived in Baltimore, but I got down there and she'd moved. Found some people living in a viaduct under the interstate. That's when I met Joe here." She gestured with a fresh piece of pizza. Beth seemed to be able to enunciate and chew at the same time. "Joe Thackery."

"No need to be telling them anything more about me," the burly boy grumbled. "Must say I was sore you gave Becky fifty bucks for the kid, though." He harrumphed. "Could have used it for training food." He was free with information concerning Beth but tight-lipped about himself, it seemed. *Is Thackery hiding something more?*

"Don't mean to split hairs, Mr. Thackery." Carolyn's tone was ironic. "But we do need to know everything, since you almost burned down the studio on my property."

Thackery's neck muscles tensed. He thought a few seconds. "It was a fire to heat some water for Grace Ann Before we left here. Guess you better keep telling 'em, Beth."

"I stayed in the homeless camp to help Grace Ann's mother, before Grace Ann was born. Thought Becky would straighten herself out once Grace Ann was here…but she didn't. She stayed involved with a robbery crew, using truant kids wanting dope or liquor, boosting their friends' homes or people out working," Beth began. "She got arrested and I gave Becky the fifty dollars I'd saved from working, and then I left with Grace Ann and Joe."

Beth looked from Joe to Carolyn to Joe again. "It's not too hard on the road. Go to diners and truck stops. I can run just about any dishwashing machine made." Beth looked earnestly at Carolyn. "Joe's training to be a food-eating contest champion," she said with conviction. "I collect scraps or cook, and he eats it."

"Beth's crazy about cooking. Only girl I know who keeps bottles of spices and stuff rattling in her backpack." Joe grabbed another pizza slice. "I worked bagging groceries some…and worked as a dog walker too."

"Joe's got to break the record of eating hot dogs in five minutes. Isn't it, Joe?" She looked at the thickly built boy with the reddish brown buzz cut for confirmation.

Carolyn's brow wrinkled. She couldn't believe she'd heard the pair correctly, as if Beth had just indicated she was a lost princess or some other ridiculous notion.

"Something like that." Joe nodded meaningfully. "First contest is in four or five weeks in Philly, then it's off to New York."

Carolyn lost interest in the story. "There are *many* things to consider before any eating contest," Carolyn began. "Most certainly Grace Ann." She looked over to Muriel, who was dripping milk mixed with water from a tiny slit in a plastic bag into the baby's mouth. They'd tried to salvage baby supplies from Beth's tattered backpack, but someone had stepped on the lone plastic baby bottle, breaking it irretrievably. There was only water in the bottle. "We'll have to get some baby supplies and some things for you." She looked from Beth to Joe. "You can't stay here with someone else's baby."

"I can. I'm legal. Like I said, my ID is in the backpack." Beth retorted.

Carolyn ignored Beth's comment. "So we'll have to pretend you're some part of this family until we can find out from my lawyer, what, if anything, we can do."

Beth bolted from the chair, causing Muriel to dribble a stream of milk down the baby's cheek. "Please don't give Grace Ann away!" in a high-pitched whisper of dismay.

"Did it get in Grace Ann's ear, Aunt Muriel?" Carolyn was up almost as fast as Beth, taking a clean paper napkin and wiping the milk away.

"No, child," Muriel replied. "Just down her cheek." All the attention, faces, and eyes made Grace Ann gurgle gleefully, not noting the tense faces of the people above her.

Carolyn put her hand on Beth's, which nervously patted the baby's tummy as she continued to watch Muriel give Grace Ann the milk. "Better stop the milk, Aunt Muriel. We'll get her some non-allergic formula until we can have a doctor see her. Give her some bottled water. And get Nan on the phone." Carolyn turned Beth toward her and looked over to Joe. "The firemen would have had *to report* the situation of you having the baby if we hadn't hidden you. You know that, *don't you?*"

Cass nodded. "We could have ratted you out, and then you'd be cooling your heels in jail." Cass's words reminded Carolyn of something from a crime novel. Beth paled and her ragged-nailed hands stiffened.

"Jail ain't fun," Joe said, grabbing for the pizza box and then putting one slice on top of another onto his plate. He took a huge bite. "Worse than juvenile detention, but the food's not too bad."

Beth looked at him with anger and incredulity, Carolyn noted. *Guess this boy never thought about giving a good impression.*

Carolyn looked into the questioning eyes of her aunts and started thinking about what she needed to do - hoping she had enough information to give to Mr. Lyon. Mr. Lyon, as her attorney, and his private investigators might flesh out Beth's and Joe's stories. She knew she had enough to do on this end.

Clearly, there was no way Carolyn would let anything entangle her in this mess unless she had control of the situation - especially in this clear case of abandonment and illegal sale of the infant by the biological mother. Carolyn had to know what she was getting into. They needed to look under or near a Baltimore interstate viaduct and get legal paperwork underway so the lovely baby girl sleeping in the corner could be legally under Carolyn's care. *Guess my money from years of hard work could help with something personal besides this decrepit house!*

With a drug-ensnared hooker or worst, Beth, Joe, "Becky", and Grace Ann needed: toxicology and STD testing for the adults as well as cocaine, other drugs, and AIDS panels for them all. She'd go for a doctor's exam as well; hiding it all under the guise of making sure they were not harmed by the smoke inhalation from the fire. *What nearby city would be big enough to provide anonymity?* Probably back to Baltimore.

Carolyn hadn't pressed Becky about her education, but it was a good sign she had graduated high school, although that, too, could be a fabrication. *Why is this Beth girl tied up to a young man who doesn't appear to be the brightest bulb in the chandelier and whose life goal thus far has revolved around becoming a championship eater, with a specialty in hot dogs, no less?* They'd know in a few days.

Secondly, Beth and Joe weren't leaving with Grace Ann! Carolyn thought she could keep them hanging around with promises of warm beds, lots of food, and trips for clothes shopping in another city—without giving these two any cash, receipts, or view of their credit cards or any other sensitive information for the few days she thought it might take to get definitive information. She'd also activate the tracking devices on all the rental cars they'd need. Her aunts could act as sentries and keep Grace Ann near them at all times. She'd get pictures of both teens, and the baby, under the guise of needing more pictures for their construction efforts. Those would be sent to Lyon's private detectives to enhance information gathering. Carolyn had their fingerprints on the plastic drink glasses and she'd ease them into plastic bags that would be boxed and picked up as well. *Praise God for all the police procedural programs I watched on television!*

She'd soon know if their stories were bogus, and then she'd have to introduce a whole new set of information to Beth and Joe, if those were their true names. If they were telling straight stories, they could stay. Carolyn would help them. But one thing remained crystal clear in Carolyn's mind: Grace Ann wasn't going *anywhere* if she had any say. Carolyn would spend all the money she needed to make sure the baby stayed safe. She was seriously considering that place being with her and her aunts. *Instant motherhood?* She had some time to reconsider while they were all busy with going to Baltimore, getting the health exams and getting the information and counsel of her legal team.

"We need to get ourselves checked out after the fire," Carolyn began. "Doctors in Baltimore will have to see if we're OK." She tried to swallow and continued. "Hopefully, when we get back, Nan and Ed will have extra rooms and a bassinet and high chair available." Carolyn wanted to make sure they were all adequately housed, so she'd have time to figure out this whole mess. As far as living arrangements at the Stornel family bed-and-breakfast, that would be several days and many decisions later.

"Yes. Perhaps a portable crib." Bee smiled hopefully and pushed Cass's shoulder. Muriel looked at both of her friends and mutely followed in step.

"We'll make those calls and go pack the things we'll need," Cass said, glancing over Carolyn's shoulder to look at Grace Ann. "Bee and I will make a run to the store for baby supplies and a safety seat, so you needn't worry about those things, either. You just continue your...chat."

If Carolyn hadn't been afraid of giving the wrong impression by rolling her eyes, she'd have done so at her aunt's understatement concerning the amount of information she still needed from Beth and Joe...and about her thoughts concerning motherhood.

Cass motioned to Carolyn and Bee to go to the portico. When they were a safe distance away, Cass whispered heatedly. "What the hell do you think you're doing? A baby...and two young who-knows-where-from vagrants?"

Carolyn took a deep breath. "I know this is a bit rash...but I want to help Beth and Joe, if they'll let us." She tried to stay calm as well and looked at her aunts with pleading eyes. "But more importantly, I want to try to see, think about and all, if I might be able to keep Grace Ann."

Carolyn saw Cass's incredulous look. "We'll let out scant information, making sure everything stays on the positive side." Carolyn knew this sounded more like a fairy tale than something she could really pull off.

"Are you sure?" Cass choked in a loud whisper.

"Oh, Carolyn," Bee cried, trying to stay calm.

"I don't know anything yet. I need time, more talking to these two and help from my lawyers and investigators." Carolyn knew this was going to be a mountainous dual task of legal paperwork and infant care! Her times of infant baby-sitting were years past. She had some knowledge of children and aspects of healthy childhood practices from making her health food bar products...but Carolyn was honestly confessing she was talking about instant motherhood!

Bee looked over at the teenagers, wanting to help everyone stay calm. "Thackery does seem a bit surly," as she looked through the doorway at the gruff exterior boy who she thought might be the most trouble in this crazy equation.

"Just let me see if I can pull this off. All I know is that my heart is telling me to try!" Carolyn pleaded. "Backs of steel?" she offered, praying Cass and Bee would agree.

"Two days," Cass countered, not wanting to shatter Carolyn's hope just yet. She for one wasn't going to say "Backs of Steel" because Carolyn's move seemed too hasty. *Can this scheme actually work?*

"You might have to give the baby back, is what I want to make you see," Bee said, equally concerned.

"I hear you," Carolyn offered. "I really do. Two days and I acknowledge I might have to give the baby up and all the rest having to do with the other two as well." Carolyn hoped they wouldn't question her too closely. She had enough self-doubt for all of them in this situation...but more stubbornness than sense, it seemed. *Going on with no regrets about this, remember?*

Cass and Bee looked at each other. They'd be watching Carolyn and every aspect of this bargain like mother hawks.

"Then, I guess you've got a two-day…and two day *only* 'Backs of Steel' declaration, Ms. Reynolds," Cass said grudgingly. "Starting now."

"Backs of Steel," Bee said, half-heartedly. She didn't know what Muriel was going to say about her friends' agreeing to all this in her absence. *Two days!*

After an hour of concocting a plausible cover story and watching Joe eat the rest of the pizzas, Carolyn noticed he started getting restless. "Gotta go out in the yard. Go over the backpack. Get edgy with no more cigarettes." Beth followed him after checking on the baby.

Muriel considered two more people and a baby added to their entourage. "Need another van?"

A van and a whole lot more, Carolyn thought. *A whole lot more!*

Joe was a smoker and the Two Tea Cup was a nonsmoking bed-and-breakfast. "Better call Nan again, Bee," was all Carolyn said as she walked over to the sleeping baby girl swaddled in Muriel's sweater, lying in the clean cardboard box they emptied of their supplies. "He's a smoker. Better get some nicotine patches or gum, or the Stornels won't take him when we get back." She looked at Grace Ann's downy light brown hair and the too-large stained baby nightie with a large hole in the left foot needing to be trashed. Grace Ann needed a bath and new, freshly washed-and-dried baby clothes. Carolyn knew to avoid the starch and sizing in newly pur-chased baby things. A feeding and sleep schedule was another matter to consider.

Carolyn called in another pizza order and sent Beth and Joe out to the road to wait for the delivery truck. Grace Ann was here with her and her aunts, so Carolyn didn't think Beth would run away.

"I called Nan, told we about our shirttail relative…and she already knew about the fire," Bee began. "Told her the girl was a runaway from the far side of the family, but I didn't know what to say about the baby."

"I told Nan about Joe and his appetite. She'd already planned for more breakfast food and increased our dinner order when we get back," Muriel added.

"After we clean up, you, Bee, Beth, Grace Ann, Joe, and I are headed out of here tonight for at least two days as far as I can gauge—for medical exams and a neutral place for me to think and try to figure things out. We'll have a van here before nightfall, and the excuse about smoke inhalation and not feeling well," Carolyn announced. "Cass will keep things going here at Bayshore and stay with the Stornels. Tell Nan and Ed we'll pay for all three rooms…because we've had some unexpected things come up out of town…and we'll be back."

She looked at Muriel. "Give Cass the phone so she can call the construction company to send the rest of the contracts for me to sign before we leave. Tell them, I'll phone them tomorrow or the next day to make sure everything is in order." Keeping plans going on 39 Bayshore was a good cover to indicate to the outside world that everything was progressing normally and give her some time to research this *very* impulsive path.

"Anything else?" Bee asked.

Carolyn pushed her thumb and index finger of her left hand on either side of the bridge of her nose. She ignored the dull ache behind her eyes caused by the fire's smoke. "If I decide to go ahead with all this, I've got to get everyone to believe the story about us coming here to renovate this house and adopting a baby. Any ideas?"

Bee put her hand to her face. "If you go ahead with this…and if Beth says Grace Ann is her baby or she bought Grace Ann or some such, that beautiful baby girl will be associated with her in some respects." She tapped her finger against her cheek. "It'll all be stitched into whole cloth as the legal things are settled and time passes. But here's one thing I do know. We *all hope* you're doing the right thing."

"I'm not sure. Money can't do everything," Carolyn whispered. "But I want to try. All these things and feelings are whirling around in my head!"

Muriel pulled up a folding chair and looked up at the afternoon daylight coming through the broken and cracked windowpanes. "Money can do what is needed for now and it's a good thing to try to invest in them, I think." She pointed in the direction of Beth, Joe and Grace Ann. "No matter what happens."

"I'll keep things going until you get back from the medical exams." Cass indicated as she came through the door. "I heard the first part." She held up her note pad. "I'm still adamant. Two days!"

"By then we'll have to come up with a complete cover story or I'll give the whole thing up to the authorities," Carolyn replied as she looked into three sets of eyes that mirrored concern and skepticism. "I promise."

Cass knew that she, Bee and Muriel had to stay strong, be realistic and not let this situation go on if things didn't work out. They all knew Carolyn *could be* a wonderful mother, even in these unusual—to say the least—circumstances. They'd have to work out what was right for *everyone* involved. But this is just like the old days when we helped each other, Cass thought with a grudging smile. *Just like the old days.*

CHAPTER NINE

S healds fumed inwardly. Not so much as a thank-you from the Bayshore owner, whose life he'd tried to save. Just like the long list of society girls, colleagues, and some ill-conceived dates, as long-ago sour thoughts popped into his memory. "She's a beauty but 'to the manor born', using those blue eyes to get what she wants," he said to the air, since no one stood near his truck. Perhaps the fear and smoke inhalation booted some of the brass from Ms. Reynolds's entitled behind. Shealds wished he'd taken the time to change into his gym clothes. All of him was sooty - stinking up his truck cab!

Shealds' business smarts and prison-hones instincts told him something was wrong. The watch on Carolyn's wrist and the logo on her simply tailored blouse spelled plenty of zeroes in her bank balance, but her eyes were worried. He'd bet if any of those women knew the girl named Beth *before* the fire, he'd do all the work on the Bayshore house for free. That lovely sandy-haired prissy bundle he carried was putting on an act. *But why?*

He couldn't think about her feistiness and beauty right now. He had to concentrate on exoneration. But there might be some residual benefit to his reflexive action. S*aving the life of someone might swing the contracts for the construction work?* He'd have to work that angle...and poke around a bit.

Shealds undressed in the mudroom and headed for the shower, leaving the trash bag for his smoky clothes in the garage; grabbing a clean pair of jeans and an old sweatshirt from the folded clothes. "I'm headed for a shower before we talk, Hesse."

"Got a whiff of smoke." Hesse left the office to investigate. "You OK?"

"Kids started a fire in the studio fireplace on the Bayshore property. Probably a vermin-plugged chimney that didn't get beyond the fireplace," Shealds talked as he headed up the stairs. "Say they're 'relatives' of the Reynolds family...but I don't buy it." The sides of Shealds's mouth turned downward. "Carolyn Reynolds is a lovely woman to look at but she's probably spoiled and entitled and I can't get involved with anything besides rebuilding her house now. Nothing matters besides getting Zaugus." Shealds took a deep breath. "The fire truck got there before anything really bad happened."

"Anybody hurt?" Hesse called up the stairs.

"No one except for me and Ms. Reynolds, coughing out the smoke," Shealds called.

"Was just coming to tell you that Ms. Reynolds' representative called to say Ms. Reynolds was signing and sending *all* the completed and *signed* contracts for Bayshore in a few minutes," Hesse informed.

"I'll believe it when I see the all papers and her signature," Shealds replied. "Maybe not even then."

Shealds should have been happy, Hesse thought, now that he was assured of the work he needed to complete his plan. But he wasn't.

"Something is going on over there," Shealds continued.

Don't that beat all, Hesse thought. The job was handed to them on a silver platter! But from the look in Sheals's eyes, Hesse knew not to say anything more just then. "You go take your shower."

After his shower, Shealds went to his desk and turned his swivel chair to the wall without saying a word—another habitual indication Shealds needed more time to think. From all appearances, the thoughts weren't pleasant. No answers were coming soon.

Just work at the Bayshore place and keep your mind's eye on the prize of your exoneration and freedom. He didn't need to get embroiled in anything else. But Ms. Reynolds startled and worried blue eyes kept coming back to mind. He could work with any society woman or family member to hide his intentions, but he needed to cool down. He'd call Samples and let him take care of watching the Reynolds clan. Shealds changed his blank gaze from the office window and headed for the kitchen. He needed to push Ms. Reynolds out of his mind. "Now that we have the necessary work contracts, I was thinking of asking if we could put a double-wide trailer on the Bayshore property as a place to supervise the construction."

"That sounds like a good plan." Hesse went to retrieve his half-full coffee mug on the counter. He'd let Shealds talk. *Nothing about the woman or what had happened.*

"Ms. Reynolds has already put in several calls to reputable modular home dealers," Shealds confided.

"I won't ask how you got their temporary housing information," Hesse replied.

"I want to keep you and Molina informed. Something's going on there." Shealds looked grim. "I'm not proud of this, but I want surveillance devices in each of the modular homes, at the Bayshore house and barn as well. All three floors with several on the main floor in all the conversation areas," Shealds scowled deeply. "I'll tell Samples, and if anything happens, it's *all* on me, you understand?"

Hesse tried to keep his mind on his paperwork, willing the tension that was forming in his shoulders to stop. "I understand. I'll get it done." *Trust Shealds!*

"Even though Reynolds says they're related, those kids who started the fire need surveillance." Shealds bounded from his chair and headed for the door. "I'm not buying it...and I'm not taking any chances."

"Where you going in such a hurry?" Hesse shouted at Shealds's back.

"I'm going paddle boarding," Shealds growled loudly before he slammed the door. "Need more time to think."

Carolyn, Grace Ann, Muriel, Bee, Beth, and Joe had been back from their medical exams in Baltimore for several days. There had been a flurry of night-and-day phone calls organizing the efforts concerning Grace Ann and the Bayshore property while they were gone as well as a day-and-night tutorial on infant care theories and choices.

"We're seeing the progress you're making and we're giving you another *two weeks* to continue your plans for Grace Ann, Beth and Joe," Bee said. She, Cass and Muriel had frequent talks and they were pleased with Carolyn's actions and attitudes.

Carolyn hugged her and promised. "I, thank you, so much! Two more weeks...but I know that this will be a continuing process and unfolding story."

"You still might have to give Grace Ann up...and Beth and Joe have minds of their own," Bee warned.

"But having another two weeks, means you believe in what I'm doing...and believe I'm doing it well so far!" Carolyn smiled. "Backs of steel!"

As far as Carolyn could see, Jackson, Silver and Molina were in evaluation mode, taking over supervising the army of inspectors and subcontractors coming to see the buildings. Water and power technicians from the utilities indicated water and electrical service would be primitive for a few weeks until the new lines could be dug into the property, but they could run pipes from the Bayshore line for water if the pipes held, or work out daily bottled water deliveries if they didn't. Carolyn had chemical toilet rentals delivered for the family now that Grace Ann was with them, unwilling to revert to her Girl Scout training of trench and cover.

Carolyn and her aunts, with Beth's help, had cleaned up six of the stale-smelling rabbit hutch rooms along with the front entrance and kitchen, allowing them to begin a semblance of occupying the home in the daylight hours. Worn plywood panels were removed. Muriel and Bee washed the unbroken windows for some natural light. Carolyn and Cass wiped down walls, knocked down cobwebs, and swept floors as they all scouted the rest of the house. The construction workers replaced the spongy deteriorated treads and risers on the attic staircase, and two-by-four temporary reinforced walls stabilized the opening. "We're going to have to let the construction crew take care of most everything else here," Muriel reported.

"Most of our subcontractors for this phase have made appointments. Our preliminary schedule starts below and finishes on the next page. Priority is water, septic, and power for the modular homes. Please consider the foundation issues on Bayshore as the first structural priority here," Hesse reported. "The rock-and-mortar foundation original to the structure is cracked and settling in several places, and support beams had been undermined by beetles and carpenter ants in several others."

Carolyn said, "I'll agreed to the foundation repairs but I need to focus on interpersonal concerns right now."

Beth and Joe needed a watchful eye. So far, Beth, as well as the rest of Carolyn's clan, had cared for the baby. Joe didn't seem to be much help at all. Losing interest in the common necessary chores they assigned him, he just concentrated on eating any and all snack and food supplies within reach and going down to the cemetery where Carolyn was sure he'd stashed some cigarettes.

The investigators submitted their first reports including the state's children protective agency information. So far, Joe checked out as a minor and persistent juvenile offender, easily and frequently lead into lots of minor and several major scrapes with the law, including shoplifting and being a passenger in several stolen car incidents. That wasn't good, Carolyn knew. He was a smoker, since the age of nine, but drank beer only occasionally, he said. Pot and traces of some other prescription drugs were in his bloodstream, but nothing major since no needle marks or scars were uncovered on his extremities, and his other blood work and physical exam showed he was in good health.

Carolyn locked her and her aunts' purses in the closet, where she'd had a new lock installed. She didn't mind seeing the new utilitarian deadbolt lock set on the sturdy new door adorning the entry closet—function trumped aesthetics now. Their valuables were safe, and this made things much easier than constantly checking to see if Joe or Beth suddenly decided they were easy marks.

Beth's story checked out. From what they could see so far, Beth was an even-tempered, hard-working girl who remained mentally intact in a life filled with beyond-rough circumstances.

Beth was eighteen, not a ward of the state anymore, and the investigators were scalpel-sharp in their ability to piece together Beth's life. Carolyn had seen none of the aggressive or hyper-sexualized behaviors noted in the quick e-book perusal she gained, in her speed-reading analysis of foster children and their problems. Beth had many foster home placements but had only run away twice, which was nothing compared to some foster children. Carolyn closed her eyes, thankful the Stornel's place was wired for her electronic information requirements. She could have kept it on the computer, for confidentiality's sake, except some notarized hard copies were needed for the state authorities regarding Grace Ann and her "unique" journey, as Mr. Lyon informed them from LA. They wouldn't take e-signatures. Carolyn kept these files under lock and key in the newly secured closet as well.

Carolyn looked at the papers again. Beth had been a foster child in what Carolyn counted were more than a dozen foster homes from age eight to eighteen, after she had been turned over to the state by her incapable mother, due to persistent and continuing drug and alcohol problems. Her father fled even before Beth's birth. Beth's mother was dead now. The private investigators faxed the copy of the death certificate. Beth's aunt didn't want a thing to do with her and asked that her new address, in Cleveland, not be shared with anyone. Carolyn didn't know if Beth knew, and now wasn't the time to bring it all up.

There were several disturbing incidences in Beth's medical history: describing bruises on her face, arms, and legs at various times, in several of her foster homes, leading to placements in other care facilities, and a particularly sad notation of one visit to an emergency room...and need of a rape kit. One of the two times Beth ran away from supervision. Charges were filed in one incident, it seemed, but it led to another new foster home placement and a formal investigation.

"She doesn't use tobacco, drugs, or alcohol," Cass whispered as she reviewed the blood test results. Those couldn't lie or deceive. Beth was clean physically. "I'd like to continue talking to her."

"Perhaps, you *should* try to be the dominant female in this situation, since I'm going to become Grace Ann's caregiver," Carolyn replied.

"She does seem to be drawn to my no-nonsense approach to life," Cass agreed. "And I'm drawn to her...if she wants help. There's the rape kit to consider."

"You can help her and draw her out in some ways we can't." Carolyn wanted what was best for Beth. *Cass survived that nightmare experience. Perhaps she can help.* "I'm thinking Pastor Allred, in his psychologist capacity, might be able to help us or her as well, if Beth is willing to use him as a resource."

"Sounds good, but we'll have to give her a bit more time and space and see what *she* wants," Cass said in a measured tone. "A lot of things are unanswered."

Building on her conversation with Cass, Carolyn made sure a call to Pastor Allred was high on her list of things that day. *Does Beth need a mother, a mentor, a friend, or all three?* She and her aunts would need Pastor Allred's help in deciding how best to talk to Beth about all of it.

What was most clear now to Carolyn was that she *wanted* to be Grace Ann's legally adopted mother. She'd gone over and over it in her head. Even though she was just 35, she would regret giving up Grave Ann for an unknown future. *Wedding Bells? Children of my own?* With her mother's death and the death of all the men who were in her aunts' lives, there was no relying on the future to fulfill her dreams of home and motherhood. She'd regret stepping aside and *only* being an aunt to Grace Ann, no matter how closely she could follow the little girl's life. If the authorities agreed to her adoption plans, she was going to relish raising Grace Ann. *I can be her mother!*

So far, legalities were all on Carolyn's side. Beth, at age eighteen, with no blood ties to the baby or means of support, gave Beth very little chance to be declared Grace Ann's mother or guardian. If Carolyn left the picture, Grace Ann would be taken by the state social services in a New York minute.

The watershed moment of Carolyn asserting herself to Beth about becoming Grace Ann's legal mother needed to come soon.

She'd be forever grateful to Beth. Carolyn didn't want to seem too dramatic, but Beth had possibly saved Grace Ann's life by paying fifty dollars for her and keeping her in good shape. Not being able to give Grace Ann many baths or tend to her case of diaper rash were only very, very minor negatives. The biggest thing besides the legal situation revolved around how to present Beth, Joe and the baby to everyone in general.

If and when Carolyn adopted Grace Ann, she would be a mother, and Beth could always be part of Grace Ann's life if she remained a capable young woman…and worked on her own undeserved scars from the past. When Grace Ann was old enough, with the guidance of reputable counselors, Carolyn would make sure Grace Ann understood every aspect of her fragile beginning in this life, which included Becky, Beth, and Joe. *Could starting a journal or a diary help explain things?* Carolyn would ask Pastor Allred.

So far, in their conversations while Carolyn was in Baltimore, when they were getting their health exams, Mr. Lyon said it wasn't going to be too difficult to get a private adoption. The natural mother, Becky Monroe, faced a slew of charges, not the least of which was selling her child for the paltry sum of fifty dollars to Beth, as well a rap sheet of drug, prostitution, and other offenses, as long as her young arm. Becky didn't even know what she had done concerning Grace Ann was illegal, saying she didn't want the baby and was trying to give the baby a good home since Beth wanted her! The authorities seemed conciliatory on this point. Signing the necessary papers would keep Becky from prosecution, since Grace Ann had made it through the situation unharmed and Mr. Lyon was shepherding Becky's case.

Becky was now headed for a rehab program in California. Carolyn felt she owed her a second chance, paying for a job training program the drug counselors would help her select, a bit of cash for a year's living expenses paid under Mr. Lyon's supervision, and allocations at proscribed intervals from shares of Allied Brands stock held in trust—if Becky strictly followed the recommendations of her counselors in every respect.

Carolyn had told Beth and Joe about finding Becky and her trip to drug rehab. Beth had lots of questions that all related to Becky's welfare, which was good, Carolyn thought. Joe said little other than, "I bet that plane ticket cost a bunch."

This wasn't Becky's first baby. Another, a little boy, had gained adoption by a New Jersey couple three years ago, when Becky was seventeen. If Becky hadn't said anything to Beth and Joe about the first child, Carolyn didn't see the need right now. She'd bring it up when things seemed more stable and fold it into Grace Ann's counselor-guided learning about her past.

Carolyn hoped Becky took advantage of this opportunity and gained a solid foothold in life with work and purpose in her life. Otherwise, a wrong move on Becky's part, and everything would be gone for her...sooner than a doughnut in Joe's vicinity.

The pediatrician's exam had been encouraging—another blessing. Praise God, Grace Ann appeared in good health, considering Becky's tenuous pregnancy and birth with Beth as her midwife in the viaduct shantytown hut. *How did they manage to survive?* Becky's long history of drug and alcohol abuse hadn't, as yet, shown up in Grace Ann. Carolyn and her aunts watched closely for any of the classic motor, crying, and light and sound sensitivity symptoms, common with so many of these utero-poisoned infants. In Grace Ann's growing years, her entire life really, her health history needed to indicate her birth mother blighted her fetal experience with drug and alcohol abuse.

With Becky in good hands, tackling Beth's issues were the next daunting task. Beth had been with the baby for about four weeks before showing up at the Bayshore studio. So much had been taken away or suddenly changed in Beth's life but Beth and Grace Ann couldn't be "mommy and baby" anymore. *Could Beth change roles?*

If things didn't work out in this new scenario, Carolyn would offer Beth a generous financial and college educational package and send her off to a new future; a reward for a young woman who missed so much in life but still seemed to have hope. Joe would get a college or job-based financial package too, although Carolyn thought he might blow it as fast as he seemed to forget her well-intentioned mentoring conversations with the young man. He seemed lazy and bull-headed, not realizing he needed to get trained or educated for a future in life. His only goal as a professional eating contestant seemed farfetched and unhealthy.

"Beth? We've got to talk about Grace Ann," Carolyn said without preamble as they sat in the Bayshore foyer on folding chairs. "I want to adopt her."

"Thought that was the way it was going to be." Beth sighed, her face calm as she looked at Carolyn with wary eyes.

"You did a good job with Grace Ann." Carolyn stopped for a moment to find the right words.

"There's a place here for you and Joe, too, if you want…but you need to look toward more technical education, college, or getting work," Carolyn continued with conviction. "Have a solid future." She wanted to make sure Beth knew their love and concern for her, and her friend, Joe, were offers, not bribes or payoffs.

"I was working before I got here and…and my dream was to be able to start junior college…and work myself through the classes I needed." Beth picked up one of Grace Ann's clean bibs. "I can see you love Grace Ann…and your aunts really love her too." She ran her finger over the green edging on the bib. "Is that enough, though?"

"Yes. Yes, we do, very much to answer your first concern. I love Grace Ann." Carolyn took a deep breath. "The other question is complicated. If you mean, am I willing? Even *without* my loving aunts being in the picture, I'm committed to taking *full* responsibility and care for Grace Ann, so the answer is yes to that, too." Carolyn looked at the patched-up windows and the progress they'd made in cleaning up the first floor of the mansion. "I see her life being filled with love, great memories and a great environment for her to grow up in."

"You're still kinda' young...and single," Beth replied. "Are you going to raise her yourself...or are you going to give her to a nanny or send her off to school somewhere?"

Beth had a natural talent in negotiating, Carolyn thought with amusement, but she managed to keep her face relaxed. Beth deserved the truth, and Carolyn was going to give it to her. "I'm 35 and I'm going to be a single mother to start out, Beth. I grew up in a single-parent home. So I think I have a good idea on what will be needed." Carolyn stopped for a moment. "Again, let's not consider my aunts in this picture. I'm going to need help in taking care of Grace Ann. With this place, the grounds...and Grace Ann, who I hope to call my daughter very soon."

Carolyn looked at Beth as the young woman set down the bib. "As a starting point, if I were alone, I'd probably be looking for three people to help me on a daily basis: two people would be providing the help and services Grace Ann and I need and a third person would be assigned to supervising the care of the housing and other issues, like caring for vehicles, the grounds, and maintenance issues, inside and outside. If I start another business, I'll have personal assistants as well."

"You've really given this a lot of thought." Beth kneaded her hands.

Carolyn gave a wry smile. "Not much else, really, since I saw her delicate pink hand escape your jacket."

"But *you're* going to take care of her," Beth persisted.

"Grace Ann is going to be my single greatest priority, Beth, with my time and all the decisions I make from now on," Carolyn replied, meeting Beth's concerned gaze. "Nothing will be more important to me than *loving and caring* for her."

"What...what if you decide to get married?" Beth asked.

Well, Beth had managed to ask a second million-dollar question. "There are several things to consider." Carolyn wanted Beth to understand that Grace Ann and she were bonded in love and care as mother and daughter both legally and emotionally. "First, and foremost, Grace Ann and I will be mother and daughter. A man coming into that scenario would have to be worthy of us...and fully and continually honor the meaning of that bond." Carolyn continued carefully. "I hope God will bless us with someone who loves and cares for us, with the same cherishing spirit we have waiting for him.

"Then there's also the fact that I've been a businesswoman for most of my life, from lemonade and cookie stands as a child, to the chairman and CEO of the company I just sold." Carolyn wanted Beth to understand. "I'd like my daughter to see me as a loving mother first, but also a woman capable of supporting herself financially and working outside the home, *if* she chooses." Carolyn had to laugh. "But she's not even eating solid food or walking, so I don't think we have to talk about her college and career path quite yet."

"And...and your aunts have mentioned things about your health?" Beth wasn't going to let anything go unasked, it seemed.

"That's something I'm going to have to teach my daughter. Instruct her to lead a more balanced life...and to have a better line of ascendancy in any future corporate structure." The smile went to Carolyn's eyes. "The heart palpitations are gone since I sold the company. They were warning signs and never became life-threatening. Stress from working and overseeing the investigation about the death of my mother.

"We'll be learning about each other more...and go into things in depth about all of our history, but if we can stop talking about me for a moment, we also need to talk about you." Carolyn wanted to display her genuine regard for Beth. She was a dear girl, who, despite the uproar of a house and dealing her aunts and Grace Ann, became more part of the extended Reynolds clan every day.

"Me again?" Beth asked, riveting her gaze on Carolyn.

"We want you to stay...here," Carolyn began. "What do you want?" Carolyn left the table and walked toward a scarred wall. She turned back to Beth. "Do you need a sister, a mentor...a ready-made extended family who already cares about you?"

Beth bit her lip.

Carolyn wanted Beth to understand the depth of their feelings. "Not as some Cinderella taking care of us and Grace Ann but as a member of this household."

"This is some place," Beth began, looking around the room, not knowing what to say or if she should say anything. "Out of a history book or the storybook like you mentioned."

Carolyn kept quiet to hear everything Beth wanted to say. From the files on Beth, Carolyn knew sadness, uncertainty and servitude were always a part of her former life.

"It's not an easy choice for me. I've lived in bags and boxes all my life. One drawer, six inches in a closet I couldn't even fill. Three outfits to wear at the most, even in the places where I felt people really cared about me," Beth recited as she stretched out her arms. "Am I wanting you...or wanting this?"

"Both, we hope," Carolyn replied softly, like her words were skating on the thinnest ice. "We've had an interesting beginning, haven't we?" A slight smile again crept onto Carolyn's lips. *Where to start?* "These ladies I call my aunts aren't related by blood to me, but we couldn't be closer if they were. There's more than enough love in the vicinity...and room here for you. And room for Joe too." Carolyn looked at Beth to see if her heartfelt sincerity had registered. "You'd always have a home here and be safe to share your *authentic* self with us. Good enough?"

Beth eyes grew into saucers as she replied hesitantly. "That's quite a promise...and still not...easy."

"True," Carolyn admitted. "But you can help too."

"Help?" Beth said with incredulity.

"You are eighteen, but I've never had a young person in my family life. Sister, cousin, young friend, younger person to mentor—it *could* be a very fulfilling and fun relationship. Think of it as a final springboard for you toward maturity, not to mention another person for me and our aunts to love."

"You mentioned they're not your aunts?" The word "love" echoed in Beth's head.

"Wonderful ladies my mother met and loved before I was born," Carolyn confided. *Now isn't the right time to divulge the eccentric relationships of my aunts and me or probe into the sad, private parts of Beth's past.* Carolyn prayed Beth would allow time together with her and her aunts for that. "We'll tell you the whole story, but it will probably take a lot of time…and barrels of popcorn." Carolyn came up behind Beth's chair. She saw Beth flinch.

"If you wanted to make this a legal arrangement…that would be fine too. Whatever and whenever you're ready." Carolyn took a chance and touched Beth's shoulders with her hands. "Grace Ann needs to be adopted and protected because of her age and dependency, but you're older and wiser, so you have time to stay here, find your footing, get all your questions answered, and decide for yourself." Carolyn came closer. "Can I give you a hug?" Beth nodded and Carolyn kissed Beth on her head and slid her arms around the girl's neck for a lightning-quick hug and then returned to her standing position.

"I've been struggling with the fact that I'm not married," Carolyn confided with a sigh, going to sit at the table across from Beth again. "To tell the truth, I think I was impulsive and selfish to start Grace Ann's proceedings because I don't have a husband."

"I've thought about it—you and Grace Ann and no husband." Beth spoke slowly. "But *I* took Grace Ann and I wasn't married." Beth shook her head. "I had nothing. *That* was pretty stupid."

"Having money and resources doesn't guarantee a happy home," Carolyn replied truthfully.

"But the love you have...with your aunts, how you treat Nan and Ed and how you talk to the workers who come here. How you've treated Joe and me. That matters."

So Beth had been paying attention! Carolyn prayed Beth might. Her admiration for the young woman grew. But that didn't change Carolyn's own concern that she herself was unmarried and adopting a beautiful baby girl; making plans as a single parent with her aunts' help. In the court of life, Carolyn felt she needed to recuse herself and continue the legal and social services inquiries to see if they thought she *was* an adequate candidate for instant parenthood. She'd be heartbroken if the authorities denied her request, but she had to think of what was best for Grace Ann. *Backs of Steel.*

"Are you going to have other children?" Beth asked.

Carolyn bit her lip. "I don't know." She rested her chin on her hand. "There's the possibility of marriage, I want that, and I would consider having children...but that wouldn't in *any way* diminish the fact, my husband and I, would consider Grace Ann as our *first* child." Carolyn looked in Beth's eyes. "Does that answer your question?" Carolyn put her hands out on the table. "I'd like to have your full support in my efforts to adopt Grace Ann. Do you think you can do that?"

"I'll sign anything that you need...or do we have to have a legal meeting or something?" Beth asked.

"I don't know, but I'll let you know everything just as soon as I find out...every step of the way." Carolyn smiled, feeling the conversation had gone well. "Thinking this hard makes me hungry. I think Aunt Bee cut up some veggies and left us some dip. Want to go scrounging for it in the cooler?" She looked at her watch. "I think we have time before the next group of inspection people come." Beth's face broke into a smile, she nodded, and they headed for the food.

Beth sat quietly for a minute. Carolyn had actually hugged her...and Beth had tried not to tense up. But bad things happened when people came up behind you, Beth remembered. *If I really start talking with Carolyn and her aunts about my past, would any of them be so open and friendly?*

Joe told her they wouldn't. "You be careful. If things go bad, be sure to stash away some cash, so we can at least get some money out of this," he said rubbing his chin and furrowing his brow. "I guess taking that brat wasn't such a bad deal after all, if it gets us a bankroll." Joe sneered. "They talked about the future with me...but I want cash."

Carolyn had promised something a lot better than cash, Beth thought. She'd promised a home...and belonging. Those things had evaporated when her mother turned to drugs instead of caring for Beth. For years Beth had thought there was something wrong with her because she couldn't keep her mother's attention or warrant her love and care. Beth had been the mother figure instead: trying to wake her mother up, keeping their dump of an apartment clean, and trying to cook meals from the few food stamps and garage scraps she was able to get from the Dumpsters she scavenged for food. She'd eaten well when her mother would go to rehab, but the kaleidoscope of rooms, people, and names were so frightening and difficult to remember. When she got older, Beth figured out everything was temporary and she needed to be ready to move. *Can I consider getting it in writing from Carolyn to secure the promises when nobody has kept their promises to me before? Will that make Joe more cooperative?*

CHAPTER TEN

Carolyn thought the carousel of appointments and lists in building a business or a house renovation had nothing on learning daily baby care! The loving benefits of instant motherhood involved a seemingly endless line of diaper changes, meticulous cleaning of Grace Ann's baby bottles, and washing all the clothes she went through each day—not to mention the bibs and burp pads. Carolyn set up a schedule for using the Stornel's washer and dryer to keep everything clean, including her and her aunts' and Beth's and Joe's clothes - so glad she'd upgraded and expanded the appliance package for each modular home she'd ordered.

Carolyn had done all the talking in public conversations concerning Beth, her so-identified distant relative *and* about Grace Ann, her soon-to-be-legal adopted infant daughter, with the Stornels, and in meeting any new people in the Bayshore area. They were swimming in legal seas, and Carolyn wanted to make sure they were as calm as possible. Carolyn referred all legal inquiries concerning Grace Ann to her legal team headed by Mr. Lyon and the equally efficient, Mr. Soames, from a Baltimore law firm taking on the brunt of the work within the state under Mr. Lyon's long-distance supervision. So far they'd been able to assuage and stave off the social services department, but Carolyn knew they'd have to start their visitations soon; knowing most anything, including the Bayshore house under construction conditions and the fire-safe modular homes, would be light-years better than Beth and Joe's living hand-to-mouth.

"I've signed contracts to rent and fence modular residences while our home and our immediate neighborhood are under construction," she'd told one state investigator, showing him the pictures of the homes she'd selected.

Their workday schedule was straightforward. When Carolyn wasn't on the phone trying to guide the custody matters, there were constant details concerning the property. From after breakfast until dinnertime, everyone, including Mr. Jackson, Mr. Silver, and Mr. Molina, saw life now revolved around baby care. A steady succession of tradesmen, technicians, and local, county, and state personnel of one sort or another called the company to get their necessary forms, orders, reports, or inquiries completed for continuing their work. "We don't see enough of each other and your partners, Mr. Jackson," Carolyn quipped in one of their many daily talks.

Shealds thought better of it and didn't respond to her barb. He paused for a moment, then said, "Our construction trailer will be delivered today on the staked footprint Mr. Silver showed you yesterday."

Hesse walked quickly through the door and interrupted the conversation. "There's some brush and things we need to look at before we can do anything else." He turned to Carolyn. "So sorry to interrupt...but the inspector insists that Shealds looks at this now before we continue. Excuse us."

Shealds didn't know of any inspections due or anything interrupting their progress? *What was Hesse talking about?*

Shealds gave a small smile and excused himself. "I'll be back in five minutes to continue our discussion, Ms. Reynolds. I want to talk about the size of the dock you might need and to remove any hazardous submerged wood in the water from past structures."

Shealds and Hesse walked casually down the drive. "There's an unstable, rotten tree that's been freshly half-cut, aimed at the portico."

Shealds flinched slightly but tried to appear like Hesse was just discussing normal business.

"I've stabilized it as best I can and wanted you to know before we cut it down." Hesse pointed in the opposite direction and tried to look like they were engaged in another topic.

"Get it down and I'll make some excuse." Shealds nodded and headed back to the house.

"So you're sure your experts have determined the house structure is sound?" Carolyn was anxious to make sure they were able to save the house and not start from scratch.

What should I say? "There still are issues for you to consider, but I'm a lover of old houses, and I think Bayshore can be saved and fitted with everything for a comfortable modern lifestyle befitting the property." Shealds was worried about what the half-cut tree meant. *A warning to me? A clear signal about my plans to clear myself?*

"But how much time, Mr. Jackson?" Carolyn's brow wrinkled, waiting for his reply.

"I think I have to talk everything over with the plans in front of us and walk the whole property. Bring a camera or your mobile devise for pictures…and your boots." He looked at his phone. "Tomorrow morning. Nine a.m.?"

"Nine thirty, please," Carolyn replied, thinking she'd be able to get Grace Ann fed and happily ensconced in her playpen by then.

"In the meantime, there's a dying tree that's leaning badly and needs to be removed today. See you at nine thirty, then," Shealds replied, relieved to get out of there quickly without any further explanations.

"Good-bye, then, Mr. Jackson," Carolyn said. Grace Ann needed a fresh diaper.

"Please call me Shealds, Ms. Reynolds." He turned quickly and left.

On the list for the next morning, was keeping Bayshore free of varmints and vermin.

The most highly recommended person, Nelder Griggs, had cleaned Nan and Ed's attic of a recalcitrant raccoon and her babies the year before. "He's a humane person," Nan said as she and Beth cleaned up the breakfast plates. "Works with the parks and the forest service toward reintroducing the animals into the wild...and he's done all the animal relocation work for Shealds, Hesse, and Molina's company." Nan put her face closer to Carolyn and confided, "His house is a bit creepy, though. Nelder moved into the place of a former taxidermist, Ely Peel. Peel went to live with his daughter in North Carolina when his health failed—left almost everything as is. Nelder says it had the barns and outbuildings he needed, but the house and almost every other useable wall is filled with taxidermy." Nan reported. "Animals, fish, you name it!"

"Dead animals?" Beth said with horror-filled saucer eyes, almost dropping the coffeepot for Carolyn's second morning cup. "He kills animals?"

Carolyn, caught off-guard, had forgotten Beth's seeming interest in animals and desire to eat more vegetarian meals.

"Don't worry there, miss. I don't kill them," a deep bass voice offered. This older man, with a heavyweight wrestler's build, thick salt-and-pepper hair, and three-day facial stubble, walked closer. He took a clean work rag out of his plaid work shirt pocket, wiped his hands before extending his right one to shake Carolyn's, and then pushed his silver wire-rimmed reading glasses up on his nose. "I catch them gently and then make sure the forest service tells me where to let them loose. Habitats are important." He put the cage in his left hand down. "The *past* owner was a taxidermist."

"You don't hurt them, then?" Beth asked.

"Can't say they're not concerned and confused a bit at the beginning," the man replied as he picked up the rectangular wire cage again with what looked to be a spring-loaded latch door at one end. "They're not smart enough to know where they should be and where they shouldn't sometimes. Live too close to people at their peril. That's why I brought a clean cage in to show you."

"Do you spray any of them dead or shoot them?" Beth said with more heat, derision steeling her tone as she looked at the cage.

"Not if I can help it at all, little lady. Only guns are tranquilizer guns, and Dr. Moore takes care of that part, but those are for the really big animals. Don't think there's anything like that for you folks to worry about in your house out there at Bayshore." The man put the trap down in the bed-and-breakfast foyer and again offered his weatherworn hand to Carolyn. "But some of them are sick or dying. Can't let them suffer if the vet can't save them. When it's a problem like that, it's his call." The man looked from Beth to Carolyn. "I'm Nelder Griggs. From the wildlife relocation company you called."

Carolyn's hand was dwarfed in the man's work-roughened grasp. "Have you had enough time to evaluate the other buildings?"

"I've still got the last one to evaluate, Ms. Reynolds," Griggs replied after unfurling a job order from his faded jeans. "Going to need plenty of relocation boxes." Nelder gestured to the cage by his feet. "You've got the standard raccoon, bird, gopher, and rat infiltration as well some chipmunks and perhaps even a skunk or two. You've also got some old bee, wasp, and hornet digs that have to be destroyed, so they'll only nest away from your place."

He looked down at his list. "Are you going to be living there while I'm working?" He looked around at the assembled group. "Suggest you double wrap your garbage at all times and seal all your food because every pest, including the field mice, will bring themselves and everyone else for a free meal, right up the food chain."

Carolyn cringed when the man talked about rats, thinking of the exposé she'd seen about urban businesses and their constant fight with the Norwegian rat. Some as large as healthy cats, the report had indicated, if she recalled correctly.

"I'll be helping on the property. Can you show me all the cages when you catch them?" Beth asked with wary eyes. Turning to Carolyn, she continued, "Can I go with him to release the animals?" Carolyn's brows lifted in surprise. Beth certainly wasn't thinking about rats, Carolyn hoped.

"Is there a safety issue, Mr. Griggs?" was all Carolyn could think to say. "Would Beth be a distraction?"

"I'll have to see," Griggs replied. "I've mentored plenty of people wanting to get into the business."

"I'd be careful," Beth promised in a strong voice. "I'm eighteen."

"If you think so," Carolyn said with slow trepidation. "In answer to your other question, I was hoping to have the young gentleman in our party live in the main house for a few days. The Stornels are booked here, so we have to give up one room."

She'd already been trying to think of how to get everyone shelter even before Mr. Griggs had arrived. She pressed her thumb and forefinger to her nose.

"We now have four rooms here with the Stornels until our modular homes come." Carolyn started. "Baby Grace Ann and I have to stay together." She wasn't going to say anything about this being ordered by the state regulators. "My other aunt and Beth have a room with other two aunts having another…and Joe has another room. Putting my three aunts and Beth together doesn't meet fire code…and the rest of the rooms at the Stornel's place are taken."

"How many need better bunking?" Mr. Griggs asked.

"Only Joe," Carolyn replied.

"I wouldn't be too sure of that, missy," came an accusation from the door. A gray-haired, thin, military-erect, and decidedly irritated man, just a tad above five feet tall in his vanilla-white suit, stood indignantly at the threshold. No one had heard the door open while they were discussing the animal control problems at Bayshore. The man dropped his two suitcases on either side of him with a bang. "I'd only travel this far in Robin Lee's dear memory," he said dramatically, as if he were making his initial entrance in a stage play, needing to project his dismay to the people in the balcony. Only the absence of a theatrical key light, instead of the sunlight coming from the windows, marred his performance.

"Darby!" Carolyn exclaimed, half in greeting and half in horror. "The fan club!" Carolyn's hand hitting her forehead was the only other sound in the room. *Just great! Another person has shown up needing housing somewhere.*

Not seeming to recognize someone had addressed him, Darby continued. "If you don't recall, I'll reintroduce myself." The man walked regally to the table. "I'm Darby Fisher from Hollywood, California."

Carolyn knew the worst was coming because when Darby acted in such a theatrical manner, it always meant trouble. At the very least, Darby Fisher had traveled all this way to berate Carolyn about her lack of care concerning her movie star aunt's memory and stored possessions.

"You did get my memo regarding the storage facility after leaving LA, darling?" Darby questioned in a slow Southern drawl. He mentioned her leaving LA, which meant he might give her a break from his wrath, but his tone appeared a bit too silky to her ear. Alarm bells clanged in her head. Carolyn thought she knew, in all her years of dealing directly and indirectly with Darby's southern, low tenor voice, that she could tell his mood. *Will this flow of honey-tinged well wishes hide bristling bourbon malice?*

Either way, fair or foul, Darby's eyes shot sparks of amber fire, indicating he was not pleased. Carolyn watched his rigid body language, looking for his signature flowing or chopping arm gestures, which indicated his mood, like flesh-bound instruments of languid contentment reminiscent of a long-haired, bored Persian or the open-clawed rage of a feisty alley cat. This wasn't going to be good.

Carolyn tried to remember the gist of the information in the memo—something about the storage facility changing hands or wanting higher rents for her aunt's things. Carolyn didn't quite recall as she rubbed her forehead.

"It's nothing, really, darling," Darby began with exaggerated slowness, raising his hands slightly. Carolyn knew his style seemed too understated. This was bad. "They're just going to throw all of your Aunt Robin's things out on the streets if you don't get your navy pumps back across country, is all."

Carolyn's mouth dropped, and her aunts looked stricken as well. "Throw it out?" she said, her voice wobbling.

"In a few weeks," Darby whispered with a pained shudder. "Billie put me on all the storage contracts except the last one when I was gone to visit my family in Louisiana years ago." Darby walked slowly to look at the dining room. "The very dear one passed before it could be changed and, legally speaking, I've been locked out." He walked around and looked at his audience. "On another note, the insurance company says it's time to get everything in *all* the storage spaces re-cataloged and properly stored or they won't insure *any* of it—any longer." His voice quavered in banked outrage, and Carolyn wondered if he might shove his fist into his mouth to keep from sobbing. Instead Darby bit his lip, looked to the floor, and seemed about to burst into tears.

"Why don't you just truck it all out here?" Nelder suggested, affected by the small man's grief. "They'll be plenty of room in the barn when it's free of chipmunks and it's cleaned up a bit."

Darby's face contorted in horror. "Barn? Barn!" he cried, first in incredulity, and then, in outrage. He started walking, almost stiff-legged, to where Nelder was standing, showing the group the difference in height and size between the two men. Darby had a decided advantage in emotion. "You, sir, would relegate the prized possessions and collections of the inimitable Robin Lee to a mere"—Darby grabbed his chest as if he were feeling heart pain—"baaaarrrn?" Then Darby lifted his arm as if reciting a Shakespearean soliloquy, ending with a meaningful downward motion and fist clench.

"Now, Darby," Muriel said soothingly, having dealt with the International Robin Lee Fan Club director for many years. "Mr. Griggs made a plausible suggestion, not knowing the stored items belonging to dear Robin needed such special care." She came over to pat Darby's shoulder, which matched with the height of her own petite frame. "Please don't be so upset. You'll become ill." She looked at her niece. "Carolyn will think of something."

At that very moment, Carolyn's universe shifted to an elongated remembered moment. Muriel pronounced those very same words in that very same tone to her mother, Billie. Fifteen, perhaps, eighteen years ago when they were going to get Aunt Cass out of a scrape—only the names were changed.

Cass came over to Carolyn. "Joe's impressed with the mention of your Aunt Robin," she remarked.

"How can you tell?" Carolyn asked sardonically.

"He's stopped eating," she observed with a voice as dry as the martinis she used to drink with her friends when Billie was alive.

They'd driven out to Bayshore to continue that day's appointment schedule. "Got anything civilized to drink?" Darby asked, after they'd figured everything out in the accommodations scheme. He'd used his charm to great effect when he and Mr. Griggs had driven to the house in his truck. Darby and Nelder Griggs appeared on cordial terms, since Griggs agreed with Darby's half-persuading and half-coaxing efforts into letting Beth and Cass stay in a small, unused guesthouse at his home. The former taxidermist, a Mr. Peel, had housed his mother there during the summer before her passing so she could avoid the heat and welcome her myriad group of nieces, nephews, and grandchildren to her home without disturbing her son's taxidermy work.

These plans allowed Carolyn and Grace Ann a room at the Stornel's bed-and-breakfast, with Muriel and Bee in another, leaving the third available for Joe and Darby. They'd make strange bedfellows, Carolyn knew, but preferable to having Joe sleeping unsupervised at the mansion or in a tent, easing Carolyn's mind about Joe's erstwhile smoking to *really* burn down Bayshore. Carolyn's thoughts snapped back into focus as she heard Darby remark, "This young fellow has finished just about everything else eatable." Darby looked over at Joe.

"Miss having some cream soda to wash it down," Joe said to the last twelve of the eighteen doughnuts Carolyn had bought at the bakery this morning.

"Do all growing boys do this, or does he just have a tapeworm?" Darby asked languidly.

"He's training for an eating contest in New Jersey," Muriel replied.

"Well, that explains it," Darby retorted drolly as he leisurely flopped onto one of the folding chairs. "Managed to save a pretzel stick from the bag," he said proudly as he showed the group his snack. "But a salty snack cries for something with a malt tang."

"It's still a bit early for beer and wine," Cass drawled back.

"The mimosa and gun fizz hour goes with brunch, and that's long past," Bee observed.

"How about a dog and a beer? And a soda for me, of course," Pastor Allred teased from the threshold.

"So you're the padre the ladies have been telling me about." Darby didn't miss a beat at seeing Pete's clerical collar, welcoming the man as he headed across the floor by thrusting out his hand like the lord of the manor. His bright greeting echoed in the hollow open space. "Darby Fisher, friend of the family."

"Pete Allred." Pete smiled, looking at the man in the white suit pants as well as seeing the positive changes in the house around him. "Things seem to be going well."

"We're coping." Carolyn sighed. Her slight smile didn't betray her sour mood. She crossed an item off her list. If Cass and Beth's trip to Mr. Griggs proved satisfactory, the pressure of getting the temporary sleeping arrangements settled her attention on her newly revised to-do list. But now Darby's crisis loomed.

"We'll have to take up other things," Darby said in a singsong manner. Overtaken by his need to get his concerns immediately on the agenda, he dispensed with his usual manners at keeping family things private.

"Well," Pete said, knowing to come to the point quickly, if other things were pressing on Ms. Reynolds's schedule. "I was just coming over to make the appointment you wanted…and to meet your baby." Information about the baby had become part of the town gossip, as Pete saw a portable baby bassinet in the corner. Ms. Reynolds hadn't mentioned a baby, nor had Beth or Joe confided in him. This new wrinkle of a baby, who seemed the center of excellent attention and care from his quick perusal, required some surveillance as well. "What's the baby's name?"

Carolyn stepped closer to the pastor. She'd face this challenge directly and with strength. "My daughter's name is Grace Ann. Her loving family here can't wait for the legal steps to be finished." She enunciated clearly in her best executive-level tone. She looked back at Beth, Darby, and her aunts, plus Joe, who seemed the only clueless member of this scene with his slack jaw and confused expression.

Best get Joe out of the way before he can muddle things. "Joe, why don't you go out to the SUV? There're some snacks there for entertaining." Carolyn hated keeping this ruse going, especially to a pastor, but if Pete became some kind of stickler, his objection might keep the legal proceedings from going smoothly. *As a therapist, could he feel that I'm trying to undo some 'wrongs" from my mother and aunts' past...with their babies by adopting Grace Ann?* She'd thought about that – many times. She didn't need any unnecessary monkey wretches being thrown into the plans. Carolyn wanted allies, not enemies. So now seemed the time to find out which way this pastor would lean. "Pastor, can we look in your appointment calendar and see if there are any empty dates for Grace Ann's baptism?"

"My secretary is in the office if you need any help or need to reach me," Pete replied. "I'll look in my book now and also have Betty check the calendar in the church office."

"I'll see you to your Jeep, then." Carolyn felt relieved as she headed to the front door. *I hope this man is someone I can admire as my pastor.* They walked a few steps and over the threshold. Carolyn looked to make sure no one was following them. Then she spoke in a softer tone. "There are a few more things to cover, Pastor, but I wanted to speak to you privately."

Privately. "Something beyond the baptism?" Peter asked.

"I'll get right to the next point...because this is awkward. It's all such a rush, but I think I'm unexpectedly going to have to devote a lot of time to care for the stored memorabilia of my aunt, so we'll set the baptism date after that...and I, my other aunts, and Beth are going to need group counseling sessions when we return to town." Carolyn turned to see if the pastor had followed her quick change of thought. "Perhaps separate sessions for Joe Thackery too."

"Group counseling? Family counseling?" Pastor Allred repeated, trying to understand this new request.

"Yes. There are some extenuating circumstances and personal issues I'll need to share and discuss…for all of us to go forward." Carolyn looked around again to make sure no one was listening. "Could I have an individual preliminary session here, before we leave, to explain things?" Carolyn wanted to introduce her aunts and their eclectic family history to Beth so she could have a true context of their history and relationships, just as Carolyn had promised, before Beth made final decisions concerning staying here or going. This might also unlock a Pandora's Box of Beth's sad history…and Carolyn wanted to identify what Beth might need in order to deal with in her past and work toward a sure-footed future.

"I don't know," Pete hedged, still off guard. He looked keenly in Carolyn's face. There were so many questions he wanted— needed—to ask before any therapy session could begin, but in these rushed circumstances, now wasn't the time to get to the answers. "I don't have a handle on what you're trying to accomplish, but I'll set an hour in my schedule for a first session, perhaps two. I'll need to call you if I have other thoughts on the matter…or there needs to be some tweaking. There's still a lot I need to know."

"Perhaps the day before we're scheduled to leave for Los Angeles?" Carolyn asked. *As if I can even begin to explain things, even to myself.* Instead she added, "Thank you. I'll call your church secretary on both matters."

"I know there's need of a baptism and to get this place straightened out, but Robin's treasures are going out in the gutter if we don't get things taken care of," Darby whined, continually imagining the sacrilege of Robin Lee's personal possessions and memorabilia blowing down the streets of LA, adjacent to the storage lockers. Excavation of a new office complex in LA was scheduled on the real estate where the storage facility sat. Darby shuttered at the nightmare of picking paper and trinkets from the street and the trees for weeks to come if Carolyn didn't get off her sassy ass and do something. At best, Darby hoped they wouldn't have to re-purchase the contents of the lockers if they went up for sale.

"I'm thinking. I'm thinking," Carolyn said. "You say I can't send an agent with legal authority to handle the situation?"

"You could," Darby replied. "But as you must remember, some of the boxes are worn, and items need special handling and pack-ing in things like acid-free paper even before they're moved, or they might be damaged or lost forever. Billie wouldn't have wanted that to happen."

Carolyn flinched inwardly at the mention of her mother's name. *Not another duty,* Carolyn thought as an angry red mist covered her vision. She momentarily thought losing all of the memorabilia for-ever wouldn't be so bad, but then, almost immediately, she chided herself for her negativity. Aunt Robin's work had kept her and her mother afloat in the hard times and there remained, many fans, old and new, devoted to her aunt's film work and memory. Darby Fisher stood as a long and staunchly loyal case in point.

"Where I go, Grace Ann and Beth have to go." She'd have to get an OK from the lawyer here and Mr. Lyon back in LA before she did anything. "How long?"

"A little over two weeks, I think," Darby said, giving her his best-case scenario. "Perhaps a few days less." He saw her blue eyes darken to almost slate, exactly the same color of Billie's when she'd looked displeased. "We'll need a secure site, someone to pack the boxes for moving, and a curator to assure the process meets the proper insurance company standards."

"So you're planning for us to fly out and drive everything back?" Carolyn said, her CEO mind-set kicking in.

"At the very least, we'll need help with the boxes the curator wants us to use, a large truck, and a licensed truck driver," Darby concluded, knowing he'd been planning this presentation for days. "At this time, until other arrangements are decided legally, the family member, which is *you*, must decide, what to do with these treasured things."

"Why can't you come back with the truck driver...and we'll fly back?" Carolyn asked.

"If there's trouble, what can I do? You've never wanted me to take responsibility over Robin Lee's things? Why now?" Darby asked.

As if Darby couldn't see the situation had changed. Darby had never had children...and neither had Carolyn until a few days ago. If the care for Grace Ann and Beth worked out, all she needed, as if she were a magician, was: a trustworthy, strong truck driver; a memorabilia expert; plane tickets for as many as seven with Grace Ann, Darby, Bee, Muriel, Beth, and Joe in tow; hotel reservations for two weeks, a rental van or two for LA; curator supplies; a large rental truck for the return to Bayshore; an itinerary to get the truck, van, and them all safely back to the Bayshore house, plus proper storage for Aunt Robin's things. *That's all!*

Carolyn just had to remember that she was, until recently, the president of a large food company and could use those skills to face this challenge. *I can manage this!* She had the business know-how and the financial resources.

"Cass is staying behind to monitor things here." Carolyn was so glad Cass had volunteered. "She wants to make sure the landscaping and tree demolition go as she's planned. We're already had one dead tree close to the house cut down."

Darby cared more about Robin Lee's things than any of the spindly trees outside. "We need a permanent solution and to see if Nelder's suggestion about how to *properly* house everything...to keep her prized memorabilia close to you, as you're Aunt Robin's heir. Think some of your barn space can be converted?" Darby supposed they could find a temperature-controlled secure space somewhere close to Carolyn's impending new digs here if they couldn't put the memorabilia on the property. He was just glad he'd convinced Carolyn to save Robin Lee's things. "We could keep it in LA."

"*We* could," Carolyn replied with a bit more emphasis and sarcasm than she'd wanted. "But it's my responsibility, so I guess I better keep it close." She looked out toward the overgrown backyard. "I'm going to get everything done to insurance company standards *and* keep everything together so this doesn't happen again." She could just envision a caravan of moving trucks traversing the country if she kept having difficulty deciding where to put down roots.

"I'll just keep Muriel company and throw around a few bags of refuse until you're ready to talk further," Darby replied, relieved Robin's things were a priority now, and on the road to safer storage. Besides, this would be delicious and incredible news for the fan club newsletter. As editor in chief, he intended to tell all of Robin's loyal fans, who loved their fallen screen goddess, that each and every one of Robin Lee's possessions *finally* neared his grandest dream of proper cataloguing and care!

"Perhaps Mr. Silver might know some company near here that can possibly do the conservator space," Carolyn said as she grabbed at the yellow pad list of all the things needed for the trip to LA. This was also a reason to get back to LA to check on her mother's case—a positive aspect of this good-news-bad-news situation. "I'll call Alice, my former assistant, in LA. Hope the new owners of my former company won't mind me taking her time to set up our itinerary." She grabbed the pen from its holder and went over the items she'd scribbled, casually piercing her thick sandy hair and aiming to catch the pen on her right earlobe.

Bee called from the increasing pile of filled garage bags. "Mr. Silver is here for your appointment, Carolyn." After wedging the bulging black plastic bag into the soldier-like rows of trash, she added, "When did you say the Dumpster was coming?"

Carolyn headed for the door so her aunt could hear her reply, and ran almost directly into Hesse's rock-hard chest. Some air left her lungs, half from shock and half from meeting the brick wall of the man's hard frame. Long, muscled fingers steadied her off-balance body in a lithe catching and lifting motion. "Most of our clients don't usually jump for us. We jump for them," he said with a low, molasses laugh.

"This is a rather unique situation." Carolyn stopped for a beat. "Let me start over again. Things have changed. I'm looking for an additional bid from your company to make part of the barn into a temperature and access-controlled space for my...my art collection."

Hesse could catch a con in the first few sentences. Ms. Reynolds fumbled through the reason for the work. Hesse blinked, because he'd expected her to talk about the house instead of a barn conversion. Hesse didn't like liars. *Shealds mentioned something fishy was going on out here.* Hesse got ready to make some excuse, so he could go back and tell Shealds he was right about this woman being into something. Carolyn speech sputtered a bit. "It's...it's not an art collection per se. It's my late Aunt Robin Lee's film career memorabilia collection. There's a need to move it all...and it might as well reside here for the time being."

Art? Memorabilia? Death? Hesse still wasn't sure what to say, but he remembered hearing something once about a movie star named Robin Lee. Shealds would want to check this out.

Carolyn kept talking. "I know we were only talking about the house, but I need the estimate from your company on this additional memorabilia project, and I need it...yesterday." She consulted her list and grabbed for the pen.

"When do you need the space?" Hesse asked, intrigued she confessed the deception.

"We should be back in about three weeks from today," Carolyn replied as she considered the dates. "Darby can tell you the size of the current storage facilities and have you call the storage company in California, but as I looked at the drawings, we should have enough space on the south side of the barn area, if it can be converted."

Hesse kept his face blank and concentrated on his breathing. He replied as if she needed something simple, like asking him to fix a wobbly doorframe. "We'll give you an estimate." He made some notations on his pad. "We might have to consider a double move from storage units here in the area and then onto the property...but we'll do the very best we can."

"I'm sorry. I don't have anything more concrete to give you...or a longer time frame. Again, you'll have to talk to Mr. Fisher." Another thought popped in her head. "Oh," Carolyn said. "Since you're going to be supervising the barn job, do you know any reliable man to come with us to retrieve the collection from its current facility in LA? Someone equipped to help with packing, cataloging, and moving the boxes, when I find an expert to tell us what to do." She looked down at the list on the table. "He also has to drive the truck back from California."

"Of course. I'll inquire and get back to you tomorrow, at the latest," Hesse replied, wanting to seem unruffled and wanting to keep the work momentum here at Bayshore going. "I'll check to see if someone in our subcontractor crews will be able to help you." He looked out to the front lawn again. "I'll have the bid back to you by this time day after tomorrow. May I speak to Mr. Fisher now?"

"What?" Shealds exclaimed after the good feeling regarding the specialty remodeling contract for the Bayshore house barn *before* Hesse told him about the impossible deadline. "Let me get this straight. About three weeks max! We have to do an impossible amount of work on the barn in three weeks, find someone to drive to LA, pack up how many square feet of stuff, and get it all back here while babysitting a real baby and how many adults in the process? These people, may I remind you, tried to burn down the studio on their own property."

Hesse stood there with his arms crossed, not even bothering to sit down at the desk before he delivered what he thought was great news. Any man other than Shealds would have been intimidated by such bulging biceps sheathed in black T-shirt cotton, as Hesse wound one arm over the other and back. Instead of getting angry or leaping over to the desk to strangle his erstwhile partner, Hesse gave Shealds his cold-as-dry-ice stare, hoping his friend's anger ebbed before his own patience gave out—otherwise, there was going to be a dry wall hole to repair when Hesse punched the wall instead of his business partner.

Getting the Bayshore barn job completed was about all that was going to get done, except for a few slim hours of sleep each night for he, Molina, and Shealds in the job site trailer if they were going to get the barn space completed in three weeks. Hesse raked Shealds with a shout like a drill sergeant. "You 'bout finished, boy?"

Shealds stopped in mid-fume. His temper boiled over like molten lava. "Who you calling boy?"

"The idiotic man who's not happy with what the good Lord delivered to him, and what he'd been asking for, that's who," Hesse spit out. "I don't want it at my doorstep, mister." Hesse unfolded his arms, spreading them wide across his side of the dual office desktop and put his forehead about six inches from his business partner.

Shealds's temper eased a bit. "Since you say it like that, I guess I'm out of bounds."

"You said you needed a cover for attempts to salvage things and dealing with Attorney General Zaugus. Let's try to put things aside and straighten your life out. Let's grab it while we can...and not blow it." Hesse's tone sounded more conciliatory now, with diminished heat. Shealds was getting the picture.

"Just tell Ms. Reynolds that you're going to LA...until we find an adequate replacement," Shealds asked.

"Why me?" Hesse blustered.

"Trust, Hesse. Trust," Shealds replied. "Like you said, we can't blow it."

CHAPTER ELEVEN

Carolyn knew there was another announcement to make, and with everything else going on, she was edgy. Things seemed to be settling down after the furor of the fire and her decision about considering instant motherhood. But now, she was going to try to introduce another seemingly unorthodox infant care idea. She'd been researching this from the first few days after finding Grace Ann. It was now or never. Carolyn was going to tell them she was going to try to *breastfeed* Grace Ann.

Carolyn wanted to try to breastfeed because no matter what anyone said, dear Grace Ann might be her *only child*...and she surely had more time to attempt to breastfeed since she wasn't working outside the home.

Carolyn knew it sounded *unusual* for a woman of thirty-five with some years of child-bearing years left, but she'd been studying the information on the Internet and breastfeeding seemed like an excellent way to give Grace Ann a dual nutritional and bonding experience. Time and interest seemed like the major needs in breastfeeding, so Carolyn kept on researching.

Carolyn called the pediatrician. When she'd pushed Dr. Wells, he admitted that breast-feeding was the best form of infant nutrition...but not to stress on the issue because many babies could not be breast fed and did very well. Although Dr. Wells didn't have any firsthand knowledge of the process of adoptive mother breast-feeding, he'd given Carolyn the list of homeopathic supports to aid lactation and the number of the local La Leche group, who helped breastfeeding mothers. They had been quite enthusiastic and made some helpful suggestions. After getting all the information, Carolyn wanted to try. Overnighted equipment and supplies were due to arrive today. So to avoid any further uproar or suspicion, Carolyn needed to tell her aunts immediately.

According to the online diagram, small bags holding formula would rest on either side of a neck strap to bring formula down a tiny tube that Carolyn would keep near Grace Ann's mouth while the baby clasped on for the "breast" milk. Grace Ann's suckling would stimulate Carolyn's hormones and promote breast milk production, so Carolyn could try to truly give her daughter and herself the gift of breastfeeding. "Don't expect to be able to have enough milk to meet her needs immediately," the kind, disembodied volunteer's voice said during the call. "But it's a wonderful idea, and both of you will gain so much from the bonding time and closeness."

She'd ask her aunts, Beth, Darby, the conservator, and Mr. Silver to do the work in LA on Aunt Robin's things, and Carolyn could take the time to gain success in breastfeeding Grace Ann. She saw Cass was coming over to speak to her.

"I think *both* Beth and Joe should stay behind," Cass began. "I'll supervise them."

"What?" Carolyn exclaimed as she looked around to modulate her tone.

"It's the perfect set up, getting them both to work with Nelder while you're gone." Cass leaned closer and whispered, "You know

Beth and I both share the experience of being raped." Cass waved away Carolyn's stricken look. "It will give her a few weeks for us to talk and to transition from being Grace Ann's 'mother'…and time for you and Grace Ann to be *together* as mother and daughter."

Not only did Carolyn understand Cass's idea, she was so thankful of Cass's thoughtfulness and willingness to share her experience with Beth. Before she could say anything, Cass continued, "I'll get to see just how attached she is to Grace Ann in her conversation…and find out more about any problems, her personality *and* her intentions."

"There's also the other matter," Carolyn said gently.

"I know. As I said, being a victim of rape is something we both know personally." Cass was going to see how and if she could bring up the subject with Beth.

"I hope you can help her," Carolyn said, hugging her aunt's neck. "Besides being a good person and a fine aunt, I always said you'd make a great private investigator."

The talk about the breastfeeding had gone well, better than Carolyn expected. She thought her aunts and Darby might think she'd dove off the deep end - again. Now, with Cass taking care of Beth and Joe, Carolyn could *definitely have* more time to Grace Ann on their trip to LA. Darby, Muriel, and Bee promised to make sure Grace Ann's care and schedule were everyone's first priority on the trip, which Carolyn thought seemed like a great concession for Darby.

Carolyn shook her head, grateful that Mr. Griggs had bowed to Darby's persuasion—letting Cass, Beth, and Joe rent his guesthouse for the time they were going to LA. Mr. Griggs also sympathized with Beth's animal rights sensitivities. Although Beth seemed horrified by the former taxidermist's walls of animal trophies in his residence, Cass mollified her concerns, buying all the bolts of bleached muslin the craft and fabric store stocked and draping each and every one of the wood, fur, and grass-eyed relics of another era. Carolyn could just see each specimen swathed in cloth!

"Nelder's got a moose head above the fireplace in his house, which we've left untouched," Cass confided, laughing. "I think he's kind of cute, and I call him Charley, but don't tell Beth on me. It's a wonder she listened to me and didn't cover him up too!"

"What do you mean, I'll have to go instead of you?" Shealds thundered. "I've got to plan for Zaugus...and we've already *told* Ms. Reynolds you're going with her."

"It's the only way to keep your plan intact," Hesse shot back, looking at his clipboard. "I'll be needed here for installing the air-conditioning and dust filtration in the Bayshore barn. You've got no experience in that. Molina's your best dry wall and framing man." Hesse tried to ease the blow of the decision. "Do you want the opportunity to stay under the radar or not?" Hesse left the weighty issue hanging in the air for his partner to consider. "Yesterday's damage from the sugar in the gas tank of our trencher is proof positive that someone or some group isn't happy with us. The tree, too, remember."

Shealds's eyes clouded and his jaw clenched. He remained uneasy about the accidents happening; first the slashed tires weeks before the Reynolds arrived, the tree, and now, the trencher damage. "Nobody else?" he growled, grasping for someone in the truck driver's seat beside himself. "What about Smithfield?"

"Family wedding in two weeks."

"Parker," Shealds returned hopefully.

"His daughter is the lead in a high school play."

"Stornel?" Shealds wheezed in exasperation.

Hesse harrumphed incredulously at this suggestion. "You want a man with little construction experience to give up work at his own bed-and-breakfast to keep you from going? How you going to talk him into that...and not affect our reputation or your plan?"

"I don't want to be away from work...or my plan," Shealds' anger rose again.

"I know," Hesse said in exasperation. "I even called my uncle Jim, but my aunt is so ill now, and he can't leave her." Hesse started pacing. "We can't slip one of Samples's men into the picture now. He'd be a stranger to the Reynolds family and the neighborhood. There'd be no way of explaining our connection to a *new* man, if the Reynolds, Stornels or Pastor Allred start asking questions!" Hesse folded his arms. "Sometimes we got to do what's needed...no matter what." He shrugged. "Just have to keep your head low. Have you made arrangements for more protection?" The extra layer of private investigator protection seemed a wise choice now.

"I've got Samples on it," Shealds replied, still bristling. "I should never have suggested that you would go."

Hesse nodded. "Granted, it was an improvisation on your part to make us look like we were doing our best on this whole Bayshore deal...which is necessary to get *your* mess done."

Shealds ignored Hesse's logic. "Samples's men will be watching things here and along the trip, I'm sure. Is the plan to get Molina closer to their niece, Beth, over at Nelder Griggs's place underway? With Ms. Reynolds and most of the family gone, that should go smoothly. *If* I go, wonder if I'm the only one packing up all this memorabilia?" Shealds said as his sour tone returned. "There's a baby to care for and this Darby character, who seems like he'll argue with Ms. Reynolds the whole time." Shealds knew he was grousing now. "If I have to do it all myself, it'll take more time."

"You know Ms. Reynolds shows herself as a hands-on type, and her aunts and Mr. Fisher seem the same, although I doubt they could do great feats of heavy-lifting," Hesse replied. "If you decide the progress is too slow, ask for more help. Have one or two of

Samples's men get on the job then. There'll be no problem with inserting a stranger in LA. That should help with the work and the surveillance."

"But I'm still uneasy about this," Shealds grumbled.

"We'll do the switch-out between you and me the day before we're supposed to leave. Hopefully, Ms. Reynolds won't balk too much." Hesse turned, leaving no time for Shealds to protest further.

"Thanks for your time," Shealds began after he'd set several architect's canisters and his briefcase down next to the table at their 9:30 a.m. meeting in their newly installed construction trailer, across from the 39 Bayshore front portico.

"Yes, Mr. Jackson," Carolyn replied. "I want to talk over your plan."

"We've gotten everything through both the coastal people and the permitting people so far as well as working on the hazardous submerged piling removal for your new dock." Shealds's gray hair passed into the sunlight as he moved to unfold the drawings onto the table.

Carolyn looked at out at the trees.

Shealds thought Ms. Reynolds and Ellen were close to the same height as he watched Carolyn sit down on the desk chair. They both had quick intelligence. *Just conversation, Shealds. Let's get back to the plan.*

"As some people might have told you, my partners and I considered buying this place…and we had some plans made to restore it to its original structural configuration, including building an adjoining wing, which might give you and your family the advantages of both access to public rooms and privacy with modern fittings and conveniences." Shealds opened a large document canister and spread the thick, layered drawings over the other plans. "I'll take you through this set of plans to see if this is what you'd like to consider for your home."

Shealds poked his finger at the white and blue plans also flashing on his computer. "I've rethought a few things. I'd like to talk to you about bumping the kitchen out, giving it a slight L for a reading nook with the view of the trees and making the kitchen eating area less cramped - under the roof lines with no structural changes."

Carolyn eagerly looked at the footprint of the other wing on the plans. "I need to bring up the other issues...which are rather unusual. I might need to talk to Mr. Silver." Carolyn didn't think she owed Mr. Jackson any facts about infant bonding and breast-feeding, so she would keep it minimal. "Since, I've adopted a baby girl, I'll need time and privacy to be with her on this trip." Carolyn wanted to make sure he understood. "I'll help and supervise when I can with my aunt's possessions, but I'm leaving most of the work and protection decisions to my aunts and Mr. Fisher."

"Protection?" Shealds said, trying not to appear concerned.

"Poor choice of words, Mr. Jackson," Carolyn countered. "I've hired a firm to help us decide for the best *preservation* options of the articles in the storage units."

"I see." Shealds wasn't going to say *anything* about the change in drivers. "So while you're gone, our company will finish the septic work for your modular housing units, build the temperature-controlled storage unit for the items coming from Los Angeles...and I'm hoping we can have some of your thoughts on the work for your other Bayshore structures, so we can get started on the permits for those as well. Cold weather, Thanksgiving and Christmas are coming."

Carolyn nodded. She could only think about the next few weeks. Shealds slid the amended contracts to her. "Where do I sign?" She hadn't been in the holiday spirit for many years. *Christmas!*

Muriel knocked on the door and called for her niece. "Grace Ann needs you."

Carolyn got up quickly and headed for the door. "Thank you so much, Mr. Jackson. I'll look over the plans while we're gone and get back to you. Can you bring the canister over to the house, please?" She stopped for a second and turned. "As you know, we'll be leaving day after tomorrow. I'll get the final itinerary to Mr. Silver this afternoon."

For breast-feeding, Carolyn kept drinking another glass of water even though, at times she felt she was drowning. The pediatrician said she needed to be adequately hydrated if this idea of adoptive breastfeeding had any chance of working. An iffy proposition at best, but several Internet chats with women who had been success-ful breastfeeding their adopted infants gave Carolyn some hope.

Grace Ann had gained adequate weight from her regular bot-tle feedings, didn't seem tired from the experiment, and seemed willing to try to help things succeed. With Grace Ann's suckling and the use of the breast pump to stimulate breast milk produc-tion, everything had started on schedule, but who could predict what might happen on their cross-country trip?

The small tubing from each bag on the shoulder harness had provided formula while Carolyn and Grace Ann waited for nature to supply the rest. Two to four weeks, maybe more, had been the guesstimate of the professionals and helpful volunteers. Grace and Carolyn were on their second *day*.

Today she and her aunts had successfully decided on the best layout for the Bayshore kitchen. Most of it was going to be a com-plete gut job. Cass thought the dated knotty pine cabinets with the original shellac finish could go in the barn for garden storage.

After about an hour of planning, Grace Ann had fallen into a deep, easy sleep, and it was time to put her down in the travel bed to complete her nap. "Now that we've done the kitchen, we'd better get started about thinking of our own personal living spaces, don't you think?"

The three aunts stopped cleaning up the discarded pencil sketches and looked at one another. They'd had this conversation outside of Carolyn's earshot, knowing she had ordered the work started on the barn and grounds, yet her aunts hadn't said one word about their living quarters in the house or personalizing *any-thing.* As far as they could tell, Carolyn was doing the project...but might still be thinking of this as a spec home. "I've got a few ideas of my own." Carolyn's brow crinkled. "I'll edit any ideas if I get time on the trip?"

"Sure thing," Cass said, trying to sound relaxed and natural.

"Fine with me," Muriel replied.

"How about trying to bake some cookies for the trip? But let's not start another fire," Carolyn quipped. The gas company said the stove was safe.

Bee nodded, happy to do anything that would keep a smile on her niece's face. "I'll start my list and get started on the cookies." She had a few more ideas for the kitchen now that she knew that Carolyn might consider living at Bayshore.

"I'm no architect or contractor, but the site plans seem to coincide with my topographical concerns. I've walked the acreage on the other two lots," Cass said.

"So the next steps, when we get back, are to bring your aunt's things to the place in the barn and move into the modular homes...and moving here?" Muriel asked.

Carolyn just nodded, admiring the kitchen space design they'd draw up.

Bee headed for the old gas stove she'd worked on for ten hours cleaning, hoping the sugar cookies she'd be putting in a suitcase for LA didn't burn...and everything else would take care of itself in its own good way. "I might have some more ideas for the kitchen."

The next morning Carolyn's arm muscles ached from the marathon breastfeeding efforts. Her thoughts turned to Billie not seeing her first grandchild, leaving Carolyn with a depressed, low-energy feeling. At least, the endless yellow lists had shrunk, and she only needed to get through her meeting with Pastor Allred before they left.

Carolyn yawned into her steaming teacup. Grace Ann could sleep between suckling efforts, but Carolyn couldn't. How Carolyn wished she could have some coffee, but she'd read caffeine might interfere with breast milk production, and now she was an herbal tea drinker. *Would a few sips hurt?*

Carolyn didn't feel she had the energy to drive into town to get a java jolt just then and the coffee was gone with all the other foodstuffs to the Stornels since they'd be in LA since Mr. Griggs said food encouraged "critters" to come back into the house. *Didn't Mr. Silver have a coffeepot brewing constantly?* Carolyn thought it was still in the barn and not the new double-wide construction trailer at the edge of the driveway. Perhaps he would take pity on her and allow her a small sip from his pot. If there wasn't any coffee, at least the walk in the brisk morning air might revive her enough to get the rest of things done before the flight tomorrow. A walk, instead of a call, would also suffice, to notify Mr. Silver when the van was coming to take them to the airport.

As Carolyn climbed the slight rise to the barn, she thought of her intended conversation with the police detectives and her private investigators about her mother's case when they got to LA. Something more, even a shred, about the hit-and-run driver, the truck, some other witness, or something from the tire marks or paint on the curb by her mother's fatally injured body. New forensic techniques? Cost was no object.

At least things were falling into place about caring for Beth and Joe. Beth readily agreed to stay in town. She felt Joe needed her support in his training, and he shouldn't be left alone. Besides sitting around and eating extremely large quantities of food, Carolyn couldn't identify just what Joe's training entailed. Nan Stornel promised to help Cass take care of Joe's food and give an extra set of eyes on his activities so Cass could concentrate on

Beth and make a smooth transition to the mother's house at the Griggs's place.

Cass had called to break the news. Carolyn was glad she was sitting down. "I don't know how she talked Nelder into it, but Beth's going to have funerals and bury the animal heads and such."

"What has Mr. Griggs said?" Carolyn asked as blood left her face. *What is Beth thinking? I thought the muslin was enough!*

"He was quite calm about it, saying he'd purchased everything from the former owner, and as the *current* owner of the property, Beth would have to speak to him before she did anything more. He said he respected her feelings about animals, but she must respect his feelings and his belongings."

"First, the moose head cannot be touched or covered," Cass advised. "There can only be one or two funerals a week, and if Nelder is expecting company, the muslin covers on the animal heads, etc. have to come off the walls." Cass thought a minute about the rest of the negotiated items. "The walls are darker where the plagues holding the animal trophies were kept. We're still thinking about what to do about that problem." "Problem" was an understated way of expressing the situation as a whole. Beth's and Joe's futures were on top of Carolyn's list of concerns when she got home from LA.

It seemed strange, though, that a teenager wouldn't jump at the chance to fly first class out to LA. Carolyn had chosen first class to have enough room for the baby. It seemed unfair to make the others sit in coach or have people so close if Grace Ann didn't handle altitude changes or travel well. It would also be an airborne "treat" before the long hours of sorting and culling because Darby constantly harped, "Every shred of Robin Lee's belongings is priceless." They'd have to see.

Darby suggested a curator of reputation he'd investigated, whose references were impeccable. At the very least, this Mr. William Hazeltine, would be able to settle any argument between her and Darby about matters of historic and memorabilia worthiness as well as satisfy the insurance company. So Carolyn, Grace Ann, Bee, Muriel, Darby, and Mr. Silver would hopefully enjoy a few hours of in-the-clouds pampering before they sat with dusty and yellowed trinkets of another era.

"Mr. Silver? Mr. Silver?" Carolyn called, standing several feet from the barn door, which was propped open with rocks.

"He's not here now," Shealds's whiskey-strong disembodied voice replied. Startled, Carolyn almost stumbled, still caught in her other thoughts. Her eyes darted to her feet, trying to make sure she had her footing. All she could see were work-scuffed boots and worn, frayed hems of blue jeans in the intense, dust-mite sunlight through the loft window as his arm shot out to steady her.

"Whaaat?" was all Carolyn managed. "I just...wanted a sip of coffee."

"Easy enough," Shealds continued with a slight smile as he eased his grasp.

"I..." Her voice trailed off.

"Is that you, Ms. Reynolds?" Carolyn's attention turned toward the door. Hesse moved past her and turned on the temporary construction light stapled to the exposed wood.

Carolyn blinked a bit. "No. I wanted...a sip of coffee," Carolyn said hesitantly. "And to confirm the airport arrangements for tomorrow." Perhaps coming over to the barn had been a bad idea.

"Tomorrow," Hesse said in a serious tone. "I was coming over to speak to you about that. We've got several things to consider before you leave. First off, Mr. Jackson is *coming* with you, instead of me."

"Mr. Jackson?" Carolyn said in confusion, not comprehending what Mr. Silver was saying at first. Her plans had not included Mr. Jackson.

"Mr. Jackson will be accompanying you to Los Angeles, Ms. Reynolds," Hesse said, praying he would be able to convince this woman to take Shealds on her trip to LA.

"What?" Carolyn exclaimed, looking back and forth between both men.

Shealds shoved a chipped mug filled with steaming hot coffee toward Carolyn. He retreated quickly into the shadows, hoping to make things less complex.

Carolyn looked up from the mug, now in her hands. "He's going," she said in a dust-dry statement, looking toward Shealds now. "Why?"

Hesse clamped his jaw down tightly. This wasn't going to be good. "You know Mr. Jackson as well as you know me, Ms. Reynolds."

"I suppose, Mr. Silver," Carolyn began, relying on her hard-edged business persona to take over this rocky ground in the discussion. She was the boss and had been caught at a disadvantage. She needed time to consider this drastic change. Carolyn turned her eyes, which were now like smoky blue lasers, to meet the sorghum brown ones of Hesse Silver. This situation seemed to her to resemble a bait-and-switch maneuver. She wasn't going to roll over at this news. "You made no mention of anyone, other than yourself, since we began talking about the trip."

"I realize that, Ms. Reynolds," Hesse replied evenly. "The storage your curator expert says is needed has been reviewed by permitting officials. Their instructions require *major* unexpected changes." He pointed to the county documents to that day's date on the notice. "I *must* stay *here* to make sure the job will be done...or there's not a chance it might be ready before you get back. I'm the person with the expertise in these areas." He looked at her unblinkingly and prayed she would reply in a positive manner to his next statement. "You can, however, hire another company, but I think the answer would be the same from anyone you contacted. I'm the one in our company to deal with these latest *problems*."

"There's another thing." Shealds walked back into the conversation. "We *also intend* to get the utilities and placement pads for the modular homes in working order for you before you all return." He pointed to the plans sitting on the large plywood table. "With your approval, we're proposing to concentrate on the necessary hookups at a cost savings for you. Our associate, David Molina, will spearhead that project."

Carolyn took a minute to think. She turned to look toward the barn loft's window and fumed inwardly. *Blast this house, and blast my late aunt's memorabilia!* Carolyn needed to calm down and remember her health. As she shifted her weight on the cement floor, and in a voice more controlled than she felt, she replied, "I'm going back to the house to consider the change in plans you've outlined. I'll call you with an answer in a few hours." She looked at both men. "Thank you for the coffee. I'll bring back the mug, clean and washed."

As Carolyn walked across the grass, she considered how she was going to couch her questions about Mr. Jackson in the conversation of her overall objectives and efforts with Beth, Joe and Grace Ann with Pastor Allred. Perhaps, she was putting her pastor, who was going to be their family therapist on the spot, but she had to get his input into letting Mr. Jackson instead of Mr. Silver accompany them to LA.

Carolyn looked at Pete as he sat down on a folding chair.

"This meeting is fortuitous because I have *another* issue to discuss with you, Pastor," Carolyn began, smiling her welcome as she came into the room. "In an effort to bring items from California, we enlisted the help of Mr. Silver to accompany us." Carolyn looked for any telltale warning signs. "But it seems with the intricacies of our construction needs here, Mr. Jackson will accompany us instead."

"An unexpected agenda item?" Pete considered the information calmly. "So you're asking *me* about Mr. Jackson?"

"Exactly," Carolyn returned, unrepentant for being careful.

"Let me assure you. If I were in your situation with my daughter, my aunts, and me, I wouldn't worry. I've personally put my faith and reputation on the line for these men." Pete bent to get his yellow pad to take up Ms. Reynolds other concerns.

So that's settled, Carolyn thought. Pastor Allred was vouching for Mr. Jackson, so Carolyn couldn't identify any other reason not to agree to Mr. Jackson coming on the trip.

"Thank you for being straightforward, Pastor Allred. I'm grateful for your input, so let's go on to the next issue." Carolyn wanted to choose her words carefully in this as well. "My daughter came to me in a *unique way.*" Carolyn took a deep breath to bolster the truth telling. "Beth and Joe were unknown trespassers on the property when I discovered Beth had an infant, who'd been purchased from the biological mother in a communal homeless situation in Baltimore." Pete took in the information and kept eye contact. "My aunts and I would like to include her in our extended family, but she's had some rough times as a foster child with verbal…and physical abuse."

"Are you saying…?"

Carolyn only nodded, not wanting to verbalize the ugly word. "So my aunts and I want to provide a safe, therapeutic environment for them and to share our family story, as it were…and for them, especially Beth, to feel safe to share hers, when and if she chooses."

"And you'd like to start this when you get back from California?"

"Yes. Adding in any information Cass gets from conversations with Beth while we're gone. Cass, Beth, and Joe are staying over in Nelder Griggs's guesthouse." Carolyn put her hand up in a blocking motion. "Don't worry—this arrangement is *not* to isolate or interrogate Beth or force her to say anything she doesn't want to share willingly." Her eyes and demeanor remained calm. "You can keep an eye on them if you're concerned, and identify if she might need one-on-one sessions with you."

"Any individual sessions for any of you?" Pete said gently.

Ms. Reynolds looked thoughtful. Then she tried to banter. "Pastor, the rest of us might be well *beyond* therapeutic help."

"OK. All lost causes besides Beth and Joe." Pete smiled while continuing his notes. "So now I see why you need group help. The idea of *two hours* for the first group session, with a break or two in between, seems like a good one. We'll stop whenever *I feel* like we should. That might be two minutes…or it might be the full two hours—but no more."

"We'll check things out with Beth and let you know if we'll all be ready for the first group session." Carolyn looked down at her list. "There's also Joe to consider. He might need extra help too…but at a different forum."

Pete included Joe in his notes.

"If you'll excuse me, I'll see you out and call Mr. Jackson."

"You're certainly in a pensive mood, Carolyn," Bee noted gently as her hand touched Carolyn's hair and then sank to her shoulder. Bee noted Carolyn had pushed around her food on her plate during the planned bon voyage party. Bee didn't want to be harsh. "Is it Grace Ann and the breastfeeding?"

"Not really," Carolyn said finally. "There are several things. Construction concerns for the storage space." They'd all been taken aback from Carolyn's announcement that Mr. Jackson, and not Mr. Silver, was coming on the trip. It seemed Carolyn was more bothered by the switch in the escorts than the barn construction concerns. She gave a slight shrug. "Sometimes plans need to be altered."

"Are you sure?" Bee asked.

Carolyn patted her aunt's hand. She didn't want to talk about Mr. Jackson, working with him in LA and getting to know him wasn't part of her plan. Mr. Silver was supposed to come to help with Aunt Robin's things. "Mr. Jackson's coming seems like the only practical substitution for our LA trip." She had so many things to do. *Why don't I want to get to know him?*

"But something's still bothering you?"

"No," Carolyn lied, flushing at her idle thoughts. "I want to get into the modular housing as soon as possible." Carolyn rubbed her forehead. "This side trip has complicated things." Carolyn shivered inwardly, not wanting to think of Mr. Jackson anymore. "Think I'm just tired. A good night's sleep will help my outlook." She got to her feet, hugged her aunt, and climbed the stairs to her bedroom. Carolyn turned around and smiled. "I've already left a wake-up call for five a.m. with Nan."

Bee knew she was almost all packed except for her toiletries. She and Muriel had packed Grace Ann's things, including putting identification tags on the stroller and baby seat. They'd had a play-pen, some toys, and other supplies drop-shipped to the storage unit office in LA. Muriel assured her Darby had been packed and ready for two days, and they knew Beth, Cass, and Joe were already well taken care of over at Nelder's.

Beth seemed like a young woman of her word, becoming a more integral part of the family as each day passed. Joe, on the other hand, wasn't a joiner, and needed a lot of assistance and cajoling in most tasks. He hadn't helped out much or mentioned much about the New Jersey contest he'd been so concerned about when he'd arrived at Bayshore. Carolyn said she'd talked to Pastor Allred about counseling him. None of them knew what he would do. He'd resisted all their conversations regarding furthering his education or setting future goals. From what Bee could remember, the contest would be over by the time they all got back from LA. But all that could wait. They needed to concentrate on Carolyn, Grace Ann, and the cross-country work ahead.

Bee knew it wasn't going to be easy for Carolyn to breastfeed her adopted child in a travel situation and going through her aunt's things with Darby fretting over every piece like lost treasure.

Then there would be the heartbreak of going over the cold trail of the investigation of Billie's death. Just thinking about it brought tears to Bee's eyes.

She still missed Billie. They all did. It was little wonder Carolyn looked a bit sad and tired at times. She'd spent five years with little resolution. Billie's death had torn everything apart...and things weren't back together yet. If Bee were to fulfill her helper responsibilities, she needed to shake off her thoughts and go to bed.

"I, for one, am glad we're leaving for a few days, or I think I'd really come to blows with Mr. Clem," Muriel confided. "Even though he's the mayor, he's in my way and pestering the blue blazes out of me whenever I go to the historical society."

"He's here a lot too," Bee agreed. "Always looking nervous and asking questions about the construction and the digging."

"Cass said she saw him out on the property past the side lawn with a shovel," Muriel recounted. "He said something about hearing of some work that had been done about thirty years ago, without permits, and he thought an unauthorized septic tank might be in the spot where he was digging."

"That would mean trouble, wouldn't it?" Bee noted. "I was surprised when Mr. Clem said his original family business was started with outhouses, then septic systems. I thought he was in real estate and busy being the mayor. Why not just tell the construction company people and not go digging around by himself?"

"He says he's a septic expert and feels some 'hangover' responsibility after being the conservator and all," Muriel said, "and a 'real love of local history.'"

"Well, if he continues to be a nuisance when we get back, we'll talk with Carolyn." Bee looked to make sure her bags were ready to go.

"Or we can assign him to Darby," Muriel said. "He should be able to keep him occupied, perhaps get our mayor interested in

Robin Lee history." Muriel's bags were in front of Bee's. "I'm going to enjoy the architectural research concerning the Paynes and the Dornes when I have more time."

"We'll be leaving in ten minutes for the airport, Mr. Silver," Carolyn called as she inspected the grease pencil lines he had put down indicating the rest of the rough walls they'd erect for her aunt's possessions in the barn. "You've done a nice job coordinating things with the current storage facility in Los Angeles."

"From what I can understand from Mr. Hazeltine, it's best to plan for more space, in caring for older cloth and paper items," Hesse replied. "And, Ms. Reynolds...?" He waited until she was finished looking at the black lines and could turn toward his voice. "It's Hesse please, and no more Mr. Silver. Same goes for Shealds and David. Please."

Carolyn flushed at that. "I know you've told me a number of times, and I will try to remember. It's just that I was taught to use Mr. and Mrs., etc., when I spoke to people. I'll get it straight." Her entreaty ended in a smile. "Now, *Hesse,* just where is the new door going to be?" Carolyn headed toward the large barn interior. Frightened, furry feet scrambled over her shoes, as Carolyn let out a startled shriek, sending her running through the barn door and into the sunlight. *I have to call Nelder again!* Hesse followed her. Just as he was just about to turn and reenter the barn, loud echoing thuds shook the ground as dust plumed from the barn entrance for several seconds.

"You OK?" Hesse side-armed her, pushing Carolyn away from the barn to keep her safe. Carolyn could only nod and swat at the dust cloud. "Stay here," he ordered as he headed back into the barn. "I've got to see what happened." In an instant of long strides, he was gone, and then, he reemerged. "The temporary office door's wedged shut with whatever happened. You stay here while I go through the set of barn sliders." Carolyn knew Hesse was headed toward the large double doors previously built for horses and wagons on the middle of the building on the opposite wall. She stood there looking at Hesse's back as he loped away, while brushing the dust from her hair and clothes. She wouldn't have time to shower, if the group were to have to time to make their plane.

"What happened?" Carolyn heard Shealds's voice coming from the direction of the construction trailer before she saw him as he ran past her and followed Hesse's path to the sliders. Carolyn should have known. *Did Shealds Jackson always sound so authoritarian?* Another reason for her dissatisfaction, knowing Mr. Jackson was going to be accompanying them, and not Hesse.

Shealds's eyes darted, trying to assess what had caused the thundering noise he'd heard from inside his truck as he'd turned off the ignition. He'd yelled for everyone to stay by the luggage for safety while he investigated. His plan, to transfer his bag from the curb to the shuttle rented for their trip to the airport, evaporated when the loud noise rang out.

At that point Carolyn decided she was getting tired of such declarative male sentences. *Do they think I'm going to go rushing into the barn like a woman superhero?* It might have taken a bit more time, but she probably would have gotten a few breaths of fresh air, dusted herself off, and followed a safe path, first to survey things from a window or the entrance door where she was standing and then, perhaps to the other barn door. *Should I start to ask questions now?*

Best to wait, she thought, until they came out to report about what had happened. Then she'd confront Hesse and Mr. Jackson about their strident orders and demeanor, for want of a better term. The testosterone slinging would have to stop—*more on the part of Mr. Jackson.* Otherwise, it was going to be a very long trip, and their construction company was going to lose the job on her house, no matter if they did own one of the other lots on the property.

"It's one of the heavier timber jousts," Hesse pointed to the ceiling. "It's freshly sawn almost through and came down under its own weight."

"Sawn?" Shealds repeated as Hesse nodded. "The size of the tampering might mean there's more than one person. Could have killed somebody."

"Seems so," Hesse replied. "Perhaps, one man could do it. Remember, nobody's here at night, and the security system doesn't get completed until Thursday."

"What do you want me to do?" Shealds looked into the dimness, his face taut.

"We'll say it was a rotten timber, which we were going to reinforce this morning and a couple of scaffolding slats and sections fell," Hesse replied. "I'll investigate here, and you watch your back out in LA."

"Better get outside before we raise any suspicion," Shealds agreed. "Send some of Samples's men over in construction gear or dressed as inspectors to investigate. Jack up the infrastructure and get another joust in place at our cost." Hesse nodded.

"Remember, no one says anything to anybody," Shealds said. He didn't look back for Hesse's reply.

CHAPTER TWELVE

Carolyn looked at her group of travelers, including Grace Ann, who'd captured the Baby Congeniality title. Even some of the crusty first-class business travelers smiled at Grace Ann. She couldn't complain about Mr. Jackson, either. *So what is bothering me?* Mr. Jackson was now silently efficient. Rather than being put off or bossy in the hustle-bustle of the airport environment, he had known all of the protocol of getting them through every challenge from the curbside to their seats. Guess he thought it best not to speak too much when she was around. She closed her eyes and fell asleep.

Darby looked around the first-class compartment as he sipped his glass of chardonnay.

"Want me to take a turn with the baby?" Shealds whispered. Ms. Reynolds was asleep, and Shealds had held Grace Ann for a few minutes at the beginning of the flight.

"No. I think it's time for a bit of rest from all this passing around. Getting overtired with too much stimulation is one way to change Grace Ann's mood and everyone else's," Muriel replied.

"She's a trooper, just like her great-aunt Robin," Darby spoke up in a whisper, craning his neck to see Carolyn's head turned toward the window in relaxed slumber.

"And her mother," Bee pointed to Carolyn's seat. "Getting a lot done."

"About that," Shealds said, trying to remain casual. "It's nice to be adding to your family."

Muriel and Bee had gone over the cover story they'd concocted in order to tell the most truth as possible. They'd all agreed Grace Ann would be told the *whole* truth when, and as, she was mature enough to understand it. "It was a family opportunity for all of us. We all decided—to take care of this beautiful child."

These women should have been actresses, Darby thought as he listened to Muriel. If he got off story about Grace Ann and Beth, he could plead ignorance or misunderstanding, invoking distance in his knowledge and relationships since he was, truthfully, only Robin Lee's fan club president. Everything they said sounded plausible. Beth was from the estranged side of Carolyn's family. Carolyn had been trying to adopt…and now Grace Ann was here.

Carolyn had signed, checked, and filed the mountain of forms, reports, and other legal paperwork concerning Grace Ann with what Darby knew was reminiscent of her late mother's skill and concentration. When Billie was alive, she frequently mentioned her pride when she talked about Carolyn and her business. It would take a bit of time on court dockets, and the last of the home visits, to make everything legal. All state and county employees given jurisdiction in the matter were happy with Grace Ann's situation and awed by the magnitude of the restoration plans for the Bayshore place. Darby had wrapped his professional and personal life around perpetuating the work and memory of a long-dead film star so he could certainly understand wanting to preserve bygone architecture!

Besides the fan club, Darby had simple needs except for occasional splurges on gourmet food and finely tailored clothes. His job in textile design allowed him to travel and live comfortably if not lavishly. Coming to visit Carolyn was now the underpinning of next spring's seaside collection of washed damasks and chenille, textured upholstery, and prints having a dash of autumn-hued Portofino and Provence, like the mulched leaves on the Bayshore grounds. He'd already sent several samples and his intentions in a memo to the marketing department of the licensing company.

Darby heard Shealds ask another question. "So you're intending to settle down at Bayshore?"

"Young man," Muriel said, seeming to indicate she was in her eighties rather than her well-preserved early-sixties. "We're heading for Los Angeles. I, for one, would like to think about resting a bit." She looked down her nose in a fine imitation of a nineteenth-century English aristocrat. Darby seemed to remember such a character in the period piece where Robin Lee was cast as the scullery maid—one of her first bit parts. After a final pregnant pause, Muriel concluded, "I think I'm going to take a nap." Darby would have to ask Muriel when they had a moment away if she had seen that movie.

Carolyn thought the first day had gone well as she dabbed at the perspiration on her forehead. They started working with Mr. Hazeltine, an impeccably dressed, black-haired, and mustached man. By renting two larger, vacant storage units for the supplies and tables, nearby the three they were sorting, they also had room to put the boxed items as they were packed. While arranging work stations with rented tables and chairs delivered to the storage units, Shealds assembled and stacked an array of various sizes of flat boxes, which sat on the periphery. Several screens and a more heavily upholstered chair with a high back and rocker mechanism were rented for Carolyn and Grace Ann, as well as another travel playpen and bed, matching the one they had at the hotel.

Mr. Hazeltine seemed like a much taller carbon copy of Darby in his approach. He was fussy, giving lessons on how to pack and label things, while he monitored their progress like a disapproving French chef. "Work precisely." His pencil-thin black mustache contrasted with his green eyes, which would twitch slightly when they failed to understand or follow his exacting directions.

"I'll have to investigate what to do with some of your items with my colleagues. They should have been cataloged years ago," he said in a dark tone and angry look for emphasis. "Handle them gently; put them flat on the acid-free tissue. I'll bag them and transfer them to the proper people after each working day. Place the photographs needing restoration over here." He lifted his hand over his eyes and scanned the back of the unit. "We might need more tables."

"I am glad you rented the biggest truck available for the transfer." Hazeltine walked over to pick up a measuring tape and looked at a costume placed on a clean muslin cloth tarp. "I am taking these to experts who have impeccable credentials in specialty inspection and cleaning. But I should be able to estimate the amount of space they need before you get to the new storage facility."

Carolyn tried to tamp down her impatience at Hazeltine's attitude. She realized they were dealing with what he and Darby said were important items, but they weren't priceless artifacts or bombs needing to be defused. She was willing to wear the white cotton cloth gloves Hazeltine insisted were necessary whenever they touched anything, but using large tweezers for paper and smaller items seemed a bit much. Hazeltine also wanted the clean white gloves discarded when they got soiled.

"Don't worry; I'll take the gloves to the hotel laundry," Shealds offered, "if we don't have enough." No one had to know Shealds could use this as a possible opportunity to meet his surveillance contacts or make calls.

"You'll do no such thing," Hazeltine admonished, shaking his left index finger for emphasis. "To re-use gloves requires a special soap, not the cheap packets you buy in those coin machines at the hotels." He pointed to himself. "I will do them."

"Do what you think is best, Mr. Hazeltine, but I'm sure Shealds was only trying to help," Carolyn replied, trying to mollify the situation.

"I'll take the van to get other supplies. Whatever is needed," Shealds said, trying to keep his temper in check...and his options open.

What a morass was all Shealds could think of when he considered what he was doing. "What junk" would be another term he would use, not understanding why a piece of paper with a few scribbled words or something on an ordinary cloth cocktail napkin required such care. They weren't excavating King Tut's tomb. Shealds knew about dealing with papers, mountains of them, in his investment business and then with the court case. They had to be safely stored—but nothing like this. He kept reminding himself to keep his mouth shut and his eyes open as he doled out the specially treated wrappings, plastic sheath envelopes, acid-free papers, and made boxes.

Darby Fisher acted like Hazeltine, only in a friendlier histori-cal manner, rhapsodizing while he sat in a shady corner of the slump-block structure, following Hazeltine's numbering system and electronically narrating his, Carolyn and her aunts' recollec-tions about any item in an effort to describe the meaning of each piece of cloth, paper, newspaper, magazine article, photograph, or miscellaneous item. Muriel took on the task of letter labeler and Bee took pictures of every item leaving the premises so nothing would be lost or misplaced.

There would be a lot more anecdotal work needing to be done when the boxes were delivered to the Bayshore barn, Hazeltine informed them. He'd be flying out with his assistant to continue the process. "I have other clients waiting in two weeks, so you can carefully unload the boxes in the storage area, but don't touch the contents until I get there," he ordered. "Will the unit have adequate humidity regulation?"

"Yes," Shealds replied. "The unit's been changed as you suggested."

"I've kept my records in meticulous order," Darby sniffed. Evidently, Hazeltine's dismissive pickiness was razing Darby's twill-suited hackles. "Mr. Jackson knows all about the archive unit as the contractor." This lead to a twenty-minute discussion of what Shealds and Hesse had designed for the barn space.

Carolyn was glad the operation was going smoothly but bemoaning the fact there was so much of it. Her aunt had been such a hoarder! Mr. Hazeltine would ask for what he needed, and Mr. Jackson...Shealds made sure supplies and the daily necessities of food came as requested.

"Let that trinket go for now, Darby," Carolyn called, looking at a piece of costume jewelry Darby was inspecting. "Shealds got the food truck he's called, to include us in our route, while we're here. If you don't come now, the drinks will get warm, and you know you like your hot beverages, hot, and the cold ones, cold."

Shealds sat on the asphalt with his back on the cement block storage unit wall. The driver from the food truck said there would be a file from Samples concerning Carolyn Reynolds on his computer when they got back to the hotel. He'd told everyone he needed it to keep up on his business work...in the evening to catch up on things back home. So far, Shealds knew about Carolyn's professional life, the recent demise of her company ownership, and the death of her mother. She was much different than he first thought!

Ms. Reynolds was a mother hen now as she slathered sunblock on them all, including him, in her every four-hour ministrations. The first time he'd met her, her skin was covered in soot, so all he was able to see were her blue, with a hint of amber, eyes in her fiery gaze. Ms. Reynolds wore some designer labels and some cheaper off-the-rack clothes, but she was all washable cotton and denim for her job days here.

Her face was an elongated oval, a bit too long by classic standards with an equally long, aquiline nose that fitted her bone structure. Ms. Reynolds's lips were generous, with a distinct Cupid's bow upper lip. She frowned frequently, Shealds noticed, or looked out into space, as if something tangible floated in the air. Her thick sandy hair had some natural curl or she frequented an expensive hairdresser.

She spent a big chunk of time behind a set of rented screens with the baby girl she'd adopted, when Beth Seavers came on the scene. Shealds was floored when he'd nosed around and saw Ms. Reynolds trying to breastfeed Grace Ann with some tethered pouches around her neck. He'd quickly and silently gone back to work. *What was that all about?*

Excluding Shealds and Hazeltine, everyone kept Grace Ann entertained, dry, and fed while she was awake. After talking with Muriel on the plane, he remembered he was an employee and not a friend. He hadn't offered to interact with Grace Ann again, except to guide her stroller in a pinch. He'd cooperate, keep to himself, and wouldn't invest in interpersonal relationships. Nothing beyond the information he needed to do the job...and keep everyone safe, if these accidents and problems back at Bayshore and the construction company were directed at him. Getting into relationships made you sloppy. *I remember what happened to Ellen.* He didn't want Carolyn or anyone to get hurt.

Carolyn had two unexplained absences, Shealds noted. She'd been gone for several hours each time with no explanation, asking for reports and updates when she returned. Darby, Bee and Muriel, as he now called them, seemed more concerned and on edge when she returned from wherever she went. There weren't any bags indicating she was shopping, although they might be housed in her hotel room. She seemed to be such a protective adoptive mother, so he couldn't think she would go off without the baby if more family were involved to acquaint her baby with relatives, friends, and the like. Probably visits to the cops or investigators about her deceased mother.

Shealds asked Samples's food-truck driver to make sure about his hunches and check on her whereabouts in these absences. He'd have to palm a door card from Muriel at dinner just as they were getting ready to order. She always kept the plastic pass in the pocket close to the top of her bucket handbag. Shealds would get Muriel's card, have them pack up his meal, and bring it to him after they were finished, pretending he needed to go back to his room to call the construction company on business.

He did have to report in with Samples, but this evening would be devoted to finding out more about Ms. Reynolds, her extended family, and if there was anything else he needed to know about their LA visit.

The two older women here in LA were each unique, but Shealds didn't have any information about them above the ordinary—yet. Cass Williams, the one left behind with the Beth Seavers and Joe Thackery, with a dark, dyed mane of hair beyond her shoulders, wasn't bringing up anything of note either.

These women were as different as night and day in most respects, yet by all accounts they'd been together for a number of years. There were public records on their childhood and addresses and job records. Cass and Bee had husbands, now decreased. Darby Fisher was a colorful personality in his long-sleeve shirts and khaki pants or white twill suits, even while working in the storage units. Fisher had shared that he'd lost his wife of eight years, which checked out, but nothing about the failed court case and confiscation of his retirement home several years ago for high-rise coastal vacation hotel construction in Central America. Shealds could relate about failures of justice. Fisher kept afloat with textile design jobs and some design consulting.

The teenage vagrants were another matter—just wild cards, complicating things. Thackery had a juvenile detention record a mile long. The girl, Beth, was supposed to be a distant relative. Samples had uncovered the lie, which smelled to high heaven even before any one did any investigation...and the true history of Beth's foster care and abuse record. *Is Beth Grace Ann's real mother?* Those court records were sealed, but Samples was investigating in Baltimore. That seemed like more of a likely scenario, Shealds thought, but if the Reynolds clan needed to make their explanation to society with their fudging of events, that was their business.

As far as being in Los Angeles, there wasn't much to say, except they had decent, basic hotel accommodations. He'd expected Ms. Reynolds and her family to stay in more luxurious digs, especially after getting the first-class plane ride to LA. With the converted Four Almonds stock, cash, and settlements, the Reynolds clan were *very* wealthy and could well afford more luxury.

They were all together on the same floor of this midlevel-priced hotel near the storage unit. Ms. Reynolds and Grace Ann stayed in one room, and her two aunts were in the adjoining room. He and Darby were across the hall. They all piled into the rental van after breakfast at 9:30 a.m. sharp. Ms. Reynolds always asked him to drive. Their schedule was eight hours a day at the site with one meal and two breaks. Grace Ann stayed with them the whole time.

Back at Bayshore, Pete's worry lingered as he spoke into his office phone. He'd worked hard on this, as Pastor Bill had suggested, but had little to show for his efforts. "I've got everything I can think of down on paper. I'm hoping my impressions are correct," he said in a half-apologetic tone after he and Pastor Bill had finished their prayer asking God's blessing on the information. "No guilt about my past so far."

"That's OK. That's OK," Pastor Bill replied as he put Pete on speakerphone to have his hands free to write down what Pete had to say.

"It's all rather a jumble, but I want you to hear them." Pete tapped his pencil on the pad with the first observation. "Since we've talked about the injuries and experience from my youth, the only thing that's stayed in my consciousness, is that this started before I purchased the Bayshore lot."

"We can get back to your purchase in a few minutes, but is there any other reason you can think of concerning its importance?" Pastor Bill asked as he wrote down the property name on his pad.

"All I can say is an elderly spinster lived out there, and she died about three years ago. I visited her as a shut-in before she died, chatted, and gave her communion before a layperson took over some of the visits." Pete tried to think of more as he scanned the list. "I looked at the property initially when the conservator asked if the congregation if we would like to buy the place. Except for the beautiful view, it was never suitable because of the cost, acreage, and distance from town."

"Anything else?" Pastor Bill asked.

"Well, as you know, my aunt, who is going to build on the lot, is the person who took me in after my mom died and my father went to prison—as soon as I was out of the hospital. She was single and my mother's sister. I think I already told you, she's a surgeon who's getting ready to retire in a few years." Pete considered if anything else might be important. "She's really happy with the lot, and she's going to start with her architect soon on a plan for her house."

"Your relationship?" Pastor Bill wanted to know if there was anything more there.

"She was great…and continues to be great. She raised me, and even learned to enjoy baseball and rugby when I played them in high school and college."

Pete sounded truthful and that he had good feelings concerning his aunt, so Pastor Bill tried another track. "Anything going on there now?"

"Renovation and subdividing of the estate land by a woman and her aunts. That's how I got the lot I just mentioned," Pete replied. "There'll be three homes there within about two years or so: renovation of the original mid-nineteenth-century mansion, my aunt in one house on the second lot, and a spec home on the third. The spec home is being built by a contractor who's remodeling the mansion for the new owner."

Pete felt disappointed and wished there were more to tell. "What I'm feeling now are these different levels of sadness, like there are several sad people or situations. Does that make any sense?" He tapped his pencil on the pad again. "Carolyn Reynolds, the new owner, seems like a really nice woman—single, bright, and smiling—positive, not negative feelings…from her and her family." He thought a moment more. "She's got her three aunts there and a niece and her niece's boyfriend…and Ms. Reynolds has adopted a baby girl."

"So?" Pastor Bill wanted this to be open-ended. Perhaps, this had more to do with the woman, this Ms. Reynolds, than the lot for his aunt. He wanted to know if Pete might be interested in this woman, which might explain why he was thinking about the Bayshore place. *Did Pete's problems have something to do with love or the lack of it?*

"She's a lovely woman inside and out. I might consider asking her for a date, but I don't think that's got anything to do with my feelings about the Bayshore place." Pete thought for a moment. "Actively thinking about the Reynolds family makes me feel happy.

So it's not them. The impressions that keep bubbling up make me feel sad and confused, with a kind of foreboding at the edge, sometimes…and I'm trying to get more. But it's not coming yet. That's why I'm frustrated."

"So you think its multiple people or situations. Do you think you're sensing something bad from the past or something that's going to happen in the future?" Pastor Bill was trying to get things as clear as possible. People sometimes were bothered by negative impressions, just like they were bothered by phobias, like heights, snakes, and spiders.

"I don't know," Pete replied, trying to describe things. "I'm just trying to dig down and find exactly what's going on." Pete looked out the window at the calm sunny morning. "I've also got something on the physical angle."

"Physical angle?" Pastor Bill asked, not understanding what Pete was saying. He was still writing down *sad, confused, and foreboding.*

"I've tried to evaluate the fear I'm feeling. I don't think it comes from my family or any of my personal baggage," Pete replied. "Mine's about grief, shame and personal stress, this other 'thing' that's happening is sadness mixed the dread."

"So, at this point, you're saying it's something different…and not from your past?" Pastor Bill wrote down "says it's not from his past".

"I guess that's it. I'm really just talking out loud…and I need more time to edit and consider things." Pete wanted to be clear about what he was saying. "At this time, my physical impressions are splintering in different directions." He bit his lip. "I really want to concentrate and really make sure." Pete winced and tapped his fingers on the tabletop. "But enough about that." Pete wanted to change the subject. "I also want to talk about something else. One of our members has volunteered to look at your materials to guide our new ministry effort."

Carolyn almost hit herself in the nose with her arm thrusting her body toward the alarm clock. After a very tiresome day of packing Aunt Robin's things, Carolyn had fallen into bed after Grace Ann's last breastfeeding attempt. Her neck and back hurt, and she wasn't even going to think about last evening's breast discomfort. A hot soak in the tub had helped. She'd dozed off twice in the water and fallen exhausted into bed. "It can't be morning yet," she whispered hoarsely, simultaneously batting at the air and tumbling from the bed as she gained consciousness from deep sleep. "Think, think," she ordered herself, groping for her robe. She was in the hotel room. This wasn't an alarm clock; the piercing loud sound was the fire alarm or some kind of an alarm coming from the hall. Grace Ann was in her travel crib between the sitting area and the desk.

Carolyn hit the nightstand lampshade, probably putting it askew as she as she got on her feet, when Muriel and Bee came through the inside door of the adjoining room.

Coming through the door, Muriel ordered. "Is there any smoke coming from under the door? If not, feel the door to make sure it's cool. If it is, try the door. We'll take the stairs if there's no smoke in the hall. Get Grace Ann."

"Perhaps it's best to stay here since we're only on the third floor, and the fire ladders can definitely reach this far," Bee countered. A loud knock made them all jump and sent Grace Ann wailing, being startled from sleep now with hearing the shrill siren.

"Open up. It's Shealds. There's no smoke in the hall." Bee went to the door as Carolyn tried to soothe Grace Ann by holding her close, rocking her, and cooing calming words into her pink shell-like ear. The alarm only got louder when the door was swiftly opened and closed, causing Grace Ann's cry to escalate. Carolyn looked up to see Shealds and Darby rushing in. The travel baby bed and other paraphernalia blocked most of the walking space from the center aisle of the room at the foot of the two beds to the window. Shealds charged to the back of the room. "Let me go to the window. Darby, wet some towels and put them under the door jams just in case. Stay off the phone."

Carolyn looked askance. Seeing both men with their hair mused and haphazard dress made her think of all their dishevelment. Bee had managed to get a blouse on over her nightgown. Muriel had her robe and black flats on - not her slippers. Darby was not his usual dapper self, but his matching pajamas and bathrobe with the small blue stripes seemed to be the most fashionable of the group. Carolyn was sure she looked less than put together. Shealds was in his jeans, white-sleeved undershirt, and loafers. The men were definitely better dressed than the women. She looked down at Grace Ann, now recovered from her fright. "Well, you, my lovely, might save us from designer hell with your delicate pink-footed terry cloth sleeper and sweet baby smell."

Shealds half growled, still acting all business and looking black-eyed, like an automaton. "No sign of flames or smoke from this vantage point. Firemen are here and the deployed hoses are snaked into the building, so we're going to have to wait this out."

"We've got light for now," Carolyn remarked. "Keep the drapes open wide so we can use the streetlight in case the power goes out. Shall we all stay in here?"

"I'll go get the desk chair from the other room so they'll be enough seats for us all with the bed. Then I'll recheck the door and the towels." Shealds looked around again. "This room is closer to the stairwell, so I think we should stay here." He started into the other room.

"Do you remember, if there's smoke, we're supposed to crawl on the floor where the air is most breathable?" Darby remarked.

"I do remember, Darby, but thank you for the reminder," Carolyn said gratefully. Then her face contorted with alarm. "How do you crawl with a baby?"

"Don't think it'll come to that," Shealds said as he reentered the room. "Walls and the door are still cool in the other room. No smoke coming from underneath either one, although I covered it for safety's sake."

Carolyn listened to the alarm still blaring in the hallway.

"Well, it looks like it's going to be a long wait," Muriel said, her voice filled with fatigue and apprehension. She looked directly at Shealds. "If you don't mind, I'm going to sit on the bed until the 'all clear'."

"I agree, Muriel," agreed Bee. "Just standing in the way here." The bed sagged.

"I'll take the baby bed and put it between you," Darby offered. "That way, the path from the window to the door will be open. I'll use the facilities before first watch."

"Just wanted to call and tell you we're not going to get much work done today—false fire alarm," Carolyn said in a bit of verbal shorthand to Cass. "Didn't get back to bed until about four a.m., I think. Just got Grace Ann down for her nap."

"Are you all OK?" Cass asked, concern lacing her tone.

"Just feeling a bit tired. We all are…and it will put us behind schedule. We'll be going over to the storage shed about one p.m."

"Don't mean to add to problems today, but I have to tell you that Joe's gone," Cass announced. She rubbed her tired eyes, waiting for the information to sink in.

"Gone. Gone where?" Carolyn asked, alarm coming into her voice.

"Joe left a note last night on his bed. Beth found it this morning. The gist of it saying all 'our activity' was interfering with his training and he had to get up to New Jersey," Cass replied.

"How's Beth taking it?" Carolyn asked quickly, hoping Beth wouldn't run after Joe, whose appetite seemed to be much larger than his good sense or concern for her. "We were going to broach the subject of a job for him with Hesse, Shealds, and Molina, or perhaps something with Mr. Griggs, when we got back in town."

As before, Joe seemed long on lazy and short on gumption. "Beth vacillates. Doesn't seem too sad about it, other than she hopes he's OK, safe, and wishes him well. Then she's angry about him leaving and not saying whether he'll keep in contact or afraid he can't take care of himself." Cass stopped to consider if she knew anything else to tell. "If I was a betting woman, I'd say Beth provided for the three of them on the road." Cass stopped again. "Nelder took her out on a raccoon family relocation to keep her busy."

Now, it was Carolyn's turn to rub her tired eyes, trying to think of what to do about the new development. "I guess keeping her busy is the best thing." Carolyn tried to think of what to do next, or any advice she could think of, being so far from the situation and her aunt. "I know you're doing the best you can."

"The sheriff's been notified, but I can't file a missing person's report yet since he's over eighteen, there's a note, and he left voluntarily," Cass added.

"Just tell Beth to call me as soon as she gets back. I'll call Mr. Lyon and have him contact the private detective agency he's using here to track Joe down." Carolyn stopped for a moment. "Shealds has been a big help here in LA...and took over to make sure we were safe last night."

"Glad to hear it," Cass replied, glad someone else could help Carolyn shoulder the work there. Carolyn's goal was to be with Grace Ann and Cass hoped she was telegraphing that Shealds was helping to make that happen.

"I didn't even get a chance to thank him," Carolyn said. "I'll tell him later."

"Sounds good. Try not to worry," Cass wanted details about Grace Ann. "How's the breastfeeding coming?"

"I'm still convinced I need to keep trying, but I'm tired, sore, and with getting all of Aunt Robin's things moved, I'm not sure if I'll be one of the lucky ones to get this to work..." Carolyn's voice trailed off.

Cass tried to be reassuring. "Just keep going, honey. I know you're trying your best. Lean on the others to get things done." She wanted to give Carolyn some uplifting news. "We've scheduled a funeral for the twenty-pound bass plague today, when the kids in the neighborhood get out of camp this afternoon. I'm even making punch and cookies for the reception after the service."

Carolyn tried to find some humor and solace in Cass's calm words. *If Beth, my so-called niece, goes running after her wannabe food-eating champion, what are we going to do?*

"Jackson," Shealds barked into his mobile phone.

"It's me," Hesse's familiar voice intoned. "We've got a possible problem. Don't know how serious, but I thought you should know." He continued without preamble. "Beth Seavers's boyfriend skipped town. Griggs informed me when he went out on an animal relocation job this morning. Good thing you told him we wanted to look out for the Reynolds family. What do you think?"

"If this so-called shirttail niece leaves, we might be in trouble," Shealds replied. "If the family pulls up stakes, Samples won't be happy. More people to track. Get him on Thackery." Grimness etched Shealds's tired face. As long as he was on the phone, he might as well tell Hesse. "False fire alarm kept us up a good part of the night. No problems with anyone. Lost sleep. Carolyn was a champ with rearranging things. Might be a day or two longer. I've called Samples, and he was already on it."

"It's something else for him to bill you for. Anything we can do?" Hesse joked. "Griggs mentioned they're burying one of the taxidermist's trophies over there, trying to get the girl's mind off Thackery."

"Tell Molina to get over there to keep an eye on things. He's closest to the Seavers girl's age," Shealds said. "Tell him he's developed an animal conservation streak and to keep his eyes open," Shealds replied. "The Seavers girl can't go anywhere because if the Reynolds clan leaves, we'll have blown the protective cover off my plans for cleaning my name. Understand?" Hesse knew exactly what he meant.

Pete squeezed his eyes closed, putting direct pressure on the bridge of his nose. Griggs, Cass Williams, and both of the Stornels had called to tell him that Joe Thackery was gone. The Bayshore place again! There was something in the pit of his stomach and flitting on the edge of his mind. It started when he was driving his Jeep past the Bayshore property and ever-so-slight tugs of sadness came to him, expanding as he pulled into the dirt road by his aunt's lot and turned off the ignition. This time the sadness came to him in one single, strong impression like a scalding flame. His hands went ice-cold and sweaty.

"OK, OK," he said to the empty Jeep interior. Strong, but was just another feeling and nothing to be scared of, as Pastor Bill had said. *Concentrate.* He was hoping and praying to see or feel a concrete basis for these Bayshore episodes. He needed to follow Pastor Bill's advice. The reason for the drive over here this afternoon was to follow all of these impressions and physical symptoms without anyone connected to the property to interfere...and write everything down.

Nothing bad, shameful, or fatal had happened to him, besides some lost sleep. So he had to be more open and let things flow in or out to keep getting clearer impressions—like the one right now. Nothing more came as Pete sat there. No more concrete information—just sadness of scalding intensity.

Pete looked at his watch. He only had a few more minutes to get to the Griggs' place to see how things were going. He was about to turn the key to the ignition and leave.

Suddenly it came to him like a lightning bolt! These feelings were all from *women*, especially this current one! Pete fumbled for his phone to call Pastor Bill.

The sugar cookies, lemonade and stack of paper cups for the neighborhood kids were ready as Cass started the coffee for her and Nelder. Everything was ready for the first bass specimen burial from Nelder's living room wall. No peanut butter cookies because the Jimiss boy's nut allergies, Cathy Bean couldn't have milk products, the Radley boy was allergic to strawberries and the Press boy had ragweed and pollen troubles. This was the new world of children identifying themselves by their health problems, along with their current interests. Cass considered foreknowledge might be all well and good because Carolyn didn't need to hear about any allergic reactions of visitors, along with everything else.

Nelder welcomed the neighborhood kids over since he'd moved to town. Like Beth, the kids were attracted to the animals he caught and released. Every type of local animal, and a few exotic animals, stayed there before he released them back into the wild. Nelder had proper food and information on what and how much to give each animal as he waited for orders to relocate them in the natural forest areas or to the state park - farther away from people. On occasion, the animal was banded and tracked for scientific wildlife research. He got his instructions from the authorities or academics. Other times, and thank goodness, they weren't often, the animal was ill or injured, requiring veterinary care before being released or euthanized.

There was a knock on the screen door. "Can I come in?" Cass looked at the door to see Pastor Allred.

"Why, hello pastor," Cass began as she welcomed him. "Nelder's in the woods."

"You've just come in time, like a real gift from heaven," Beth exclaimed. Pete was a bit startled and turned questioning eyes to Cass.

"I just came by to see if you all were doing well," Pete started, trying to hide the fact he knew about Thackery and wanted to know how Beth was reacting. "People told me Ms. Reynolds and the rest of your family are out of town."

"Well, pastor. You might as well know Beth has the idea to bury as many of these poor stuffed animals on the walls as Nelder allows—one at a time," Cass informed him in verbal shorthand, grateful he had come to check up on them.

"You have to help us give the fish a proper burial, since you're here," Bradley Jimiss exclaimed, bursting through the screen door with several of his friends.

"I…I," Pete stammered, not knowing quite what to say.

"You don't mean you're not going to help. You being a pastor and all!" Kenny Radley exclaimed. Pete had never officiated at an animal funeral, let alone a stuffed animal funeral. But as he knew from his infancy, some people respected animal life, just as much as they respected human life. It was an extreme stance, but people loved their animals, whether pets or in the wild. In Pete's own case, he'd left all his father's long-ago ill feelings and the shouting about animal habitats, saving the rainforest and other ecological fights behind him, to see what he could do for the people around him instead. But…after all, this animal had been alive. They just didn't know how long ago.

"I'll help in this one, but you pay attention so you can do the future services yourself. OK?" Pete wanted to make it clear; this coincidence was not going to be his ongoing ministry. "What were you going to do without me?"

"I looked up something on the Internet about how the bass lives and breeds. I was going to talk about its life, read some Bible verses, and say a prayer," Beth said, looking at her notes.

"That sounds fine," Pete said. "Shall we try to sing a song or a hymn?"

"Nice," Beth said, smiling, trying to think of something to sing. "Can you think of anything more?" There was a knock on the door.

"Please come in," Beth said, opening the screen door. Cathy Bean and Emma Fellows walked in. "You know Pastor Allred and Miss Cass, don't you?"

"You got the pastor?" Emma Fellows said, with surprised owl eyes.

"We'd better get started," Beth concluded, heading down the hall to the living room. "I've got my part of the service on some paper, and I'll go get the poor bass."

Cass whispered to Pastor Allred, "She's been through a lot, Pastor, and just she adores animals." She took a breath and added succinctly, "Her friend Joe left with only a note this morning, and we're trying to keep things settled here while everyone else is away. Thanks for being so understanding about this."

Nan Stornel answered the registration phone. "Two Cups of Tea Bed and Breakfast, how may I help you?"

Detective Drake had chased down this number through the Allied Brands corporate offices, wanting to know if Carolyn Reynolds, whose mother was named in one of the group of Lucas Crandall's last cold case effort, might have some information regarding his death. They'd come up with nothing so far and this lead was about the last one to consider before the Crandall homicide hit the inactive case file. "I'm looking for Carolyn Reynolds."

"I'm sorry but we don't give any information regarding guests here," Nan replied.

As Drake was about to tell this woman that he was inquiring about an official police investigation, he was interrupted by his partner, Andersen. "Lead on the Lauson investigation, line two."

"Thank you. I'll get back to you," Drake said as he hung up. The active Lauson case was making headway, the months' old Crandall case was not. He'd call back later.

CHAPTER THIRTEEN

Molina knocked softly on the kitchen door. At least Beth thought it was a knock on the door, still thinking about the twenty-pound bass they'd buried two days before. The poor fish's mouth gaped; glued open for who knew how many years. His beady, glass-eyed stare came from what looked more like a cold dead marble rather than anything resembling a real eye. They were going to bury a smaller bass plaque today.

Beth looked around again. With her time on the streets, Beth relied on her sense of hearing to avoid being surprised or cornered by predatory men. People who saw her in town called her "fresh-faced" with her peach-hued, creamy skin, a straight-toothed white smile, and doe-colored hair and eyes. Beth thought she looked plain and wanted to keep it that way, trying to avoid unwanted attention. Her fingers placed her shoulder-length hair on the right side of her face behind her ear, listening again. Another gentle knock sounded, so Beth looked through the ecru lace door curtain to see the pensive, quiet face of David Molina, who they all called 'Molina', one of the construction owners Carolyn had hired to work on the Bayshore house. *Isn't he supposed to be working on the barn to get Carolyn's aunt's things a storage place?*

Robin Lee! Beth tried to see the famous aunt's features or mannerisms in her niece Carolyn. The movie star on the forty-foot scene was so full of life, voluptuous in both her figure and her attitude. *Who would have known?*

There had been one time when Carolyn looked down at Grace Ann sleeping in the crib at the rented room at the Two Cups of Tea. In her relaxed profile, Beth thought she saw the same look of peace in Carolyn's face, which matched her famous aunt's expression when Robin Lee's movie character decided to keep her child. In the film, even though Robin's no-good husband, who Robin's character shouldn't have married in the first place, and his second wife were scheming to get the child and lying about Robin's character every chance they got. But the truth won out, and the toddler stayed with Robin. It was a two-handkerchief chick flick.

Beth had watched the film, as she planned to run away from her foster home, because a brother of the couple where she was assigned to had tried to grope her a second time. She decided she wasn't going to be touched improperly or be raped ever again!

When she'd told the husband at that foster placement, he had taken offense and given her a backhanded whack. During that Robin Lee film, Beth thought about the situation, cleared her mind, and decided to leave. Beth thought she was lucky, because with the marks on her face, she was back at the temporary shelter before nightfall.

Now that part of her life was over. She'd gotten out and away. But she was still worried about Joe. Joe was decent to her, and she could protect him with her brain power while he protected her with the threat of his brawn. There was nothing like love between them—just the mutual benefit of each other's strengths.

Beth thought Joe might stay here and make a place for himself. Joe's leaving without talking to her indicated he didn't have much sense, or sentiment, at all. Time would tell. Beth wished him the best, and Carolyn and her aunts said they'd try to find him. Beth hoped he'd come back, and she shrugged her thoughts away as she called for Cass as she opened the door. "Aunt Cass, Mr. Molina's at the door." She congratulated herself, remembering to be polite and use the name "Mister" as well as using the term "aunt" when speaking about the women involved in giving Grace Ann a home.

Beth didn't know Molina at all…and it seemed strange calling someone only a few years older than she was "Mr. Molina," but he was one of the owners of the construction company. Beth couldn't imagine why he was at the front door of Nelder's house. She just saw his solemn face and neon-carrot-red-streaked hair through the filmy ecru curtains shirred on the window.

"Mr. Molina?" Cass inquired, taking off her canvas apron as she walked from the front parlor.

"It's Mr. Molina from the construction company," Beth repeated as she stepped away from the door and let Aunt Cass take over. Cass started to release the old chain latch before she turned the deadbolt lock on the door.

Beth remembered she'd heard Molina was near mute, and she might have to guess what he wanted, although his face was quite expressive. Beth hadn't had any difficulty in communicating with him the one or two times they'd come in contact at the barn. She hoped she'd be able to understand him now, starting with a rush. "Aunt Carolyn's not here," Beth said. The broad-shouldered young man shook his head and brought a bouquet of spring flowers he'd been holding in his hand up to viewing level. "You're bringing us flowers?"

Molina's lips firmed. His eyebrows creased over black-amber eyes. "Yes." His body moved slowly, taking a few steps over the threshold while looking for his unknown target, his eyes darting over the walls and surfaces in the room. Unafraid of the large silent man looking to be in his mid-twenties, Beth and Cass turned to look at his intent face and the path of his vision. A few seconds seemed to take longer as they tried to understand what Molina wanted. His face relaxed and, using the bouquet as a pointer, he indicated the fish plaque on the freshly pressed dining room tablecloth between the silver candlesticks. "For the fish," was all Molina said.

"Are you here for the burial?" Beth asked.

Molina nodded this time and gave a thin, sad smile, his eyes flashing in the affirmative as he slowly nodded once more.

"You can talk here," Beth said bluntly.

Molina handed the flowers to Cass, drawing his hand up in a wide expanse, gesturing to include all the muslin-covered heads and plaques on the three walls. Beth's face turned sad as she shook her head. "Tragic, isn't it?" She sighed audibly. "We'll do one or two a week until they're all safe and buried. Aunt Cass says we can make this like the old tradition of Irish wakes."

"Two?" Molina repeated.

"You've got enough here for quite a while, Beth...and I don't know about the winter," Cass remarked with a warning.

Molina lifted his brows at that, heading to the pine panel wall. There was a distinct difference between the color of the wood-paneled wall where the former plaques had been and lighter overall wall color. Molina ran his fingers over the missing plaque pattern.

"Besides taking the nails out of the walls, we haven't figured out what to do about the marks," Cass informed, forgetting about the ceremony in order to talk to their visitor.

"Needs blended shellac." Molina looked at his watch.

"You can tell Nelder," Cass replied. "We should be starting in about ten minutes. Several other children and teens volunteered to help."

"We've already made some lemonade. Would you like a glass?" Beth asked.

Molina gave another slight smile and headed toward the kitchen, stopped, and beckoned both ladies with his arm to precede him in a courtly manner.

Bradley Jimiss and Kenny Radley came bounding through the back door after only a split-second cursory knock. "Guess who we found?" With that, Pastor Allred came through the door. "Is he coming for the funeral too?"

"Didn't you say you'd only do one funeral?" Katy Dell observed as she made her way to the kitchen table to get a sugar cookie, but then stopped talking because, for once, she remembered her mother saying it was impolite to talk with her mouth full. Katy wanted to tell her mother later that she'd made a good impression in front of the pastor.

"I stopped to schedule Mr. Griggs's services for inspecting the church attic, but I see there's another burial today," Pete remarked with a rueful smile, assessing what he'd heard around the neighborhood: that more people were excited about the burying of Nelder's inherited taxidermy collection.

Katy chewed and swallowed swiftly so she could make this overheard observation with a clean mouth. "I remember Mrs. Smythe saying that one summer Sunday, the scratching and chawing of a nest of birds in the eaves ''bout drowned out the last preacher's sermon.'"

"That would be a problem," Pete observed, seeing Beth, Cass Williams, and Molina standing in the area between the kitchen door and the dining room as well as the young members of the Jimiss, Dell, and Radley families.

"Nelder, err, Mr. Griggs, is over getting some possums out of a barn," Cass said, reminding the younger participants to mind their manners with using people's full names and getting themselves settled down for the ceremony. She ushered the pastor to the window to see the makeshift ceremonial space in the wooded section of the property beyond the grass.

"Today, it's another bass plaque," Beth reminded the assembly. Pete went into the dining room and saw the open-mouthed fish plaque on the tablecloth between the two unlit candles in their silver candlesticks.

"They are God's creatures," Pete replied.

"You a vegetarian, Pastor?" Bradley Jimiss blurted with some skepticism, not wanting to give up his hamburgers and spicy barbecued ribs his father made on their built-in brick grill in their backyard.

"My family and I have always loved animals. I know some people prefer not to eat meat," Pete replied gently. "But I *do* eat meat." Beth looked disappointed. Pete wasn't about to get into any heated arguments, saying a few quick words of prayer for wisdom in this situation. He tried to smile to soften the blow. "As far as I can see, it's a personal and health preference. It seems to me God allows the humane raising and using of animal products." No one knew how long and how hard a time he'd had in coming to these conclusions.

"Seems to be my feeling about things," Bradley said with solemnity beyond his years, wanting to put the fish plaque to eternal rest, yet happy to keep his taste buds ready for his future hamburgers and barbecue, as well as the cookies and lemonade waiting for them after the ceremony.

He could have kicked Cathy Bean when she'd come quietly through the door and into the room. "I'm not so sure about how I feel." Bradley had thought it was all settled, and he scowled at her.

"I've got a few minutes again to help with this if you like, if we can get started now." He let the last nonjudgmental words hang in the air. "I'll be happy to show you the Old Testament and New Testament scriptures having to do with food after we've finished the ceremony," Pete offered, seeing the large Bible on one of the built-in nook shelving units on either side of the long wall in the dining room.

Molina had already headed to the large square box of wooden matches, rasping one against the side to light the candles.

"The words have been said for centuries. The Lord created animals and saved them two by two in the ark with Noah," Pete said as he stood near the center of the dining room table.

Beth took the pastor's signal and said her passages from Genesis and a short prayer about God loving all living things. Molina picked up the bass plaque and headed for the back door. Pete looked at Cass.

Everyone followed the solemn procession with Bradley Jimiss holding the door open for everyone and Paul Dell, who played on his baseball team, following in their wake after grabbing Molina's flowers, taking care not to slam the door and interrupt the solemn procession.

Molina wondered about his orders from Hesse and why he was here. There was all the work still to do at the Bayshore barn, yet he was supposed to keep a closer eye on Ms. Reynolds's niece and aunt out at the Griggs's property, now closer than his already four-times-a-day surveillance he'd been doing since Shealds had left for LA. Molina guessed it was because the Thackery boy was gone…but he didn't ask.

Molina accepted this new assignment as he watched them and all the other children trail after the preacher in a duck line to the sparsely wooded land in the back of the yard.

In the bigger picture, Molina didn't want to have to leave here if everything went wrong with Shealds. Leave the business. Leave this beautiful seaside area. Go back to prison. Have to start all over again years from now. Interrupt his search for a future and who he was—deep inside. Such things took time, resources, and…watchful silence.

After the lemonade and cookies, Molina nodded his good-byes, offering his handshake to excuse himself to go back to the

Bayshore work. Hesse said they'd need to work most of the night and bunk in the construction trailer, concentrating on finishing the special storage work before Shealds got back in a few days' time. They were pressed between the need to have things done on time for the rental truck to arrive and this new order by Shealds and Samples to watch out for the safety of the Reynolds contingent here in town. Molina shrugged. He'd need to think of a cover story for his presence at the Griggs's home by tomorrow.

Chalking up the experience at his first taxidermy funeral, Pete was relieved his feeling of sadness vanished during the entire mock funeral and time at the Griggs's home. *Women's feelings! What a surprise!* But no matter how hard he tried, he couldn't elicit the reason for the women's soul-deep sadness. Not a whit. He'd just keep investigating and keeping his lists going. But the lists didn't point in any particular direction yet except the Bayshore place. *Past? Present? Future?* Pete would tell Pastor Bill…and keep working.

"Who's in the backyard?" Beth asked, the next morning, as she rubbed the sleep out of her eyes and headed for the smell of coffee in the kitchen. As she parted the lace café curtains Cass had washed and ironed the second day they were at the Griggs's house, she hopefully asked, "Is it Joe?" Beth guessed her sleep-mussed mind was hoping to have closure with her friend's sudden departure. Joe was not a morning person, she now remembered. If the sun was still low in the cool sky, Joe was in bed. Cass lifted a glass of orange juice in her direction.

"No," Cass said flatly, still waking up too, even though the coffee was made. She'd already tramped through the dew-covered grass and identified the person working in the wooded field beyond the backyard grass. It was Molina—the one and same surprise mourner at the burial of the stuffed bass yesterday afternoon.

Cass tried to look casual and nonchalant as she investigated. She shaded her eyes against the brightening sun. The neon-headed man, Cass noted, busied himself setting up a portable worktable with an array of long-handled tools, each with a different-size curved head. In front of him was a sandpapered wood oval. Cass looked again. No, the shape was more like the elongated oval shape reminiscent of the silver-chained wine bottle medallions she's gotten as a gift—somewhere in limbo-storage waiting for her new home here.

"An art project?" Cass asked. If her memory served her, specific questions would be the best way to get information.

Molina already knew by her steps: it was Cass Williams. Beth Seavers had lighter, colt-like strides, and sometimes a tendency to intermittently hop when she was pleased or agitated. The older woman's steps were unhurried and casual as he listened to the cadence and sound of her weight pressing the grass under her rubber-soled boat shoes. He didn't look up at first, pretending to be engrossed in his activity. Her face was relaxed in questioning interest. *All the better,* he thought. If she was hostile, he didn't know how he was going to explain his presence there. He gave her a wide smile.

Molina lifted his head as his flaming hair caught the sunlight. He'd drawn a small sketch of a bass in open-mouthed flight and in profile above what seemed to be lake water—the same size as the marked round space on the plaque. He handed it to Cass and watched her scan his plaque and wood-carving tools, hoping she'd be able to see he was going to carve a plaque, as it were, for the taxidermy specimens as Beth buried them. These could replace the specimen plaques on the wall and hide the shellac mars until the walls were bare and he could repaint the rooms. Best to have everything set up to make it harder for Cass to consider throwing him off the property. *How will I explain things to Shealds and Hesse if I'm not welcome?*

Cass had left without much comment, and he could now hear Beth's quick strides and the return of Cass behind her.

Beth had to run up the stairs and thrown on some clothes, grateful she'd planned ahead last night and knew what she was going to wear.

Beth stopped at her new aunt's side as Cass turned to show her the picture. Cass tried to push her thoughts together. "Molina took pictures of the fish plaques on his phone and is making plagues for Nelder's walls," Cass began, looking alternately into Beth's pale brown eyes and the amber-brown stare of the neon-haired Molina. Molina nodded once, still straddling the work stool he'd brought from the garage. *Stay in a submissive position and keep working.* He set the bottom of the carving tool on the wood and shaved off one piece, and then another, and another, sending each wood shaving scurrying into the light breeze.

"It's a wood carving," Beth noted with delight, now understanding Molina's efforts. "Instead of stone, he's doing it on wood!" Molina was pleased by her enthusiasm. "Are you going to put their names here?" she questioned, pointing to the rest of the space on the wood plaque. Molina nodded at the question, looking at the golden-yellow flecks in her brown eyes sparkle with pleasure. She was happy. Her aunt seemed calm with a slow, normal-appearing breathing pattern, Molina noted. All the better.

"I'll get you some orange juice," Beth said, turning for the house. "If you haven't brought breakfast, we'll get that for you too."

Cass caught her arm before the girl could bolt. "Now, wait a minute." Cass appreciated art, and Molina's project, but there were some things that needed approval. "Molina, you know I'll have to call Hesse on this. Carolyn needs her storage more than Nelder's walls need plaques right now. These specimens have been on the wall for heaven knows how long and can wait. The storage issue can't." She stared down the beginnings of the mutinous light in

Beth's eyes, adding, "When you want to work here, that's fine, but if it gets the barn project's behind schedule, that won't do."

Molina's eyelids closed thankfully but sprung open again to his work as the woman and girl walked quickly back to the Griggs's house. Beth's chatter, alternating between excitement and pleading, for Cass to understand, was only stilled by the banging of the aluminum screen door on its frame. He could keep his watchful eye on the Griggs's place, like he'd been told, with the possible reward of two breakfasts this morning instead of one. Homemade food now eased the memory of hunger he'd known…before he'd met Hesse and Shealds.

The phone rang on his side of the partner desk. Hesse absent-mindedly grabbed the sleek silver cordless receiver on their landline, concentrating instead on Molina's drawing for the redo of the Bayshore mansion's rear porch. They wanted to retain the period style of the home, returning to original shingle-style facade, but still offer more protection from the sun and wind that contemporary homeowners wanted. Molina also added fencing and gates with child-safe locks to all openings, using authentic-looking latch hardware he'd uncovered on the Internet. A nice touch for authenticity and safety, Hesse thought, but they'd have to change the overhang columns. The old columns, done in an ill-conceived earlier redo at some point, looked out of place. He *also hoped* Molina ingratiated himself with the Seavers girl with the same skills he saw in these drawings. "Hesse, here."

"Make sure Molina makes a report as soon as he hits the door," was all Samples's gruff voice said. "Got a lot going on with all of Shealds's requests." There was a loud click, and the phone went dead.

CHAPTER FOURTEEN

Carolyn closed her eyes in gratitude – uncertain and happy at the same time. She thought she'd never say this…but she was glad to leave LA. At last, they were headed back to Bayshore in the rental truck!

"Ms. Reynolds, before we start back to Bayshore, I'm glad you've starting calling me by my first name." Shealds looked at her through his dark glasses.

"And I want to thank you for being such a help at the storage units and through the fire alarm, Shealds. Handling all this is a hand-full and I'm glad to have had your help." She looked back at the comfortable vacationer's van she'd rented, to make the cross-country ride easier for Grace Ann, her aunts, and Darby. She sat in the truck with Shealds now, wanting to be able to help him spot the navigation system instruction landmarks through the maze of interstate interchanges toward the open road. She'd go back in the van with Grace Ann when they got to the rest stop for gas.

Overall, Carolyn knew she should feel better; have a sense of accomplishment. They'd almost gotten everything done in the two allotted weeks with two days tacked on. An extra two days with everyone being too tired to work from staying up till the 4:00 a.m. "all clear" notification from the fire department, in the person of a brawny fireman in boots and jacket, coming to their door for a room audit. "I'm Jackson, and this is Fisher from the Room 393 across the hall. These ladies are from the adjoining rooms—Muriel Porter and Bee Elders, and this is Ms. Carolyn Reynolds and her daughter, Grace Ann." The man had checked off the names on his list and said it was a false alarm. Carolyn didn't know whether to be mad or happy. She decided on happy, considering she didn't want to think of the alternative, what danger they might have faced.

The other lost day she attributed to learning how to pack and catalog everything. Carolyn was pleased that chore was over and they were finally on the road. Hazeltine would come with the costume boxes, which they'd guesstimated for size and space. She hoped the barn space was large enough and met Mr. Hazeltine's exacting expectations.

Thank the Lord, her aunts, Darby, Shealds, and she worked their way through everything under Mr. Hazeltine's tutelage, giving Carolyn some good emotional days and some bad ones. Most of the time, she enjoyed the anecdotes needed to catalog her aunt's things. Others hit too close to the bone. She didn't know why, but she frequently felt on the verge of crying.

On second thought, of course, she knew why. Things reminded her of Billie. Plus, the morning trip to the police station, and the second one, to the private investigators' office, brought no news on her mother's case—another dead end. Then there was the complication of Thackery's leaving, and the stress of wondering if Beth would go chasing after him. The roller coaster of hormones from the breastfeeding attempts and discomfort didn't help either.

Nothing had been too trivial or demeaning as far as jobs were concerned for Shealds, Carolyn noted. In contrast to her earlier concerns, he'd really been a great help.

Carolyn closed her eyes and burning telltale moisture seeped from under her lashes. She became uneasy and embarrassed. Her face flushed, and she slowly raised her arm, trying to wipe the tears away surreptitiously. Thankfully, the third short visit, to the cardiologist, had been uneventful. He was pleased with her progress.

Carolyn frowned, and the tears kept flowing.

Shealds noticed, wondering if he should make some comment. He flexed his hands on the truck's large black steering wheel. His face flushed, feeling a bit of remorse about going through this woman's personal papers. His preconceived notions were bent quite a bit. He'd fed names, addresses, and facts to Samples. Samples reported back the same narrative they already knew: Reynolds was a former owner of a health food company whose mother had been killed in a hit-and-run accident still under investigation by the LAPD. She'd come from humble beginnings with a single mom. Not much more information on Beth Seavers, who Ms. Reynolds masqueraded as her niece, or Joe Thackery. Not a drop of familial blood between them, as Shealds expected. DNA tests indicated Carol Ann was not Beth's child or Thackery's, for that matter. Thackery had hightailed it for now. They'd still try to find his whereabouts.

The Reynolds clan were really nice people…but caring wasn't in the mix right now. Feelings made you sloppy and careless. Too many accidents and too many unknowns. He had to keep things at a level of respect and admiration. But he had to admit Carolyn had been though the ringer.

"You OK?" Shealds rasped, noticing Carolyn trying to swallow her tears.

The question seemed so ridiculous to Carolyn, her heart raced as she started to laugh and couldn't stop. Concern changed Shealds's brown eyes to black, making them look like onyx, the same color Carolyn saw in his eyes on the morning of the false alarm. An odd combination, she thought, while trying to control herself. His head moved to look at the large rearview mirrors. He was going to pull over, Carolyn thought alarmingly. She lifted her hand to his forearm, choking through the waves of laughter as the tears kept falling. "Keep going…I'll…be…fine. Keep going. I get this way sometimes, when my heart starts racing." Shealds' knife-straight brows crinkled in thought, considering her words. "Please…please." His frown would have stopped a charging bull in his tracks. He kept looking over at her as he kept the truck in the slow lane of the interstate. "We need…to go east…at this exit," she wheezed.

At least she was still making sense at this juncture and she wasn't turning blue, Shealds thought. *Is she hyperventilating?* He needed to keep a good look at her in his peripheral vision and feel safe guiding this loaded truck. Besides, the van hugged his bumper, and traffic was thick behind them and to his left. "Too much traffic now to pull over," he spit against clenched teeth, thinking about the safety of the van.

He took a deep breath and looked in the rearview mirror, glad Carolyn seemed at least to be breathing between her waves of fighting the unrestrained glee. He wanted to do something, and tried to think of all his long-ago Red Cross training. "You can't take off your seat belt, but you can bend over a bit, put your head down, and try to ride this out. Lean over and support yourself." Shealds didn't need her flailing around. "Try to concentrate on getting your breathing back to normal. If your fingers start to tingle or get numb, you're breathing too fast. Since you don't want me to pull over, you're going to have to listen to my instructions and cooperate."

Having him talk to her harshly wasn't as surprising as having him talk to her at all, Carolyn thought. Shealds was always serious and businesslike. A short fuse, in times of crisis, if the time when he thought he was saving her life on the Bayshore property was an example or when they'd had the false fire alarm at the hotel. They'd never gotten back to the fact she was capably using the two home fire extinguishers she'd purchased at the local hardware store to put out the fire Joe had set in the studio fireplace. Before they could talk about the incident, Carolyn was embroiled with Grace Ann, the cover story, and more than a little wary of the strength and acumen of this man with a criminal past. For his part, at Bayshore, and here with her Aunt Robin's storage units, Shealds seemed to be content to get his orders, do his work, and keep to himself.

Any answers to polite conversation were monosyllabic but he was always kind. He'd give an opinion when asked. Something hard for a man who was used to giving orders, Carolyn thought. Everything he suggested saved time and money. Hazeltine took credit for Shealds' ideas like a preening peacock, which didn't seem to bother Shealds. He just kept his head down and did what was needed. All in all, Carolyn knew firsthand, Shealds was a capable man. *Wonder if he would ever be husband material?* The idea made her jump a bit at its absurdity and caused her to cough as well as laugh!

"If you pay attention, concentrate on your breathing, and do as you're told, I'll tell you some of the ideas we have in renovating your Bayshore property."

Carolyn nodded, thinking she needed to get her mind off absurd thoughts about Shealds and she'd settle for continued détente through the trip back to Bayshore.

Carolyn was jarred awake by the truck turning a corner. She seemed to claw at the air. *Is Grace Ann safe?* A steadying hand gently caught, and then, brought down her forearm. "Just stopping for gas," Shealds's voice whispered. "You're OK now."

"Where are we?" Carolyn asked urgently, forcing herself awake, trying to sound more in control than she felt. She'd been dreaming of a wetlands meadow with dragonflies. The sun hit their wings and radiated a rainbow light, but now her eyes focused on an oversize corrugated sunshield over the pumping stations at the truck stop. Their truck looked like a dwarf next to the eighteen-wheelers rumbling in and out of the line of bays.

"The van's over getting gas at the roadside section of this place. Grace Ann is fed, diaper's changed, and she's sleeping in her stroller in the air-conditioned diner. I'll be along in a bit for lunch. Darby's got us a table and ordered you an ice tea," Shealds said matter-of-factly as he stepped up on the fender step to wash the windows. "Like I said, I'll be there in a few minutes." He turned his head back to his job. Carolyn felt disoriented as she looked around, seeing the gas pumps and the tall, bright yellow sign with the arrow underneath indicating the soldier line of plate glass windows, which must be the diner. Carolyn watched her step, dwarfed by the colorful cabs and silver trailers emblazoned with carrier advertising.

Carolyn's cheeks turned scarlet at the thoughts of what had transpired before they'd rolled into the truck stop. She'd had a heart episode, something she despised and something even more hateful with uninformed witnesses! She'd hoped all the confusing and bottled-up emotions assailing her were gone for good. Would this affect the business relationship she had with Shealds and his two partners? Perhaps she should consider cutting her ties with the construction company. Carolyn didn't need more complications.

"Guess I…" *Why do I sound so lame?*

"Probably the strain of the baby and all the work that got done." Shealds tried to sound supportive, but he was in the role of employee. With the packing and the unsuccessful trips to the police and the private investigators, Samples had outlined in his last report before they headed back to Bayshore, Shealds could understand Carolyn's reactions – fatigue, sadness and stress. Samples was getting more detailed medical records, and Shealds would have that report soon.

"That must be it," Carolyn half said and half whispered as she bolted for the diner.

Shealds concentrated on the tank nozzle and returned to filling the fuel tank. One thing he'd have to say, he admired Carolyn and her getting *through it all.*

Carolyn enjoyed her soup and grilled cheese sandwich, although she was concerned about missing her breastfeeding with Grace Ann…and her episode in the truck. "Did the truckers say anything about the weather…Shealds?"

Shealds was taking a long drink from his ice water and tried not to take note of Carolyn's uncharacteristic sheepishness. "Yeah, clear weather, unseasonably warm, really, through Gallup." His expression softened a bit. "You're OK."

Carolyn's brows came together. *I trust and hope Shealds is right!*

Shealds saw her at her worse and didn't panic. *Were his eyes and manner now indicating that he understood?*

Darby sat in the truck on this leg of the trip. Shealds hoped starting a conversation about Robin Lee would also get him some information about the extended Reynolds family. Knowing Carolyn's past history and stresses made this all the more imperative for Shealds. Darby talked expansively about everything concerning Robin Lee and her career. Darby corroborated what Shealds already knew. Carolyn's mother, Billie, Robin Lee's younger sister, died in a hit-and-run accident in LA about four years ago. "Those ladies seemed really close and concerned for one another." Even though a small headache was expanding behind his eyes, Shealds hoped this open-ended observation would get Darby to talk more. He needed to pay attention.

"Muriel, Bee, and Cass, who's back with Beth, have been close since they were young, I think," Darby offered.

"So they met in school?" Shealds asked trying to get some concrete facts, names, and places.

Darby looked thoughtful, knowing Billie was private about the past. "I think they've been close for many years." He nervously repositioned himself. "Mind if I get some shut-eye?" Shealds didn't bother to look at the small khaki-suited man. It seemed unusual the man would want to sleep. He hadn't stopped talking since they flew to LA. Shealds shrugged, willing to bet this might be an evasive tactic, but he couldn't press things unnecessarily. He just had to hope there would be other opportunities to talk. He'd set the groundwork slowly to gain trust and access. He'd continue to be both careful and watchful...and wait.

"Maybe just passing the time," Muriel noted as she lifted her baby great-niece's bottom for the fresh diaper. "Asking a lot of questions again."

Carolyn was putting away the breastfeeding apparatus, looking thoughtful as she handed Grace Ann's clean pants to her aunt and put the baby wipes away.

Muriel smiled as Grace Ann cooed. "Just trying to be friendly, you think, since we've been together for over two weeks?"

"Don't know," Carolyn replied, not wanting to alarm her aunt. *Was Shealds trying to find out about her health issues? Something else?* They were free to talk in the motel room. Shealds and Darby were off getting the truck and van gassed for their early morning departure.

"Right easy on the eyes," Bee observed in an ironic tone.

"Don't get your hormones twitching, Bee dear," Muriel warned with a wry smile, although she, too, had noticed Shealds's masculine appeal. *Had Carolyn? What about his history?*

"We may be in our middle years, Muriel," Bee replied, "but it doesn't mean we can't enjoy the scenery."

"He's got such nice eyes. Don't like his wearing those sunglasses all the time—makes him look like a biker or a robot with his gray hair." Muriel kept smiling at Grace Ann, trying to keep her tone from becoming more wary. Babies picked up on tonal changes. "Don't you think, Carolyn?"

"He's got good qualities," Carolyn replied evasively. "I just want to be careful about *everything*," steering the conversation back to the specific, back to the informational considerations and away from gender issues...or his felonious past. She remembered thinking about Shealds as marriage material...and her neck flushed. "I'm not proud of it, but I might as well tell you, so we will be ready if it comes up to bite us." She stopped for a moment. "I...I had a bit of a heart episode in front of Shealds...in the truck."

Both older ladies looked at each other before Bee remarked, running her lavender-flowered voile-clad blouse material through her fingers. "With all the pressure of late, it's understandable."

Muriel nodded too. "Just put it in context, and it's nothing more than a blip on the screen of life."

"Shealds might be doing all the work on our house and the other homes on the property for that matter," Carolyn remarked. "Anybody who's going to do the work is going to have to know many things, not extremely *personal things*, but many things about us, our preferences...and he'll be working in such close proximity to us all."

Bee heard her niece's words and kept distractedly fingering the sleeve hem.

"He didn't seem to be star struck with Robin Lee's things," Muriel observed. "Don't think there's trouble in that direction."

"He was very helpful during the fire scare in LA...and when Joe set the fire back on Bayshore," Bee added.

By this time, Carolyn was biting her lip. Both her aunts had seen this expression on their niece's face since she was a youngster. *Carolyn needed to talk things out.*

"I don't know what to say." Carolyn knew this was silly, yet she couldn't shake the feeling. *Thinking about Shealds made her nervous. Because he knows too much?* She pictured Shealds in her mind. There was the angular gray-haired head on a strong, square skull and, sometimes, a jutting chin when he was angry. His lips were generous and not thinned by what seemed to be his continual silence and displeasure with the world in general. His brow was prominent, and he had an angular nose. His nostrils flared as well when he couldn't express his anger, if she had been accurate in her observations. He was tall and muscular and...there was a scar on his jaw. She didn't want to know where he'd gotten it, but she guessed it wasn't from *this side* of prison bars.

"He does look like some of those biker rock stars," Bee said. "Perhaps the one from Wales who got all the press last October for wading in that fountain in NYC?"

"Perhaps," Carolyn thought aloud, as she mentally added looking up the singer's picture on the Internet when she had time.

Carolyn thought she could get past the fact Shealds and his partners were ex-cons – emphasis on the "ex". The three partners slowly built their fledgling company in the community. Their work was excellent, and they paid their bills on time. Kept to themselves, it seemed, which was understandable, since Ed said they worked seven days a week, except for church attendance. Billie had always said not to trust a man who couldn't be respectful to Sunday worship and clergy. Pastor Allred as their pastor *and* counselor, remained decisive and strong in his post-incarceration approval of the men...and he'd vouched for them all.

"They were at church since we've been at the Bayshore place," Bee noted, not knowing Carolyn was now thinking about Pastor Allred's endorsement.

If there was one thing sure in her life of changeable things, it was that Billie had taken them to church almost every Sunday of their lives together—unless she or Carolyn had been sick.

Carolyn still felt uneasy, and it wasn't because some social work-er might by some astronomical chance go to the construction site and Shealds might spill the beans about her hyperventilation epi-sode. Something else nagged at her.

Carolyn couldn't afford to make any more mistakes. She was trying to be a mother to Grace Ann and be responsible for Beth and the new track in her life. *Shealds has always been respectful but is he too close now? Or rather, am I too close to him?*

CHAPTER FIFTEEN

Shealds took a deep breath. What he knew about the Reynolds family and their activities was mundane chatter, nothing to appease his need for gritty information that might be behind the two incidents in the construction yard, the sawn tree or the barn beams or anything to do with the false fire alarm. So far, the Reynolds family had been like rocks in not disclosing personal information. *Is someone in the Reynolds clan helping Zaugus, or is the Reynolds clan now in danger because of his efforts to clear his name?* He'd try to find out *again* now that Ms. Reynolds was riding in the truck with him.

Carolyn had been silent for the first few minutes after making sure Grace Ann was belted in the van and relaying GPS instructions for the morning's phase of the trip to her aunts and Darby. "Those slate rocks remind me of the stone in front of your house," Shealds began, almost wincing at how false this observation sounded, given the fact the rock they were looking at was wren-dull; nothing like the color of the Bayshore stone and slate.

"Oh?" Carolyn said, trying to see what Shealds referred to. She thought she could count the words he'd said to her on two hands, aside from the ones during and after her heart episode, since they'd left LA. "You'd like to suggest something?"

Shealds replied, "As I've said, we always like plenty of input from our clients about their likes and dislikes. Less guesswork." Again, Shealds winced. Talking had been so easy for him once. Now the words came out like pained swipes of a rusty blade.

"Tell me about the house plans," Carolyn said.

Shealds's brow wrinkled. Perhaps he was getting somewhere. *How else will I be able to tell Samples yet again I've got nothing useful to report?* Best talk a bit and get the conversation redirected.

"Did you see the big gourmet kitchen drawing with the appliance specs I e-mailed?" Carolyn asked.

Shealds made sure the road ahead was clear and turned to give Carolyn a quick look inviting her to talk. "All top-grade professional chef's kitchen equipment—on the north side of your first floor." Shealds couldn't close his eyes, but he could imagine a spacious cherry wood or white Shaker cupboard space with a fireplace down a bit, several comfortable seating areas on the opposite side of the counter, and a mix of cozy and bright spaces with a rustic chandelier or a spaced cluster of individual hanging lights in the middle of each of the two large kitchen islands. Expansive enough for multiple work spaces, lavish buffet dinners, or family dinners indicative of pictures in glossy magazines—not like any in his recent past. Shealds shook his head, willing useless thoughts from his imprisonment to evaporate.

He conjured up colors and construction ideas in his mind. A few couches with overstuffed chairs in front of the floor-to-ceiling stone-clad fireplace with two walking paths from the kitchen to the expansive, casual living space, looking out on an uninterrupted estuary view to the east through a span of several sets of ten-foot slider panels. On the opposite end of the seating area, set apart by a beefy sofa table in the corner next to the kitchen, would be a large banquette with a heavy, custom-made barn board and iron rectangular table with benches and chairs. There'd also be room for another seating area with four chairs and a low, large rectangular, almost dining-size table with a sofa depth cushioned love seat, recessed in the wall. Behind the kitchen would be a pantry, large bathroom, the laundry and a crafts room leading to the garden and garages with a state-of-the-art private home office with views of the woods.

"Ours seems like a group home of sorts," Carolyn said as she thought of all the tastes and people needed to be housed there." Cass and Beth want space out by the barn, nearest the gardens, I think, and Muriel and Bee would live in the main house. I don't know what we'll do with Darby yet, but I'm thinking of the barn area for his space, as well, since he's so tied to Aunt Robin's things. I haven't even asked what his plans are. He's rather a vagabond with all the bygone celebrity conventions he attends and his textile work." Carolyn considered her ideas. "To keep the feel of the house authentic, we'd probably have enough room with the addition you've proposed, reminiscent of the former servant's structure—as you indicated in your set of plans."

"Seems like you've done this before," Shealds ventured, hopeful she might stay in the truck cab for a while, so he could get some answers.

"No, not really," Carolyn replied. "A bit of remodeling for an LA house I just sold and some interior design for personal and business spaces." No space would be needed for her mother, she thought. It made her heart ache and her stomach hurt. A sad flush stained her face.

A look like a cloud came over Carolyn's face, Shealds noticed, but he didn't want to lose momentum. He took another hasty glance. "Should we talk more about the barn or do you want to stop?" *You fool! How can you get her to talk with giving her permission to stop!*

Carolyn gave a weary sigh; her thoughts were now drawn to her mother and the failed attempts to find her still-at-large assailant. She forced herself to return to the conversation at hand. She picked up a pad. "Keep your eyes on the road, please. You'll be able to look at these thoroughly during our stopovers, or we can discuss them later when we get back to Bayshore." She quickly drew an overhead line drawing the shape of the current barn structure and added a two-story front porch area. "I was thinking of a big second-floor porch on the front facade several feet above the barn doors on the front wall with living quarters in the loft expanse. Perhaps, there could be some usable space over the artifacts storage. We also might keep some horses, a few for riding, perhaps some miniature ones or small donkeys. I'm not sure yet.

"We'll be in our modular cottages soon, so we don't have to rush any decisions." She bit her lip and continued drawing. Carolyn flipped the page on the pad. "For the main house, I'd like to maintain the integrity of the current structure with second-floor bedrooms for Grace Ann and me with two bathrooms. I'd like one big room facing inland with a deep window seat and storage and a smaller bedroom facing the water." Carolyn drew some more intersecting lines. "I'm thinking of a life-size, two-story playhouse on the second floor into the attic and a crawl space large enough for adults so Grace Ann and I can have a play area, year-round, and a tunnel between our bedrooms that can be converted to storage after she's grown."

Shealds continued to look at the road with a few short glimpses at the paper. Most people were ill equipped to do space planning. They always overestimated the amount of space they had. "The playhouse sounds interesting," Shealds had to admit. "So you want the big bedroom facing the land, and your daughter will get the small bedroom."

"Oh, no," Carolyn replied. "Grace Ann gets the big bedroom, and the playhouse space will be behind a large floor area. Where else will she be able to have sleepovers and tea parties?" Carolyn looked at Shealds with a laughing smile. "Needs plenty of room!"

Wasn't that a surprise! Shealds felt sure the woman was going to occupy the larger space. He swallowed his shock. He shouldn't care what she wanted. He was there to build whatever she wanted as a cover for his plans against Zaugus. *Now, I'm getting emotionally involved. Back off or I'll mess things up!*

"I want to make sure everything is child-safe in Grace Ann's bathroom until she's older. Bathroom accidents are a leading cause of injuries for children." Carolyn started drawing again. "Hope there's enough room for a small fireplace and a window seat in my room," she said with shining eyes. "Just tell me if I'm going overboard."

Another surprise, Shealds thought silently. Clients with her kind of money were usually telling him to fit things in no matter what! This woman was different.

"Grace Ann and my rooms will be over the kitchen and family room area, so I want extra sound-proofing and...could we have a pull down staircase encased in the new back porch so we can get up to our rooms from our terrace?" Carolyn asked. "But I don't want a permanent staircase blocking the landscape and garden views from the kitchen."

"You mean like a Murphy bed or pull-down attic-type staircase?" Shealds asked, wondering if he could provide such a convenience and retain the views and porch aesthetic. He'd loathe it if it made the exterior look like a tenement building fire escape! He tamped down his misgivings. "Perhaps a small spiral staircase with a child-safe gate might be an option."

Better have her put all this down on a list...and agree with everything just to keep her talking. Perhaps he'd try throwing out some of the ideas about his modifications to a personal plan he'd had for Hesse's and Molina's place when he'd hoped the

Bayshore house would be theirs. "Would you want a game room in the addition?"

Suddenly a large bang jolted the truck, forcing Carolyn painfully forward against the seat belt strap, followed by a hard swerve to the left. A small gust of fear sprang from her throat. Her hands grabbed the dashboard to steady herself, while hearing the squeal of the truck brakes, and turning concerned, questioning eyes to Shealds, who was engrossed in avoiding an accident as the truck drunkenly swerved on the pavement.

Carolyn knew nothing about Shealds' driving skills, except he'd managed well so far. His white-knuckle grip on the truck's steering wheel was the same color of his lips, which were pulled over gritted teeth while wrestling to slow down the loaded truck on what Carolyn surmised was one less tire. The truck decelerated, cutting a path toward the interstate shoulder as it slowed to a stop. Carolyn sat for a moment, realizing she needed to breathe again.

"We're OK." Shealds looked to see where the rest of their party was and was glad he'd taken those high-speed Formula One driving classes, as a lark, years ago. "How's your heart doing?" Carolyn nodded that she was OK. "The van's behind us. Watch yourself and head for the grass while I call for help."

"Please. Please. Before you do, can you hand me the tissues? Carolyn asked.

Shealds grabbed Carolyn's arms to look for blood.

"No. No," she said trying to hide the telltale signs of wetness that might be on her white cotton blouse. "It's not blood," she said still shaking from the accident, yet feeling somehow joyful and relieved. He deserved some explanation. "I've got to get to the van, Mr. Jackson. My breast milk has soiled my blouse."

Breast milk! Shealds knew next to nothing about breast milk. *Did that mean she was injured?* And she was calling him, "Mr. Jackson" again. *Great.* All his brownie points would be gone. *Back to square one and I don't like her not calling me Shealds!*

"Well, a good thing and a bad thing as Cass would say, if she were here," Muriel mused as she put Carolyn's soiled blouse and bra in a separate plastic bag and into their travel dirty clothes container. "You've got breast milk, but we'll be delayed with the flat tire." Carolyn ignored the sounds of the tow truck's arrival.

Muriel stayed in the van with Carolyn and Grace Ann, who was blissfully unaware her new mother and the truck driver, Shealds Jackson, had luckily avoided any injury in the blown-tire incident, or that she was now breastfeeding—for real.

"I'll be able to look back at this incident with thanksgiving to the Lord for safety and some fondness," Carolyn agreed. "I want to get as much milk supply as possible."

"Do you want some formula poured into the sacks and tubing?" Muriel asked, looking at her niece and grandniece. Each of the aunts had become as adept as Carolyn in filling the neck halter plastic bags delivering the formula Carolyn alternately held to her breasts. Carolyn nodded as she smiled, feeling the physical release of the beginnings of her own breast milk supply. Carolyn couldn't even put the peaceful euphoria of this into words as she tenderly cuddled Grace Ann to herself and gently stroked her infant's cheek, hair, and ear with her other hand. She began to rock slowly back and forth with joy.

After a time, Carolyn thought Grace Ann needed the formula, so Muriel helped her put the plastic bags on each side of her neck.

When they finished, Carolyn shifted Grace Ann to her car seat, straightened her clean clothes, put on the restraint device, and they both fell asleep.

Everyone looked at the shredded rubber and the braking marks on the pavement.

"Lucky thing, young man," Darby said with the more-pronounced southern accent he had when he was under stress. He thumped Shealds's shoulder.

Shealds remembered noticing Carolyn hunching over and mumbling she wanted to go to the van to hold Grace Ann. Shealds had enough to do here and didn't want to chase her. It would be some time before his adrenaline rush died down. His thoughts were interrupted by an oversize wrecker stopping in front of them.

"Highway patrol sent us. See you've got a flat," the driver said unnecessarily. "Anything else?"

Shealds shook his head. Another man came out of the car cab and tapped Shealds on the shoulder, bidding him to follow him with a clipboard. "I'm not the renter."

"Doesn't matter, bud," the man said, looking around. "Just need some information from the glove box on this rental, and you're all set."

Shealds shrugged and got the rental papers as instructed. The man looked at the papers and said, "Keep looking at me and nod a few times. Samples had us follow you and we've rented the tow truck." Shealds's neck drew up reflexively. "Better keep it normal. Good thing you had a high performance driver's training class seven years ago."

Shealds tried to keep his startled reaction hidden under in context of running his palm up and down his jaw. "What do you want?"

"Have they said anything of interest, Mr. Jackson?" the man inquired in a bland voice, never looking up while writing the information down on the wrecker slip.

"Nothing," Shealds replied. "How do I know you're for real?"

"I'm as real as that tampered-with tire, Mr. Jackson," the blue jump-suited man said as he walked away from the truck. "Inside sidewall looks slit near the rim—real professional like. We've already called Samples."

"Can I call Hesse?" Shealds asked, feeling his throat tighten.

"We'll do that, Mr. Jackson," the wrecker said. The man turned back to the wrecker, hiked himself into the cab with ease, and appeared to be finishing his paperwork as if working with broken-down trucks was part of his everyday life. "The fire at the hotel was a botched arson attempt near your rooms that burned out before it could cause any damage—not a false alarm." The man wrote down a few words. "Needless to say, someone will be following you all the way back to Bayshore."

The blown truck tire had a silver lining, Bee mused as she glanced to make sure Carolyn was sleeping. "She's got the look back."

"Yeah," Muriel replied, tapping the last drops of gasoline from the spout before replacing it in the pump holder, noting the price and checking the paper receipt. "Her eyes *are* different...and serene as she was nursing Grace Ann. Like she's living again, not just working...and existing. Successful backs of steel!" Bee lifted an eyebrow as Muriel got back in the van and Bee eased the vehicle onto the roadway. "It's like the time she was starting Four Almonds. Measuring all the ingredients and packaging the bars. Her enthusiasm's back too, as if *all* the lights in her brain are on again."

It might be silly, but both ladies knew they had good intuition, especially since they'd known Carolyn, from the minute she was born. Billie had called that look "seeing the sunlight"—when the darkness was lifted, and a clearer path was in sight.

"I haven't taken an unconcerned breath for years," Bee said. "I hope we're right."

"A few prayers in the matter wouldn't hurt anything either." Muriel sent up another short prayer and straightened in her seat.

After the accident with Carolyn in the truck during the blowout, he and Samples had scratched her from the list of possible Zaugus conspirators. Her aunts wouldn't want her to be harmed, so they were out as suspects, too. That just left Darby. So now, the information gathering changed drastically to protect him *and the*

Reynolds' clan. Whoever wanted to hurt them was willing to undertake drastic measures!

The evening of the blowout, Shealds was tense. Carolyn stayed in the motel room and had her dinner sent to her room. If Carolyn didn't get back in the truck because of the mishap, Shealds wouldn't have blamed her. But to his surprise, Carolyn was back in his passenger seat the next day.

"I hope you can drive the truck and talk construction again," Carolyn began the next morning. "It will be easier to finally decide what to do concerning the Bayshore project if you can. We were interrupted when you said you had some ideas." Perhaps losing the Bayshore house was why Shealds had been so silent and brooding about the work, she surmised. Carolyn knew about grief and losses. "I don't think you'd gotten started."

Shealds had thought hard about it last night. Parrying her verbal thrust, he took a breath and replied tentatively, "I've also been thinking about telling you about our other work. It might give you some more ideas. The slate roof you mentioned might require extra trusses. You also might need measurements for antique furniture niches and other special art placements you might be considering. Do you have any pieces you'd like to place that way? Any interests or hobbies we need to be aware of? You need to feel comfortable telling us more about what you want for the Bayshore place or it might mean expensive changes later."

"I can give you some rough ideas," Carolyn offered, "but on your part, I'm also interested in finding out about the other two property schemes as well."

"Oh," Shealds replied, thrown by the word "schemes" and ignoring her wanting more information about the other two lots. Carolyn's face seemed interested and friendly. She mustn't mean anything about the *real* plans he was undertaking, just what his company was planning for their one subdivided lot above her property and Pastor Allred's on the other. *Changing the pieces on the chessboard now! Concentrate on Darby!*

"In speaking about rooms, we don't like surprises, so we measure everything out with chalk biodegradable spray paint and cardboard or plywood mockups depending on the size of the project. We used chalk for the construction trailer, and we'd use that or the biodegradable paint for the outlines for your temporary housing." Shealds felt responsible for putting her and her family in danger. The arson fire and the truck sabotage showed they all were in more danger.

"Sounds good. On another subject, I was wondering if we can make the Bayshore place at least livable with some electrical wiring and plumbing. The holidays are fast approaching, and the main floor area on Bayshore would be better for the larger-scale entertaining we have planned. Perhaps, since we already have a stove, you could provide one rudimentary indoor toilet and sink as well as central heating now that it's getting cold."

"If those are your priorities, I think we can get one main floor sink and toilet safely replumbed with some cheaper fixtures, if you don't want to move its location...but heating and air conditioning is something else. We could get one fireplace relined, but not much more." There would be some problems, Shealds knew with century's old systems. "What were you thinking about as far as Mr. Fisher?"

"I don't know about him, as I said before, and as far as lighting is concerned, I guess we can use some of the battery lanterns we have. Thanks for getting us the gas line for the kitchen stove by the way." Carolyn was looking down at her note pad as she pinched her nose with her right thumb and forefinger. Shealds reminded her, she'd have to talk to Darby!

Carolyn looked at her phone. "We're only about an hour behind schedule. Think we'll be OK to get to the motel on time this evening." She rubbed her forehead. "Glad we didn't plan a more ambitious driving schedule."

Now that Carolyn was talking, it was back to Plan A. He had skills and intellect. Shealds had to find some way to dig up what he wanted. Like the times he was up against tough competitors or clients…

"I've been thinking," Carolyn burst out. "We've already talk-ed about the general layout of the kitchen and family room area, haven't we? You know which walls can come down and which are load bearing, don't you?" Carolyn asked. "I'd like an uninterrupt-ed bank of windows with French doors or paneled sliders to the ceiling, across the entire foyer back wall on the inlet side, and a wide porch you've suggested in the plans, so the family room gets bright indirect light most of the day." Carolyn closed her eyes, also seeing the cottage-white painted windows with deep crown mold-ing gracing the space between the wall and ceiling. "I also want all the baseboards patterned after the fragments of the ones already there. Do you think you can get the proper impressions from sam-ples in the house?" She looked at Shealds's honed profile.

"We think we should be able to get enough samples." Shealds stopped for a moment. "I'll just take some from the floorboards and various moldings. We'll mill them ourselves, but we need to send out to get the right blades made from the initial profiles. Do you want wood or composite?" *They'll be sitting ducks with all those windows.*

Shealds was talking like a rusty door hinge. He'd been able to talk, persuade, order, and cajole any number of people, with some deals involving huge sums of money, he recalled. "We want you to be a part of every aspect of our work, if that's what you want. We don't want problems for you or your family about your home or the barn."

Carolyn gave a nod of understanding. "It hasn't been easy." Those four words were an understatement. Before she turned toward the passenger-side window, Shealds noticed the clouds passing over her eyes again. "Reminds me of my mother."

Carolyn started telling him the story about her mother's death and the gift of the Bayshore house. *Why am I so interested in this woman beyond my own plans?* It didn't matter. *All that mattered is freeing myself, right?* All he had to do was report what she said. And for once, it wasn't his veracity that was being questioned.

After dinner everyone in the Reynolds entourage was in their motel rooms, and Darby left for the room he and Shealds were going to share. Shealds wanted to get gas for the truck before they headed out in the morning, so he pulled the truck into the roadway. His phone rang. "Pull into the first station on the right. Beige van." Shealds did as he was told. He got out and started to fill the tank, walking over to the beige medium-size van behind him. A man he'd never seem before got out of the passenger side, patting him on the shoulder while looking at a sightseeing brochure, pretending to study it as Shealds talked. "Her story stays the same. She's been given the place from her aunts…and her mother died some years ago in LA. Hit-and-run, like we already knew, from the investigation. Not much yet, as far as information from the others. Nothing from or about Fisher." Shealds strained to think if there was anything more.

"Did Ms. Reynolds say anything else?"

"Seems her aunts sold the lots, unbeknownst to her, to make sure they made enough money to ease the dent in their retirement funds, if Carolyn was opposed to staying." Shealds was tired. All this in-the-dark stuff was getting on his nerves, and the problems of the near-accident on the road and the arson in LA didn't help. He'd been used to being in control from his helm behind a desk. Those times seemed like centuries ago. Shealds scanned the other man's shadowed face, hoping for some sign this information would get him and his partners some answers.

"Did Ms. Reynolds say anything about a broken window at the bed-and-breakfast where she was staying?" The man pointed to the map and then west with his finger.

"No. No, not a word." Alarmed, now Shealds wanted to ask some questions himself, when the man tilted his head, still looking at the map.

"We'll see what happens. Don't look or sound concerned...but we have to consider people are trying to get to them...*and not you*," was all he said as he raised his hand to start folding the brochure.

"Them?" Shealds whispered in incredulity. *It couldn't be!*

"There's also something about sabotage to their rental car before they got to Bayshore." The other man looked uneasy. "Adds up. About four years ago an unsolved hit-and-run in LA killed her mother. The ballistic tests are back from the pieces of the two shattered windows and broken casing we tested from her room at the bed-and breakfast. Everybody thinks the damage was caused by a bird, but it was *really* caused by bullets. Then there's the tree thing and falling scaffolding at the Bayshore house, the failed arson fire at the hotel, and now the truck tampering. Do you see a parallel pattern here?"

"What about *our* slashed tire and the sugar in the gas tank?" Shealds asked.

"The way we see it, those were also *after* your company expressed interest on working with the Reynolds family," the man replied. "Chicken doo-doo, really, next to the life-threatening accidents, which have escalated since *they've* come to Bayshore place."

"So, the Reynolds might be the target..."

"Or you both might have bull's-eyes on your backs," the man concluded.

Shealds was shaken by this new concept. "After the Reynolds? Samples agrees with you? In your estimation, we could be looking at one, or perhaps, two *separate* threats?"

"That's right." The man poked at a place on the printed brochure several times. "Don't forget there's also Pastor Allred's nutty father to consider." He drew an invisible line with his hand. "You're all involved in a remodeling scheme putting *you all* in his crosshairs. No sightings of him…yet." The man dropped his arm, coughed once, and covered his mouth. "We haven't been able to locate the Thackery kid either. We've looked hard…but there's still a few days until the second eating contest he mentioned, so he still might turn up."

"So his disappearance is another item pointing toward the Reynolds? Even with the note?" Shealds added glumly as he pretended interest in the brochure information.

"Should have been able to find him by now," the other man said as he looked around and folded the paper up when a couple of truckers walked by. As he moved to go, he whispered, "Stay alert…and like Samples asks, get more information." The man faced in the direction of his camper, saying loudly, "Thanks for the help in finding my way. You all be careful now."

"I guess you could say it was kind of a personal epiphany," Carolyn continued, trying to explain what she'd been considering since the truck tire blow-out. Carolyn looked at Bee and Muriel. "In those few fleeting seconds of near-disaster, I thought I might die when the tire blew out. Although I'd been doing better, it suddenly occurred to me that my grieving for Mom had gone on for years…and, I finally, *truly realized* she wouldn't have wanted that!"

Carolyn was in one of the backseats with Grace Ann strapped in her car seat next to Bee and Muriel with Darby driving in the front seat of the van, looking like their chauffeur with no one next to him. "I just can't live by defining myself in somber negatives: the *ex*-owner of Four Almonds, the daughter of the *deceased* Ms. Billie Reynolds, or a *once*-healthy person now with heart problems.

I've got to look at these things as parts of my past, not things *stopping me* from living." She looked at her aunts. "I only hope all this negativity hasn't rubbed off on Grace Ann." She looked over at her daughter, who smiled up in her mother's face as Muriel tickled her tummy.

"Grace Ann certainly looks deeply affected," Bee said with a sidelong glance and a dry tone laced with Cass-like irony.

"You know I was a mess after my husband died," Bee admitted.

"Felt that way myself for several years after Robin died," Darby admitted, not taking his eyes off the road, the steering wheel held tightly in his small hands. "Just sat and stared at the television, not seeing anything and crying for all I was worth when I was home. Happened a second time, when my wife, Sally, died. If I hadn't had work and the fan club to get up for in the morning, I'd have been frozen there under the covers or on the couch twenty-four-seven."

Darby said - the "second time." If Carolyn remembered correctly, Darby and Sally had met at classic movie nostalgia meeting or convention as she tried to remember what Billie had said about it. Neither had been married before, followed career paths and melded their hobbies concerning their love of the black and white cinema and Darby's absolute passion for everything Robin Lee. The couple moved down to Central America somewhere, where the prices were so much cheaper and they could own a place where the beach was their doorstep. Billie, Darby, and Sally kept in close touch, and Darby remained as the newsletter editor and fan club president emeritus.

Then the letters came about litigation, eviction, and other legal troubles down in paradise. Darby and Sally spent a great deal of money on their fruitless litigation, and their cottage was torn down for the seaside cabanas of some industrialist's spa and hotel. The rest of the money went to try to stop the incurable problems Sally discovered shortly after they returned to LA. "Glad I could go back to my work with my fabric designs," Darby sighed.

246

Carolyn had had twin losses too, and had handled both badly. Now was the time to change things and her outlook. "I'm dropping the private investigators…and harassing the LA detectives about Mom's case," Carolyn announced. "Darby, I'm going to looking forward to seeing your new fabrics brighten your set of rooms at Bayshore."

Gratitude radiated from Darby's eyes. "I thought you might never ask," he remarked quietly. Trying to hide his relief behind his well-polished acerbic, drawling sophistication, he added, "I might do many fabric collections inspired by *our* domicile."

Carolyn smirked. She really did love Darby, his Southern drawl and colorful vocabulary.

Knowing neither he nor Carolyn were soppy sentimentalists, Muriel broke in. "We all needed time to bear our sorrows. You just needed some extra time. We hoped the construction project might help you work it all though in your own mind."

"Mom would have kicked my butt instead," Carolyn noted.

"You're being too hard on yourself," Bee replied kindly. "As you said, you were facing several losses and ill health; just not dear Billie's passing."

"So you got the surprise gift from your aunts and came cross-country to find a grape-colored mansion, meet Beth…and get your bundle of joy here," Darby interjected, smiling as he looked in the rear view mirror at Grace Ann and knowing he now was a real part of the family.

"So we're off to a great new start," Muriel stated.

"We'll be back at Bayshore tomorrow and we'll celebrate," Bee interjected. "But now we have to call Cass and Beth with the great news!"

Carolyn believed they hadn't been home two seconds when Beth came bounding in, telling her some jumbled things about burials, plaques, Molina, and Molina's silent periods, while hugging

Carolyn, Bee, Muriel, and asking to hold Grace Ann, ending with, "I saw the truck and I was so excited."

"Slow down. Start from the beginning, Carolyn laughed. "*Well, so much for getting acclimated!*

Beth stopped her chatter, took a deep breath, and did as Carolyn asked. "As we told you, Mr. Griggs agreed we can bury all those poor unnatural taxidermy animals. So we're burying each animal with a nice service, and then Molina is carving a wooden plaque for each animal and putting them on Nelder's walls *instead*." She stopped and rummaged into the snack bags Darby had just put on the folding table. "Don't know how long it's going to take, but we're going to give every animal a decent burial. The modules are coming tomorrow, right?"

Beth's expression became somber. "Joe's gone and he hasn't contacted anyone."

"It's been an interesting time while you're been gone," Cass said dryly as she entered the foyer. "Nelder dropped us off when Hesse gave Molina a note, saying Shealds called, and estimated you'd be back about this time."

"The storage facility in the barn is ready if you'd like to see it," Hesse said, coming into the foyer as well. "The module pads are *also* ready as Miss Beth said."

Carolyn looked at each of the faces before her and suddenly felt tired. "We'll talk about everything, but it's been a long day and a long time on the road. I know it might be selfish, but I need a shower, a good meal from a menu that doesn't include chicken-fried steak, and a night's sleep where I don't have to be up at five a.m. to get Grace Ann up and shuffle things into moving vehicles." She turned her attention to Hesse. "Just humor me and tell me everything is ready. We've got the specialty movers with the modular homes arriving tomorrow, midmorning. Right?" Carolyn checked her list. "I'm sure your work on the barn has been done to your exacting standards and we'll put things in there, starting after my inspection tomorrow. Does nine thirty a.m. sound OK?"

"We prewashed all the bed linens for everyone when the modular homes come tomorrow," Cass reported, taking one small item off Carolyn's list.

"We missed you both," Carolyn said in a whisper as she grabbed the whisk broom and twirled her arm comically in the air. "As Major Princess of this run-down castle, I declare a holiday for everyone this evening and we'll get started again tomorrow." Carolyn headed toward the door with the diaper bag and her purse as she looked at Hesse.

"Well, it's settled then. I for one am headed back to the Two Cups. See you for dinner after we're rested a bit and have looked at all of tomorrow's lists. Only then can we all talk about what's happened the last few days." She looked again at everyone, stabbing with the broom handle again. "Only then."

"Have they told you anything about the accident with the truck?" Hesse said as he absently stirred at a cup of coffee gone cold. Like the endless trips of the old spoon around the rim of the mug, the conversation was going nowhere. Shealds's look became grimmer.

"As I said, everything indicates there's someone coming after the Reynolds, or me, or both of us, which includes increasing violence and more frequent episodes." Suddenly sitting in the chair was too confining. Shealds headed toward the fading light at the window.

"So we really don't know if someone's after you, them, or both of you." Hesse looked out at the dusk and turned.

"Tell me again about Mrs. Williams and Beth Seavers," Shealds ordered.

Molina shrugged. "Thackery left the Griggs's house. I stayed near them at the Griggs's place without them getting suspicious.

No accidents or trouble there. I'm carving plaques. I've got nothing more to add."

"Everything else stayed quiet while you were gone to LA." Hesse shifted in his seat and looked up at Shealds.

The answer seemed clear from the information they had. Whoever was staging the mishaps and accidents were targeting Shealds *and* the Reynolds now...remaining undetected thus far. Whoever they were, they were close now...and lethal.

CHAPTER SIXTEEN

I t had been a week since the Reynolds family returned from LA as the Reynolds' women came to their first appointment, Pete noted. The modular homes had come for Carolyn, Grace Ann, Muriel and Bee without incident and the two remaining homes for Darby, Beth and Cass were arriving tomorrow. The women and Beth had shown up...all sitting in a circle of folding chairs in Carolyn and Grace Ann's modular. Grace Ann had cooperated with her morning nap.

There had been some startling revelations in their two hour session —all given with great honesty and candor, Pete thought, as he shook his head. Carolyn wasn't kidding when she said they were going to be honest with Beth. The aunts had laid out their lives as unwed mothers and carefully shared every aspect of their, Carolyn and Billie's lives.

After he left the session, Pete was glad he had permission to record the session because he knew he was going to be going over his notes and audio for another few hours, at least!

They'd started quickly, and Carolyn spoke directly to Beth, who was sitting at the opposite side of the small circle. "We're going to lay it all out as best we can, but we'll all be interrupting each other and adding things, so you'll probably have lots of questions." Carolyn looked at Pete for confirmation to speak in this way.

"Can she ask us things outside of the sessions?" Cass asked, looking at Pete.

"Let's see how this goes," Pete said, hedging. He didn't want to promise anything and then regret his words.

After almost an hour-and-a-half of soul-baring revelations with two breaks, Cass noted. "Well, all the bones of the skeletons in our closets are out for everyone to see."

"Guess it's time for me to say something," Beth said.

"You don't have to, Beth," Pete remarked. "This is a safe place, and there's a lot to think about with all the information shared from Carolyn and your aunts." Pete didn't know if it was right to brand the situation with familial associations, but it felt right.

"I knew we were going to talk today, so I want to say something too." Beth looked around. "Cass and I have been talking and I'm sure you're come over the part about my rape." Carolyn, Bee and Muriel looked sheepish, a clear sign to Beth that they knew her *whole* history. "Thought so," she said more softly.

"Only if you feel comfortable, Beth," Pete reminded her, wanting her to feel safe and that *everyone* cared about her well-being first. "May I repeat, you don't have to say *anything* just because Carolyn and your aunts contributed personal information."

"I know that." Beth talked quickly as if walking over hot coals. "The welfare agency psychologist and the rape counseling center helped me some. I've talked a bit with Cass." She inhaled and held her breath for an instant. It came out in a soft whoosh. "I was fourteen…and the brother of the man of the foster couple who caught me in bed one night. He'd sent his sister and brother-in-law out on the pretense of a dinner and movie date night, and for me to stay with the kids." She swallowed. "He came over saying he'd left something after the kids were asleep, and I let him in. He pulled a gun and backed me into the bedroom. He had the gun in his hand and a put a big knife from the kitchen on the floor as he pinned my neck down to the mattress so I could hardly breathe.

"The only light was the moon shining in from the window, and I couldn't see much except the knife on the worn bedroom carpet when he shifted his weight and I struggled to turn my head. 'What you're feeling here on your right side is the loaded revolver. You know the knife's on the floor. Don't try to scream or I'll snap your neck like a chicken bone.' The man shifted his weight again, and the mattress creaked. 'If you're feeling lucky, you can try to get one of my weapons, but if I win, I'll just throw you in the dump. Lots of runaways are never found. I like it rough. You still feeling lucky?'"

Beth took another breath. "I lay there like a board while he rubbed my breasts a few times and then raped me. He didn't kiss me or anything, just jammed himself into me, grabbed the gun in his hand, looked at the wall, closed his eyes, and started grunting—like the pig he was." She looked at the crying faces of the other women. "He got up, pulled on his pants, and said, 'Don't say a thing to anyone or I'll kill you.'"

"Oh, Beth, what did you do?" Carolyn cried, wiping her eyes. Muriel was already holding Beth's hand.

"I ran away two days later...and told the counselor I was raped down by the railroad tracks but I couldn't identify the man," Beth said. "The rape kit didn't show anything, but I still had some internal and external marks."

"You mean the guy's still out there?" Cass asked.

"No. I got over being scared. At sixteen, I reported the exact details to social services...and several other girls came forward when they started investigating," Beth said. "Think he's still in jail."

"They have to inform you if he's released, don't they?" Bee inquired.

"I'll get Mr. Lyon on it. Just give me the names," Carolyn said. "You're safe here with us."

"And all of this alone," Muriel said with an astounded tone.

Pete could hardly believe it either. All these stories of resilient, thoughtful women and abandonment, murder, and rape! He'd adjourned now. "I think we all need to think about this information you have shared and consider where to start next time."

"Thank you. We'll get back to you in a few days," Carolyn said as Pete put on his coat and put his notebook in his briefcase. "Can you just wait a minute? Bee's made a casserole for your dinner. We'd invite you to stay but…"

"I understand. It's been intense," Pete replied. "If you need anything, just call."

"Thanks for your help today. I'll let you know." Carolyn waved good-bye.

Everyone went to Bee's modular, as planned, for dinner. Even though they'd talked in their session, there was lots of conversation as Grace Ann sat contentedly in her infant high chair.

"You know, Thanksgiving was Billie's favorite holiday," Carolyn remarked to Beth.

"Even better than Christmas?" Beth responded.

"She loved Christmas, don't get me wrong, but people get so tied up in presents and the hoopla of it all." Carolyn chose her words carefully. "She thought they'd forgotten the real meaning of Christmas. My mother thought Thanksgiving was just on the cusp of all that…and people still used it to celebrate thankfulness of family and friends and used it as a time to carefully plan what simple things she could do for others at Christmas."

"We're old-fashioned in that way," Cass added.

"We have a big breakfast and a big Thanksgiving meal," Carolyn informed Beth. "We watch all the sports events and parades in the background as we're cooking…"

"And we start planning what we're going to do for Christmas," Cass said, finishing Carolyn's thought.

"It's our one-hundred-dollar tradition," Bee said. "It's really a lot of fun!"

"Really?" Beth asked. "Tradition?"

"Well, we started with just pennies years ago, but now, we've tried to keep up with prices, and we budget one hundred dollars each," Muriel offered, setting the vegetable bowl down on the table.

"We each have one hundred dollars to provide a side dish and dessert for Christmas dinner, and we've also got to make one tree ornament or house decoration, and something for the animals for winter care." Bee ticked off the categories on her fingers.

"Whatever is left is included in our Christmas charitable donations we give for that year," Muriel, their resident treasurer, said.

"It's not a contest. Nobody is judged on anything, but we have fun telling everyone what we're planning as we help each other," Carolyn said.

"We help each other...and it all gets done," Cass remarked.

"Can I help?" Beth asked. "Darby and I can be a team."

"Well, that would be a fine idea. I was going to team up with him because he's new at this tradition, too, but your teaming with him would be fine." Muriel smiled as she looked into Beth's eyes. "We'll help you...or you both can just help us!"

"Sounds like fun," Beth agreed enthusiastically. "I'm in...and I know I can persuade Darby."

"We've also budgeted fifty dollars for Christmas gifts, bought or made." Bee got a pad of paper. "We pick from a hat. Pieces of paper have our names on it, and we list several things we want for Christmas gifts, so whoever gets the name knows what the person wants!"

"Thank the Lord for gift cards if we run out of time!" Muriel laughed and the others joined her.

"I almost forgot, we also like to wrap the gifts with all kinds of ribbon and doodads," Bee said. "We bring the boxed gifts to put under our Christmas tree."

Carolyn reached for the church bulletin. "We've already contributed to Pastor Allred's church for Thanksgiving, but we also work on the gifts we've selected from the women's, men's, and family shelter list, as well as the people the church says need help at Christmas. As before in our other church homes, they give us all the gift ideas and sizes."

After dinner, as they were talking about Christmas plans, Carolyn looked at her watch. Time for Beth and Cass to drive back for their last night at Nelder's. Carolyn asked to speak with Beth. "That's enough of our Christmas plans. Let's get our coats."

They walked down the four porch stairs. "That was really brave of you today, Beth," Carolyn said, looking at the late-autumn moon. "I wanted to tell you before you left."

"Yeah?" Beth replied, listening to the crunch of leaves under their boots.

"Yeah," Carolyn said, thinking her words were an understatement. "It's going to be Thanksgiving soon, and besides sharing all our plans, we'd like you to start thinking of us as your family...and this as your home." She stopped for a moment. "Is it all too soon? Are we pushing you?"

Beth took a few more steps. They'd almost reached the end of the three tidy modular homes that looked like seaside cottages. There would be five tomorrow, Beth knew.

Carolyn stood still. "The two-bedroom cottage for Darby and the three-bedroom cottage for you and Cass are coming tomorrow, if you still want it."

Before she could say any more, Beth wordlessly flung herself in Carolyn's arms and hugged her tight. Carolyn swayed a bit before regaining her balance and hugged her back. Carolyn smiled in the moonlight, so glad Beth's nonverbal answer was an emphatic yes.

Darby, Cass, and Beth settled in at the Bayshore property in the next few days. Beth asked for one-on-one sessions with Pete to help her explore her abandonment issues and the rape. They also celebrated Grace Ann's private adoption completion. Mr. Lyon sent the information via computer. The official documents would come in overnighted mail.

"We've got a lot of things to celebrate. Do you think you can manage a pinochle game with Nelder on Friday, Darby?" Cass asked.

"We're thinking of a having something in the line of a girls' night out here," Carolyn said. "I've already told Shealds and Hesse we don't want anyone working in the main house this Friday or Saturday."

"No work?" Darby replied. The work stoppage seemed strange since they were thinking of having appliances in the first-floor kitchen and wallboard in the family area finished to celebrate Thanksgiving and Christmas *in* the Bayshore house. If they were going to get that job done, they'd need time to get the new windows in, a bathroom retrofitted, and the electrical work finished.

Taking possible construction workdays away from the project seemed strange, but Darby kept his questions to himself. Being together was what mattered, even if the place wasn't ready in time. They always had the kitchens in the modular homes for making food. "Anything I can do besides making myself scarce?"

"Just not saying anything to Beth and staying in town would be great! We're still setting up our plans," Muriel said vaguely, not wanting to give Darby too much information that might spoil things.

Surprise indeed! Now that Beth had agreed to make her home with Carolyn and her aunts, they all wanted to welcome Beth in a special way to affirm her as the truly remarkable young woman they'd grown to love. Shealds had been disgruntled, to say the least by their work stoppage request, saying after the windows were replaced in the back of the house on the first floor and the footings were set for the new patio, the patio roof Carolyn wanted needed secure anchors within a few days before the outside temperatures plummeted. Because of two days of heavy rain this week, he'd already had to postpone both putting in the replacement windows on the second and third floors, and setting the footers for the new addition to the house - reminiscent of the size of the former Bayshore servants' structure slated for Bee and Muriel.

"We don't want to have a mess this weekend," Carolyn said with finality. "We understand the financial implications of our decision and the effect on your schedule for our Thanksgiving and Christmas needs. But don't work this Friday or Saturday!"

All four women remained tight-lipped - only letting Grace Ann into their planning sessions.

"Something's going on at Bayshore," Hesse said.

"I know," Shealds replied. "They're not letting us work on Friday or Saturday, and Nelder said Darby's going over there on Friday night."

"Think we should be concerned?" Hesse said.

"Five women and a baby who might be targets against me or targets on their own?" Shealds replied sarcastically. "I can't believe the microphones at Bayshore or the modular homes aren't working!"

"Must have been the electrician when he got the temporary lights working on the first floor or we cut something when they dropped the last two homes in place. Don't know if we can get it fixed by Friday." Hesse bristled. "Can't you pull the trigger on Zaugus and get your thing over with? Then we'd have *your* problems out of the picture."

"Wish I could, but I can't," Shealds replied wearily.

"Can we listen by surveillance antenna?" Hesse asked.

"Don't know...we're a long way from stopping anything that happens at the house whether we chose the barn or the trailer, and we'll have to get extra equipment in the trailer to hear what's going on before Friday. 'Bad angle and fuzzy signal,' Samples says," Shealds began.

"We won't be close enough if something starts happening on the other side of the house. There's a lot of seaside windows now for people to see in," Hesse continued. "I wish I'd been able to convince them to get temporary window coverings, so they wouldn't be such sitting ducks."

"You did the best you could, but there's still a lot of construction left...and even you couldn't guarantee the shades, drapes, or whatever they chose wouldn't be ruined in the dust and debris. Saying we'd pay for replacements might raise a red flag." Shealds folded his arms. "You did your best. They decided against it."

"So we'll just have to pretend to work on other things here in the work trailer on Friday as long as possible, keep our eyes open, and sit in the dark in the construction trailer on Friday night when they think we've gone." Hesse walked over to the window looking at the rainy sky.

"At least you talked them into getting the security lights around the house and the modular homes," Shealds replied. "We've got the heater in the trailer, so at least we won't be cold...but no pinochle."

"Everything set?" Bee said for the fifth time.

Muriel rolled her eyes, knowing Bee repeated herself when she was nervous or excited. "You got the dinner ready?"

"Stove's set, I've got several crockpots hidden away in the pantry, and the portable folding screens will look more festive," Bee replied.

Carolyn walked quickly from the foyer. "Stapling the sheets on the open stud walls make things look better." She checked her watch as she admired the Misty Tree sheets they'd selected to camouflage the walls. "If we need to, we can use these for the holidays." Bee and Muriel both nodded. "We better get dressed."

Hesse watched the women go back to their modular homes. "Cass and Beth are not here."

Shealds spoke into the microphone wire hidden in his jacket as he looked through the night goggles on a higher ground perch in the woods. "Molina says they've just finished burying the wild turkey specimen in the woods, and he's started carving the plaque for the porcupine they buried on Tuesday. He'll leave soon." Shealds looked at the clock. "Darby's been there about an hour. They changed their plans for the both of them to go to dinner in town before they come back to play cards. Molina confirms that, says there's no dinner being prepared in Nelder's house."

"There's been a lot of nervous looks out of the door by everyone at the Bayshore house in the last half hour, but no calls for police or fire," Hesse reported as Shealds's mobile device vibrated.

Shealds listened and gave a few affirmative nods. "I'm headed back to you. Cass and Beth are headed in this direction and should be here in a few minutes." He bent down as he started the walk to the trailer. "Molina will go back to the office at home and wait to see if we need backup. Our vehicles are hidden."

Cass tried to hide her nerves as they climbed the steps to their new modular home. She tried to think of something to say. "Doesn't feel like a modular home, does it?" Cass asked, making sure she gave Beth time to find the large note taped to the front door.

"Muriel asks for us to come up to the main house for pizza," Beth began.

"I'll start ahead," Cass said, "to see if they need anything. Will you go in and get my favorite Parmesan? You know I don't eat pizza without it!" Cass almost ran down the steps as she called back over her shoulder. "Should be on the second shelf in the refrigerator."

"They just pulled up…and Cass is running up to the house. I think something is wrong." Hesse put down the night-vision goggles and was about to leave the corner of the dark construction trailer.

"Wait a sec!" Shealds hissed. "If there's trouble, we're on it, but let's let this play out a minute or two. We might be wrong."

"You sure?" Hesse hissed back. Shealds could hear Hesse's apprehension.

"Sure." Shealds voice was like steel. "Don't want to bring out the guns unless we have to. My gut says Cass wouldn't abandon Beth if there were trouble."

Hesse silently readjusted the goggles and went back, thinking of the hidden large-caliber guns taped to back of the office cabinet—within easy access. "Those guns are going to send us back to prison if we get caught."

"Can't defend ourselves with fly swatters," Shealds remarked dryly, holding the lightweight night-vision camera with the close-up lenses. He wanted proof and the identity of who was behind the attacks. He hoped he'd find out tonight.

"Everything's ready," Bee said loudly as she opened the door for Cass. "Your dress is in your bedroom as we promised, and everything for Beth is all laid out in her bedroom in the modular as well. She just has to go into her room to find them." Bee called out over her shoulder. "Muriel, just turn on the lights as we've planned as I let Beth through the door when she comes."

Cass looked up to see Muriel, Bee, and Carolyn dressed in white, as was Grace Ann, in her white-flowered headband, bib, and dress, covered in the down-soft white blanket they'd bought. "Here she comes," Bee whispered. "Grace Ann doing OK? Everyone set?"

As the others nodded, Beth came through the door and Cass closed it behind Beth, against the cold night. "Surprise!" everyone yelled as Beth blinked and frowned in puzzlement.

"It's a surprise party for you!" Cass smiled. "We wanted to do something special."

Muriel walked up with a large shiny white box tied with a wide, shiny white satin bow and extended the package to Beth. "Would you wear this for us?"

Beth took the box and put it on the linen-draped table closest to her. The smiling women crowded around. Beth reverently removed the bow and box top with shaking hands to reveal a white satin and tulle strapless gown with scattered crystals sewn and shining on the gossamer net skirt. Seemingly endless yards of candy-cotton soft tulle made up the knee-length skirt. "I've never seen anything so beautiful." Beth breathed as she lifted it from the box and hugged the dress to herself. "For me?" she whispered as the misty-eyed women nodded silently. Bee grabbed for a tissue, tucked under her sleeve to wipe away a tear. They knew Beth had never gone to a school dance or prom, turning down every invitation because she didn't have money for a dress or even knew if she'd be around to attend if she was asked.

Cass hugged Beth. "Put the dress back in the box so you can go back to the house to get dressed...and *then* we'll have dinner."

"The other things you'll need are under a sheet on your bed and on your desk," Carolyn announced as she laughed. "Grace Ann was particularly vocal about the shoes you should have."

"That is certainly a fact." Muriel remembered Grace Ann cried when they were thinking of another pair from the assortment the personal shopper had brought to the room they'd rented for the afternoon at the Stornel's bed and breakfast several days earlier. Carolyn had allowed Jessie Stornel to pick out her dress for the winter formal dance from the rest of the selection...under strict orders not to say anything to Beth.

After hugs and kisses were shared by the group, Beth and Cass went to change.

"Cass and Beth are going back to their modular, it seems," Hesse reported. "Beth's carrying a box—a white box that looks like a present. What gives?"

"Don't know. But hold your position. So far, so good," Shealds replied.

A few minutes later, Hesse spoke. "Cass and Beth are going back to the house, and you're not going to believe this, but they look like they're going to a party."

Shealds looked puzzled. "Let me see." He looked at the camera screen. "I don't get it?" He looked out the window, and Cass and Beth were almost in the house.

"So we'll stay put and see how it plays out?" Hesse moved to get a better look at the front door.

"I'm waiting for another call from Samples. After that, we can circle around the barn and studio and see if we can hear anything," Shealds replied, "and make a decision from there."

"In the meantime, there's the tuna sandwich I picked up for you for dinner," Hesse remarked. "I've got a roast beef. I'll give you half in exchange if you want it…and a warm soda because the light in our frig here might raise suspicion."

"Forget the sandwich. Let's go now," Shealds growled after hanging up from his call with Samples, "or we might miss something important."

Hesse nodded and followed Shealds's route to the back of the Bayshore mansion. *What was going on?*

The long table was set with a white damask tablecloth and matching napkins in silver rings over white silver-edged china and sterling place settings. Lit white tapers flickered from numerous silver candlesticks of different heights around several oblong silver bowls filled with white roses and other white and green flowers. Besides several floor lamps, the fireplace was filled with several levels of white pillar candles lending a soft golden glow.

Canapés and two kinds of sparkling fruit punch in crystal pitchers sat on a silver tray on a coffee table by the couches Carolyn had rented. "Let's sit down and talk before we start dinner."

"I don't know what to say," Beth said shyly, looking like a young beauty in her formal clothes. The crystal accents on her dress sparkled in the candlelight. "I've been so stunned since you surprised me at the door."

"No need to worry about that." Bee picked up an envelope on the table and gave it to Beth. "Come, sit down and open this."

Beth opened her mouth and closed it again, not knowing what more to say. She did as Bee asked and found a certificate promising cooking lessons from Bee. "Oh, that's so wonderful," Beth said as tears formed in her eyes again. She clutched the paper to her heart. "You know I love cooking as much as you do!"

Indeed they did, as Beth peppered Bee with her questions regarding food, preparation, and cooking techniques since her Bayshore arrival. Both would be glad when Bee's full collection of books and folders came out of storage. "We'll get a good start in our houses, so we'll be ready when everything is built here."

They waited a few minutes before Cass gave Beth another envelope. It was a certificate for sewing lessons...and a promise of an appointment for a spa day and makeup lesson for everyone on Thanksgiving weekend. "There's more to it, even if you don't want to learn to sew," Cass said practically. "You need to know how to look at the way clothes are constructed and the material in them to indicate value and how long they will last."

"I'd love to learn how to sew...and perhaps I could work on making something for my bedroom," Beth replied.

"That's what we like to hear. I'll also help you with any gardening interests," Cass said, holding up her champagne flute for a
toast. "To Beth!"

After more laughter, Muriel's certificate promised help with
any research Beth might need as well as assistance with any craft-
ing projects. "Can you help to find out about Joe and Becky?" Beth
asked. "I'd like keep in touch with them, if I could."

"That goes without saying," Muriel replied. "We want to be
transparent about everything...and help you with anything you
need."

"We'll tell you everything and anything you want to know,"
Carolyn agreed. "Now it's my turn." Carolyn looked to see that
Grace Ann was comfortable in her port-a-crib. She handed Beth
the fourth envelope. "I promise to be your mentor, big sister, or
friend in anything concerning our life, yourself, or your plans."
She looked at the others. "I know you've just really met us, but I
hope you know you can come to any of us, or all of us, and we'll
respect you and protect anything you'd like to say with complete
confidentiality...and we hope you can come to love us, as we are
learning to love you."

"Oh, my gosh." Tears rolled down Beth's cheeks as she hugged
Carolyn. Muriel grabbed some tissues, and they all ended up in a
tearful group hug.

After a few minutes, they composed themselves, and Beth
looked at the certificates again. They managed to sit down to their
salmon dinner complete with endive salad, chive biscuits, au gra-
tin potatoes, and French-cut green beans.

"You'll be able to prepare this meal in no time when we start
your cooking lessons," Bee said as she shooed Beth from the kitch-
en as they removed the dinner plates. "We'll take care of this mess
tomorrow. Now it's time to go back to the sitting area." She took
Beth's hand as they headed for the couches.

"There are a few more things," Cass said as they sat down.

Carolyn brought another tray, a white one this time, with several small silver wrapped boxes on them. "These are for you."

"But you've given me so much already. I feel like crying again." Beth looked at them all. "I've never had so many presents at one time. Honest."

Carolyn kept smiling, but her heart broke to think of this beautiful girl not getting the kind of love, attention or gifts in her life thus far. Carolyn put down the tray and handed Beth one of the boxes. Beth carefully opened the shiny wrapping, lifting a pearl necklace from the box and letting it dangle from her hand.

"It's the most beautiful gift I've even gotten." Beth seemed mesmerized as she looked at the string of pink-hued, white pearls.

"We don't know if they're in style today," Muriel said. "But we think pearls are timeless, and since you can wear them from anything from jeans to the dress you're wearing, we thought you should have some." Cass helped Beth put the necklace on. "Earrings, too."

"I want to see them in the reflection in the window," Beth said. The others followed, enjoying seeing Beth so excited with their gift.

"Time to open another one," Cass said after they'd admired the pearls.

The protective cotton covering on the second box held a sporty silver and gold metal watch with the inscription, "To our bright and shiny Beth!"

"We know people tell time by their phone and gadgets today, but sometimes people need watches," Muriel said. "Let me help you with the clasp."

Beth cried, "I love it!"

The third box held a bracelet. "There are five rectangular sections made of five different metal filaments with five gold rings to connect them," Cass announced. "Which represent the five of us."

"We know with Grace Ann, there are six of us…but we decided she'll be the next generation," Carolyn said, smiling at her daughter sleeping in the portable crib.

"Oh, how beautiful," Beth said. "The five of us."

"You can put the bracelet on, and there are several more things we'd like to add, like getting you a phone," Carolyn said. "But the rest is going to require some time and planning on your part." Beth looked into Carolyn's eyes. "If you like, we're offering to give you driving lessons for driving the household vehicles."

"Oh, my gosh. I never thought…" Beth began.

"It's the start of your future," Bee offered.

"Driving?" Beth wanted to comprehend this. *Driving?* "I've never tried."

"Well, no way but to start," Bee said. "There's a written part and a driving part you can learn in the classes, and behind-the-wheel lessons we will set up soon."

"That would be…beyond belief." Beth gasped. She'd have to pinch herself to see if she were dreaming.

"You've proved yourself to be intelligent and resourceful," Muriel said.

"As well as kind, polite, and thoughtful," Cass added with a smile.

"You're capable of much more than just staying around us," Bee noted.

"For that reason," Carolyn began as she handed Beth a thick legal-size envelope, "we've set up a trust fund for you."

"What?" Beth said, looking confused.

"It's a nest egg for you, dear…but it's got some stipulations," Bee warned.

"Stipulations?" Beth didn't understand. "I don't know what you're talking about."

"Scoot over, Bee," Carolyn said. "I think we've confused her again." She sat down and took Beth's hands. "Let's start over on this part. OK?" She looked into Beth's eyes. "We're asking you to think hard about a plan for your life. You've already said you were looking to go to junior college for more education but now you have *more* options." She looked at her aunts. "Here, with us, you can take *one year* to decide what you want to do...figure things out...without having to worry for your safety, housing, or anything. We're your family now, and we can help you...or get the help you need in your planning."

"College, a business, or whatever you want to do, so you can support yourself...and make your *own* dreams come true," Muriel said, adjusting the pillows behind her as she scooted forward on the couch.

"It's going to take some kind of classwork, dear," Bee said. "Even if you want to cook for a living, I would suggest a rigorous culinary school."

This was almost too much for Beth to take in as she put her hands to her temples. "Let's see if I understand." She bit down on her lip to concentrate. "I get to learn to drive *and* you're going to give me a year here to help me find a career?"

"That's right, dear," Muriel said. "Although I would suggest we start with the premise that we need to learn all the time...and are really *life-long* learners."

"Find and pursue my passion? Is that what you mean?" Beth asked.

"Muriel is right about being curious and learning all our lives," Cass agreed, trying to be practical—thinking of the taxidermy burials. Something like that, although from the heart, would not pay the bills. "You should concentrate on something that provides an adequate salary for you to be able to pursue *all* your interests. We're you home base...and an emergency shelter and bank of last resort, after you've established yourself, just like family."

"Each of us has been lucky enough to find enriching careers...and that's what we want for you," Bee said. "That's what we *all* want for you."

"You're my family?" Beth asked softly.

"That's right," Cass replied. "We gladly volunteer. You've got us...but we want an independent life for you. Also, you're young with no life mate on the horizon...and, of course, on that subject, we'd all have to question your young man when you've found him, concerning his intentions and ability to help support your mutual relationship and a family. You should know that *well* before you consider marriage."

"Perhaps we're being premature on this aspect, Beth, but Cass is right," Carolyn noted. "You're at the age when you should be filling out applications for careers or colleges and thinking of your goals *first*." She was supportive of Joe, they knew, but now she needed to think of herself.

"But we don't have to talk about these things anymore," Bee said. "I'm sure you'll have a lot of questions in the next few days and weeks to follow...and we'll be here to answer them or find people to answer them with you."

"We're going to make mistakes, Beth," Carolyn parried. "We're not perfect." She looked in the eyes of each of her aunts. "But we'll try our best and hope you will give us second, third, and fourth changes as you figure things out."

"There's one last gift...and kind of old-fashioned," Muriel said, lifting a book from the table. "We're got two volumes of memory books for you. Volume one is from your birth to now...with interviews and documentation of your life thus far."

"Volume two is from today on, and the space should last for a few years," Cass said as she handed the second leather-bound book to Beth.

Carolyn smiled and got up from the couch. "You can look at them both later. Think it's time to ask Bee for some of that cake and ice cream she has ready for us." Carolyn put her hand to Beth's back and went to start taking some pictures with her camera. "We know strawberry is your favorite!"

"No candles on the cake, darling, because we reserve those for birthdays," Bee said over her shoulder as she headed for the kitchen. "But with this cake, consider yourself initiated as the youngest member of the Reynolds clan!"

Shealds hit Hesse with the two finger sign on his shoulder, signaling it was time to move. He could have done it long before, but he'd wanted to hear everything the women were saying. They got back to the construction trailer. "If that don't beat all!" was the first thing out of Hesse's mouth in a soft exclamation. Shealds just nodded. They'd witnessed an "adoption" party for the orphan runaway who had been squatting on their client's property. They were no closer to finding out whom, if anyone, was trying to harm him or them. *But who would try to harm a group of ladies who acted with such care and generosity?* If this was all a put-on, these women were great actresses. Shealds believed they were truly good people now…and so did Hesse.

"This makes things harder, my friend. It raises the stakes," Shealds whispered as he put the guns back in their hiding place. "Now, we're *really* getting to like them, which is dangerous." *How will I react if anyone hurts them?*

CHAPTER SEVENTEEN

L et's stop for lunch," Nelder said, as he and Beth finished relocating the raccoon family.

"I brought the library books in my bag," Beth said, remembering the volumes on wild animal husbandry and animal care she'd been reading. Nelder had suggested she learn the habits of the animals native to the area.

"Speaking of that. You got everything straightened away about your high school diploma and all?" Nelder grabbed the cage, and Beth tied burlap-covered box.

"It's done," Beth replied. "Cass faxed the documents back and forth between the people at the school, the lawyers, and Carolyn." She turned to Nelder and gave him a big smile, holding the box up a bit higher. "So now I can go talk to guidance counselors and get started on a career. Something dealing with wildlife or culinary arts, I don't know."

Nelder had to smile a bit at Beth's continuing process. They'd had some long talks. He'd even heard Beth talking away to the silent Molina, when Molina was over at the house chipping and whittling away on the animal plaques. Nelder had to hand it to the neon-headed young man. Not only was Molina doing a fine job on the animal plaques, he said a few words in counseling Beth in what Nelder thought were the right aspects concerning her career questions.

Beth's voice changed into an almost whisper. "You know Molina's speaking more and more to me."

"Humph, you don't say," Nelder said. He knew Molina had a voice, but he hadn't heard it much. Being a man of few words himself, Nelder just treated him like anyone else. Perhaps he'd only hoped Molina could speak more because he'd be sad if Molina was really ill in some way and couldn't communicate. He had heard someone say Molina chose to be mute at times.

Nelder wasn't big on getting into other people's business. Most people talked too much, especially that Clem fellow who was the mayor, pestering Nelder with all kinds of questions about the Bayshore property and his work there. Said it had something to do with zoning. Yep, Nelder liked quieter folk. Molina seemed to communicate just fine with his expressions and infrequent words.

"That's all of them all right." Nelder heaved the burlap-covered cage agilely into the truck bed. He hadn't wanted to push Beth in any course of study, but anyone with two eyes could see the girl was a natural with animals.

"We've got problems...or should I say I've gotten a solution," Shealds began. He wouldn't have admitted it to anyone, but reliving the eaves-dropping event last Friday night had affected Shealds. *Getting out from under Warren's cloud of destruction has taken forever – from prison and back! How many years has it been since I could talk freely to my family?*

"What?" Hesse replied, not understanding what Shealds said.

"It's Ellen," Shealds replied. "We had a long phone conversation...and she wants to visit after the holidays."

Hesse still didn't know whether to happy or sad about the news. Ellen had been a big part of Shealds losing almost two years of his life in jail and even more in planning his exoneration. They still didn't know if it was going to work or not. And now, Shealds was talking to Ellen!

"She's interested in the idea of the home we're going to build on the 41 Bayshore lot...and she's going to bring the boys when she comes to talk things over," Shealds stopped, looking to gauge Hesse' reaction.

Hesse saw the optimism in his friend's eyes and he didn't want to squelch it. "You said she was a lovely young woman when you first met her, so I hope, after everything, that same person reemerges. It's been a tough road for her."

"I want her and the boys to have a good home...and make a good life here," Shealds said earnestly. "After I clear my name, everything can be in the past." He shook his head. "Besides you, Molina and Samples, they're almost the only family I have."

Hesse wondered if this was an early Christmas gift or someone giving Shealds coal in his stocking. He'd talk to Molina so they could help Shealds in either case... and prayed, now more than ever, that Shealds's plan to clear his name would work!

"I'm going to talk with Ms. Reynolds after services on Sunday," Pete said. "I still can't shake all the sad spots in my emotions, although confronting and understanding them with your help has improved things immensely."

"Still getting strong feelings of the female gender when you're near the Bayshore property?" Pastor Bill asked.

"Yes. They're jumbled but I feel more peace and I'm sleeping much better." Pete felt encouraged or he wouldn't be taking this step...or telling Pastor Bill about it.

Pete trusted he was doing things in God's time. "I'd like to extend my relationship with Carolyn *outside of* being Carolyn's pastor and counselor, since only Beth needs further help from me."

Pastor Bill had to be blunt in his questioning. He didn't want to compromise his ethics. "Has there been anything between you and Ms. Reynolds before today?"

Pete knew and accepted the reason for the personal question. "I've only seen her a few times outside of Sundays...and only in an informational or therapeutic vein." He had to think about it. "She's an attractive and likeable person."

"As a person...and not an avenue in this part of this puzzle?" Pastor Bill asked, marking a pencil line doodle he followed back and forth on the paper.

"As a person," Pete replied. "That's why I'm asking for your opinion on this."

Pastor Bill mulled over the information and offered his advice. "Then I think you *could* explore this relationship on a personal level...but, as with anything, go slow with lots of thought and prayer. If I have any more reservations, I'll let you know, since she is directly a part of Beth's life. I hope you will, too."

Sunday services had gone well, and the Reynolds family was there. Pete had heard a few hungry squeaks from Grace Ann's baby carrier during the communion time. He shivered a bit, chiding himself silently, hoping the chilly morning would warm up before his parishioner greeting time at the sanctuary door. If his rugby-injured knee was any barometer, they were going to have a very cold winter. Fortunately, Pete felt his sermon had gone over well. Evangelism was always a touchy subject. He'd tried to ease into the topic and elongate the process in the members' minds by giving each of them an index card.

Pete had told them at the end of the sermon. "Pray on it over the next few weeks, ask God to tell you who you might approach to speak to about our Lord, write down any people God brings to mind, and perhaps, even invite them to church. You've already heard me speak about the Christmas and Easter Christians who only step into church on these two holidays. So if they're thinking of coming, it shouldn't be too hard to jar their thinking about it between now and in December." This had brought a few startled glances and widening eyes in reaction to his challenge. Comfort zones were difficult to change. Who wanted to be thought of as different, pushy, or *weird*? This was an ever-increasing secular society with increasingly little time for their Creator and Comforter. Pete had prayed all week the Lord would soften people's hearts to react positively.

Now he needed to face the *other* personal "speaking" challenge—asking Carolyn to go out with him.

Grace Ann needed a feeding and diaper change, so Carolyn and her family were some of the last to leave the sanctuary.

"May I speak to you for a moment, Carolyn?" Pete asked, trying to remain casual. Carolyn smiled and handed Grace Ann in her carrier to Beth and followed Pete to the other side of the narthex. "I know this isn't exactly the place to carry on casual conversation, so I'll get to the point. I wanted to ask you if you would come out to dinner with me this Thursday night."

Carolyn's mind reacted quickly. She considered a number of different things in lightening rapidity regarding his profession, her interactions with him, and his personality. *He's asking me for a date! Who would have thought?*

"I haven't gone out on a date since I've moved here," Carolyn replied candidly. She looked at her family. People might have thought she was entering into an area of unusual circumstances and to carefully consider things because he was a pastor...but Carolyn was wondering if he's considered everything carefully that he knew about *them* before he asked her out? He must have, she thought...since he's been our family counselor and advisor. "But I think going out to dinner with you would be nice."

"Fine, then," Pete said. He'd been holding his breath. "Would six be OK?"

"I think that's a good time," Carolyn laughed. "I've got plenty of babysitters!"

Pete looked over at the aunts and Darby to continue the quip. "It looks like you do." *Do I know what I'm getting into?*

"I don't know what I was thinking," Carolyn said with a shake of her head. "I wasn't nervous or anything when he asked for a date. Perhaps I was in shock!"

"Were you thinking that even though he's a pastor, he's a nice guy?" Bee asked.

"That's what Nan said about him…and it's turned out to be true." Carolyn looked in the rearview mirror for a second. "He's helped so much in the counseling sessions."

"So this is a pity date?" Cass had a sour look.

"Not at all, Cass," Carolyn replied. "*I* think he's a nice guy, not only a pastor, and I'm going to treat him like one, starting at six p.m. on Thursday."

"Anything else?" Muriel asked.

"The 'anything else' I'm interested in is that Shealds Jackson is also very easy on the eyes," Cass noted.

"We're talking about Pete Allred," Carolyn said pointedly.

"Well, all I'm saying is, if it wasn't for his felonious background, he might be another potential candidate." Cass tried to sound conversational with an innocent tone.

"Hesse is a nice man, too," Muriel added.

"I'm *changing the subject* to note, I've only had one episode of my heart problems since we've come to the Bayshore house…the time we were coming home with Aunt Robin's things," Carolyn said.

"And who was there to get you through that?" Cass said, pressing further in her comments about Shealds Jackson.

"Let's just be happy we're headed home for Bee's chicken pot-pie," Muriel said, seeing the fiery look in Carolyn eyes, to return to more neutral subjects.

"Here has become *home*, Carolyn." Bee smiled. "*Here* has become home."

"I must say I'm a little bit more than nervous," Carolyn admitted on the ride to the restaurant in Pete's freshly washed Jeep, wondering from the time she accepted Pete's invitation if her decision would muddle things. With her new status as mother to Grace Ann, guardian-friend to Beth, and new resident on Bayshore, did she possess enough time, energy, and emotional space left to start dating? But she remembered Billie always saying, "You'll never regret taking a chance because you should never live with regret." So…here she was in the passenger seat on a date with her pastor and Beth's psychologist.

The sign on the small restaurant door said, it was only open Thursday through Sunday.

"Please tell me about this place," Carolyn asked.

Pete smiled. "This is a private culinary school owned by Henri and Rachel Bushon."

"Really?" Carolyn said. "Might be some place I want to bring Beth. Culinary school you said…and so close to Bayshore?"

"Not only that, but I've enjoyed every meal I've had here," Pete said simply as he out pulled her chair out for her to sit down. "They have a Bananas Foster here that in my humble opinion is as good as any dessert I've ever tasted."

Carolyn looked at Pete with a twinkle in her eye. "Then should we eat dessert first?"

The other diners heard their conspiratorial laughter. "Perhaps, the endive salad first to wake up our palate," Pete suggested with a gleeful glance. "Definitely after that."

"Good secondary strategy," Carolyn replied. She was really having a good time!

Carolyn didn't have much time to think about Pete, even though they'd gone on another date to the movies. It was, now, almost

Thanksgiving week and they were starting their festivities in a new place...and with Grace Ann, Beth, and Darby!

As her aunts watched Carolyn's new dating life with interest, they also shepherded Beth and Darby into their Thanksgiving routine, which included each guest selecting a side dish or dessert recipe to be prepared for everyone to try.

"Can't believe we're so close to Thanksgiving week already!" Darby exclaimed.

"We can have at least two types of dressing because we never stuff the bird! In my opinion, it dries out the white meat," Bee confided. "If you've got a recipe that's special to you, dear, we'll try it out today, if you like, so everything will go smoothly next Thursday. We'll put the dried bread on trays in the cupboard."

As she, Bee, and Cass continued to talk, Beth remembered dry turkey from previous Thanksgivings...and trying to be thankful in years past. This year was going to be different, Beth knew, as she felt the string of pearls she'd worn every day since she'd gotten them. She prayed they signified a personal banner of hope, like a flag planned after a battle or on new territory. "I read about a cranberry relish from an old magazine that I'd like to try. I can check on the Internet. I'll add some cinnamon that I think came from Ceylon." She had a few rows of fresh spices —in her and Cass's modular home.

"Sounds good," Bee said. "I'll get four bags of cranberries. Just remember to start slow and taste. Fresh spices are powerful until you get the hang of it. You can always add more, but you can't decrease flavors easily."

"Remember when we almost put twice the amount of salt in the oyster stew because of that recipe typo?" Cass said, folding the last farmers' market bag.

"So glad we caught it," Bee replied as she held the refrigerator door. "We didn't have the luxury of extra money to replace our culinary mistakes back then."

"They were just working their regular jobs before Carolyn sold her company," Darby said as he took the bag containing the carrots to the sink.

"That's right," Cass said. "Working women, now retired…to do more work."

"But life goes on…and speaking on life going on, Carolyn seemed to enjoy her time with Pastor Allred, if I might change the subject," Bee noted.

"Two dates in a week and a half," Darby replied, walking to the Bee's refrigerator.

"I'm not so sure," Cass cut in. "There are more than one horse in this race."

"You mean Shealds?" Darby asked.

"You've seen them together!" Cass said, arching her brow. "A dark horse I say."

Muriel didn't want the conversation to descend into gossip, so she tried to change the subject. "Wish these modular homes had garages. With all the power tools in the Bayshore garage, it's going to be a long walk when the real winter weather comes," Muriel said. "If the snow gets deep, I won't be easy to get over to them to work on the Christmas projects."

"Mind if I pay for a snow shoveling service? Nelder said he uses a guy in town to come and plow," Darby offered.

"That's very kind of you," Muriel replied. "I'll ask Carolyn and see what she thinks."

"We'll be in the mansion before you know it," Bee said, "and living here in the cottages is like being in our new home already!"

"How are you doing, Beth?" Darby asked. "Your counseling sessions?"

"They're OK," Beth started, grabbing for one of the last fall leaves on the ground that she'd put on the counter. "I'm still talking with Pastor Pete. He asks good questions. Hard sometimes…but good."

"Even with the…" Cass began.

"The rape?" Beth felt she could speak freely to everyone here—even Darby. He'd never hurt any woman like that. "I still feel I can talk to Pastor Pete…and I'm not shy or uncomfortable. But if I don't feel I can talk to him anymore, I'll tell you. Honest." She looked at them all. "Pastor Pete keeps telling me that too."

"Well, that's good, dear," Bee said, feeling relieved. "This counseling is supposed to help you…and we're praying it does."

"Guess even though I felt I'd gotten through the past without all this, I know you care about me and I should talk about it… and make sure I deal with it all," Beth sighed.

"You've read the articles on the Internet we've all sent you…and the experts say you still might need guidance." Cass grabbed a coffee mug from the cupboard.

"Are we all set for the spa day?" Bee asked, wanting to allow Beth some time to consider their words - so glad Beth didn't need to be pressured to continue.

"I've confirmed everything for the Saturday after Thanksgiving…and we can keep Grace Ann with us," Cass reported with a smile. "They'll just slow things down when Carolyn has to breastfeed." They were glad they'd encouraged Carolyn in those efforts.

"She persevered through the discomfort and all that mess of getting her Aunt Robin's things back here," Darby said as he remembered traveling across country and back. "I'm sorry about the timing."

"It was quite a tussle but you weren't responsible for the timing," Muriel noted with a smile as she brought the freshly ironed table linens into the kitchen. "Bee, have you got all the Thanksgiving recipes?"

"Yes, right on track." Bee wiped her hands on the dishtowel tucked in her apron waistband. "Beth wants a new cranberry relish and Darby wants sweet potato pie."

"Before we write down the menu," Cass said, "who's accepted our invitations?"

"Carolyn said Pastor Allred is going to drive to see his aunt after the evening Thanksgiving Eve service," Muriel reported.

"So far, we've got acceptances from Shealds, Hesse, and Molina." Bee looked at her list. "I'm crossing off Pastor Allred."

"Shealds asks for cornbread stuffing, which we were going to make already, Hesse wants pecan pie, and Molina wants a savory Aztec pudding but he doesn't have any recipes," Muriel said looking down at the list. "One side and two desserts."

"I'll look up Aztec pudding on the Internet when I make sure about my cranberry relish," Beth offered as she jumped off the counter stool and headed for the computer. "Think we should try to make that pudding today to see if it's sweet or savory."

The older women exchanged glances, knowing Beth and Molina had spent a lot of time together with his work on the Bayshore house and their burial efforts at Nelder's. "You don't think she's seeing too much of him?" Cass whispered.

"Always a gentleman...and we've been keeping our eyes on him," Muriel replied.

"No need to get all riled up." Bee grabbed for the clean dishtowel. "She's talking about her future plans...and there's nothing in them concerning him or any other man."

"Jessie told me their bed-and-breakfast expects to be full...and they're hosting about twelve people for their own Thanksgiving dinner," Beth said in a loud voice as she waited for the server connection. "They're having an early dinner and want to try to come over for desert on Thanksgiving evening...and they'll call if they can't come."

"Don't forget my two friends, Wesley and Emerson Beals, are coming for Thanksgiving," Darby said. "Friends from my late wife's side of the family."

"I've got two extra numbered spots for them. Do they want or need anything special for their dinner?" Bee filled in the names on her paper and counted the number.

"They said anything homemade is what they want," Darby replied.

"So that's eleven for dinner, not counting Grace Ann, so far!" Muriel counted the names on her list. "I'll start the place cards tomorrow."

"Can we keep a spot for Joe?" Beth asked, holding a page from the printer.

Cass came over to hug Beth. "You miss him?" she asked.

"No, it's not like that," Beth replied. "I just want to know what happened to him since he was with Grace Ann and me until we got here. He needs a family, too."

"You're right. So let's make sure *everyone* has a place card and Grace Ann will be fine in her high chair," Muriel said, adding Joe's name to the list.

"Glad we'll be finishing the covered porch before winter sets in," Hesse said looking at the construction schedule on their kitchen table for the Bayshore house.

"Glad the weather held out and the rain stopped to pour the footers." Shealds picked up his coffee mug and headed for the window. "The Reynolds are celebrating their Thanksgiving in the main house too."

"Would be a shame, being invited guests at their home this afternoon…and not to have their fulfilled their wish," Hesse remarked as he rolled his neck and readjusted his shoulders. "But those clouds in the south sure look more ominous than what the weather forecaster is saying."

"Are you feeling it in your bones, old man?" Shealds quipped, coming back from the kitchen. "I better get out for one last paddleboard trip before the weather changes and we have to leave for dinner."

"I'm not saying anything more or less than I feel the weather is changing toward winter." Hesse gave a fleeting slash of a smile, not rising to the bait. "No one's going to be at Bayshore on Saturday, and we can work on the monitoring systems."

"I know they're going for their spa day on Saturday. Samples checked," Shealds replied. "But it's a good time for someone to try to cause trouble with *everyone* gone."

"You nervous because you're dropping the hammer on Zaugus on Sunday?" Hesse ventured.

"Let's just say, Thanksgiving is going to be the last holiday Attorney General Zaugus is going to enjoy...for a long time." Shealds didn't want to admit he was nervous and needed to have some excuse to exercise and not to sit and worry. "I'm thinking of after the holidays, too. Ellen and the boys are coming."

"There hasn't been any more trouble," Hesse ventured, trying to calm Shealds. Thinking of a bright future was good.

"Then some might still be coming...and I don't want that to happen for them...or me." Shealds grabbed his jacket and left without saying another word to check his wetsuit and paddleboard. These last few days of waiting were going to be hell!

Shealds dragged himself up on the spit of land after beaching his paddleboard. He checked his leg. The calf wound bled sluggishly but could be covered by some of those Steri-Strips from the first aid kit back at the house. He hadn't drank too much brackish water in the struggle and was able to keep his wits about him in the surprise attack from what he guessed was a six-foot man with a full rubber suit, scuba gear and mask, who tried to pull Shealds off his paddleboard. *Do I need a tetanus shot?*

There was only one man. Shealds kept his assailant turning around in the water, as they struggled, to make sure there was only one attacker. After the element of surprise was gone, the fight had only lasted about thirty more seconds before the other man escaped. His assailant had dropped his knife in the water and fled. No swim fins and the cramping, from the wound and the compromised wetsuit, kept Shealds from chasing the man down.

Shealds wasn't in too bad a shape, but not willing to take any chances of another attack. He ran as fast as he could in his swim shoes to his truck and gunned the engine.

"I'm telling people if anyone asks about my leg that I slipped or lost my balance and cut it on the rocks down at the cove while I was paddle boarding," Shealds said after returning from the urgent care center and drying his damp hair from his shower.

Hesse held a cup of hot coffee for him.

"I don't have much of a limp and no one will be able to see anything under my dress pants."

"Molina's picking up your equipment and he should be back soon," Hesse offered, folding his arms. "What did Samples say?"

"He'll have his own men down in the water tomorrow to look for the knife and anything else that might identify who was after me," Shealds said grimly. "No police."

"So this proves people are after you now…and they're getting desperate?" Hesse asked.

"Seems so," Shealds replied after taking a sip of the hot, strong coffee. "No more paddleboard excursions or other solitary pursuits until this is all over."

"I can't feel my feet, I'm so full," Molina said, plopping down onto the sofa now that they were back in their home.

"Must say you cleaned up good," Hesse noted, liking the navy pullover, white button-down shirt, khaki pants, and regimental tie Molina had worn. Molina had surprised them. His hair was now a natural dark-brown shade.

"Great time," Shealds admitted. "We're going to have to up our game when it comes to barbeque season…and invite them to come over here."

"You hear that, Molina," Hesse bantered sarcastically. "Think Shealds wants to show off his charcoal skills to Ms. Reynolds!"

"Ms. Reynolds and her family, Hesse," Shealds replied. "Ms. Reynolds and her family."

"Don't give me that," Hesse said skeptically. "You've mentioned her in positive terms many times now that we've gotten to know her. Don't deny it!"

"She's seeing Pastor Allred now," Shealds replied. "I'm still an ex con."

"Only for a few more days, Shealds," Hesse persisted. "Then it's an even playing field, my friend. An even field."

"Take a chance," Molina said solemnly.

"I'm so sorry, Beth," Carolyn said. She hugged the girl and kissed her head. "Grace Ann seems to have her first cold, and I need to stay with her." She looked over at the port-a-crib in the corner of Bayshore's old kitchen, glad her baby daughter only had slight flushing and a low-grade fever. The pediatrician said Grace Ann needed to rest. "Tonight, we'll all celebrate with our annual Thanksgiving leftover casserole."

"Maybe we can reschedule everything for later in the afternoon," Beth suggested. "It's so early…and that wouldn't hurt would it?"

Carolyn tried to appear unfazed, but all the preparations and having Thanksgiving plus a sleepless night with Grace Ann's fussiness and the doctor's office visit, left Carolyn exhausted. Grace Ann was finally resting. "I'll miss being with you all, but I'll do some paperwork…and some prepping for Christmas." She looked into Beth's sad eyes. "Lots of homemade presents, decorations and all our cottages will be brimming with activity!"

"Better try to get some rest while Grace is sleeping," Bee said as she brought in the casserole and Carolyn's favorite canned artichoke side dish. "Set the oven for three hundred and seventy-five degrees, and we'll take care of dinner."

"I brought magazines, one of books I bought at the church rummage sale, and a sack lunch for you," Muriel said as she walked through the front door.

"Shealds, Molina and Hesse brought in enough wood for ten fires before they left on Thursday night," Cass offered.

"They're just glad for some home cooking...and to be able to help in some way, I'm sure." Bee looked at the three piles of logs on the tarp, not wanting to discuss Cass's opinions about Carolyn and Shealds. "Hesse said it won't hurt the floor since the sanding, floorboard, and gas firebox replacement projects aren't on the schedule until after they start the kitchen in January." Now, these men were friends as well as their contractors.

"They were helpful, complimentary, and blended well with us," Cass said. She wasn't going to give up easily in pushing Shealds forward as a dating consideration for Carolyn.

Carolyn didn't notice, it seemed. "I'll get the information if we want a gas insert when the man comes to see it today," Carolyn said. "We'd put the gas line in at the same time as the one for the outdoor kitchen and be able to forget about all this wood."

"If we're *are* going to keep all this wood in the family room, we're going to have to deal with these piles much more ascetically," Cass said. "Looks like a fishing cabin."

"Perhaps we could put a large slab of Plexiglas on it...and use it as a coffee table or credenza." Muriel laughed.

"I'll have Hesse price it out both ways," Carolyn replied with a smirk.

Bee looked at the sky through the bank of windows. "Better get going before the rain starts." She looked around the room. "You sure you're going to be OK?"

Carolyn smiled again. "I've got all the emergency numbers. Nan knows I'm here with Grace Ann, and Pastor Allred said he'd be coming by this afternoon."

Bee frowned. Carolyn still used the pastor's full name frequently, even after two dates. "He knows you're here alone with Grace Ann?" *Have things fizzled between them?*

"Yes. Don't make it sound like I'm on a desert island," Carolyn mused. "*Besides* the fireplace guy, Shealds has slated some other potential subcontractors for estimates on the exterior of the house." She looked at Grace Ann again. "I won't need to jostle Grace Ann because we're already here...and they'll help if there are any problems." She checked her watch. "If you don't get going, you'll be late...and I thought this was supposed to be a restful day."

"Carolyn's right," Bee said. "Besides, when we get back this afternoon, we'll let Beth drive again on the entrance road if it's not raining." She knew the promise of afternoon driving might short circuit Beth's sadness.

"Only if it's still light out," Carolyn said with outstretched arms as she herded her aunts and Beth toward the door. She hugged each of them as they put on their coats and opened the door. "Brr, it is a bit chillier than I thought it was going to be."

"Feels like the warm autumn we've been having is over," Cass replied. "Glad I covered the plants we're going to try to save."

"You sure you don't want us to move you and Grace Ann back to the cottage?" Bee asked. "We'll call Darby and tell him to come home from sightseeing with Wesley and Emerson."

"You'll do no such thing. We're fine," Carolyn replied strongly. "Get going." She would fix a hot cup of tea while looking at the patterns for afghans they might knit for such occasions when they were living in the house. *It is cold.*

Shealds looked up from the architectural drawings he was working on in the construction trailer and saw the Reynolds family's SUV drive up the road and turn right on the highway. Hesse and Molina had left an hour before, looking at the new small welding setup Molina wanted for their company.

Shealds remembered the women said they were going for the spa day. Nice family. Something like what he wanted when everything was out and settled down concerning his wrongful conviction. He thought it might take another year to get out from under everything: a careful orchestration of identifying the *true* facts of the situation of Zaugus's artful manipulation of the law using Shealds's sister-in-law's vulnerability plus several glaring examples of Zaugus's failure to disclose not one, but three documents that clearly exonerated Shealds's concerning the charges, not to mention the other offenses of document tampering and forged signatures.

Even if Shealds had wanted to throw his life away and go to prison, Zaugus had a duty, as a representative of the court, for this information to be disclosed. Zaugus and one, probably two of his aides, with equally blind ambition, had decided to withhold the truth. That wasn't all. Shealds hadn't even brought up the knowledge he had of Zaugus's personal life indicating unbecoming conduct.

The retired yet highly respected former national news anchor who had interviewed Shealds before the debacle, quietly researched and authenticated all the new documentation Shealds and Samples gave him. He'd secretly taped an interview with Shealds on Tuesday evening, at the Baltimore house Shealds had rented for the occasion, asking all the skeptical and hard-hitting questions Shealds had expected. Samples provided the security detail as everything had gone flawlessly, from the private jet picking up the news crew, to flying them back to their New York destination, as they prepared their broadcast information, including hotel rooms and catered meals right through Thanksgiving. Their reward might include television news awards if everything went well. After the broadcast, the television segment and all the documentation would be personally couriered to the Justice Department and the governor's office.

Shealds saw the increasing energy and excitement in the anchor's eyes and body language with the realization that this news story was going to last from the post-Thanksgiving doldrums, well into the New Year. Shealds hoped the man had his Christmas shopping done—or had this story been the "present" the newsman had been waiting for?

Christmas. Thanksgiving had been Shealds first "real" holiday celebration in years. He'd been wrong about Carolyn Reynolds...and remembered what Hesse had said. He *could* see a relationship happening...if she might be interested in him. The last of the *real* barriers to anything good would be *gone.*

Shealds was going to be vindicated and he could start the healing with the rest of what was left of his extended family...and start his life again. He thought of Carolyn's blue eyes and her warm smile as he rubbed his neck. He really needed some coffee.

CHAPTER EIGHTEEN

"It's a surprise nor'easter," Cass said with more than a bit of anxiety in her voice when she called Carolyn. It had started snowing hard when they'd arrived for their pampering. The spa owner rescheduled all their appointments and sent everyone, including his staff, home.

They'd tried to drive, and it had taken four long hours just to get to the Stornels' bed-and-breakfast from the spa, exhausted from the white-knuckled drive, in trying to get back home, calling Carolyn every half hour or so. "The roads are impassable, the highway patrol has closed everything...but we're safe here for the night. We'll take one room and use two rubber mattresses if other unlucky travelers need somewhere to stay."

"None of the people with weekend reservations got here before they closed the roads," Bee informed. "But that doesn't mean there won't be people walking in from their stranded cars and trucks. Wanted to tell you that Darby and the Beals got here too."

The news reports indicated the weather had changed almost the instant Carolyn's aunts and Beth left Bayshore. Three weather systems had converged; an unexpected cold, rain-soaking system from the south was caught between a cold front with high winds in the west, and an unexpected strong eastern system which developed and headed up the seaboard. Energy from the three fronts merged, pushed by the stronger southern flow surging north-northeast, and produced blanketing sheets of cold, heavy wet snow over their region with forceful winds from the interplay of the three systems.

"Should we put you on the list for emergency evacuation?" Muriel asked.

"Certainly not. We're fine here. Grace Ann's fever is gone...and we're trying to celebrate her first snow...from the inside of course," Carolyn reported, trying to reassure her family. "The electricity is still on, but if we lose power, you know I've got the generator in the garage...and I know how to use it. I've got plenty of food. We're fine."

"You know we'll get back there as soon as we can," Cass announced. "We've got chains, and I told the highway patrol to call us at any hour if they're getting a caravan together once the road is cleared for one lane of traffic."

"I know you're anxious to get back...but just be safe," Carolyn admonished. "You know yourself; you talked about all the firewood I've got here. I've got that going, too!"

"We're not the one alone with Grace Ann," Beth fretted.

"Please, I've already told you we're fine...and you can call me on my cell phone as often as you'd like if you're concerned," Carolyn assured.

"Like you could stop us," Muriel grumped. "Grace Ann would be a better weather forecaster." She shook her finger in the air. "I said the clouds looked 'funny.'"

"Thank Nan and Ed for taking care of you. Stay safe," Carolyn replied.

"Sending lots of prayers," Bee called out as Carolyn ended the conversation.

"What do you think, Grace Ann?" Carolyn said, lifting the baby from her port-a-crib. "Let's take a walk in the room, stretch our legs, and see if the blizzard has tapered off." Carolyn could see from the outdoor light facing what would become the outdoor kitchen, spa, and kitchen garden, that the storm was still raging. They'd have been in their modular cottage if the mansion's windows hadn't been replaced, its chimney and hearth fixed and the wiring redone.

Thank goodness, the water heater and furnace were safe and workable, too, Carolyn thought. She and Grace Ann could be safe until everyone got home.

Shealds couldn't figure out where he was. He wanted to go back to sleep but felt cold as hell, as if he was immersed in an ice bucket - although he remembered hell was always very warm by all accounts. Shealds's mind felt funny and slow, like he'd been on a weeklong bender...drinking some really cheap booze. His mouth was dry, and there were no pillows or any blanket on his stomach-sprawled body. Had he kicked everything off during this pitch-black night? Was the electricity out in the house? He'd have to get out of bed and rouse Hesse and Molina to help him check the furnace and pipes.

When he tried to move his arms and legs, they were numb, as if he'd had a stroke. He felt like a beached whale trying to find traction on dry ground. The effort to turn his upper body to one side caused beads of cold sweat to spring up on his forehead. As he tried to rock back and forth, Shealds's flaccid legs bumped into what he thought might be his desk, and then his chair. Now he remembered he was in the construction trailer. *What the hell is going on?*

He felt pressure sensations in a few places but no pain as he continued his struggle. He tried to fight to sit up with no success—only getting his right shoulder to turn slightly. His body wanted to stay put and go back to sleep, but his mind knew he couldn't stay still if he wanted to live. He'd been beaten up, drugged, shot or something. *But what?*

"Concentrate. Concentrate," he whispered as he rested for a few seconds. His face and neck felt so cold...and his shirt and T-shirt were gone. *How did that happen?* All he knew was, he was in the work trailer at the Bayshore property, the heater and lights were off, and he was probably near naked.

He thought of trying to throw up if he'd been poisoned but wondered if his throat muscles were as useless as his arms and legs seemed to be, and he didn't wanted to choke. Shealds felt lucky to be breathing as he tried to swallow with great difficulty. Then he tried rocking and rubbing himself against the trailer's industrial carpet for warmth as the burning, piercing pain of nerve reawakening made tears come to his eyes. He didn't want to moan to tip anyone off that he was awake. But he couldn't help panting against the twin agony of his efforts to move and his skin feeling as if it was being pricked by needles or was on fire.

Shealds clumsily rolled his right shoulder down and under on the floor, trying to twist his torso because his lower body was still dead, wondering if this was like the pain he thought fellow inmates might have felt when they secretly branded each other's skin in gang rituals in the prison. "Keep going. Keep going," he admonished himself silently. Hypothermia would kill him if he couldn't escape from the cold.

Shealds remembered seeing the weather change and the first sheets of sleet, then snow, hit the trailer windows. He'd decided to pack things up and get back home before the roads became impassable. But he wasn't at home; he was here in the construction trailer, helpless and in deep trouble. The next thought was as cold as the floor. *Someone wants me dead.*

Shealds could clench several finger joints on his right hand, and that forearm twitched in cramping response to his flexing attempts. He felt like he'd already run a marathon, perhaps two, and neither his left arm or either of his legs worked yet.

He kept pushing his torso with all his might, against the dead weight of his legs, first to his right side, then to his back and then to the left, hoping to push some warmer blood down his body. For what seemed like hours, he kept up the agonizing routine and cadence of the movements until sharp pains started shooting first to his stomach, then his thighs, and then down to his calves. The accompanying muscle spasms sent tears to his eyes and agonizing pain to his brain.

Shealds's hands didn't have much dexterity yet, like the signals from his brain weren't getting through. His arms didn't seem to have enough strength to brace his weight either. He thought he might injure them or break bones if he tried to push too fast. He was a bit warmer and covered in sweat from what he could feel…and so thirsty with little hope in getting anything to drink or even being able to hold anything down until he and his muscles were more awake. The snow outside could be quick drinking water, but that would induce more hypothermia…and going outside to the snow would make him a target if anyone were watching the trailer.

He wished he had music or something to keep his mind active against the dulling fog still swirling there. He wouldn't talk to himself. Best not telegraph that he was awake to whoever did this.

Taking another inventory, he could now feel painful needlelike sensations in his left hand and forearm. He tried to get to his back as well as test the strength and feeling in his right hand and arm. At this rate, he hoped to be able to stand in a few hours, at least sit up and see if the guns were still behind the desk drawer. Shealds wasn't going to die without trying to put up a fight.

Thinking about prison and the injustice of being put there and being so close to vindication, got Shealds through the hot, searing pain of finally being able to get to a partially seated position, in a drag-and-rock motion, like a seal lion. It had taken innumerable unsuccessful, awkward attempts of "batting" his desk chair to anchor it to the side of the desk—with him trying to persuade his burning arm muscles to work like recalcitrant flippers. Using the braced chair, Shealds pulled himself up with his head, neck, and "flippers" to various wobbly leaning positions from his waist up, retreating to the floor again to stay flat if the pain became too unbearable.

Shealds knew his knuckles, hands, and forearms were scraped and bloodied but he hoped to be able to raise himself to a balanced, sitting position soon. He also hoped Hesse and Molina had missed him by now, probably suspicious of numerous unanswered messages and were working as hard as he was, to get him out of this predicament. Other possibilities were shoved from his mind. Shealds told himself Hesse and Molina were safe.

Pete didn't know why, but he had this overwhelming feeling he needed to get to the Bayshore property. It was so strong it felt like an elephant on his chest. He knew he'd told Carolyn he would come by, but there was blizzard out there, and all the roads were impassable. He'd prayed about it for several minutes, fixed a cup of tea, and looked out the window at the whipping winds and the snow pelt the windows.

He had storm gear, snowshoes for cross-country exercise...and many years of tutelage by his now-crazed father on survival techniques. *What will people think if I get caught out in the storm or get hurt?*

Pete kept lecturing himself about keeping the roads clear for emergency vehicles and only letting the paid professionals be out in weather like this. He didn't even know if there were any problems at the Bayshore mansion. *What will I tell Carolyn if I get there and nothing is wrong?* She might think he was crazy as well.

Pete wracked his brain. Bee and Cass told him they were going for a spa day today with the ladies? Carolyn and Grace had the shelter of any of the new modulars…and the Bayshore house. Pete tried to convince himself they were as stable a situation as anyone in this storm, maybe better! *Right?*

In his attempt to call Carolyn, he was greeted with an "All circuits are busy message". But instead of lessening at this attempt to reach her, the impressions became more nagging and strong - like an angry lion clawing at his chest.

Pete looked around hurriedly. He had a clean water pouch in the closet and some energy bars. His phone with GPS was charged, and he had his all-weather flashlight and a small shovel in the closet. He'd need his walking poles and other set of lighter, retractable ones in his pack just in case. This was madness, but he could take the path through the riverbed and climb the crude stepping-stones by the bridge on the Bayshore property to keep away from the worst of the winds and deep snows. He could also turn around and come back home if the feeling left…and call Pastor Bill for an emergency counseling session if the phone still worked.

He prayed he wasn't worse off psychologically than he imagined. Before this episode happened he'd thought that he might be getting better.

In the short rest periods between testing and trying get his muscles working again, Shealds planned his next moves. See if the truck was there. Check to see if his mobile phone was still in the trailer. He'd need some light. The flashlights, matches, and light sticks were across the room in the tool chest, and he didn't know if they were still there or stripped, just like him from his clothes.

Clothes. He'd have to see if the coat pegs were empty. If his coat was gone, Shealds knew they didn't have any extra clothes in the construction trailer, only metal tools and drawings. If the utility knife was still there, cutting carpet sections to cover himself would take too much time and energy, sapping what was left of his strength and be too cumbersome if he needed to move quickly.

There were two full garbage bags he'd put by the door to take to the construction waste bin by the driveway. He could rummage around in them and see if there was anything more he could use and or even use the bags themselves—one over his head for his body and one for briefs. Shealds didn't know what to do for his feet. Anything too big would shift with his steps, be too slippery, or cumbersome, but he wanted to prevent irreversible frostbite. He was in survival mode, trying to save his life.

Shealds's first efforts to corral the trailer chairs as braces failed as waves of vertigo and nausea assailed him. Even in the inky darkness, he needed to shut his eyes. The rollers and pivoting seat on his cushioned office chair bucked him off like a Brahma bull, giving him a small bump on his forehead and a bloody lip from hitting the drafting table as he fell. In a second attempt, the chair almost fell on top of him. The armrests of the chair made it impossible for him to get his body onto the seat. Shealds regrouped and changed his efforts to use one of the straight-back, stationary office chairs.

After numerous attempts, Shealds successfully hoisted his torso weight over one of the stationary desk chair seats braced against the wall. A crab-walk effort to hold on to the chair seat and push the chair legs across the carpet caused his awakening legs to cramp painfully, budging the chair only a few inches. Next he tried to hold on to furniture and pull himself along the floor—another failure. Finally Shealds alternately shifted, pushed, and twisted his weight in the direction he wanted the chair to slide. He guided its haphazard course by getting whatever pressure he could with his torso, arms, and legs; congratulating himself that he going in the right direction toward the tool cabinets and construction desk.

Clumsily, he pushed the chair into the tool chest nearest him. Shealds didn't count the number of times it took him, but he was near enough the chests and the wall to twist his body to try to sit up in the chair. He swiveled his torso with tingling, weak hands, and pulled himself into a sitting position. He wondered if he could tie himself to the chair, but there wasn't any rope. Shealds carefully assessed his position on the chair seat and bent over to slowly check the wheel locks on the chests to make sure they would not roll away.

Now, Shealds could start his hunt for useful supplies. He almost laughed at his snail-slow progress. His fingers felt like they were breaking as he got one of the drawers open. He slowly inched his fingers to find the large rectangular box of matches he knew were stored there.

After ten unsuccessful attempts and burning himself several times, Shealds managed not to start a fire as he kept searching for things he could use with each small flame. Although he was hampered by the pain of the bright light of the flaring matches and dizzying images before his eyes, Shealds was able to find a utility knife, two rolls of duct tape, some old plumb lines, and a sheet of sandpaper. He slowly gauged the distance to move each of these treasures from the top of the chest to a smaller table, next to the drafting table, where there was more space and at a better height to work.

Shealds started to shiver and tried to rub what he could of his skin with his fumbling hands. His efforts produced more pins-and-needle sensations that were less painful this time. He'd have to get moving because of the cold. Now was the time to try to stand up and see if he could hold his weight. He'd have to be careful.

Weakness still assailed his lower legs and feet as he rubbed them as best he could, cold sweat stinging his eyes. He put one hand on the top of the tool chest, and then the other as he heaved himself up and forward. In the first try, he bent a bit at the waist and gasped for breath. He almost fell, but he held as tight as he could to the tool chest drawer, locked his knees, and strained to hold himself up, waiting for the vertigo to lighten. Shealds sat down heavily and almost fell off the chair. He kept trying in a focused attack plan: deep breathing, making sure his bracing was steady, and pushing up slowly toward a normal standing position and balancing his weight. At last, he was able to stand erect, bracing himself with his hands and locked elbows. Weakness forced him to sit down again and rest.

Now Shealds could pick up the supplies he had and pivot to transfer them to the small tabletop. He started, trying not to drop anything.

That accomplished, he needed to try to walk.

Shealds sat on the chair, wiggled his toes, and rubbed the bottom of his feet on the carpet. He tested them by turning them to the right and the left, accessing the feeling in each toe and gauging his abilities from his knee movements to see if his brain and feet could now accurately communicate where his feet were in space. After that was mastered, he felt the areas around him. Nothing had been moved, so he'd have to try to chair scoot to the trailer door, turn the knob, and see if he could get out. If not, he would resort to freeing himself with other tools...or if that didn't work, if the guns were still there, he could try to shoot off the door handle, closer to the time he'd be making his breakout.

Soon, he'd try to use his wheeled office chair as a makeshift "walker" in front of him, get to the door, and use a stationary chair to sit at the side of the door. No sense in giving anyone a kill shot by standing in front of the door.

Now it was time to start working. Shealds lowered himself to the floor, using the chair as a ladder to slowly sit down as his legs and arms continued to shoot pain signals to his brain. Shealds needed to remove the desk drawer to see if the guns were in their hiding place against the wall. He let out a sigh of relief as he felt for and found the two handguns in their hard foam cases. At least he had some defense and a few rounds of ammunition. He loaded them clumsily, but kept working because he needed protection, if whoever it was came back now. Otherwise, he would carry one gun and tape the other to his body, on what he proposed would his run over to the house, barn, or studio. It all depended on any gunfire or hints of other trouble he might see as he ran from the trailer.

The wind seemed to be buffeting the other side of the trailer, although there were some consistent swirling winds. If the door was unlocked, Shealds thought it best not try to gauge the level of snow against the door right away. Any changes would signal he was awake. Shealds closed his eyes, thanking the Lord that he and Hesse had zip-tied barrier cloth on the stairway rails to keep construction debris from the landing. Now it was his snow and sleet barrier as well.

He'd test the door now, and then again, right before he was ready to leave. He'd thought of using the utility door on the far side of the trailer, but its stairway lead to a steeper incline, right where the wind was blowing. With any drifting snow, if he misjudged its depth or drift size in the storm light, he'd emerge snow-covered with no protective clothes. Besides, it was facing the open land with nothing he might use as shelter or cover against gunfire.

Shealds turned the door handle slowly. It was open. So he needed to lock it from the inside, to make sure he wasn't surprised by anyone coming to check to see if he was dead. He set the lock. Now to get to him, whoever it was who did this, would either have to fire shots to see if they could kill him through the side of the trailer, shoot the lock, or use a key to unlock the door. He'd have warning.

Next he quickly looked out the door window to see if his truck was there and to assess the snow drifts by the front door. His truck, which he had parked with its nose to the trailer steps, was gone, so there was no reason to look for keys. After searching the charging station, his phone was gone as well. Whoever had done this wanted everyone to think he was gone and the trailer was empty. He made another quick look just to make sure his eyes weren't playing tricks on him. Shealds guessed the snow had drifted to four or five feet deep in places with some taller towering drifts away from the house; the snow seemed well above the first stair risers on the trailer steps as the dim barn light illuminated the white ground.

Shealds checked his food supply. He'd found a flat, half-full plastic bottle of cola in his trash survey. He'd try to see if his stomach would welcome the sugar water as much as he craved something to drink. He sipped slowly against his parched throat, waiting for telltale signs of nausea or for his other post-drugging symptoms to worsen. He thanked the Lord that, after a few sips, he felt a bit better.

Shealds grabbed for the plumb lines. He fumbled at cutting the line from their canisters. Some of the sting from one canister would be used to tie the Bayshore shore property keys around his neck and the rest would act as a belt to keep the garbage bags cinched to his body, along with the string from the second canister. He laid the chalked strings across the desktop, knowing he was making a horrible mess...thinking of what Hesse and Molina would say when they discovered what had gone on.

Shealds now had to consider what to do with the duct tape. The extra gun and ammunition should probably be taped on the outside of the garbage bag clothes, Shealds thought. If he got pinned down, he didn't want to have to fight the plumb line belting and the plastic to get to it.

The rough sandpaper was the only thing Shealds could think of that might give his feet some traction as he swathed them in duct tape, so he carefully tore the sheet in half. He was sweating by the time he finished wrapping toes and ankles, first in duct tape, and then, taping the sandpaper to the duct tape already on his toes and around his toes and ankles. Getting out of the trailer and having some time against the cold were more important. If he lived, he'd worry about cutting the tape off his body—not now. *Will everything hold up if I need to run?*

Next he put two holes in the first garbage bag and stepped into the holes. Shealds pulled the bag to his waist and pulled on the bag ties to close the top. He put several rows of tape on his waist and more rows farther down on each of his thighs to keep the bag from interfering with his movements. He put the other garbage bag over his head and arms. Efforts to get some covering for his arms like sleeves and allow enough freedom of movement weren't as successful as he'd hoped. Neither was his attempt to use the plumb line sting for a belt of sorts, so Shealds wreathed his torso with more duct tape to keep the garbage bags secure. Some of the first plumb line did work as a neck lariat for the Bayshore property keys, so if Shealds could make it across to the buildings, he could get in. So his "clothes" were secure as he could manage and he'd drink the rest of the cola and rest for a few minutes.

Shealds did a few practice jumps in place and almost fell because of dizziness and cramping muscles. The pain is good—he felt awake and warmer. So he held on to the table and chair and started jumping again. He took his pulse. Shealds needed to get out of there. Getting awake and ready had taken a long time. Whoever was trying to kill him, might want to come back any second.

Shealds needed a better place to fight for his life. The main Bayshore house was his first choice—lots of rooms, lots of hiding places, and more time to defend himself. As he taped the extra gun and ammunition to his chest, Shealds gauged the distance he needed to run. It was about thirty yards to the nearest the side of the house. He'd be fully out-in-the-open as he was running to the house, so he'd have to try evasive maneuvers to get to the front door. The biggest banks of windows were in the kitchen and family room side of the house as were most of the doors. Another spot any gunman or gunmen might be. So would it be better to run to the denser bushes on the left side of the house and get back to the portico steps, perhaps to spot where the gunmen were or go to the back to the house under the protection of the shrubbery. A second choice for a hiding place was barricading himself in Robin Lee's storage area in the barn. He knew the combination of the security lock, and it might be a bit warmer in there, although all the utility cords might be cut.

These people weren't dumb. They could burn down the barn and the Bayshore house, too. But the house was bigger with more places to hide before smoke and flames took over. Thankfully, everyone was gone to the spa. No lights from the modulars.

The snow was getting deeper. It was time to move. Shealds didn't think his makeshift clothes or duct-taped feet could stand the cold for long. He'd come close to hypothermia already.

If he got to the house without being spotted, he needed a plan. He needed a barricade to block an area on the window side of the house. He hoped the rental furniture was still there, and he had the plastic garbage cans the construction crews used for their trash. He'd tape them together once he got in the house. Bullets hitting the wooden braces between the glass panes and glass shards could injure him. *Can I get a defensive position together and not make too much noise? Perhaps I can use the Lee storage area for something?* There was a gas can over there and a small chainsaw—maybe he could make some Molotov cocktails if he had the time and protection to get back to the house without frostbite or bullet wounds.

He said a few prayer words, asking for self-preservation, and got ready to open the door. There wasn't much snow against the trailer door, so he opened it and started running.

Shealds stopped at the first hiding place behind a Hemlock tree, the scraggly bushes, and rock mound Cass argued should remain for aesthetic value. He was going to have buy Cass a dozen roses, no, two dozen roses every week for a year for fighting for her position to save those plants and stones. He looked around and didn't see any protruding heads, sentries, gun barrels, or strange vehicles. The sandpaper was making him slide, not giving him any grip at all, so he tore it off his feet. Should he run again or throw up something small, like stones, to flush out the killers?

Shealds cursed himself for not bringing something extra for that purpose. He should have looked at the garbage more carefully, although he was at a rock pile. But with the strong winds, no one would hear the sound of a rock, so he was wasting precious time. Shealds decided to make his next run. He was starting to lose feeling again in his legs and his feet were stinging and getting numb again. He couldn't wait any longer. The terrain was slightly uphill, and he'd have to make it to the far side of the portico because everything to the door was open ground. Shealds rubbed his ankles as best he could and took several deep breaths. He grabbed the gun and ran the second route up the small rise to the three bushes beyond the portico, making sure he gauged the level of the snow as he dove for the ground. He slid a bit too soon, like he was trying to steal second base on his belly, and the gravel lacerated his right thigh and tore at the garbage bags. The imprint of the other gun bruised his ribs. At least he hadn't broken any bones and the ground seemed a bit warmer here.

Again, no gunshots or sign of anyone around, but he couldn't be sure, and he couldn't take any more time to think. Someone had tried to kill him. Killers didn't care about scaffolding, hotels, fire, out-of-control trucks or intended deadly overdoses. They'd be back to try again, if Shealds and his would-be protectors didn't get them first. There was going to be a deduction from Samples's bill for all this, Shealds thought, as he raised himself to his knees for the final assault. This was going to hurt; even if he didn't get cut down by gunfire. Aim for the lock and a quick turn of the knob. *When they find out they haven't succeeded, what would they do next?*

The newly installed reproduction door had been carefully leveled and shimmied into place, and the weather stripping on both sides had been stapled and nailed per manufacturer instructions. Shealds prayed it opened as easily and quickly as the manufacturer bragged in their instructions. He hadn't remembered if it had opened smoothly Thursday when they had come for Thanksgiving.

The key slipped in and the door opened. Shealds jumped through the doorway, fell to his knees, and swatted the door closed behind him. He needed a few breaths before he turned to lock it. His legs felt like jelly again. But he needed to look out the window to see if anyone was following him and start on his defense plans in the kitchen area. If he couldn't get that started, he needed to get up the stairs and hide.

As he got up, Shealds heard a sound from the hallway by the windows. He raised his gun. Carolyn Reynolds walked into the foyer. She was holding her daughter, Grace Ann. "You're not supposed to be here," he croaked, lowering the gun. "Why aren't you at the spa?"

Carolyn recoiled when she saw the gun, instinctively turning to protect Grace Ann. "Why are you *here?*" she exclaimed, looking at her escape options.

Taking Grace Ann and running out the door into the teeth of a blizzard wasn't an option, Carolyn thought, as the first thing she saw was that Shealds had a gun. She might be able to get to car, but the drifts would stop her before she was fifty feet from the house. "Why do you have a gun?"

"I was left for dead. We're in danger. Call the police," Shealds rasped. "I'll tell you what I know later."

Thoughts careened in Carolyn's mind. Shealds had a gun and was a paroled felon, but he looked like he'd been beaten to a bloody pulp. Shealds was also oddly dressed in tattered, duct-taped plastic sheeting with duct tape on his feet. His exposed skin was scraped and bleeding. *What should I do?*

Shealds was telling her to call the police, but what if it was an elaborate ruse to get her to come closer? She wouldn't be able to defend herself...and she had Grace Ann to think about. "I'll do what you say," she said, thoughts swirling in her mind. "My phone is by the kitchen table."

Shealds put his arm up in a blocking motion. "Stay here and away from the windows. I'll get it." He started moving in a crouched, crawling movement toward the kitchen. "If you can get through, call the sheriff's department and the town police. I've got to look and see who's out there," Shealds ordered. "Tell them shots have been fired in the construction trailer on your property." He couldn't catch his breath, and his arm caught his body as he fell forward. "Then I have to use the phone to call my private security people."

"Private security people? What private security people?" Carolyn ran forward, not able to resist her instinct against helping this man.

"I'm OK. You and Grace Ann just get down and stay away from the windows," Shealds wheezed. "Get down. I'll explain everything. I just need the phone when you're done." Shealds needed to get his strength back and call Samples. Now there were two more people to save in this mess. "Sit on the floor and stay here with Grace Ann. I'm going to crawl across the floor, turn off the lights, and get the phone." Shealds didn't want to think of how his enemies could use two hostages against him. "If shots are fired, don't come after me. Run up the stairs to the third floor with Grace Ann and get to the attic crawl...until the sheriff arrives."

"We'll *all* be fine," Carolyn said as she watched Shealds squat and head for the doorway, praying she was right. She knew she'd be doing a lot of praying. Carolyn couldn't think of any reason why she'd be in danger. Carolyn's mind went to several police and espionage novels she'd read. *What is Shealds's part in all this?*

Shealds was clumsy but he got what he needed quickly plus a clipboard and pen. Fortunately, Carolyn hadn't argued—yet. Shealds kept his eyes on the windows and door as he handed her the phone.

Carolyn had the police and sheriff on her emergency speed dial. She did as Shealds requested with a few embellishments. "Someone's been firing a gun at or near the construction trailer at Bayshore...and I don't know what to do. I believe one of my contractors, Mr. Jackson, was in the trailer, but the storm came up so quickly, I can't get out there. I'm here alone with my baby daughter, and she's sick with a fever. I think there's a bullet hole in one of the trailer windows." Carolyn looked at Shealds, daring him to make any changes in her story, wanting to convince the police to get here as soon as possible. "My aunts and Beth Seavers are at the Stornel's—waiting out the storm." Carolyn ended the call. She scrunched her mouth, indicating her dislike of the situation. "They need to know."

"I think a blizzard and gunfire are enough," Shealds said. "Don't you?"

Even though she didn't want to, Carolyn could see the logic of his argument. *What can Beth and her aunts do from the Stornels?* When they found out, she hoped they'd start praying! *Did I only manage to make them frantic when the police tell them?*

Carolyn changed the subject, wanting to take her mind off the police notifying her aunts and Beth. "You're a mess, and you need some clothes. I think there are some paint coveralls in the other room from when they were working down the hall...and some old boots the plasterers left on the third floor." Carolyn looked at the doorway. "They're almost as full of duct tape as you." Carolyn looked down at Grace Ann in her arms. "I also think you need some hot water, the first aid kit, and some scissors to get the tape and mess off you."

"We can't risk many trips to the kitchen because of the windows," Shealds replied. "Let's make a list of what you and Grace Ann need, and then we'll talk about first aid. I'll disable the refrigerator light."

"If we need protection, we can cut through the new wallboard in the back hall to the kitchen so we can get food and water...and anything we forgot," Carolyn offered, not knowing if she should be helpful or keep her mouth shut. *How did Shealds put them in danger?*

"Good idea," Shealds said, trying to sound encouraging.

"I'll wait till you're cleaned up to find out the rest," Carolyn said. "You can't take the time to clean up in the bathroom?"

"Think I saw some buckets for hot water in the old pantry," Shealds offered. "I'd better be as ready as possible, and you need to stay put so I know where you are."

After he'd belly-crawled to get all the supplies they needed from the family room to camp in the foyer, they started building the defense perimeter. Shealds got three plastic garbage cans and blocked the doorway between the foyer and the family room. He dragged all the bags of patching plaster from the two rooms off the foyer hallway to block the front door. Woodpiles and the plastic bags they put on and by the windows gave them about three feet of cover in the family room.

Carolyn did as Shealds asked and now looked at the guns: first, the one now in his hand again, and the one sitting next to his leg, as he leaned his battered body against the scarred foyer millwork. He wasn't in good shape. "Are you warm enough?"

With all the physical labor, Shealds was the warmest he'd been since he'd wakened in the trailer. He only nodded.

"I think it's time to get you cleaned up." This was an untenable situation, but Carolyn wanted to stay calm and rationale. For what other reason would a person like Shealds run in the blizzard looking like a plastic bag and duct-taped warrior? "Perhaps two layers of coveralls."

"Later. I'll start cutting the drywall to the kitchen," Shealds replied. There was a pocket door leading from the kitchen hall to the garage as well as the pocket door in the foyer assess, which Shealds wanted to keep closed for their protection. Getting to the kitchen by using the door was too dangerous. "I'll nail the doors shut after I've made the hole." He got to work as Carolyn listened to the hammer bashing the drywall.

Carolyn spoke as Shealds came through the doorway. "I'm not a nurse...but let's start cleaning you up. I'll get the coveralls and do the best I can."

Shealds didn't reply, he just kept working and watching, until he was through with their protective perimeter.

As he sat down on the floor, Carolyn dipped Grace Ann's washcloth in a clean plastic bowl of water. She wasn't going to use a wash bucket as Shealds suggested. *What good will cleaning his wounds with water from a dirty bucket do?* "I'll only be able to do a few at a time. The grime is really deep. It's going to hurt."

"I'll make two trips for water...but no more," Shealds replied, trying to keep Carolyn on task and calm. "Then, I'll put on the coveralls."

"You'll make as many trips as necessary," Carolyn retorted. "You can't protect us if you're septic with a raging fever."

Shealds seemed to be scraped and bruised everywhere Carolyn saw as she assessed his injuries. "I'll put antiseptic on, and I've got some wound adhesive. Bandages at this point with all the crawling won't work." She washed a few scrapes on his right shoulder. "So far I don't think you need any stitches."

Shealds winced in pain as Carolyn cleaned a deep wound on his shoulder. He shook his head. Shealds couldn't believe Carolyn hadn't asked him a million questions already about this crazy situation and the guns. "I had nothing to do with the drug-running and such on my company's planes."

Carolyn lifted one eyebrow skeptically but kept her eyes on her work. Shealds kept talking, wanting to get it out. "I haven't told anyone, well...only a few people really, but my sister-in-law was pregnant, had several threatened episodes to miscarry. She was a widow and had a young toddler as well—two premature children in twenty months. Will was born at seven months gestation to his widowed mother and was in the NICU for a long time—so there was a toddler, Devin, followed by a preemie...and a dead husband.

"My stepbrother, Warren, was behind everything at the company and kept it secret...but I was the leader and owner of the company...and the government came after me." Shealds relaxed his hand as Carolyn started to disinfect his right knuckles and fingers. They'd be raw for days, if he lived, he thought. "Warren was living way beyond his means…and I *do* admit I wasn't paying attention to his lifestyle." Shealds winced more at the thought of Warren, than the wound cleansing. "And it looks like he wasn't a faithful husband, either."

Carolyn's lips puckered and her eyes narrowed, but she kept doing her first-aid work and let Shealds talk.

"My sister-in-law, Ellen, collapsed under the weight of the grief, child-care for Devin, and trying to take care of a preemie." Shealds turned his head and looked toward the family room windows, seeing the blizzard still raging outside. "Ellen collapsed and was placed in psychiatric care postpartum depression." He winced a bit as the swab loosened a tiny stone in the heel of his right hand. "I pleaded guilty to save them."

"So, you went to jail…prison," Carolyn said, still concentrating on cleaning the wounds. She and Grace Ann were in danger and she wanted to know why.

"I met Hesse there," Shealds said. "He saved me with a strategic fight and a few scars." Carolyn had always noticed the chin scar, and she thought there was a deeper-than-nature-given groove in his frown lines.

"I was released, and Hesse and Molina joined me in our construction business…and I got working on exonerating myself with the help of several bright lawyers and an innovative private security and investigation company I used, even before I was in prison."

"The Mr. Samples you mentioned," Carolyn detailed.

"He's the head of his firm. Yes," Shealds replied with a frown. "I just taped a news program segment for a national broadcast on Tuesday, blowing the lid off of everything…and it seems word has gotten out about it and the Sunday broadcast…and we're all in danger because of it." This all seemed so strange, Carolyn thought. *Should I ask more questions?*

Grace Ann started to squirm and fuss. "It's time for Grace Ann's feeding," Carolyn said, clearing up the first aid debris. "Is that all right?"

"As long as the storm is raging, I think we're OK," Shealds replied. "Hopefully, Hesse and Molina are trying to get to us."

Carolyn picked Grace Ann up. "I'll put her on blankets, nearer the floor." Grace Ann settled in her arms. "Keep talking."

"Ellen's diagnosis was grief reaction and postpartum depression." Shealds stopped for a moment. "The state's attorney general had documentation and audiotapes from the undercover sting where Warren and his cohort said I knew nothing about the shipments on the company plane. But Zaugus needed the conviction...and a *live* defendant, so I was the patsy."

Carolyn listened to Shealds's bitter tone.

"You want me to clear out now?" Shealds's asked.

"If you're saying, should you leave because I'm breastfeeding, my modesty cover here is enough for me," Carolyn offered as she adjusted the roomy material with the tie over her head, sounding much calmer than she felt. "On the other hand, if you're saying, should you go out into that gosh-awful storm outside, my answer is still no. You say you're innocent and you certainly didn't think *your* trouble would include us. But I'm still scared." No, she was terrified...and she didn't like guns! "You know how to use that gun, Mr. Jackson?"

Shealds was taken aback that she was using his full name again. Carolyn lifted her head and looked meaningfully into Shealds's eyes. "I'm just praying the cavalry gets here before the bad guys because I don't want to see anyone get hurt."

CHAPTER NINETEEN

Hesse and Molina were snow-covered and cold, but they'd gotten to the Stornels' bed-and-breakfast after trudging the last two blocks after pulling their truck into the restaurant parking lot.

"You must be as cold as two blocks of ice," Nan said as she shook the snow from their parkas into an old blanket. "Put your boots over there, and come get some coffee."

Hesse and Molina looked at each other. They were trying to get back to the Bayshore house from the welding supply company even before they heard the Bayshore distress call on their special police scanner, provided by Samples, about Shealds, Carolyn, and Grace Ann…and the shooting at the Bayshore house. No one around them seemed upset so they were sure the Reynolds family hadn't heard the news…and they weren't going to say anything to get people any more riled up by telling them.

Hesse and Molina both shook their heads almost imperceptibly—a trick learned in prison. Samples said he was going to meet them there, but they didn't know how he was going to get through the storm, when they were stuck here despite their heavy weather gear, snow tires, chains, and deicing spray. So they'd sit tight for another ten minutes and then tell everyone they were going to go and search for stragglers caught in the snow.

"Hey, listen. Listen!" Muriel shouted. "They're talking about Mr. Hazeltine."

In a break from the storm and regional news, the brown-haired woman commentator was saying something about a body being identified followed by two pictures of a man with a caption underneath. "Authorities now say the dismembered body found in various places in an LA county landfill over the past month has been identified as curator and appraiser, William Hazeltine, who specialized in movie memorabilia, costumes, and studio set valuations." The picture changed, and the woman was on to another story about a Southeast Asian typhoon.

Bee was as white as the blizzard snow. "That wasn't Mr. Hazeltine!" she shouted. "That wasn't the man who helped us with Robin's things. Run the program back!"

"Get Muriel and Darby out of the kitchen. Can you roll the broadcast back and freeze the frame where they have the picture?" Cass barked.

Jessie grabbed the remote for the wall-hung flat-screen and did as Cass asked, while a chatting Darby and smiling Muriel, who was wiping her hands on an apron she borrowed from Nan, was calling back to Nan in the kitchen. "I used two cups of sifted cornmeal."

"Muriel. Muriel, come over here," Cass ordered. "Look at the screen." Cass pointed to the picture of a man the commentator had just mentioned. "They're saying that's the picture of Mr. Hazeltine!"

"No, that's not Mr. Hazeltine," Muriel replied.

"Darby?" Cass continued.

"That's not Mr. Hazeltine," Darby said emphatically. "This guy is short and Slavic-looking. The man who helped us was taller, thinner, and had a mustache. The head shape is all wrong. You can't change that."

"What's going on?" Beth asked.

"I don't know. I don't know yet," Bee said as thoughts ping-ponged in her mind. "The newscaster said this picture is of Mr. Hazeltine, the curator who helped us in LA. But it's not him! It's not him *at all*! Let's roll it back and listen to it all again."

Jessie rewound the footage. As the others watched her, Hesse whispered to Molina, "Two minutes."

The gist of the story was the same—dismembered body parts found in a county dump had just been identified. The mystery had required DNA recognition tests.

"Did they say the body had been dead for over three months?" Beth said.

"That's not too far from the time frame of going to LA to pick up Robin's things," Cass noted.

"You've got to call the police," Darby said. "What was an impostor doing looking through Robin's things?"

Hesse wanted to bolt out of the house but willed himself to stay relaxed and calm. Molina was sitting looking mildly concerned and squeezed Beth's shoulder.

"This isn't a local emergency, but the authorities in LA need to know," Muriel said. "Do you think we would be unnecessarily tying up the phone lines or mobile towers if we made a call?"

"Looks like a police matter…and they *need to* know." Hesse tried to infer that they should take action. "While you're calling the authorities in LA, Molina and I are warmed up enough to help other stragglers who might need help. There's concern here, too." The altruistic excuse almost caught in his throat, as the facts indicated the recent accidents and troubles on the job site, might *clearly* be directed at the Reynolds family and Samples needed to know.

"I'm giving you a thermos of hot chocolate," Nan said as she moved quickly to the kitchen door. "You or whoever you find may need it."

"How long are you going to be gone?" Beth said, looking at Molina.

"If we don't find anyone in an hour, we'll come back here," Hesse replied.

"Don't worry," Molina whispered to Beth. The action brought a momentary pause to the aunts' dialogue about Hazeltine.

"First things, first." Bee got her phone from her purse. "I'm calling the LA police." All eyes were on Bee as Hesse and Molina slipped out the door.

"I've got the special GPS beacon on me," Hesse said as he stuffed the small box in his inside breast pocket, not taking time to zip his parka.

"Too bad we kept both the guns in the trailer," Molina replied as they ran to their truck.

"Bad for us, but good for Shealds. If more trouble finds him, at least he can protect himself. I'm sure when Samples shows, he'll have a lot of firepower." Hesse opened the truck door, hoping Shealds was still alive.

"What's that?" Molina asked. Snow was flying everywhere from the sides of two vehicles—both appeared to be low-slung very large snowmobiles.

"There're skis on the front and tank treads in the back," Hesse said as he stared into the windswept snow, trying to see more.

The white and black vehicle pulled up next to them and the tiny driver's door opened. "Get in," Samples barked. "Bellamy's parking here and is going to guard the Stornel place. He's a karate master and has two handguns strapped to his thigh and behind his back in a belt holster." Samples looked out at the white sea of snow. "You're both coming with me."

"Do you know about Hazeltine?" Hesse asked as he got in the snug passenger seat and Molina squeezed in the tiny backseat, next to a long black box.

"That's a *new* reason I'm here." Samples turned toward Molina, remembering his rap sheet. "Can you put together an assault rifle and stand, kid? With a silencer?"

"Yes," Molina replied. "Ammo?"

"On the floor," Samples said.

"Keep it in one piece or two?" Molina worked on getting the gun case to his lap.

"Two," Samples said. "I think we'll have some time…to pick the right place on high ground. No shots at the Bayshore place. Guess Shealds just wanted to make their situation a priority."

"Great!" Hesse said with a sigh. Trouble, yes, shots, no.

Samples said still looking at the road. "Molina, you're going to watch for intruders on the ridge facing the road. We've only got about fifteen more minutes, and the storm is going to blow out to sea…and I think whoever is causing all the problems will make their move."

CHAPTER TWENTY

"Don't blame yourself too much, Mr. Jackson," an unknown woman's voice said. Carolyn guessed she'd fallen into an exhausted sleep on the couch after helping put up the safety barriers in the house and breastfeeding Grace Ann.

Shealds' wrists and ankles were tied to one of the folding chairs with his arms extended behind him. As the woman whisked the hood down from her white-winter quilted coat, she signaled her male companion to step closer to her and Grace Ann. He had a gun pointed directly at them. It looked like a cannon, Carolyn thought as she reflexively held her sleeping daughter tighter.

"We had keys," the woman said with nonchalance. "Must say the leftover turkey in Bee's refrigerator was tasty. We sat out the storm in relative comfort." She looked at Shealds with a slight smile.

"Thought we gave you enough drugs and horse tranquilizers to kill you," the man said.

"You're Hazeltine!" Carolyn exclaimed.

"Well, yes and no," the man replied. "I impersonated William Hazeltine."

"We need to keep the surgical gloves on," the woman said as they watched Shealds and Carolyn.

"It's all because of you, dear," the woman said as she turned to Carolyn's questioning face. "All because of you, Billie and Robin Lee."

Carolyn's head jumped up at her mother and aunts' names—the woman had mentioned Bee and now her mother and Aunt Robin. *Is this some crazed groupie couple? Do I know them?*

"I can see that you don't remember us, which is some comfort," the woman continued. "Too bad the plan with Hazeltine unraveled…or we might not have to be here. We could have waited." The woman stopped talking. She gave the gun to the man and took off her coat. "I'll take it back now."

Carolyn didn't know if she should react to the woman knowing her mother, her aunt Robin Lee, or Bee. *Should I stay quietly seated like Shealds?* She looked over at his face. He lifted his chin a bit. "What do you want?" Carolyn said trying to sound cooperative.

"Nothing more now, dear," the woman replied, equally polite and devoid of information. "We'll be gone soon. We've already made a really plausible story about being here."

"So let's try to put together the puzzle. Seems I've got no part in this," Shealds said in a loud, sarcastic tone. He had to keep them talking so he could try to balance and collapse the folding chair for a belly strike at the guy, and perhaps, a chance at the woman, too. The intruders sounded like they meant to kill them. Shealds figured he could take one or two shots from the small caliber gun the intruders were holding before his efforts were through. Hopefully, Hesse and Molina were close now, and they could save Carolyn and the baby if he were dead.

"As a supporting actor, you've very much a part of this," the woman replied coolly. "It's going to be a murder-suicide, I think."

"What!" Carolyn shouted. This woman was talking like this was a screenplay.

The woman shrugged. "It happens all the time in fiction and in life. Mr. Jackson is a hot-tempered yet handsome ex-con who falls in love with you. You're attracted at first by his interest, and proximity, especially on the LA trip, but you've brushed him off after a few trysts and chosen Pastor Allred. You tell Jackson at Thanksgiving, and he shoots you in a jealous rage—leaving behind a helpless infant who can't tell anyone anything."

"I could feel the chemistry between you two when we all were in LA," the man Carolyn knew as Hazeltine, offered with a smirk.

"But my aunts will deny anything of the sort! Darby's friends and the Beals are outside witnesses from our time at Thanksgiving dinner. No one will believe it!" Carolyn retorted angrily.

"They'd better be convinced or the baby dies!" the woman raged. "Now get over here!"

Carolyn started crying and shaking.

"Get some lipstick on," the woman ordered.

"Not before you tell me what this is all about!" Carolyn shouted back.

Shealds wasn't ready, and he hoped he didn't have to move. He didn't know if he could get on his feet…and then his plan would be ruined. They'd be dead. "I think we both deserve an answer!" he said, hoping for more time.

"He's got a point, El. Since they're going to die anyway," the man said.

The woman shrugged. "It's been many years since we've met, Carolyn." The woman stepped closer. "The first time I believe it was in the office."

Carolyn squinted and strained as she looked in the woman's eyes. "You were Aunt Robin's agent's secretary—Miss Raymond!"

"I always knew you were a bright young woman." Miss Raymond smiled briefly and then frowned. "Things were going so well when I sent your mother down to the unwed mother's home." Miss Raymond looked to make sure Shealds was sitting passively in his chair and not causing any trouble. "The matron was supposed to sell you to the highest bidder, and Billie was supposed to come back to California and meet her unfortunate demise years *before* she passed. But patience has its rewards."

The facts slammed into Carolyn's brain, and she jumped up from the couch. "You killed my mother!"

"If you're going to be so impolite, I won't continue with the story," Ms. Raymond said with a huff. "Sit down!"

"El tells such great stories." The man shooed Carolyn back to a sitting position with a wave of the gun.

Shealds tensed a bit. He still couldn't get his calves firmly on the back of the folding chair seat so he could get to his feet. The pain of the effort was almost unbearable, and he hoped he wouldn't start to sweat and give himself away. "I for one would like to hear to rest," he said in a tone he hoped was dispassionate enough to get the woman talking again. He hoped Carolyn could hang together for a few more minutes.

"It started before that," Miss Raymond picked up the thread. "Carl and Robin Lee said they *fell in love* during the time of her last film shoot. Carl called me into his office to say *they* were going to get married." Miss Raymond waved the gun a bit. "Before that, he said he loved *me*...and this new, little romance between the two of them was going to cut me out completely." She turned and swung the gun. "I gave him four years of my life at a lousy salary...and I almost had the ring on *my* finger!"

"Couldn't have that," the man said as he shook his head. "Secretary's salary and not being Carl Springs's bride."

"That's where my dear brother, Mel here, came in," Miss Raymond said with a smile. "A sedative and a bit of a few narcotics in the wine for Robin Lee and Carl, Mel drove her car up the road and put a concrete block on the accelerator and off it flew over the embankment. Drug addiction and unfortunate deaths are always a problem in Hollywood."

"Worked better than we thought it would." Mel laughed. "Had to put other concrete blocks and bricks on Springs's boat for Springs's body when we killed him and buried him at sea. No one suspected nothing."

"But people saw Mr. Springs," Carolyn said.

"You saw what we wanted you to see," Ms. Raymond replied. "We dyed Mel's hair and he started growing a mustache two weeks before we killed them."

"Mr. Springs even remarked I was going to have a nice one, once it grew in." Mel chuckled.

"Mel and I "married" in a private ceremony and told everyone of our marriage an appropriate amount of time after the mental breakdown we staged. Nobody suspected. Everyone seemed happy for us and we lived quietly." Miss Raymond looked at Shealds.

"But that wasn't all," Shealds said loudly. "It couldn't be." His brow furrowed. "There's got to be something else." He looked more thoughtful. "You got copies of Robin's will...and changed it somehow."

"A few signatures from Robin, I hid them in contract papers for her next film, and it was *done*," Miss Raymond spat.

"So take away the contract papers you knew she'd never film, keep the will...and you've got Robin Lee's inheritance," Shealds theorized.

"True enough." Mel moved toward Shealds. "Billie thought things were on the up and up and never even asked for anything."

"But we were always prepared," Miss Raymond interrupted stridently.

"You stayed worried. With the homicides and lots of money to fight over if Billie or her daughter ever decided to snoop around and get their hands on the millions of dollars in licensing and royalties concerning Robin Lee." Shealds stopped for a beat, wanting to keep the conversation going. "What's coming in? About a million dollars a year?"

"None of your business," Mel growled. "The stuff in the storage units caused a concern."

"The thought never occurred to me to check," Carolyn said bitterly. "I made my own money."

"And you kept digging and digging into your mother's death, like a real pest!" Miss Raymond shouted. "We couldn't be sure you wouldn't come calling one day and mess with our setup. Crandall wanting to take your case meant he had to be killed."

"So we can't be here and be Mr. Hazeltine and his assistant, since he's dead. But we can be Carl Springs's assistant, Miss Raymond, and her brother, Mel. We've got our DNA all over the place." Mel sounded pleased with the plan. "We've come in a surprise Thanksgiving visit to see the storage facility and visit you right before you get in your argument with Mr. Jackson."

"So Mel came here one day...as a worker?" Shealds theorized. He wasn't going to say they'd already called the police and tell them Carolyn said "shots were fired" yet. He might need to tell them that information later, to see if it might affect their homicidal plan.

"I palmed the mansion keys. Made clay impressions and had the keys duplicated by people who didn't ask any questions for the right price..." Mel grinned at the thought. "And here we are."

Pete had just climbed the uneven stones to get to the top of the rise by the Bayshore bridge. Before he caught his breath, Pete was body-slammed into the snow. Pete dodged a right cross, as the unknown man's other fist headed for his face. He saw a bit of the man's profile and shouted. "Stop, Molina. It's me, Pete!"

Molina stopped but didn't take the restraining pressure off as he lay atop Pete's body.

"Don't get up or I'll have to hurt you, Pete," Molina rasped, begging Pete to understand. "Shealds and Carolyn are in trouble in the house. I've got to get into position by the front door or they might be hurt. Hesse says its two people in there with guns. The cops can't get here."

Pete blinked a bit and looked into Molina's cold-reddened face. "I'll help you."

"Do you think you can help me break down the front door?" Molina asked. "Hesse would do it with me, but he's got to help Samples."

"Who's Samples?" Pete asked.

"No time now, Pete. Will you help me?" Molina asked. "I've already wasted time coming to stop you from messing things up."

"Tell me what to do," Pete said simply as they got up off the ground.

"Follow me," was all Molina said as he loped through the snow to the mansion.

"Help us, Lord," was all Pete had a time to whisper.

Shealds continued to try to keep the pair talking. The more they talked, the longer he and Carolyn were alive. "So, Hazeltine?" Shealds asked. *Where are Hesse and Molina?*

"I guess we're getting a little old and rusty with all this. They found part of his remains in the county dump about three weeks ago. But we've only got you two to go, and then we are free and clear." Mel looked at Carolyn. Carolyn felt cold. "I botched the burial of Hazeltine. Got a bad back now and couldn't dig a hole deep enough, so we tried the dump. We sold the boat years ago, so there was no clean way to dump him at sea like we did with Springs." Mel shrugged.

"Darby Fisher was frantic when the storage place was sold. We tried to buy it, but the family who owned it were all hot for the redevelopment plan their nephew pitched...and we couldn't seem too interested," Miss Raymond added.

"So you hired Hazeltine, pretended to be representing Carolyn and the Lee estate and found out how to do the conservator work," Shealds began.

"He came over to dinner several times, and we hired him as our conservator. Had several other meetings as well...and he was very informative before his death," Miss Raymond said.

"Well, you used your back some more, Mel, because I've got a feeling you're behind the shattered window at the Stornels', the fire in LA, the tire failure on the interstate..."

"The tree and the barn beam collapse." Mel finished. "That was a tough one on me. Aimed to keep you away from LA for a bit to get Carolyn alone. Thought we'd get a construction collapse investigation, but you were too fast and had everything cleared before the inspectors arrived."

"The paddleboard incident?" Shealds asked.

"Hired that dunce Thackery, a day after he left the Griggs' place. He almost ate us out of house and home. But he botched it," Mel replied. "And paid for it with his life."

Carolyn felt a bit faint at this revelation. Beth would have to mourn the death of her friend, and his stupid betrayal, if they got out of this alive.

"But now we're nearing the prize." Miss Raymond walked toward Carolyn, keeping her eye on Shealds.

"Might be *more here* than we thought from the old days," Mel hinted. "Nice property after all the investigating we've done. More here than you think."

"Shut up, Mel," Miss Raymond ordered. "We've talked enough. You'll both be dealt with, we won't have to worry anymore because the last of Robin's relatives will be stone-cold dead and we'll have the cover of Mr. Jackson's criminal past and your affair."

Shealds wondered if he should say anything about the television expose. He needed more time to think, and getting Carolyn closer would cover him wanting to stand.

"Now stand up and get that lipstick on or I'll take the baby," Miss Raymond shouted.

Carolyn again reflexively recoiled at the idea and hugged Grace Ann tighter.

"Do it, Carolyn," Shealds ordered, hoping to get her cooperation to buy them some more time.

Carolyn reached for her purse and thought of swinging it, but she looked at Shealds and saw a big "no" in his eyes. Above all, she didn't want her daughter hurt. So she took a deep breath and reached one-handed in her makeup bag. "Any particular of the two shades I have here?"

"The one you've got on now," Miss Raymond replied.

"I don't have any lipstick on now," Carolyn said in a low tone.

"Your choice, then. Just do what I say. Walk over here," Miss Raymond ordered. "Bend down and kiss Mr. Jackson hard on his mouth and on both sides of his cheeks."

"Be sure she gets some lipstick and DNA on his collar, too," Mel advised.

"Do what my brother says." Miss Raymond looked closely to see that Carolyn followed instructions.

Carolyn felt both embarrassed and resigned. She wanted to be kind to Shealds, but she also knew she had to follow Miss Raymond's orders or she might take Grace Ann from her. Carolyn tried to pucker her quivering lips as she held firmly on to her daughter. This move of endearment would be wonderful between a husband and wife...but not here. She felt more like she was reacting to bitter lemons rather than kissing a man.

Carolyn looked down. Shealds eyes were sympathetic and comforting. He surprised her by making the first move to greet her lips as she came near his face. Shealds captured her lips, and she sank into his kiss. Grace Ann's blanket touched his neck.

Shealds sat back, lowered his chin, and broke contact, seeing the myriad thoughts and emotions in Carolyn's eyes. He knew now. This was a woman he wanted to know; he'd just been concentrating on first things first—his family and his name. If they got through this, he hoped to have time to explain.

"Do it again like I said." Miss Raymond flicked the gun.

Tears were coming to Carolyn's eyes. Shealds hoped any tears in Carolyn's future would be happy ones. He moved again, and this time Carolyn was ready with willing, pliable lips. Her right hand went to his shoulder as she broke the kiss, looked into his eyes, and silently wiped her lips on the right collar of the painter's overalls. Grace Ann was still asleep.

Carolyn regained her balance and looked at Miss Raymond with contempt.

"I think that's enough, don't you, Mel?" Miss Raymond said smirking.

Carolyn wondered if her eyes were deceiving her or did she see a shadow on the porch? *Is it just wishful thinking?* She backed away and headed to the place where she had come. Tears came down her cheeks. *What's next?*

In a split second, Shealds was on his feet. He head-butted Mel into his sister. Miss Raymond recovered and got off a shot into Shealds's shoulder. He stayed on his feet.

The door splintered, wood and glass flew onto the foyer floor, reminding Carolyn of the incident at the Stornels but with less glass this time. Everything was in slow motion. She looked at Miss Raymond. The woman's face was blank and a bead of blood was coming down her nose from a round wound in her forehead. Her body crumbled like a rag doll.

Her brother, Mel, was screaming and shot his gun twice as the two men who broke through the front door wrestled him to the ground. Another shot rang out, and Mel stopped moving.

"You OK, Molina?" Pete asked.

"Yeah, no blood," Molina replied. "You?"

"You owe me a new parka," Pete replied.

"I owe you a new parka," Shealds quipped, but he couldn't hold himself up anymore. "Can you cut these off of me?" He tilted his head toward his zip-tied wrists and feet. "Balancing with this chair tied to me is getting tiresome."

Carolyn found her voice. "He's been shot in the shoulder."

Pete and Molina saw the blood and moved in tandem. Molina put pressure on the shoulder wound as Pete quickly cut the ties with the survival knife in his pocket and got the chair legs opened so Shealds could sit down.

"Samples called for the police and an ambulance," Molina said. "Maybe they'll get a chopper."

Pete was taking Shealds's pulse, asking him a few first-aid questions about his pain, while trying to stop the blood loss from the shoulder wound. "Who's Samples?"

"He's Samples," Hesse said, seeing Samples coming through the broken door. "He got the head shot on Raymond, and I see you cleaned up with her brother."

Pete looked sad, thinking of his boyhood wounds. "Molina got his arm and turned the butt of the gun...and it went off. He could have killed us both otherwise. It was self-defense."

"They confessed to it all," Shealds said, sounding tired.

"Got it all on digital from the storage area," Samples said, feeling for pulses in the brother and sister and finding none. In this murderous masquerade, Samples felt like kicking himself for thinking this couple was Carl Springs and his wife, Eleanor Raymond— *not* Eleanor Raymond and her *brother*, Melvin. But who could think these two people, much older than they all were, would keep these paranoid plots going, even when no threats existed?

"He's the security and investigation guy," Molina said simply, knowing he owed Pete an explanation.

"There's more, but that will do for now." Shealds's shoulder was starting to hurt.

"The man just said an indistinct word before he died. I think it was 'Gold here'," Pete said questioning.

Samples shook his head. "Probably 'cold here' from shock and blood loss," Samples replied.

"I'm quite sure he said 'gold'," Pete insisted.

"Suit yourself, padre," Samples turned and looked around. "Lots needs to happen before we continue this discussion. Leave everything where it is. Nobody's going to bother anything." Samples looked at the clouds and then at Shealds. "We're going to drive you to the hospital before you loss any more blood or get an infection." He lifted the lapel of the painter's coverall. "Looks like a simple through and through to me, with not much damage."

"Thank you, Dr. Samples," Shealds replied. "It feels better already." He owed Samples his life and would talk to him later.

"Grace Ann and I are coming, too," Carolyn said in a strong voice. "We've got to get out of here."

Samples looked at the other three men. "It might be a little tight, but I can put you and your daughter in the backseat of my ride, if you hold pressure on his shoulder wound. Will you guys help us?" Pete helped Carolyn get her purse, coat, and diaper bag as Carolyn put Grace Ann in thick throw.

"Have my aunts and Beth get to the hospital," Carolyn ordered as she straightened her coat, checking that Grace Ann was properly covered.

Samples shrugged as he looked at Carolyn holding Grace Ann and standing by Shealds's chair. "Molina, I'll drive the Sno-Cat with Shealds and Ms. Reynolds and the baby. Bellamy's coming here and you three can drive his ride to the hospital and catch up to us."

CHAPTER TWENTY-ONE

Getting into the vehicle was painful, but Shealds didn't care now that the crisis was over. Carolyn held Grace Ann in the crook of her right arm and reached from her backseat position to hold pressure on his injured shoulder with her free hand.

Shealds felt like his injured shoulder was on fire, and shooting pains were radiating to his back, but he didn't move. The allusion of something so complete and missing from his life, even for a few minutes, felt good. Hopefully, in a few days, he'd be healing from this injury and the injustice of his false imprisonment and he could hope for more moments like these - Carolyn and Grace Ann...with Ellen and her boys. He closed his eyes and lost consciousness.

Carolyn looked stricken when Shealds closed his eyes. She held tight to Grace Ann and didn't wipe away the tears falling silently down her cheeks.

Samples looked in the rearview mirror. Samples admired Carolyn Reynolds. She'd been through so much in the past few hours and hadn't fallen apart. He'd finally gotten a good look at the Raymonds in the Bayshore house waving their guns through his high-powered gun sight, while listening to their ranting in his earbud. Samples was glad Shealds and Carolyn had gotten out alive…and Eleanor Raymond had moved far enough away from Carolyn so he could get off his shot. Mel was next, but Hesse, Molina, and Allred got to him first.

The two people who tried to shoot Shealds and Carolyn and anyone else in their way were dead, and Shealds would get his multiyear nightmare behind him. *Not a bad week's work,* Samples thought to himself as he pulled into the hospital parking lot.

There were other costs. Shealds was going to have to pay for the two vehicles, the broken window, and all the equipment and the disabled burglar alarm at the Sun and Snow shop in Averyville. But this was all worth it.

Samples hoped Carolyn Reynolds could put this all behind her and stay at the Bayshore mansion with her family. It was none of his business, but that was one solution to thwarting every evil thing the Raymonds had wanted.

Carolyn left the comfort of the armchair and stood by the doorway as the nurse checked Shealds's pressure monitor, confident his shoulder dressing showed no further blood loss and his IV was dripping at the prescribed rate.

"I'll be out of here soon," Shealds said as he tried to pull himself up in the bed. "You should go home to your family. I'm OK now."

Carolyn's hands were still shaking a bit. She was happy to be alive and anywhere after this horrible experience. "I will in a few minutes," she said, trying to be calm, thinking she wanted to go back to her cottage and do some normal things, like put a load of laundry in the washing machine or brew a cup of tea. Even though she'd lived through every horrible moment, she still couldn't internalize that Raymond and her brother had killed her mother…and were so close to killing her. It all seemed like a nightmare.

"You OK?" Shealds said, worried about the blank look in Carolyn's eyes and her chalky skin, seeing the cloudy gray creeping into her blue eyes.

"You're asking about me?" Carolyn retorted without heat. "Seems to me, you should be worried about yourself."

Might as well try humor, Shealds thought. "Just being here with no handcuffs is good for me." He lifted his forearms as far as they would go. His other shoulder and arm were fine, so he caught Carolyn's hand as she walked closer. "Sure *you're* OK?"

Carolyn would attribute her next move to a tinge of post-trauma shock mixed with gratitude as she lowered her head. "Are *you* OK?" She leaned over the bed rails. Her lips were aiming for Shealds's forehead or temple but gravitated like an unwilling magnet to his mouth. Even after all they'd gone through today, his kiss hinted at remembrance and fire. She lifted her head. Shealds just stared at her, waiting.

"As I recall, it was supposed to be on one side of your mouth, then the other, and a mark on your collar," she whispered.

"Stay close and let me touch your hair," Shealds whispered back, almost smiling at Carolyn's smoky look. "I wanted to do that then, but my hands were tied."

"It won't hurt your shoulder?" Carolyn asked.

"Not touching you will hurt more," Shealds said as he aimed his kiss for the side of her mouth and moved his forearms up and over her shoulders in a light embrace.

She rested her forehead on his after the kiss, not wanting to move away. "At first, all I wanted was to take all the terror out of it," Carolyn explained.

"I understand," Shealds whispered, "but I'm hoping for something more, much more now." Shealds thought he might be hallucinating, but he thought of silly images of summer picnics on the Bayshore lawn and kite flying. *Does Bee have a killer recipe for fried chicken?*

"To be continued," Carolyn replied with a soft hug of promise as she pushed away from the bed. "I've got responsibilities to Grace Ann, Beth, my aunts, and Darby. We're a box set."

"Some assembly required?" Shealds said with an equal mixture of humor and irony.

"Chemistry is only part of what's going to be expected," Carolyn replied, trying to make her situation clear. Any man, no matter how much she knew she owed him, had better know what she needed, if this was to go further.

"I *fully* understand," Shealds said seriously, putting words to what she needed to know about his situation. "Same with me. Ellen and the boys, will be part of things, if we can mend fences when they come in January as well as Hesse and Molina." He pressed his lips together. "You'll need some time to *really* see how you feel when everything shakes down after tomorrow."

Carolyn was afraid of the answer but had to ask anyway. "Would you like to be with people who care for you when it's broadcast, or would you like to be alone?"

"It's been so long with nothing beyond Hesse and Molina," Shealds said guardedly. Being vulnerable again was almost as painful as all his wounds from the trailer and the gunshot.

"I know the feeling," Carolyn said. She was wary too.

"How's Grace Ann?" Shealds changed the subject but really wanting to know.

"Her pediatrician got through the snow. Grace Ann's fine," Carolyn said, not able to look at Shealds's face. "My aunts and Beth took her back to the Stornels."

"I'm glad," Shealds whispered, worry in his eyes. He tilted his head. "Come back over here...to me."

"I'm here," Carolyn whispered, coming back to the bedside. "Can we *do* this?"

"After what we've been through, we can do anything," Shealds said with a laugh as he pulled her back down and kissed her again. "Now we've got time."

"Backs of steel!" Carolyn retorted. She laughed at Shealds' confused face.

"It's something else you'll be learning if you stick around the Reynolds' clan," Carolyn said, finally relaxing as she saw some color returning to Shealds's face. "Something else you'll have to learn."

A lot to come. Shealds thought as he looked at Carolyn. There'd be their relationship to consider, Ellen and her boys and getting his financial business and licenses back. Shealds had heard the dust-up of Samples and Pastor Pete's concerning Mel Raymond's last words. His coming freedom was going to present them all with interesting opportunities! A lot to come!

Pete didn't know exactly what he'd walked into as he looked through the window in Shealds's patient room, but he knew one thing. Carolyn Reynolds was off the dating market. His instincts in seeing the kiss and their gestures he inadvertently saw said it all.

Pete felt sorry for himself for a split second. Carolyn was a lovely woman with a lovely family who'd embraced him warmly. He genuinely liked them all.

His concerns about his mental health and the pull of the Bayshore property had dissuaded him from saying and thinking just how much. *I was distracted by the psychological issues I had to attend to!*

He'd excused himself after Grace Ann's examination, had a shower, some food, and a ten-minute power nap in the clergy room there at the hospital, exhausted by his several-mile trek in the snow coupled with the aftermath of the adrenaline rush of disarming the Raymonds and getting Carolyn and Shealds to the hospital.

Praise God, they all were OK.

Another thing - he was still thinking of Mel Raymond's last words about gold which was strange for him. He'd argued with Samples about it! Pete wasn't usually as entrenched or argumentative about his point of view in such issues, either as a pastor or a psychologist. But his impressions about the Mel Raymond's last words were *as strong* as his impressions about the sadness he grappled with! *Oh no! Is this like the impressions of sadness I've had at Bayshore?* He closed his eyes and thought for a minute. A strong, lingering feeling, indicated there *was more* for him to do at Bayshore. He'd have to talk to Carolyn, Shealds, Hesse, Molina and Samples. They were with him when the new feelings started. Perhaps they could help. He needed to learn more before thinking of calling Pastor Bill. *More?*

ABOUT THE AUTHOR

In addition to *39 Bayshore*, Donna J. Grisanti is the author of two historical novels. *Wandering Hearts* is about a community at the cusp of World War II. *Paths of Promise* takes place on the front lines of the civil rights movement. She loves reading, especially history, biographies, and fiction.

Grisanti has previously worked as a research analyst, technical writer, nurse, and nursing instructor. She has a bachelor's degree and master's degree in nursing as well as an MBA.

Grisanti lives in Arizona and enjoys visiting her two sons (one on each coast!), spending time with friends, following sports, attending church activities, and taking classes to broaden her horizons.

www.ingramcontent.com/pod-product-compliance
Lightning Source LLC
Chambersburg PA
CBHW061324170626
46817CB00001B/298